STIG DALAGER was born in Copenhagen in 1952. He made his literary début with a collection of short stories in 1980 and has since become known as a prolific author of novels, short stories, poems, plays, radio plays and literary criticism. One of the most distinguished Scandinavian writers of his generation, he is gaining international recognition with a body of work that has been translated and performed internationally or adapted for cinema.

JOURNEY IN BLUE

A NOVEL ABOUT
HANS CHRISTIAN ANDERSEN

Stig Dalager

Translated from the Danish by John Mason

PETER OWEN
LONDON AND CHESTER SPRINGS

PETER OWEN PUBLISHERS
73 Kenway Road, London SW5 0RE

Peter Owen books are distributed in the USA by
Dufour Editions Inc., Chester Springs, PA 19425-0007

Translated from the Danish *Rejse i blåt*

First published in Great Britain in 2006 by
Peter Owen Publishers

© Stig Dalager 2004
Translation © John Mason 2006

ISBN 0 7206 1269 1

Printed and bound in Great Britain by
MPG Books Ltd, Bodmin, Cornwall

Peter Owen Publishers acknowledge Hempel-fonden
and Jorcks Fond for their contribution
to the publication of this book.

To Niels Andersen, Nina, Ida and Sidsel

'Against the vastness of the All, we are nothing.'
– Hans Christian Andersen

HE WAKES IN the darkness alone and for some moments does not know where he is, who he is. His right hand, flat and bony, grips something with its long fingers somewhere under his sweating body – something wooden, a board in the bed-frame. The hand clutches the board in panic. The image of his grandfather's demented face recedes; the large nose, the little eyes, the sensitive mouth that slid across his own features on a wave in his dream and obscured his face have disappeared. Is he awake or is he dreaming? Has it come to claim him now, his grandfather's madness?

There is a roaring in his ears; he recalls having his head measured in Steglitz – it was too big . . .

Twenty years ago . . . No, more . . . Why remember that now?

He turns his head. The white rose in the vase that Fru Melchior has placed on the nightstand shines.

The rose shines in the night. Night flames in the rose.

Fru Melchior's calm smile balancing his madness.

They have given him a bell; his left hand reaches out for it, takes hold of the handle, swings it back and forth, the sound clashing in his ears; the silence in its wake is unnerving as the pains in his stomach suddenly drown out all else, and he drops the bell. Steps sound in the passage as distant as the summer drone of bees among the flowering borders in the garden of Villa Rolighed . . . Is it not summer now?

The servant, his face ashen, stands in the doorway.

'How can I help, Councillor Andersen?'

'Fru Melchior!' he whispers, clutching his stomach.

The servant disappears. As the centuries pass, pain racks him on the bed. Is he going to die? A moment later she is standing in the door – the only person who can give him relief. Without a word she approaches in her white nightgown, places a hand on his forehead. That hand. And that smile.

'I am pitiful, I know,' he says. 'What is to become of me?'

'You will manage,' she says and pours him two large drops of morphine from the small brown bottle on the nightstand. She reaches out the teaspoon, and he swallows the sticky liquid.

She sits down on the chair beside the bed. As she takes his hand, her outline seems to dissolve. Why is there all this mist?

*H*E DOES NOT *remember falling asleep again, but when he wakes it is lighter in the room; night is not yet over, morning has not yet come, but he senses the blue in the sky behind the window facing out towards the balcony and Øresund. Shadows ghost the furnishings – the glass cabinet full of books, the dark surface of the writing table along the wall, Marstrand's painting of the ruins of the Forum Romanum, the washbasin on its three-legged stand, the wardrobe with his black coat and top hat and his starched white shirts. The pain has gone; he feels light as air. Will he ever get up on his feet again? Get out on the balcony? Out to the view across to Malmö, Landskrona, Hven? The white sails?*

Ah, yes. Whiteness. He is light as air. Gliding. Like a swan.

With hair the colour of flax, long loose-jointed body and clogs, he sits under his mother's white apron slung across a broomstick between the gooseberry bush in the yard and the pale yellow wall of the house; he is counting leaves, picking berries, one by one, enjoying the bittersweet juice when he bursts them between his teeth.

No, now he is walking the cobbles in Odense with eyes half closed. Where is he heading? Is he walking through a dream?

He is sitting on the wooden bench at the kitchen table, dressing and undressing his dolls, while his father's pale face reads to him. Holberg. His mother stands with her back to them in the small kitchen under the row of pewter plates, polishing a mug; the white curtains blaze. His eye is caught by the pictures of trolls and fairies and elderberry flowers painted on the doors. Suddenly his father gets to his feet, lifts the drum down from the wall, pulls the drumsticks out and begins to beat a rhythm. His mother turns, laughs, starts to dance. Dancing towards him. Tatata. Tatatata.

HE IS GLIDING, *weightless. Like a swan.*

The slope chalk-white, chill in his ears, his sled careering down-hill with the hoots of boys in pursuit, then slithering away out of control under him, flinging him off to roll down into a pool, icy cold in the instant, wet through; as two boys pull him out they are laughing. He tears himself away and runs all the way back home across the brittle grass to the house in Munkemøllestræde, where he is made to strip off his clothes, angry and ashamed, as his mother hangs his clothes to dry by the fire and finds a dress for him to wear. He hides so that neither his mother nor his father can see him.

Isn't that him standing there at the door to the Greyfriars Hospital chalking out drawings for the old folk and in full flow, words pouring out of him in a ceaseless stream, when Johanne embarks on his story about a water sprite with a lovely voice who lures a girl from Odense down to the water to marry him? The poor girl was found floating in the river early one morning, but some say she has joined the water sprite and borne him several children. Johanne has seen one of them in the water at twilight.

HE IS FLOATING. It's the morphine. Is he awake? The door out to the balcony keeps rattling in the wind. He feels a rattling in his heart. Why is his right hand so cold, his left so hot? The scent of seaweed has entered the room; his nostrils catch it. If only he could just get up and walk down to the water's edge.

Winter. He heats a copper penny on the cast-iron stove and presses the hot coin against the frozen pane so that it makes a peephole out into the dark and the driving snow piling itself in every cranny and hiding the beggar doubled up under the roof of the lean-to across the road.

Like small swarms the beggars in the streets move from door to door, their hands outstretched for bread, small coins. That evening one girl sent out to beg sat down, faint with exhaustion, by the bridge over the River Odense and fell asleep; returning home in the middle of the night barefoot and empty-handed, she was thrashed for her pains. The girl was his mother.

SHROVETIDE CELEBRATIONS. WITH their white aprons, red caps and the sun glinting on the axes they have buffed up for the day, the butchers lead a plodding ox decorated with festive birch-rods and red ribbons. On the back of the ox rides a boy who looks like an angel with his wings of golden paper and his white shirt. A butcher's boy holds on to his sleeves to stop him falling off the ox. If only he was that shining white angel-boy! He runs after them, following what is now a whole procession, with street urchins, women and beggars bringing up the rear. They arrive in the market square among the cobblers' stalls, their tables overloaded with unwieldy shoes and thick-soled boots. He sprints through the hatters' quarter with its booths and streets to the shops with fancy goods, stalls – wooden booths and canvas tents in turn – where the goldsmiths and confectioners display their jewellery, their many-coloured cakes. It is teeming pandemonium. Bullocks low and bellow, unbridled horses whinny and caper, the shouts of boys, somewhere a violin is playing. Peasant girls walk in long trains down the street clasping hands so that he cannot pass and they laugh at him. He gets confused, arrives among tents full of pottery and the displays of turners and saddlers. He must get down to the toy stalls and try out the small trumpets, wind up the musical boxes with the other children. Hawkers make their huge right hands meet in the air with a resounding smack as they strike their bargains. Everywhere the air thick with stench, and in the midst of it all comes the sweet scent of honey cake. He feels faint.

HE HAS SEEN them! The lunatics with sailcloth shirts worn over their clothes and iron chains on their arms and legs; sees the cells of the madhouse – cold, foul-smelling rooms with hatches in the doors fastened with padlocks. He walks round the kitchen garden with Grandmother, who collects the rubbish, and, sneaking into the corridors where the cells are, is all by himself with the echoes of their voices, their breathing – no guards. He crouches down on his haunches and looks through the crack in a door. A woman is sitting on a straw pallet singing with a sweet voice. Suddenly she stops, listens, hears him breathing and jumps up with a screech, hammering her hands against the door so that the hatch flies open and she is reaching out her hands for him, her mad eyes staring down at him. He dives to the ground, screaming.

The fear of her is still in his body. He is like water in which everything is reflected. A floodgate. Everything that has flowed in is dammed up, presses from the inside, must find a way out.

IsN'T THAT HIM standing there underneath the windows of the huge prison building, listening to the inmates' rough-cut voices, their strange songs and the turning of the spinning wheel so far away, so near? He is at once frightened and fascinated by these prison-uniform people who are treated like dirt. Stories of their murderous deeds run round the whole city.

His father leading him by the hand to the frozen windows in the little house, where there is an ice fern on one of the panes and behind it a maiden who seems to be reaching out her arms. 'She must want me!' he hears him say with a chuckle.

Gone he is.

HIS GRANDFATHER COMES singing down the street with flowers in his hair, holding the wicker basket full of his strange woodcarvings, Sphinx-like winged creatures and people with the heads of beasts. Most likely he has grain and ham in his basket, given to him by peasant women in exchange for his wooden figures, and he swings the basket from side to side, mumbling to himself and staring towards the house as if he cannot decide where to go. The street urchins surround him bawling at the tops of their voices, tugging at his arms, 'It's Traes from Killerup! It's Traes from Killerup!' so that he turns to stare at them, too, with his unhinged smile. And walks on. He is frightened of the old man, hides behind a stairway as he and the hooting boys throng past.

He sees in the mirror his grandfather's face looking back from his own. Is he mad, too? Have his grandfather and that toothless old mouth caught up with him?

THE OIL LAMP and behind it, rounded in its highlights and shadows, his father's face reading aloud from August Lafontaine's *The Reprobate*; he falls silent, and his thick hand passes over his forehead as the lamp goes out; but the face still shines, smiling.

Brown-eyed and dark, his mother bent over the wet washing draped across the washing stone down by the river. Big-boned and lean in her peasant's bonnet, she slaps the clothes on the stone, her hands blue with cold; her movements are strong in the icy weather, the sky grey, the leaves chased into piles across the cobbles. When she comes home, her face is flushed with drink, and she talks and talks. It is better when she washes out the bottles at the apothecary's. Then her hands are warm when she folds him in her arms.

*HE IS FAR away and close to; outside the light is growing. Is it not blue?
Is time still passing?*

To sit in the schoolroom of the Jewish school, staring at the faded
paintings of Moses and Jeremiah until they seem to move their
eyes; to sit by the gravestones, spelling out the letters until he can
hear the dead down under the earth knocking on their stones; to
watch a swallow cut its sharp flight in under the vaults of the
school building and to think of the invisible spirits playing with
the chickweed. There is a little girl at school – black hair, brown
eyes just like his mother – who comes up to him. She is older than
him. She says, 'I go to school to learn to be good at sums, for my
mother says that then I can become a dairymaid at a great manor.'
He says, 'You can be a dairymaid at my castle when I am famous!'
She laughs, her head to one side, her hands on her hips. 'But
you're just a poor boy!' One day he shows her a drawing of a
castle and tells her, 'Here it is, here's my castle. I am a changeling,
a child of noble parents. God's angels come and talk to me.' She
gives him a strange look and says to a boy standing near by, 'He
is crazy just like his granddad!' He feels his blood run cold.

HOW MANY PEOPLE have crowded into the square outside St Knud's churchyard that evening? He clings to his mother's hand in the midst of this buzz of voices that seems to come from a frightened animal. And now high in the sky a fireball shoots across the heavens, trailing a flaming tail, and everyone is talking at once, even his mother, about the awful things about to happen. It is an evil omen, the day of judgement; the end of the world is at hand. His father joins the crowd and pushes his way through to them. 'This is just nature's way,' he says, 'when a heavenly body burns up.' People give him suspicious looks, shaking their heads at the unbeliever. His father laughs out loud and leaves. How frightened he is that his father is lost beyond redemption. Late that evening he sits on his grandmother's lap. She smiles down at him, and he holds her arm tight, waiting for the comet to strike.

Dark forces are everywhere, ghosts, creatures of the night. His mother and grandmother teach him the words, the plants, the special waters that keep them at bay. On midsummer's eve he walks the half-mile to the sacred spring outside the town, where he pours water into the bucket his mother has given him. He carries it back home without spilling a single drop. And now there it is, standing in the sitting-room guarding them against misfortune and sickness. The sprigs of St John's Wort that his mother has stuck in a crack in the beam grow day by day and promise him a long life.

IN THE POOR school, in the reading room of the old building, the walls are covered with paintings of scenes from the Bible. He sits and stares at them, falling under their magic spell until his teacher's harsh words rouse him from his daydreams. Things always go wrong when his imagination runs away with him, and he talks to the other children about what he has 'seen' – snakes in the Garden of Eden with not one but three heads; Cain murdering his brother with a shearing knife covered with blood only to cast the knife from him and kneel before God to pray for forgiveness; the dance around the Golden Calf that took place not only in the Sinai desert but also among the dead lying in St Knud's churchyard (that's what he dreamt!); and what about the dove he saw by the millstream that looked just like the one sent out from Noah's Ark to find dry land? 'You're off your head,' one of the bigger boys says to him one day, and he falls silent and moves away to be by himself. 'You talk too much,' another one says and threatens to beat him because his clothes are so odd. He doesn't have a waistcoat like a number of the rich boys in the town, but his grandmother has sewn him a large patchwork stomacher out of pieces of old silk which is fastened where a waistcoat should be, and on top of that she has tied a big bow. Why does he always have to wear clogs? They ring on the cobbles, and the street urchins are after him like a shot when he has to go out of town to fetch milk for his mother. They shout all kinds of things at him, but he can answer back. He shouts back, 'You jabber, all of you – like ducks!'

DARKNESS. THE LIGHTED candles, shadows and his father's breath close by. He can hear him breathing when he pulls the thin thread and changes the pictures in the peepshow, and as they watch the backcloth changes into a forest, a castle, a night sky with tiny shining stars. Now, as he reads aloud from *A Thousand and One Nights*, the light flickers and colours his cheek.

He wakes and feels the wet. The cup has fallen out of his hands as he dozed, and the gruel has spilt, covering the duvet and his nightclothes in a thick mess. How long does he have to lie here in this pool of soup? He tries to climb out of the bed, but he is too weak and fumbles for the bell. When at last he gets hold of it and rings, there is no response, not a sound in the house except the faint soughing of the wind outside. For a long time he lies there, staring at the white painted door out to the passage and thinks of all the closed doors to all the rooms where he has lain. The space before him expands; it feels as though he is shrinking. That's what it feels like, being alone. It only occurs to him now that neither the Melchiors nor the servant nor the maid are in. The servant and the maid are in Tivoli. And Dr Meyer has already been. When was that? Two hours ago, or . . .? He coughs violently and cannot settle in the bed. How can they just let him lie here? Ah, yes. He knows. He is so much trouble for them. Wasn't it today that he wrote his will? He can't quite remember and reaches out for the pile of letters on the nightstand waiting for his signature. One of the letters has his name and address on it – King Christian IX. He smiles faintly and coughs again, letting the letter fall to the floor. Now he can hear footsteps on the stairs, a knock on the door, and the servant, Jens, comes in breathless and red-faced, pressing his hands together as usual.

'I have got wet all over me,' he whispers to him, seeing nothing but a shadow.

Jens calls the maid and they tug him up out of the bed. He stands swaying on his legs, supported by Jens, while the maid pulls his nightclothes off, until he is standing there naked in his bony frame with only one wish – to sleep. Suddenly he is shouting, delirium in his eyes, his tongue; and Jens has to lead him backwards with both hands on his shoulders, settling him on the edge of the bed; but when the maid tries to pull on clean trousers, he starts shouting again, thinking that he is being assaulted. They calm him, put on his jacket, change the bedclothes and tuck him in under the duvet.

'I am cold,' he says, closing his eyes. 'Is there anyone there?'

'Yes, Herr Andersen,' Jens says. 'Your servant and Oline, the kitchen maid.'

'Is it night or day?'

'Night. It's one o'clock.'

'There are so many shadows.'

'I can't see any,' Jens says.

'How old are you?' he asks.

'Forty-two.'

'Then you are not old enough. That's why you can't see them.'

He lies in the bed, exhausted. He can feel the pain and reaches out for the morphine.

'You can go now,' he says when he has taken two teaspoons. 'I would like to be alone.'

They wish him goodnight and leave.

It feels as though his father has just said goodnight to him. And a moment later as though no one has been there at all.

The ceiling is white, much too white, but with astonishing speed it turns as gold as henna. The sun is shining in the middle of the night.

He is flying again.

Morning has come. He is lying on the wall-bench with measles, running a temperature, sweating. His father has put on his uniform, the red jacket and blue trousers, and is singing and talking in the kitchen a few feet away. His company is to go to Holstein and fight for Napoleon. There is no more work for a cobbler, and he has enlisted for two and a half *skillings* a day and wants to go. One of the neighbours has said that it is madness to go off and get shot unless you are forced to. But he knows his father's hero is Napoleon! Now he is standing there with his crooked smile and has put on his spooned and polished boots. He bends over him, his rough sleeve against his skin, kissing him hard, again and again, and will not let him go, shaking when he lays his arm around his father's neck, until his mother has to separate them, the tears wet on her cheeks. 'Why are you going?' she says, sobbing. 'Why do you have to hurt us like this?' His father laughs a strange laugh that does not belong to him. 'I have to,' he says. 'It's for the money, too.' 'No one loves you like I do,' his mother says. 'And the boy can't live without his father, and he is your own – that I know with a clear conscience.' 'He is mine, and that he'll still be when I come home again,' his father says. 'I'll be back soon.' The drums sound across the town, and he leaves, his mother following him, weeping, to the town gates. He is lying there alone when his grandmother comes in and sits by him, looking at him for a long time, stroking his hair. And says, 'It would be a blessing for you to die now, but none know the will of the Lord.' His lips hurt. His father has kissed them raw and bleeding.

PETER JUNCKER, THE billsticker, is his friend. He was in the army and beat up his wife, which is why he lost his commission. He tried to kill himself by cutting his own throat but went to gaol instead. Later he was pardoned and now lives in Greyfriars Street just by the theatre. Every other day Juncker gives him a poster, and in exchange he hands out a small sheaf of them in the lanes around Munkemøllestræde. He would do anything to get close to the theatre! He takes the poster home and sits in a corner, staring at the title and the names of the characters, dreaming up his own play that he can then watch for hours inside his head.

HE HAS SEEN *The Maid of the Danube* at the theatre and is now Sir Albrecht, his mother's apron tied round his shoulders and a broom in his hand, riding out with lance and sword to fight his way through the sitting-room, out to the kitchen where his mother is and back again. Now he is swimming, belly-down on a stool, and is the Maid of the Danube waiting to be rescued by Sir Albrecht. He fills the air with gobbledegook, some in German, some of it made up, shouting '*Schwester*' and '*Bruder*', until suddenly his mother is standing in front of him, barring his way and saying, 'You've got to stop now! Otherwise I'll start thinking you're off your head.' But he doesn't think she is serious, and soon he is at it again.

The vicar's widow, Mrs Bunkeflod, lives in a house near by. Her son drowned in the river, in the chamber of the mill sluice near Munke Mølle. They say that the waterman demands his sacrifices. Her skin is pale and wrinkled, her fingers long, but her eyes shine when she talks about 'my brother, the poet'. 'It is a joy to be a poet,' she and her sister say. Here he finds books by Shakespeare from the lending library; he reads *Macbeth* in her sitting-room and the same evening stages it in his puppet theatre with witch-dolls dressed in black fabric torn from a worn blouse his mother has thrown away. The witches scream their curses in rhyme, and many die. His whole body quivers with excitement.

FIRST *ARIADNE OF Naxos*, then *Medea* followed by Wessel's *Love Without Stockings*. He reads one book after the other – and writes. His 'Abor and Elvire', based on the ballad of 'Pyramus and Thisbe', fills half a page. When he reads it aloud for the woman next door, she says, 'It ought to be called "A Bore and a Bit",' and laughs. He is furious and runs to his mother, who comforts him. 'The woman only says that because her own son didn't write it.'

But she in her turn gets angry with him again, threatening him with the birch when he imitates Casorti walking the tightrope and pantomimes and dances the whole of 'Harlequin Chief of the Threshers' barefoot in the sitting-room. He says, 'One day I shall be a dancer, or a hero – just like the famous men I've read about in biographies.'

HE IS IN the beech woods with his father, the dry twigs cracking under his clogs. He is picking wild raspberries, and the sky is far away, an endless blue. Why is his father sitting there on the tree stump like that, brooding and hollow? He went away a soldier and came home a broken man. Not even the comets and heavenly bodies interest him any more. Not even reading. He runs over to him now, the cup of his hands filled with raspberries, over to that grey face with its shadow of a smile. Smile, Father! Smile again . . .

Winter outside; his father in the bed, sweating, coughing constantly, fever in his eyes and in his ashen face. He whispers, can scarcely speak. What did the freezing, mud-filled trenches of Holstein do to him? The soldiers fell like flies. His father's hot, dry hand, shaking slightly, takes hold of his and points towards the frozen pane. 'There in the window. Look. You can all see the ice-maiden coming to fetch me . . .' In the night his father stands up in the bed, shaking the bedposts, shouting, 'To horse! Bridle up! Cannons forward!' The battlefield is spread out in front of him, and his mother has sent for two farmhands to hold him down. But the following morning the two men are asleep, and there he is up and dancing on the bed again under orders from Napoleon, commanding the entire army with his wild bellowing. Suddenly in the midst of his fit his father catches sight of him and shouts, 'What, boy? Can't you see my emperor? Get out of his way, will you! Get that cap off your head, you young pup, when the emperor rides past . . .!'

His MOTHER HAS sent him out to the 'wise' woman in Eiby a mile away to save his father's life, and he has found his way, half running, out to her tumbledown house by the village pond. She looks like a toad, and before she will come to his father she wants to touch him and practise her arts on him. She ties a piece of knitting wool to his wrist and gives him a leaf from 'the Tree of the Cross of Christ'. 'Is my poor father going to die?' he sobs. 'If he is going to die,' she replies, 'then you will meet his spirit on the road when you go home!' All the way home along the dusty highway and across the fields he is terrified of meeting airborne apparitions of his father, and when he arrives at Munkemøllestræde he sees him standing there in front of the door.

His father lies dead. His face is all contorted and white. He stands there, looking down at him with his mother. And aren't those long gashes he can see down both arms and legs? 'There you can see,' says his mother, 'where the devil had its claws in him to snatch him away because he said that Christ was nothing but a man!'

HE IS SWEATING, tossing in the bed. Must reach for the bell again. She is standing there, Fru Melchior.

'Can God let us disappear completely into nothing? Do we turn into nothing but dust and ashes? Blown out, burnt out like a candle?' he says.

'We do not disappear, Andersen,' she says. 'You cannot disappear. Your light burns on. Now sleep.'

He is not the shoemaker's son any more, but the washerwoman's. While his mother pounds the wet linen with a wooden paddle against one of the big rocks on the banks of the river, he stands on another, singing at the top of his voice, improvising on songs he knows, making his own sound, his own tunes, and often there is no sense in what he sings. His mother stops once in a while to look in amazement at this strange boy of hers.

SISTER KAREN MARIE, half-sister only and doesn't look like him, isn't all arms and legs and doesn't live with them any more, although she does come and eat sometimes even when they have nothing but bread, nothing. He knows where she lives but hardly ever visits, for her mother can't stand the father, and her household is just as poor as theirs. One night when his mother didn't come home and there was a storm outside they slept in the same bed, clinging to each other in the dark. He has sung for her, and when he sings she smiles and is his whole sister. When she was confirmed, he went to the church just like his mother. She had white silk trimmings to her dress, and she shone. They gave her flowers, roses. Now she is in service, a housemaid in Svendborg. He dreams about her. About her smile and about the night when they clung to each other in the dark. 'It's just such a shame for her that her father is such a swine,' her mother says. *His* mother. She also says, 'I would like to give her more, but I have nothing to give.'

THE HUGE AMPHITHEATRE, the factory floor. His grandmother goes with him when he has to start work, sweeping, being a dogsbody, but he draws the attention of the other workers by getting up and singing his improvised ballads in that high treble voice, even reciting entire scenes from Holberg and Shakespeare on the factory floor while they listen. His voice is curiously clear and high, and one day one of the men grabs hold of him and shouts, 'This isn't no boy we got here, for sure, but a little maid!' He screams and bawls as others help to pull his trousers off, howling with laughter when they have done so, and he rushes out of the factory home to his mother. 'You will never go there again!' she promises him. For several days he hides in the house, refusing to go outside.

HE HAS WRITTEN a poem for the gravestone of a little girl called Marie and has to read it aloud for Mrs Bunkeflod. He sprints across the cobbles, finds her in her sitting-room and begins to read before she has sat down:

In memory of little Marie, died 26 November 1816

Gone to rest is this bright being,
Taken in her tender years.
Earthly things her eyes scarce seeing
Ere th'untimely call she hears.
As she from earthly kingdoms flies
To Heaven's lovely marble hall
Her smile the deathly sting denies

And sees it never as betrayal
To leave these earthly realms behind,
And with the angel choirs to find
A way to God and Heaven's maker,
There to be His message-taker.
Look! I see an angel mild
Climbing upward through the skies
And it is the parting child
Spreading the joy of paradise.

Mrs Bunkeflod casts him a look of appreciation and asks him to read it again, holding a lace handkerchief to the corner of one eye with her long dry fingers when he has finished. His heart beating with pent-up jubilation, he rushes out of the house, the sheet still in his hand, to find a fresh audience.

HE GLIDES AWAY to land somewhere else.

At the theatre in Odense, the actors, the king's singers and their wigs, the hoists behind stage, the hubbub and shouting, the feverish feel of the space in semi-darkness, the sounds of instruments tuning up coming from the pit and, from the auditorium, of the audience taking their seats. And later, when *Cendrillon* unfolds on the stage, he is waiting in the wings with the voices of the altos and basses filling him and their heavy footfalls on the boards making him jump. And now he steps out in his red silk costume and speaks his lines, and everyone – thousands of eyes – are looking at him, the extra! He cannot sleep all night, dreaming about Copenhagen. The Theatre Royal.

'Guten Morgen, mon père! Har de godt sleeping?' is one of the lines in his first play, which he peppers with words in Danish, English, German and French, using a dictionary of some kind. His mother and their neighbours in Munkemøllestræde say that that's how a king and a princess would talk, in tongues of Babel, and he recites it around the town for the widows, the bishop and Colonel Høegh-Guldberg. It is a tragedy, and everyone dies at the end. He is so happy reading it out aloud. He writes down ideas for the plays he wants to write in his father's old army logbook. Twenty-five titles in all.

ACROSS THE ECHOING church floor, his father's old jacket cut down to fit him, and the whole congregation listening to the squeaking newness of his boots, he has a momentary feeling – despite standing lowest and last in the queue waiting to be confirmed – that he is the equal of boys from the grammar school, who always make him feel as though he is sticking his nose in where he doesn't belong. The archdeacon in his robes comes over to him as he has done to them and hears his affirmation of faith and blesses him – although hadn't he once said that he was not wanted there? The archdeacon looks down at him with a heavy frown, waiting for him to make a mistake in his responses, but he knows the whole thing by heart and fills with exultation. Did you see me?

He sits on the balcony. An hour and a half. A dragonfly hovers over the flowerbeds and melts away into the shimmering heat. White sails across the Sound. A regatta, Jens, the servant, tells him. The hairdresser has been, and the barber, who nicked his cheek. Perhaps it's still bleeding? The tailor will come later to measure him up for a new jacket. When is he supposed to wear it? Will he take it with him to the grave? No. He must stop this feeling sorry for himself. But, oh, he gets so tired. The doctor will come too late, and there is no wind anyway. That is why the white sails stand there as still as hundreds of doors opening on to an endless blue.

HE WANTS TO go to Copenhagen. Fourteen years old, loose-limbed and lanky, he refuses to be a manual worker, for the earth is burning beneath his feet. 'What will become of you in Copenhagen?' his mother asks. 'I will become famous, just like the men I have read about who were born poor!' he says. 'You go through so many hard times, and then you become famous.' His mother has no faith in him, and he begs her, weeping, forcing her. 'If you are going to be famous,' his mother says, 'then the wise woman from the hospital will be able to tell your fortune in coffee-grounds and cards, she'll see if you are right!' He is lying on his bed when the wise woman comes, and he goes down in his nightclothes to find her wrapped in the darkness of the parlour, a scar on one of her grey cheeks, her eyes shining from the shadows. Is she a ghost? He has to sit opposite her at the heavy wooden table and hears her hoarse breath when she lays out the cards and coffee-grounds with her thickened fingers. 'Her son will be a great man,' she says. 'Odense will be lit up in his honour one day.'

MISS HAMMER IS in town to give a performance, and the comedian, Mr Foersom, clerk at the prefect's office, is to be in the cast. He, too, seeks her out, and she receives him kindly, telling him he is to play the role of the young postman in *The Pawned Peasant Boy*. She sends him into town day after day with her *billets doux*, but he doesn't know what they are. One day he sees her on the bed with Foersom, his trousers hanging down under his naked rump as he thrusts himself into her, over her groaning wild-eyed face. Should he leave her? Behaving like that? But hasn't she promised to take him with her to Copenhagen? Hasn't she said, with that caressing voice of hers, 'I'll recommend you to my friend Miss Didriksen, the dancer!'? His mother washes her clothes for her for a whole month, and she is so grateful. But the weeks pass, and nothing happens. She has conned them. Him and his mother.

Nothing. Happens. He will live on. Live.

He smashes open his piggybank. Thirteen *rigsdalers* pour out, a whole year's savings, and enough for the journey to Copenhagen. But he doesn't know a soul in Copenhagen. He goes down to Printer Iversen's house. The printer knows most of the actors in Copenhagen, and despite being a stranger there he knocks on his door. The old man ushers him into his office. 'I am going off, all on my own, to join the theatre in Copenhagen,' he says. 'Can you help by giving me an introduction?' 'That is not a wise idea,' the old man says. 'It won't get you anywhere. Learn a craft instead.' 'That is a real shame,' he replies, 'since I shall be leaving anyway.' The old man tries to persuade him to stay in Odense, but when he sees it is no use he smiles sadly, his hands trembling. 'Of all the people at the theatre, who would you like me to write to?' 'The dancer Madame Schall,' he says. 'She is very influential.' Iversen slowly turns his back to him and pens a letter to her. In the light from the dusty, unwashed window his grey hair shines.

MORE LETTERS. MORE and more. He gets none written himself. To whom should he write? To stare out of the window, not to be able to get out. Such weakness! So much time. Oh, the expanses of time. Like millions of scents, millions of thoughts. His own have their peculiarities. Perhaps he is a little afraid of the letters the postman's footsteps bring? Perhaps they carry indiscretions enveloped inside them, comical infatuations?

There she is again, Fru Melchior, with the day's white rose. She turns towards him. She, too, in a white dress with a black shawl over her shoulders. Her skin shines. Her eyes.

'I must tell you . . .' he says.

She sits beside him, on the white chair.

'What is it . . . Andersen?'

'One day, it was around the coronation of Christian VIII . . .'

'Yes?'

He comes to a halt, searches for the way forward.

'I was living at the Hotel du Nord, when into the foyer comes a rather odd girl in a silk dress and asks me to write a poem for her mother's birthday. I tell her that she can come up to my room a little later. When she comes in, she rushes straight to my sofa and sits down, then jumps up again and steps to the window. "How incomparably beautiful your room is!" she says. "You are my poet. I love you!" She leaps back to the sofa and throws herself across it. "Embrace me!" she says. "The Lord preserve us!" I say. "Whatever are you thinking of?" She forces herself upon me, throwing her arms around me, kissing me, so I have to push her away. "Have you no mother?" I say. "What would she say if she saw you now? You must be out of your mind. You really must leave now. You frighten me – Get away!" Her face, her body – everything changes. "You are loathsome," she says. "I have loved you, but now I hate you. You think yourself a poet! You haven't a clue what a poet is!" I am shaking all over. "Go!" I say. She runs out, I put on my overcoat and hurry round to Councillor Collin, but he cannot help. I run into old Mrs Thybjerg. "What's up with you?" she asks, and she laughs when she hears the explanation. "Oh my God, you've had a woman in your room!" The next day Dr Andreas Bunzen provides the key to the mystery by saying, "But that's the hysterical young woman *lying up at the hospital. She says she loves you and quotes quite shame-lessly from your play* The Mulatto *all the time! She slipped off by mistake and must have come up to you. We will keep her shut away, don't worry." It was only then that I became calm, but for a long time I had nightmares about her coming back.'*

Fru Melchior takes his hand.

'Don't fret any more. Rest now,' she says with a faint smile. 'There's no harm done.'

His mother packs a bundle with his clothes. She has spoken to the postman, and he will turn a blind eye to his presence on the coach to Copenhagen for just three *rigsdalers*. He doesn't know what to do with himself, roams the town, bidding farewell to familiar brickwork, to the church, the river, to some of the neighbours; mute and giddy under a sky of such a strange eggshell-blue, he even says goodbye to the gooseberry bushes and makes his way back to his mother. She passes him yet another bag filled with lumps of bread. 'Don't eat them until you get over the Great Belt,' she says. They sit down opposite each other, she in the kitchen, he on the alcove bed. Isn't she crying? There is the smell of alcohol in the house. Her cheeks are flushed. He has to leave the house again, can find no peace. At last it is afternoon, a beautiful sunlit afternoon, and his mother follows him out of the door and down to the mail coach and its four heavy horses. Inconsolable she is and cries again as she envelops him in her powerful arms. His grandmother stands beside the coach with her grey hair and weeps, too, as she clings to his neck. As for him, he can say nothing, but his right hand is shaking as he pitches into the coach, where Mrs Hermansen's bulk fills the seat. The postilion blows his horn, the coach-wheels rumble, the horses whinny, the whip cracks, and soon his grandmother and his mother are vanishing out of sight, small dots far behind him. He drinks in his surroundings, the trees, the streets, the fields, and soon he is telling Mrs Hermansen and the other passengers about his plans for Copenhagen and his play, showing her his letter from Iversen, for hasn't he been recommended to a dancer in Copenhagen? Sitting there in his coarse country clothes, he is elated, talks ten to the dozen, but once out on the Great Belt in the rocking movement of the boat he feels how alone he is. They have scarcely landed on Zealand before he rushes round behind a shed and falls to his knees, praying God to help and guide him. That whole day and the following night they drive down lanes, through villages. They stop several times to repack, and he stands alone beside the coach, eating his bread, feeling far away in the world. His stomach rumbles. He bites his tongue.

DEPOSITED AT RANDOM like an unwanted guest, he wanders towards Copenhagen with his little bundle bound in cloth, passes Frederiksberg Palace with its green park and Frederiksberg Church, turns down Frederiksberg Avenue lined with lime trees and past the low gables and the gardens of Vesterbro, past the Liberty Memorial and in through the gate to the city on to lanes and streets and market squares thronging with hurrying people. People are shouting, windows are smashed, soldiers rush past with bayonets at the ready, posters on the walls read 'Extortionists, usurers, money-grubbers, swindlers'; a man dressed in a cap and filthy rags looks at him suspiciously, talks to him about 'the house of Moses and his nest of Jews which has to be made to pay' and scurries round the corner. He is terrified, speechless. The city is heaving, but isn't this Copenhagen, hub of the world? The meat market with carts heaving with the carcasses of pigs, the hoarse whooping of fishwives, the greengrocers' carts on Gammel Torv, the old market square, the Bullet mail drawn by two horses, shining black four-in-hand carriages, street urchins in clogs, girls with hoops, beggars – yes, this is the city. The canals reflecting the sky, the Exchange with its spiralling dragon-tails, the palace, Christiansborg, with its roof of green copper, the gothic windows of the Round Tower, the streets with their endless shop-fronts with their spice jars, silken fabrics, top hats hidden inside, in the dark behind the windows' reflections – this is the city. And the smells, the stench of shit in the gutters, of sour milk in wooden churns, of cow dung, of fish in barrels – this is the city. Here a stable lad is grooming his horse, here an apothecary is grinding his medicine, here a travelling musician is playing his violin, his hat beside him on the street. The gilded gleam of railings, the balconies and pilasters, the churches and the Theatre Royal, looking like an enormous collapsed elephant. This is Copenhagen. He walks around the elephant. Time and again. He feels dizzy and falls asleep exhausted in his cheap lodgings in Gardergården in Vestergade. Has only eaten dry bread and then forgot to eat.

The servant stands there holding a cup for him; he must have been standing there a long time.

'*Your gruel, Herr Andersen.*'

'*Can't eat,*' he says, turning his head away.

'*I will put your cup on the nightstand,*' says the servant and is gone again.

Was he there?

HIGH-CEILINGED STAIRWAY, plaster on the walls, wide steps with marble treads, wrought ironwork with looping roses. The door on to the clamour of the street outside slams shut behind him. He trembles, waits for a moment on the first step, clutching the letter of introduction to Mrs Schall, then up the stairs he goes with shirt-frill flapping and his dark confirmation trousers tucked into his boots until he reaches the landing with Schall's nameplate and a bell-pull on the white door. He falls to his knees and prays God that here he will find help and protection. Just at that moment a maidservant climbs the stairs with a basket on her arm and, seeing him lying there before the door, smiles to him, throws him a six-*skilling* piece and is already tripping on up the next flight before he can shout after her, 'I'm not a beggar!'. 'Just keep it,' she calls down from somewhere higher up and is gone. He returns the next day, and the next, pulling the bell-rope until at last he is let in, and the short, plump figure of the dancer, Mrs Schall, receives him in her *chambre*. He has his broad-brimmed hat with him and is quick to show her his introduction. 'Don't think I know this printer, Iversen,' she says with a little laugh. 'Now, what parts can you dance?' '*Cendrillon!*' he says straight away in his singsong Funen accent. 'That's one I like a lot.' And before she can look twice, he has pulled off his boots and, using the broad-brimmed hat as a substitute for a tambourine, he begins to dance on the polished floor. His hand gestures are dramatic and angular, his dance more of a run and glide of his spindly figure round the floor, and he sings as he goes:

> What does money mean to me?
> What is show and fine beauty?!

He sees the disappointment behind her make-up. 'I cannot give you much hope,' she says. 'You haven't shown a great deal of talent with that dance.' He starts to cry. 'If only you will help me. I have to get into the theatre, I will do anything – I'll run your errands for you!' 'You can come here and have yourself a meal once in a while,' she says, opening the door to the hall and accompanying him out. He cannot help feeling that she wants to be rid of him as quickly as possible. Once again he begs for her help. 'I shall ask Bournonville, the ballet master, whether you can come to dance and learn something,' she says, but without conviction. He hears her words but is already on his way down the stairs. Out. Out.

HE GOES TO see the chamberlain, Frederik von Holstein, head of the Theatre Royal, a military man with an arid face. He knocks on the door of his office and steps in awkwardly to stand before him, hat in hand and in his threadbare confirmation clothes. When he starts to say something, von Holstein waves a silencing hand from his desk. After a silence von Holstein glances across at him as though by chance, and he gabbles off his entire story. 'So I am looking for a post at the theatre, I can act as well as sing and dance,' he says in conclusion. Von Holstein passes him under review. Distaste is visible round his mouth. 'You are too thin for the theatre,' he says. The words escape him. 'Oh, if only I could be paid a wage of a hundred *rigsdalers*, I would soon get fat!' Von Holstein remains completely silent for a moment. Then he points to the door. 'You may go now,' he says. 'Here we only engage people with manners.' On his way down the steps and to the gate out on to Kongens Nytorv, he swears to himself that he will turn back, but his legs are shaking under him as he walks into the square.

He will have to travel home, will have to find a skipper to take him, but is certain that the ship will go down, that God will let it all end that way. He is sitting on a bench in the gardens of Kongens Have with a slice of bread and a sausage, talking to a tree. 'But the ship won't go down just on my account,' he says to the tree.

The chestnuts outside. They sing to the night. He hears them. In his night sweat.

HE CAN SING, can't he? Haven't people said that he has a lovely voice? Soprano or light baritone. He calls on the royal choirmaster Siboni, whom he read about in the papers, and goes to the mansion at 5 Vingårdsstræde. Here he finds the servants' entrance and presents his story to the housemaid, a heavy woman who offers him cake, frowning as she tries to memorize every word he says. 'You want to be employed as a singer,' she says. 'But Choirmaster Siboni might not have much time for you – right now he is in the company of genteel folk.' She disappears into the drawing-room and is gone a long time. Suddenly the door to the kitchen opens wide, and the entire gathering is standing there, watching him. Swarthy Mr Siboni with his fleshy face seizes him by the hand. '*Kommen Sie! Kommen Sie!*' he says, leading him to the pianoforte standing amid salons bathed in light, the walls glimmering with tapers and oil lamps. Here in the centre of the parquet floor he is to sing. There is complete silence. In his grey frockcoat several sizes too small, which cannot hide his emaciated wrists, he embarks on a melancholy ballad, improvising, filling the room with his clear voice while his arms dramatize the effect. His small oriental eyes close until he is somewhere else and without changing register has begun to declaim scenes from Holberg and recite his own poems. The earth slides away beneath him, and the feeling comes over him of being at the same time released and on display in a faraway loneliness, and a strange sorrow wells up in him and heightens the effect. The company applaud. The poet Baggesen grips his hand enthusiastically. 'You have traces of that true naturalness that otherwise is lost with age and human contact. Something great will become of you,' he says. Weyse, the composer, in his blue frockcoat studded with gold buttons, praises his musicality, and Siboni with an airy wave of the hand pronounces that he will train his voice. '*Sie kommen – singen – im Königlichen Theater,*' he says. He leaves the elated company, stopping on the stairs – the housemaid has to be told that all that remains of his fortune is seven *rigsdalers* Later a hat is passed around in the salon above, and the next

45

day, when he visits Weyse in Kronprinsessegade, he is told that he has seventy-five *rigsdalers* at his disposal. He is beside himself with joy. On the way down the stairs he stops in front of a window, kisses his hand and raises it to the sky to convey his thanks to God.

WAKES WITH A start after a long, blissful night. And wonders whether it was his own scream in the dark night . . . The joy and forgiveness that were within reach slide away, vanishing like sand between his fingers. He coughs up a clot of phlegm but has nowhere to spit it out. He cannot face ringing for the servant. It is beautiful sunshine outside, summer; in the vase a few feet away the white rose hangs its head.

ULKEGADE. THE STAIR passage with its creaking floor leading up to his room, wrought-iron curlicues and small roses in its balustrade which once was white, but filth clings to the lining paper of the walls and outside in the street garbage lies in heaps when people move house. Of the money given to him, Mrs Thorgesen demands twenty *rigsdalers* a month, but his room is only a small cubicle that was once a pantry. Here he has his bed and a couple of chairs standing one on top of the other and above the bed two shelves with jam jars. A thin trickle of light squeezes through the two air holes bored in the top of the door to the kitchen. There is scarcely room for him on the floor to struggle in or out of his clothes. By day he practises scales with Siboni in his mansion and runs errands or works as a *garçon*. In the evenings, sometimes at night, he sits by the candle, reading books from the lending library or the university library above the round church, where he has curried favour with the librarian, Rasmus Nyerup, who is also from Odense. Schiller, Walter Scott, Oehlenschläger, Ingemann, Shakespeare. He stitches his grey frockcoat, darns his stockings. And writes. He scrounges from the shops on Østergade and Købmagergade – samples of clothing or silk ribbons – and sits every day, sewing clothes for the dolls in his toy theatre and his peepshow, playing with them, performing *King Bluebeard*, *Macbeth*. His dolls' finery obsesses him, and he often stands still on a street corner, observing rich ladies in their silks and velvets, imagining the royal cloaks and knights' costumes he could make from their clothes. His imagination works its scissors like a thought, cutting new patterns and costumes out of what his eye sees. The lady in the room next to his, a lodger like himself, receives a guest from time to time, an uncle, who sometimes comes knocking even in the evening, and he goes down to open the door for him, standing there in the gloom wrapped in his cloak and with his silk top hat tilted down over his eyes. A fine gentleman with pointed black boots and almost no face. He hears the uncle rummaging around in the lady's room and groaning through the paper-thin walls. A bed creaks. The man is not the maid's uncle, and he feels sorry for her. In the night he dreams that Siboni is telling him off with that fiery temper of his – just seeing the grave expression in his teacher's eyes makes his voice quaver. 'No, no! *Nicht frighten, Du!*' Siboni says, but puts money in his hand anyway when he reaches the door with his heart in his boots. 'Make some fun! *Ein bisschen amüsieren, ne!*' Siboni says, smiling.

HE MUST TALK to Fru Melchior. Where is she? He has rung for her so many times now, hasn't he? There she is – no, not her after all; the door hasn't moved. But she is there, beside his bed. He whispers.

'What are you saying, Andersen?'

'I remember everything so clearly,' he says, 'even now, the faces.'

'Which faces?'

'All those I have ever seen and spoken with. I have their picture inside me, just like a mirror.'

'That is a gift.'

'I cannot remember my own. My own face that has mirrored itself more than so many.'

She lifts his head with one hand, straightening his pillow with the other. He is dribbling like a baby. She wipes away his saliva with a white cloth that shines in the darkness of the night. Her black dress rustles and catches the light as she rises to leave him. She is an angel. The wavering candle is snuffed out by the gentle draught from the corridor.

HIS VOICE IS breaking, and he cannot stay in Siboni's house. Siboni says to him, '*Lær Dem etwas mit den Hænder zu tun. Reisen Sie nach Odense zurück.*' But manual work and Odense are not for him. And he runs round town with the top hat that Siboni has given him, declaiming, reciting poems, collecting benefactors, money. His narrow leggings, given to him by someone, don't even reach his worn-out shoes, which are often wet through. A jacket donated by someone else is far too short, and a coat passed on by a fourth has a fox collar that, when he is not observed, he is busy restoring and mending. He is proud of it. Often when the door is opened, and he stands there, an uninvited guest, he gives the impression of someone with something to offer his audience – something 'from the Danish stage' – and he places his hat on the floor and embarks on his programme, breathless, exalted. At the end – exhausted – he takes a deep bow, his hair hanging in long, lank strands round his cheeks, and is gone. Professor Guldberg, the brother of Guldberg in Odense, teaches him German and grammar and gives him clothes in which he dresses up when he visits Mr Dahlén, the dancing master on 18 Badstruestræde. Pale of face and elastic of body, Dahlén listens and smiles kindly. 'I have heard of you – from Weyse and Siboni,' he says. 'Come up to the Theatre Royal, and I will set aside some time for you to dance.' He is set alight. Perhaps he really will become a dancer.

THE DANCING SCHOOL. Mirrors, *barres* where he stands every day by the long pole and stretches his legs, learns to perform a *battement*, seeing in the mirror how difficult it is for his long legs to swing round in a *pirouette*. Two girls in tutus giggle at him. When one of the girls is dressed up as a page, she scrapes his shin with her foot; he can see it on his stockings. One boy, already a fabulous dancer, often pricks him with a needle. He is dead keen and won't give up, but one day Mr Dahlén says, 'You won't get much further than being a *figurant*.' The friendly Mr Dahlén who opens his doors to him, his home, where the family plays the travel game with him or where from time to time he fetches his puppet theatre from under Mrs Thorgesen's apron in Ulkegade to perform his plays for Mrs Dahlén and her daughters. They laugh at his childishness. He knows they do.

He has a walk-on part. He hears that they need people to fill out the market scene in a musical, *The Little Savoyards*, which is being staged at the Theatre Royal. With a little make-up on his cheeks, he steps on to the great stage at just the right moment, along with the others. The rows of lights beam down from the proscenium arch in front of the dark buzz of the audience. The prompter's face is lit up like a ghost's under the roof of his little box at the front of the stage. He is wearing his badly cut confirmation clothes, his hat hangs almost over his eyes, while the diminutive jacket and the worn-out boots are faults he tries to hide as he mingles with the crowd, awkward and intoxicated at the feeling of the vast and breathing oneness of the auditorium. At that very moment one of the established actors grasps his hand and congratulates him derisively on his 'début' on the stage. 'May I introduce you to the population of Denmark?' he says and pulls him towards the footlights. In the immense darkness they are now going to laugh at him, at his oddities; he feels cut to the quick, is on the point of crying and, tearing himself away, he rushes out.

THREE TIMES UP in the night, constipated – passing blood? Each time Jens, the servant, came. Jens helps him out to the lavatory in the corridor, waits patiently and helps him back again. He tells Jens about the pain, about the letters that never get written, and Jens listens patiently. Maybe he doesn't understand what he is saying. Looks worn out the third time. Back in bed he whispers to himself, 'Poor Jens'. Does Jens hear it?

HE WRITES PETITIONS, 'To noble-minded philanthropists', to the king (with Høegh-Guldberg's help), to Ingermann, to Grundtvig. He writes: 'Girded only with my powerful desire and my trust in noble beings, I stepped out into the wide world, for my father, a poor shoemaker in Odense, had nothing to give me.' Or:

> I the steepest mountains will ascend;
> If I there but Thalia's temple spy,
> None, though he be deemed a happy man,
> Shall happy be as I.

Mrs Engelke Margrethe Colbiørnsen, widow of the high court judge Christian Colbiørnsen, has supported him with money and has a daughter who is lady-in-waiting to the crown princess. He hears that she desires to see him, has hurried out to Frederiksberg Castle and talked his way in, has forced himself upon them and is now sitting with the lady-in-waiting in the princess's salon and rises to his feet to make a deep bow in his outlandish frockcoat, as the crown princess, with long silk sleeves trailing from her dress, makes her entry. She has a pale face, lightly made up, her mouth painted red, and moves with a grace that puts him at his ease so that he immediately starts singing and declaiming. The two women applaud softly and praise him so that he bows again. And talks and talks. They give him sweets, grapes, peaches, and ten *rigsdalers* in coins. Afterwards he wanders into town and sits on a bench in Kongens Have gardens. Shouldn't he keep half the sweets for Mrs Thorgesen? The trees are green and scented around him. It is summer. His joy overwhelms him, and he begins to sing, improvising, speaking to the lime trees, to the flowers, the birds. Who else is there to share his joy with? A lad from a local stable walks past and turns to him. 'Are you off your head?' he asks sharply. He falls silent, embarrassed, and slips away from the gardens. Out into the streets. Wanders around homeless.

Off his head?

'I WANT TO have board and lodging here with you,' he says to Mrs Thorgesen in the apartment in Ulkegade. 'Where else will I be able to eat?' 'Then you'll have to give me twenty *rigsdalers* in advance every month,' she says without batting an eye. She brushes a hair off her dress; he sees her pursed lips, and the fear wells up in him, the tears. 'Then surely you can give it to me for sixteen *rigsdalers*. That's all I get from Guldberg,' he says, the palms of his hands pleading with her. 'No,' she says, 'then you can find something else.' 'But I don't know anyone,' he sobs. 'That's your problem. You'll just have to go back where you came from.' 'I beg you,' he says, 'I beg you, take the ten *rigsdalers* I have instead and wait a fortnight for the other ten. I'll make sure you get them.' 'Twenty *rigsdalers* is what I asked for,' she insists. 'You told me yourself that kind people have collected eighty for you and that Guldberg has got them. You'd better talk to him.' 'Twenty *rigsdalers* will ruin me, the money won't last the winter, and then what will I do?' he says. 'You should have thought about that before you had the bright idea of coming to Copenhagen without a penny to your name,' she says and strides towards the door out to the hall. 'I beg you,' he says, following her. She turns around abruptly. 'I know the way you beg and pray! Now I am going into town, and if you haven't got the twenty *rigsdalers* when I return, you can pack up and go!'

She goes out, and he is alone in the parlour with the portrait of her husband. It seems to him that the picture is looking kindly at him, and with his fingertip he removes a tear from the corner of his eye and rubs it into the eye in the picture. Now the man will know how miserable he feels. He clasps his hands together and prays to the dead man to soften his wife's heart for him and then collapses into an armchair in a kind of sleep. When Mrs Thorgesen returns, she is friendlier and agrees to his requests. And he does not forget to offer up his thanks to the husband before climbing into bed in the darkness of the little pantry.

HE DREAMS, WAKES, remembers – a child dried out, shrivelled at his breast. It returns to him in a morning dream, but now the child is squatting on his shoulder. From his pillow he stares at the bed-end with its rings and its two large knobs in polished brass, at his own face distorted in the large knob to the right, a sliding form without substance.

Hill House with its view of cypresses and cornfields and grazing sheep lies outside the city ramparts, and, when he is not being an extra at the Theatre Royal or practising at the ballet school, he walks the many kilometres out here, to Rahbek and Kamma, his wife. In this little Elysium where everyone is on first-name terms, all the big names used to visit, or still come – P.A. Heiberg, Baggesen, Adam Oehlenschläger, Grundtvig, the Ørsteds, J.M. Thiele, Christian Winther, Ingemann. Rahbek, the critic at the Theatre Royal, registers his presence but doesn't speak to him, while Kamma, with her fragile form and sharp wit, is all ears and listens to him recite – again and again. One summer afternoon chubby little Mr Rahbek with his sharp nose and steel-rimmed glasses approaches him as he sits on a bank outside the house. Rahbek stops a few yards away from him, stares at him but suddenly turns away and returns to the house. He is confused, wants to catch up with him, but his courage fails him. Does he fall short here, too? Kamma makes fabulous boxes, writes letters, manages to encourage flowers and plants to grow even out of season and has a homemade epithet for every known poet. Teasing and quick with her ironic tongue, she has read everything. One day as he is reading her a tragedy that he has written in his cubicle, she claps her hands together and says, 'Oh, but there are whole passages in this you have taken from Oehlenschläger and Ingemann!' 'Yes, I know, but they are so lovely!' he replies and reads on. Another day she asks him to go up to Mrs Colbiørnsen, who lives on the first floor, with a bunch of fresh roses from the garden. And she says half in jest, 'If only you would take them up, for I am sure the lady councillor will enjoy receiving them from the hands of a poet!' On his way up he stops on the stairs with the roses in his hands and tears in his eyes. Ah yes, she said it. He is a poet. Andersen – poet. The thought makes him dizzy.

HE GOES FOR an audition with Lindgren, the theatrical director, in the picture gallery at the Theatre Royal. He has told him that he has some talent for comic parts, but he wants to play the tragic roles, preferably Correggio. 'Yes, but heavens above, my dear child,' old Lindgren has said to him, 'your looks are completely against you! God knows, people will only laugh at a tall gangling hero like that. But learn the part by all means.' He practises for a week in his cubby-hole, in bed or alone in Mrs Thorgesen's drawing-room, when no one is home. With the porter's permission he makes his way into the ballet school, lights an oil lamp in the deserted practice room and stands there, posing in front of the mirror. The shadows on his face create a dramatic effect; he has wrapped a blanket around him that resembles Correggio's cloak, and with his soft boy's voice he is Correggio, exultant one moment, melancholic the next. It is life and death. All that exists is Correggio. He himself has vanished, along with the mirrors, the ballet *barres*, the doors, the school – yes, the entire city. When on the eighth day he enacts Correggio's monologue in front of Lindgren, he is exultant, as ecstatic as Correggio at seeing the wonderful art treasure, and bursts into genuine tears. The old man sighs deeply, reaches for his hand, presses it. 'You have a heart and, God knows, a head to go with it, but you must not run around here, wasting your time,' he says. 'You must study. You will never make an actor, but there are other wonderful things, great things apart from this art!' He withdraws his hand nervously. 'Am I no good at all then?' he says. 'Not even for comic parts?' Lindgren shakes his head softly. 'Oh God! I am so unhappy! What will become of me . . .?' he says and leaves with a heavy heart. Out into the town, out into the street, out into the crowds where no one knows him and where he can hide his shame. One day in heaven, the next in hell.

DR MEYER TAKES *his temperature, breathing heavily on his face as he leans over the bed. It is dark, late, the paraffin lamp flickers on the table. Meyer's distant face reminds him of Lindgren's which itself now resembles that of the stone guest. When will he pronounce the death sentence? Meyer closes his bag with a click, but he is already far away again.*

'I get filled with bitter memories for no reason . . .'

'Do you now?' says Meyer and seems to want only to leave him.

'My youth was spent in so much struggling, so much lack of appreciation . . .'

'Don't think about such things. Think about all those people to whom you mean so much.'

'I can't help it. It is a demon that possesses me. It makes me sicker.'

'You have the king and the crown prince and most of the country on your side. What more can you want?'

'I want nothing. How can you say that? You don't understand me. Doctor Collin misunderstood me, too, some years ago, when the Melchiors offered to have me in their house. He said, "But it is such a burden for strangers to have you. You have to be nursed and cared for and that's far too much trouble." Such things are beyond me. I could never lie in bed and be a nuisance to others. I remember every word.'

'Yes, it was a stupid thing to say. But I must go now. My family are expecting me,' says Dr Meyer, as he snaps shut his bag and walks to the door.

'I cannot sleep,' he says and tries to lift his arm.

Dr Meyer returns to the bed with a sigh and gives him a cup of linctus with morphine, carefully measuring out the drops, one by one.

'To help you sleep,' he says, and then he is out of the door.

SITTING ON A bench in the gardens of Kongens Have with a lump of bread and a book. Between the naked trees he has a view of the castle. The air is cold and damp; he has pulled his sleeves down over his hands under his mottled frockcoat, several sizes too small, but with every movement they creep back up, exposing his delicate, gangling wrists above his large hands. He gnaws at the bread and the next moment is reading the book again. The cold seeps upwards from his damp boots through his legs, but he is too tired to move, is strangely listless. His only wish is that the woman coming towards him along the path will speak to him, but she walks past. He wants to follow her but remains sitting where he is. What is he to say to her? She doesn't know him. He has been reading Shakespeare translated by Admiral Wulff, who lives in a mansion near Amalienborg, the royal palace. He wants to visit him . . . This evening he has a walk-on part in Kotzebue's *The Little Sailor.* His body aches all over, even his temples, and the trees crowd in on him. The dry bread does nothing to fill his stomach. He has to get back to his cubicle, to write. Write. Exhausted, he gets up. What can he do about this cold?

PROFESSOR GULDBERG HAS complained about him to Dahlén, and now he leaves the Dahléns, where he has been putting on his puppet theatre show, to sprint out to Nørrebro, where the professor receives him coolly in his library. 'You must forgive me,' he says to the professor. 'I know that I haven't done enough of my Latin homework, but I will do better.' 'Ah, you do exactly as you please, performing here, there and everywhere as a reciter, poet or whatever you call yourself – a far cry from anything I am attempting to do with you. You could be a useful element in society, but no! You would sooner declaim poetry!' 'Forgive me,' he says, and tears are in his eyes. 'You mustn't let me be unhappy.' 'Oh, so you would stand there, playacting for me, would you?' answers Guldberg. 'If you desert me, I'll have no one left!' he says. 'I have done wrong, but God knows, I *will* work harder. I never saw where it could all end and did not have a clue what Latin was before I asked you.' 'Unhappy,' Guldberg echoes him in his silk-lapelled jacket. 'Unhappy! That is just a tirade from some play that you're putting on for me. You are a wicked person, that's what you are!' Høegh-Guldberg leads him out to the hallway, slamming the door behind him. 'It is all over as far as we are concerned,' are the last words he says.

On the way back into town he stops by Pebling Lake, at a spot where the moon is shining on the water. There is no other light. Cold it is, icy. Nothing can become of him; he is no longer good. God is angry, and he must die. He stares down into the dark water, but at the same moment thinks of his grandmother, who would refuse to believe that he jumped into the water and took his own life. 'Forgive me, Lord, for my faults and for my sinful thoughts of taking my own life,' he says to himself and tears himself away from the shadow in the water. It is a long way to Ulkegade.

SUMMER WEATHER, WARM, *incomparably lovely. He wakes. The swallows fly outside with their high melodic chirrups, clipping the edges of eternity. Could he but fly with them! Lilies stand in the vase, snow-white. Jens says they are from Dr Meyer's wife. And leaves. What floodgates have opened in heaven? He wants to go down into the garden and pick a posy. Anemones, white and purple. How many of them has he sent – in letters . . .? He tries to raise himself in the bed but sinks back. Rings for the servant. Ringing, for ever ringing.*

NIGHT AFTER NIGHT he acts as an extra, laps up the words, the diction from the stage, and by day writes in the drawing-room or the kitchen at Mrs Thorgesen's. *The Robbers of Vissenbjerg*, a play written in a fortnight about Jørgen Klo, who ends dramatically on the gallows. A young woman, who went to confirmation classes with him in Odense and who is now in Copenhagen, pays to have a fair copy made without spelling mistakes, and it is sent anonymously to the Theatre Royal; it is returned with a rejection. They know who the author is. The board of directors ascribe to him a total lack of basic education and recommend him and his benefactors to 'provide him with the guidance without which the path that he is so eager to tread will and must for ever be closed to him'. He is dismissed from his position as pupil in the chorus, and his request to have access to the theatre pit is shelved. In other words, he is no longer an extra, no longer anything, just the 'poetic customer' or 'the little declaimer', as he is known. And yet doesn't the periodical *The Harp* have the first act of the play printed on its front cover? He feasts his eyes on it in his little pantry. And continues writing. On and on. Writes day in, day out; writes till he drops. Writes with a mule-like stubbornness and with a desperate musical energy to his language. *Prologue*, *The Ghost at Palnatoke's Grave*, *Alfsol*, what more do they want? *Alfsol* – a play in five acts with a dramatic climax about Alfsol, the king's daughter, who calls her father back to life:

> That morning when once more he ventured forth
> In lusty health beneath the vaulted sky!
> The pious Alfsol clasped her hands in prayer
> In thanks to Heaven for her father's life,
> And tears, like dew on lovely violets brimmed,
> Welled up and filled the softness of her eye.

He reads *Alfsol* aloud for Mrs Jürgensen and her guest, Pastor Gutfeld – who recommends him and speaks of 'true genius' – delivers it in a parcel to the Theatre Royal and prints copies by subscription – with Her Royal Highness the Crown Princess as the first subscriber. And waits. He walks the markets, the streets and lanes of Copenhagen, and waits. Hasn't he waited long enough already? He is seventeen years old.

HE DREAMS THAT he is in prison without knowing why. It is a Spanish prison – he can sense the heat outside – and he is lying on straw, the hard, insistent rhythm of castanets penetrating his cell. In his dream he wishes that it was a dream and that he may soon wake. He does wake briefly and then falls asleep and dreams again. A fairytale queen places a blue flower on his bed. He appears to wake and when he discovers the blue flower colour flows from its succulent leaves, which he uses to paint a translucent picture on the floor. A swan eats one of the blue flowers, and its intestines turn into strings that play a melody. He lays a wreath of the blue flowers around his head, and his thoughts shine so lucidly, his pictures with such poetry that he wakes in the darkness without knowing where he is.

THERE IS A meeting of the board of the Theatre Royal, and he is requested to attend. Present: Professor K.L. Rahbek with the evasive eyes and the round steel-rimmed glasses, the financial director Jonas Collin with his ginger hair and a steady, self-conscious gaze, the theatre manager, Chamberlain Holstein with his square-jawed, sculpted face, and Olsen. He is standing before the four of them, breathing rapidly with his top hat in one hand, as the sunbeams throng through the large rectangle of window behind them casting their shadows far into the room and making Rahbek's grey mane flame. Rahbek is speaking, and this time he looks directly at him as though this is the first time he has seen him properly. 'We have requisitioned an assessment of your *Alfsol*, which you entrusted to us,' he says and clears his throat. 'As a complete piece of theatre we find it inappropriate for the stage; however, there are occasional nuggets of gold which show promise. Yes, you really do have an unmistakable aptitude, but since you lack any form of education, you are incapable of producing anything that might be proffered to a cultivated audience. Since there is virtue in the piece, and since you appear to be a blameless young man, we have decided to provide for your education. Councillor Collin will put it to the king with an application, and we hope that the university will give you free tuition. Where that is to be, you will be informed in due course. Once you have studied for a few years, you will perhaps be in a position to write something that can be accepted and put on the stage. You should hereafter refer to Councillor Collin, who will take care of the matter. Are you prepared to accept this?'

The floor rocks beneath him, colour floods his face, he is dizzy with joy and can only stammer a few words. 'Thank you,' he says, puts his hat on, takes it off. 'Thank you.' The four men look on in silence. Collin nods to him with a faint smile. He turns and heads for the door, but the handle seems not to be where he thought it, and he fumbles for it and a moment later is outside. To race down the stairs in his lopsided boots and out into the expanse of Nytorv – into the thick of pedestrians and horse-drawn vehicles clattering across the cobbles of the square. Here he stands still for a moment, and then turns to the theatre building facing him at a distance and thanks God.

He has only one good front tooth left. It is loose, and now he twists it out. Afterwards all his other teeth, his jawbone, fall out one by one. Wasn't that a dream?

THE SCHOOLROOM, SLAGELSE Grammar School. He towers among the much younger pupils, and there is scarcely room for his knees under the desk. Meisling, the headmaster, stomps between the rows of desks in his sack-like trousers and his coarse, grey tails, gesticulating up at the blackboard, talking – he can smell him, his foul teeth. If only he wasn't so frightened of him and didn't tremble all over and feel the colour drain from his face whenever he approached. He is struck with confusion even before he has to answer one of his questions, and Meisling twists and turns each word of his, gets the boys to laugh at him. He feels mortified. Like a towering wave ahead, four long school years with this devil, this tyrant at their centre.

In his room in the outhouse where he has his lodgings at Mrs Henneberg's, he writes:

> In evening silence
> Surrounded by Sjøllund's glorious glades
> Where sunbeams dance
> From wave to wave
> On the gentle fjord,
> I sit here silent, sad, alone,
> All around is silence save the tree's tall crown,
> Its soughing leaves.
> But deep in my heart a dark storm heaves
> And tears are burning my blighted cheek.
> Oh, such silence!
> The sweet scent of the glades!
> The sunbeams dance
> From wave to wave
> In the crimson glow.
> Oh, such calm,
> Such soft, safe balm
> As Nature smiles at rest
> But unquiet sleeps in the young boy's breast . . .

SUNDAY IN SORØ. Sunday with the poet Ingemann and his young wife, the former Miss Mandix. Sunday in sunshine at their house by woodland and lake, vines trailing up the windows, the parlours filled with pictures and paintings, famous poets hanging in frames in the garden room, the garden itself a profusion of glorious flowers, wild herbs growing as they please. They take the boat out on the lake with an Aeolian harp tied to the mast. Here he grows. These people are human, and he is free. Along with Petit and Carl Bagger, two students from Sorø Academy who also write poetry, he feels exhilarated, hare-brained, intent on conquering poetry, the world.

And home to Odense, a hero, to meet his mother at the first street corner, she crying, unable to understand the good fortune that is his lot, wanting everyone to see him, to have him visit every family in her street – it is the least he can do. People fling open their windows in the narrow streets to catch a glimpse of him. Isn't that Marie Shoemaker's son, Hans Christian, getting money from the king to study? He can't be so daft after all! As for her, she lives in the house on the corner with a little bed, lives alone in reduced circumstances, her thick dark hair now grey, her skin wrinkled. And isn't she drinking? His demented grandfather has to be put into the hospice for the poor, and he talks to the mayor about getting him in, even though the madman doesn't want to, protests. He boats on Odense river with the town's notables, Commanding Officer Guldberg, the bishop . . . His life in Copenhagen was only a dream. His father's grave in the churchyard has been demolished. Standard roses grow where he lay.

HE FIGHTS TO be moved up into the next class, fights with God. 'Oh God, you must not abandon me, for though I sink into the dust, my soul is still with you.' He fights against a sea of troubles and obstacles. 'Lord, I could be great, could be respected by my fellow men, could spread joy.' Could become an angel. An angel or a devil he must be – either, or. God determines the fate of the despairing. But won't the unbridled power of his imagination bring him to the doors of the madhouse? Won't his violent feelings drive him to suicide? Is he not just a puffed-up fool? Why has he been created only to watch his friends rise in the world, while he himself sinks and is wrenched away from the circle of enlightened culture? Life will be without hope, a purgatory – unless he is moved up. 'Oh God, thy will be done. Confusion and clamour fill this vast world of yours.'

The house is empty, hollow, soundless. He looks at these hands that resemble his father's. Wasn't he vain? Didn't he think that he and Thorvaldsen were kindred souls, equally poor, both fighting for recognition? Is his name not more famous the world over than his old friend's? But when his name dies, Thorvaldsen's will live on. Will he discover that one day? Is eternal life not a dream of the vain, and are we not just toys in the almighty hands of God? Lord of life, do not let us go.

COULD HAVE KISSED the ground on Vesterbro in Copenhagen when he touches down again a few days before Christmas. And flies straight to the Wulffs in their residence overlooking Amalienborg Palace Square, where the lady of the house and her daughters give him such a welcome that he has to sing and recite for them. Only then can he go upstairs to find rest in his own rooms – one with a bed, the other for studying – with their high ceilings, their windows looking out on to the square and the castle. And sits there now with Wulff's elegantly bound three-volume edition of Shakespeare in his hands, looking down on the Palace Square, where they are just changing the guard. Like Aladdin, isn't he? Five or six years ago he was wandering round down there, knew not a soul. One drop of the honey of joy takes away the bitter memory.

He has been to see the Dahléns, the Ørsteds, Oehlenschläger, Collin, has recited and told stories. Oehlenschläger has praised him for his poem 'The Soul' – 'the best you have written.' Now there is a reception at the palace. The carriages rumble across the square with the guests – kings and princes among them, too – and all the cadets in their glittering uniforms. If only he could wear more finery to match everything else in the sumptuous stateroom, where the cadets take the floor with their dancing display. Who is he to think he can dance among these sheathed shapes swirling in their light and practised routines under the radiance of the chandeliers? He comes down from his room in his coat. Dare he appear in that? He asks Mrs Wulff, who casts a glance over him. 'Well, if you did have tails, it would be better,' she says. He runs upstairs and changes into his grey tailcoat, but everyone else is in black and he is in grey, and he doesn't know what to do with himself. Won't he be taken for a waiter? He runs up to his room again, cursing his fate. He has no fine clothes to put on.

EVERYTHING ELSE – DANISH composition, Religion, German, History, Mathematics, General Conduct – but not Greek. That he cannot do. It is impossible. He founders on Greek grammar. Meisling's plump figure prances around him, skewering him with his tongue. 'You live and breathe for poetry! In your holidays you run round Copenhagen reciting your own "works"! Do you not think that if there were the slightest spark of talent in you, I would sense it? Why, I am a poet myself, I know what that means. But what you have is delusion, tomfoolery, insanity. If there were the least trace of poetry in you, God knows, I would encourage it, I would forgive you for being an ass at your schoolwork, at grammar, but it's all in your head, an obsession that'll put you in the madhouse. And just say you do one day figure as a writer, I'll bet my life the public will read it as poetic posturing, will laugh you out of court and that your attempts at poetry will be remaindered in the backroom of some second-hand dealer.' Meisling glares at him with a jaundiced glint in his eye. He ducks his head, his hands are shaking, his eyes burning. 'Let me hear one single poem,' Meisling continues in fury, 'one single line of poetry that your vacuous brain has created! What you have isn't feeling, it is snivelling self-pity . . .'

The maid is at the door. What is that in her hand? Sees her face in half-shadow, chiaroscuro: the soft glow from the oil lamp warm on her one cheek. On the shapes of her body. Fire burns in his veins – his sensuality is with him, even now. She turns away, has come to his room by mistake. He cannot remember her name. When was that? What has just happened, he cannot remember. What is going to happen, he cannot see. Time is a man with outstretched wings obscuring the future.

HE HAS ASKED the admiral's wife, Henriette Wulff, which poet he should model himself on. 'You have too narrow an idea of your own talents,' she writes to him in Slagelse. 'Your poetry is all of a kind, your imagination repeats itself. Whatever you do, dear Andersen, do not flatter yourself that you will become an Oehlenschläger, a Walter Scott, a Shakespeare, a Goethe, a Schiller – and never again ask me which of these you should model yourself on! – such arrogant thoughts and vain strivings could easily crush every other good, strong and healthy shoot that was planted in you to be of credit and benefit to yourself and to your fellow man . . .'

HE HAS WOKEN, *and she is sitting there at his bedside. Fru Melchior. Darkness. His mother's face slides across hers. He reaches out his arm. It falls.*

'I didn't visit my mother. And my demented grandfather lay strapped to his bed,' *he says.*

'You were only a lad. You had yourself to look after,' *she says.*

'Do you know me?'

'I know myself and my own self-reproaches.'

'You, who are for ever looking after the needs of others?'

'Not for ever, Andersen,' *the dark face says and smiles.*

'You make much more sense than I do!'

'I didn't have to struggle as much as you. Much has been given to me.'

'I had my talent. That was my gift.'

'Your good nature, too.'

'I am not good. You do not know me!'

'More than you are aware.'

'I am vain. Unhealthily so, some people said.'

'Let the unhealthy call things what they will. As a Jewish woman, I know what I am talking about.'

'They also called me sentimental. They knew the word for it; I knew how it felt.'

'There, you see!'

'You are much too good to me. I have been ungrateful. And troublesome. I, who do not deserve the cup the Almighty has handed me.'

'Who are you trying to convince?'

'God.'

'Not me then?'

'You, too.'

'Your faults could fit in a thimble.'

'I don't even think that myself!'

She laughs, and he smiles, too, toothlessly.

Fru Melchior rises, becomes one with the wall. He stares into the wall. The wall moves. Is no longer. Gives way to his mother's contorted face. And, now, her coal-black hair. Her laughter now. As she leans over him, he is so small, is almost nothing . . . Is he breathing?

Yes, he is flying. He is a bird.

TOGETHER WITH THE grammar school boys in the top class he drives off through the night in an open carriage to arrive at daybreak for the execution of three malefactors in Skælskør. It is a holiday, and Headmaster Meisling regards it as character-building to 'become acquainted with the like'. The trio are driven to the place of execution on a horse-drawn cart under the wide blue sky, the young woman youthful and ashen resting her head against the thickset chest of her lover, while behind sits the squinting servant boy, who nods listlessly to acquaintances along the way and is given a final 'Goodbye'. The three of them have murdered the young girl's father because he opposed her marriage to her lover. At the place of execution three coffins lie waiting. They climb out of the cart and are led by a priest up on to the execution platform to stand before the block. Here they sing a hymn, as the sun's first rays touch their frightened faces. The space around them is wide and light and silent. The young woman's clear voice can be heard above the others, and standing among the group of pupils he shivers to hear this song at the gates of death and feels his legs about to give way beneath him. They kiss each other and the priest. The woman kisses her lover again. The executioner with a leather cap over his face leads the woman to the block, and she lays her head there as though she is going to sleep, but her eyes are mournful, glistening. The sharp blade of the axe catches the sun as it rises towards the sky and falls for the first blow, which smashes through the woman's neck but leaves the head dangling from the body, the blood spurting in a jet. Her head falls only after the second blow. How hard it is to end a life. On the same blood-drenched block the heads of the two men are severed from their bodies – so strangely silent. A sick boy hurries with his superstitious parents up to the block, where they have him drink a bowlful of blood, which will cure him of sickness and epilepsy. They run off as the executioner's assistants fix the two men's dead and waxy heads on stakes and their bodies on poles. As soon as they have done so, they set to eating eel and drinking schnapps, and the peasants looking on are full of talk of the fine clothes that will now be thrown in the coffins and wasted. He thinks that the two men were staring at him to the last, and when he returns to his desolate room overlooking the garden and creeps into his bed a heavy storm is raging. Outside the fencing has blown down, and he cannot sleep. He cannot escape the two pallid faces on their poles and the wondering look in the girl's eyes at the instant of death.

IN HIS ROOM late at night he corrects his poem 'The Soul':

Are you not a soul of light
That fell from heaven, errant, lost
And now from constellations bright
Buried in the bonds of dust
Waits for your new wings to rise
And lift you home across the skies.

Your greatness none on earth can prize
You see but darkly your own face
Fancies float before your eyes
And prophesy eternal grace.
When your final hour chimes
When you leave this earthly frame
Whither will the pathway climb
Whither will God call thy name
Then in death for you will blaze
A glorious dawn, eternal days! . . .

HE IS IN Odense, visiting Colonel Guldberg. 'Preserve your purity of heart,' he says to him, 'and with your genius you will succeed. My father was only a poor peasant by birth, but he still reached a position none would have dreamt of before!' Someone who believes in him, someone who believes that he has to get away from Headmaster Meisling and be set free. In the 'Doctor's stalls' among the rows of other exhausted, infirm old bodies, his mother lies in bed, clutching the bed-frame, unable to recognize him at first. Then she comes to life, wants to climb out of the bed and clasps his hand before falling back into her own thoughts, her voice clogged, her eyes averted. 'Hans Christian . . .' she says and comes to a halt, searching for something in her alcoholic imaginings, a handhold, an image of something that once was. Her large, worn hands waver, flap around her body forsaken as though looking for a perch and suddenly fall to rest. She stares at him as he looks back down decades of bruising life, into part of himself. The old nurse tells him that his mother has only a few bad days, that three days ago she was livelier, but he can scarcely believe it. He leaves some coins for her taken from his meagre travel money and leaves her and the hospital with a tightness in his chest.

Where are you? Where did you go? To pass on, to pass over, to disappear . . .

DREAMS THAT THE maid has thrown his teeth away, rings the bell loudly until the servant comes and glides around the room like a shadow with a candle in his hand but doesn't find the teeth, made so carefully from a waxwork impression. 'She must have thrown them away,' he says to the servant, recognizing a morbid anxiety in himself. 'She hasn't even been in your room for weeks,' says the servant. He becomes violent, curses the servant, who then finds the false teeth in a glass in the cupboard. Once the servant has gone, he regrets his angry reaction but cannot face ringing for him again. For hours he lies awake, imagining that the servant will hand in his resignation, that they will let him lie here alone.

The unbridled power of his imagination brings him to the doors of the madhouse . . . his violent feelings drive him to suicide . . . if his imagination and his feelings could be united, he would be a great poet . . . But that is not the will of God!

HEADMASTER MEISLING HAS made him accept that there is some gross vapidity in him, something restless and headstrong in his spirit that makes it doubly difficult for him to penetrate the mysteries of language. He is despondent and writes a letter to Meisling, begging not to be the object of his scorn for entreating him to fulfil his deepest desire: to be allowed to continue his studies. He has not been idle, he has done everything in his power, it is his poor head that places these obstacles in his way. If Meisling asks him something, the blood rushes straight to his head, and the answer often comes out wrong because of his fear. And once that happens, the despairing thought comes to him, 'I shall be nothing, shall be good for nothing.' He is desperate. What will become of him if he cannot continue? He can be put to no good use. Two days later Headmaster Meisling takes him to one side and says, 'Do not lose heart. My strictness is not intended to browbeat you but to help you progress. Otherwise it would be a poor lookout for both of us when these two years are up . . .'

Two weeks later, it is a Sunday, a day off for everyone, and he is sitting at the dinner table in Meisling's house, when the headmaster bursts out, 'I am fed up to the back teeth with you! What is more I am well aware that you have never liked me because I have told you the truth. You are a dull and stupid creature.' And three days later in class, faced with a question about Greek, his mind once again goes blank, and Meisling flies into a rage, standing in front of his desk so he can feel his spittle flying through the air on to the skin of his face. Meisling is shouting, 'You are a creature void of both feeling and honour, or else you would either show yourself to better account or pack up your bags, as I wish you would. You are a blockhead, you should be locked in a cupboard in a freak show and made to speak Greek – there you'll get an audience, I'll bet. I shall be rid of you soon at any rate, for you refuse to learn a thing . . .'

He ducks. Wipes off the spit with the back of one broad, long-fingered hand.

MIRACULOUS, GLORIOUS SLEEP! *Has slept fourteen hours and wakes to sunshine and to such well-being that he has no wish to sleep again, but drifts off anyway. Dreams that he knows a beautiful young man – it may be Scharff, the ballet dancer – his features unclear at first, ethereal, just a figure in a poem, but then he stands there chiselled in marble, fills with colour, becomes alive while at the same time they embrace. Wakes to see the servant standing before him with a tray. 'Would you care for tea?' he says. But the tea is too hot; he cannot drink it, cannot even sit up in bed but slides down among the pillows as soon as he tries and slips away into a new dream . . . He is in Paris. He walks into a house, and a woman comes up to him, a dealer in human flesh, who brings four women before him. The first is caked in powder, the second very ordinary, the third wrinkled and the youngest lovely as a rose, no more than seventeen and with pearly teeth. He asks her to stay behind, gives the hostess five francs and then goes into a room with her and just watches while she reveals her body, urges him to 'faire l'amour' with her, presses herself upon him and can't understand it when he begins to talk to her. 'Poor girl,' he says softly and takes her hand, but she doesn't understand him and, laughing nervously, guides his hand between her thighs. He feels sorry for her, apologizes, gets to his feet and leaves.*

Flying again.

A SUMMER'S DAY. He is walking in the heat along Øresund from his new school in Helsingør to Admiral Wulff's home in Moltke's Palace near Amalienborg Palace Square. He picks strawberries and raspberries along the way, reads *A Thousand and One Nights*, aware of the Swedish coastline in the distance like a hazy dream. His one cheek feels almost fried; the dusty highway is an Arabian plain. As he approaches the gardens of Dyrehaven, a landau passes, and the women shaded by their white parasols nod and wave. Everything is open; eight days of freedom, eight days in heaven. The following day he lies in his room, his face in the sun, writing:

> Look at the cliff-top where there stands a tall person
> His face as white as Werther with a halo,
> He has a nose as large as a cannon
> And eyes teensy-weensy as raisins in sago.
> He sings something German with a '*Woher?*'
> Towards Vesterlide he stares as he sings.
> Why does he stand such a long time just there?
> Oh, Heavens above! We can't know everything;
> Though one thing is certain, I have seen and I know it
> He's mad, or in love, or else he's a poet . . .

AT DINNER IN the Meisling's dining-room, to the accompaniment of the smell of stale food, he reads his latest poem, 'The Dying Child', aloud for Meisling:

> Mother, I am weary and must rest,
> Upon your heart let me now lay my head;
> But do not cry – that you must promise – lest
> On my cheek burn the loving tears you shed.
> Here it is cold; outside the dark storms near,
> But in my dreams all finds a fair repose,
> Sweet angel-children to my eyes appear,
> When I my weary eyelids close.
>
> Mother, look! An angel by me lights!
> Can you hear the music, the sweet hymns?
> Look! He has two wings so wondrous white,
> Which surely the Lord God has given him.
> Gold and red and yellow fill my view,
> Flowers that the angels scatter wide!
> Shall I be given wings in this life, too?
> Or only, Mother, after I have died?
>
> Why do you press and wring my hands?
> Why lay your gentle cheek on mine?
> Wet it is, and yet it burns and brands,
> Mother, I live always to be thine!
> If so I be, you must no longer sigh,
> For if you weep, my tears with yours will flow.
> Oh, so weary! I must close my eyes –
> – Mother, look! – The angels kiss me now!

Meisling throws up his arms and asks, 'And is *that* poetry?' He can say nothing. 'That snivelling eyewash any poetaster could concoct,' Meisling says, wiping his mouth. He goes up to his room and throws the poem in a corner. He is not a poet. He is nothing. Not until tomorrow.

THEY ARE DEFINITELY fed up with him – Jens, the maid, Fru Melchior. Has still passed nothing despite being given castor oil. Low in spirits. A soreness in his penis. Wonderful the way the white rose lights up the room.

Mrs Wulff, the admiral's wife, writes to him about a dream she has had: Headmaster Meisling had mistreated him, but he is triumphant, saying, 'I stand fast to the journey's end, like Christ, my redeemer.' She advises him to allow pictures from his imagination to come to his aid – why not Cinderella who, although hated and persecuted by her stepmother and her sisters, nevertheless bore her destiny with patience? What was her reward? But he cannot and will not be either Christ or Cinderella. He is nothing and dreams about starting all over again. And he curses all poets – the dream world they present is nowhere to be found in real life. If only his father had burnt every single book of his and forced him to sew shoes so he would never have gone off his head and would never have been placed in the situation of having to disappoint his benefactors! Will he take his own life? Happiness will never be his . . . Mrs Wulff writes to Jonas Collin, who writes to Meisling, asking about the melancholy, the terror even, that characterizes his relations with Meisling.

And now Meisling is standing there in his room early in the morning. 'How can you defame me in this way? How dare you give utterance to your despondency, to your complaints? And who has gossiped to Collin about me, if not you? You can no longer remain in my house, in my school! Do you understand! I will not harbour slanderers here!' He ducks his head again, but his blood is boiling. A door opens, a door in his unquiet sleep, a door out on to a long and dusty highroad – a road without an end. He is free! He will be free! He paces his room restlessly, wants to shout out loud, is shaking slightly all over. Free. The fever of freedom . . . Free!

WHILE HE WAITS for his liberation – and it takes its time – he writes a Danish essay 'Reflections on a Starry Night'. 'A mighty voice speaks within me saying that you must first become acquainted with this globe in all its parts, on which you wander for so few hours and over so small an area; there you must float, free as a thought, from the palm forests of the South, across the heights of Golgotha and swing through the Northern Lights across the polar icecaps where, lit by the sun that never sets, you watch the red glow of evening melt into the dawn . . .'

But how can he imagine he is a poet? Even his friends warn him. Mrs Wulff calls his poetry monotonous, querulous and asks him not to write so much about himself, to moderate himself. 'Allow me to say,' she says, 'you read badly in German but even worse in Danish. Your reading and recitation are so affected – you believe that you are giving expression and feeling, but I have to be cruel and say it: everyone laughs at you, and you do not notice.' He is so taken up with himself and his own ego, she writes, that he cannot comprehend that his dream of the 'crown of poetry' is only ridiculous. But nevertheless he possesses a noble, innocent heart. He keeps the letter tucked in among his piles of poems. He both listens and does not listen, for that part of himself where the fire burns, burns too strong. This has become his way of being in the world, his way of breathing. And if he cannot breathe, he will despair.

ON THE DAY of his liberation from the grammar school in Helsingør he walks into the school library in his grey frockcoat, reaches out his hand to Headmaster Meisling and says, 'I will now say farewell to you. Thank you for the good things you have shown me!' Meisling does not take his hand but glares at him from behind his greasy spectacles. There is a moment's silence between them, in which he senses that Meisling has noted the unsteadiness in his voice, his vulnerability, and that he hates him for it. The pause lasts long enough to wind up Meisling's aggressiveness. 'You will never pass your Higher Certificate,' he says. 'Your verse will end up as waste paper and rot in the attics of second-hand booksellers . . . As for you, you will end in the madhouse . .' 'I do not think so,' he says. 'Ah! Go to hell!' Meisling says and turns his back on him. But Meisling's wife is touched by their farewell and embraces him several times.

He is free and slips into daydreams in his new room on 6 Vingårdsstræde in Copenhagen while the barrel organ plays in the street below. How much bigger this room is than the last one he had in Copenhagen! Here there is room for all of three or four people! The attic window set in the sloping ceiling opens on to the moon and the stars at night, while by day there is a view of the houses on Holmensgade, the Butcher's Stalls and Nicolai Tower. The distant clouds are mountains when he suddenly catches a glimpse of them as he turns away from the little cupboard in the wall where he has stored his bread, butter and sausage. On the table works by Horace and Homer lie open on a pile of handwritten papers. When he is not writing – and he writes day and night – or preparing for his classes with the classical scholar Ludvig Christian Müller, who is to take him through to his final Higher Certificate examination, he sits on a hard, rickety wooden chair, darning his socks. His bed is a kind of alcove in the wall, and before crawling in under his duvet he prays in his own naïve and nervous way to God.

THE HAIRDRESSER HAS arrived. He is also a barber and is to shave him, a man of immense height with round, slightly staring eyes. The servant helps him into a chair in front of the window overlooking the Sound. So blue out there. So distant. Once in place, he doesn't think that he is sitting properly in his chair, and Jens has to place another one before the large wardrobe mirror. And now the hairdresser is splashing scented lotion into his hair, waving it, making it curl on both sides, and Jens shows him in the mirror how light and airy his hair has become, but it feels as though he is looking at someone else, a dotard with the skin of a corpse, nothing to do with him. The hairdresser's razorblade glints in the light when he sets to work on his cheek stubble, and he is lathered in cream, the barber penning him in so large and close about him that he wants to shove him away but is frightened that the barber will cut him if he does. So he sits stock-still but cannot escape the thought that the barber's look and glistening white teeth have something frightening about them and is afraid of him, afraid of assault, of human wickedness and with a jerk insists that it now be over. The servant leads him back to bed where he lies down, exhausted. He asks to be left alone. Only once they have gone does he become calm and wonders if he is going mad.

He is floating, everything in flashes, buttonholes of memory.

EVERY DAY HE walks along Holmen's Canal over Knippel's Bridge to his tutor, Ludwig Christian Müller, on Christianshavn. His handsome face and friendly demeanour are striking as long as they avoid discussing the Christian religion and the Testaments, about which Müller maintains a rigidly literalist position, while in him a desire to take issue with his Biblical beliefs bubbles like the champagne of the liberated. 'God is not a severe master,' he says to him one day. 'On the contrary, we diminish the value of God in presenting Him as such. God does not punish us with eternal damnation without salvation because we have failed to overcome a sinful nature which, after all, we are born with.' 'Yes,' says Müller, 'that may sound fair enough. But don't you think that it is the Evil One who is now speaking through you? He always comes to the aid of his own.' 'But,' he replies, 'that's just what I am saying – that there is no devil except in a metaphoric sense and that a good God cannot permit a hell in which the sinner must suffer for eternity. Now I am only human and, as you say, sinful, but I think I dare say that even I would not be able to make my enemy suffer for eternity. How then is God supposed to be able to?' – 'It says so in the scriptures,' Müller ripostes angrily, 'and that is the Word of God Himself, and God cannot lie!' 'It is not God's lie that either eternal suffering or damnation awaits,' he says. 'But suffering can come to weigh so heavy that the unhappy individual has no choice but to break, and for him God exists no more. As Goethe writes: "When man despairs, then no God lives, and without God we cannot live! Then the unhappy man throws himself into death."' – 'But that means you are sanctioning sui-cide!' Müller cries in horror. 'Who can pronounce judgement on an unhappy man who takes his own life?' he answers. 'His final struggle will surely have been sufficient to purify him for a better world. God is merciful . . .' Müller's voice cracks. 'Suffering is part of life,' he breaks in. 'Even you must understand that! Suicide is unacceptable drivel . . . nonsense. At times I really worry about your salvation and your state of mind! Are you not aware that there are forces of evil that take hold of our lives and drag us downwards into a bottomless maelstrom? That is the Devil himself.' 'I will not saddle my sins on a devil,' he says passionately. 'There is no hell, no devil, the Jews knew nothing of any devil in the patriarchal period. It was only after the encounter with the Gentiles that the concept of a good and evil being arose.' – 'But whom does evil come from then?' Müller interrupts as he paces the floor. 'In our own inner being is planted the great root of evil, but who planted it there if a good and holy God created us? It must be the Devil, the mighty fallen angel spoken of in the scriptures.' 'Now that, too, I will accept just for the moment,' he replies. 'But just tell me this. When evil crept into heaven and brought down a holy and all-powerful angel, where did it come from? Who planted the seed of the pride that was to make him into the devil? Explain that, and I will accept everything you have told me.' 'Quiet!' the other interrupts. 'Who can explain the inexplicable . . .?'

HE'S TAKEN TO light satire! Oh yes, and isn't he successful? Isn't it true that his new poems written in this bright, ironic style are published in the city's most important magazine, Heiberg's *Den Flyvende Post*? And that he has sat round a table with Heiberg himself and exchanges private correspondence with that Hegelian arbiter of taste and leading writer of vaudeville, whose good opinion everyone is fishing for? Henriette Wulff supports him, too – daughter of the admiral and Shakespeare translator, small and hunchbacked, a woman with large, dark eyes, and who has no truck with sentimentality! The reading public of Copenhagen has discovered him; he is talked about, even in Odense, and when he dreads the exam ahead he can be sure to find comfort in Henriette. She has made him forget that he is a poor, outlandish wretch and that time wears out your coat just as sorrow does the heart. One day in Moltke's palace, reading aloud for her a passage of his newest work, 'On Foot from Holmen's Canal to East Point, Amager in the Years 1828 and 1829', he confides in her. If he fails his examination now, he will complete this journey on foot, sell the work to a publisher and get down to making a name and a bit of money. With that and similar minor works he should be able to struggle through and study at the same time so that he can sit the examination again next year. And if he fails again, he has a last resort – to travel abroad, to take his own life! She laughs at him but takes him seriously. 'No more of such whinging! You'll pass your exam. I have faith in you.' She wants to hear his 'Poetic Bill of Fare' again, and unlike his contemporary Edvard Collin she is not one of those who leave the room while he recites. When he is with her, he does not imagine that every smile is applause. But nor do her smiles express derision. She puts up with his theatricality and only makes gentle fun of his weakness for performing – doesn't he enjoy making a speech, being 'interesting'? He feels himself liberated again, but she holds nothing against him. She knows – it is their unspoken understanding – what it costs to be on the outside. He steps on to the polished floor and reads:

A broth boiled on the bones of Homer's hordes
(The meatballs numbskulls all with belted swords)

89

A tragedy half roasted, a half-cooked dish,
Stories spiced by *Spiesz* like horseradish.
A side of *Hamlet* baked into a pie,
With, for dessert, young *Werther*'s final sigh.
Add flowers, Northern Lights and Singing Spheres;
Eggs *Reiser*'s hens laid when *The Boil* was speared.
Water is no charge; the best that can be made
In *New Year's Gift*s or *Flying Leaves*, it's said –
French onion soup made from *Pindaric* paeans;
A *nouveau* Roman makes us caramel creams.
The heart of *Leonora* and *Leander*,
An eggnog cure for lovers' Salamander.
Boeuf à la Recensent, peppered like the deuce
Some pork brawn drawn from *Falstaff* and his juice.
A *hexameter* cooked as carbonade;
Three *aphorisms* set in marmalade.
A heartfelt sigh in verse – we know not whose,
Naivety half baked, a Christmas goose . . .

A PLEASANT MORPHINE euphoria. It is hot, and he is walking around the Palazzo degli Uffizi in Florence, or is he asleep? Bare walls of unbroken white in every room, and suddenly – Titian's painting of Venus alongside Venus as a marble statue, the Medician. Which is fairest? The earthly or the heavenly? He stares at them, and the hours pass, and it feels like the first moments of a new existence, seeing angels above him, worlds around him full of infinite wonders. When he finally tears himself away and steps into a room next door, Leonardo da Vinci's head of Medusa hangs, waiting for him. Poison steams red-hot from her maw, the abyss foaming in the form of beauty. Was that what he was living for? He smiles behind closed eyes.

His Higher Certificate examination. Sitting before his mathematics question in a room with three others, he realizes that he has read the question wrong and in his fright cannot string his thoughts together; he recovers himself, and his pen races across the paper until the bell rings, sending its shock waves through him, and he starts, sure that he has scored a nought, the blood pouring from his nose as he collapses in a faint against the back of the wooden bench; people rush to him, someone with excessive zeal spills eau de Cologne over his face, so that he leaves the examination room with bloodshot eyes and seeks refuge at the Wulffs. He is certain that he has come a cropper.

But passes in all subjects and is officially a 'student' from 22 October 1828. And – like all 'students' – some days later in plumed pith helmet and polished leathers a soldier in His Majesty's Lifeguard. In eight days he – student, soldier and poet – writes his first vaudeville for the Theatre Royal, *Love in Nicolai Tower* . . . Drilling with the lifeguard on Amalienborg Palace Square. Did you see me?

SUCCESS. SUCCESS. HIS fellow students give him a standing ovation in the packed theatre at the première of *Love in Nicolai Tower*, and his 'On Foot' is sold out in days. Even Heiberg is behind him. He produces to live and lives to produce. He runs through the town from end to end, reading aloud, looking at the lighter side of everything, wanting only to parody any form of misery, and many clap their approval. Others sharpen their pens. Who is this upstart? Who does he think he is? The attacks mount. Why are his works read with such ardour, and why are they reprinted? Is he supposed to be greater than Oehlenschläger, Holberg and Ewald? No, his work consists of inconsequential nothings and condescending affectations. It is – writes the poet Hauch – a 'true misfortune for literature, when untalented imitators of this kind awake *such* great interest.' Herr Andersen has become cocky. The critic Poul Møller sees in 'On Foot' only powerful reminiscences of light reading executed with a fluent tongue – or rather with a self-satisfied frivolity. The work is only a Nurenberg miniature box when set beside Hoffmann's world of magic. He must be off and away – he must show his mettle in a large novel. If that is no good, he will never be able to 'deliver' anything.

Deliver, always deliver.

THE FIRST FAIRYTALE, 'The Spectre'. Johannes goes out into the world and saves a corpse from being desecrated. He is joined by the Stranger, who leads him through danger with his magic touch – the demonic princess he falls in love with releases the Stranger from his enchantment. The Stranger is the Spectre saved by Johannes – and there is a nemesis of love to be found in the world. Perhaps. Perhaps as a dream?

Is he fond of him, this Edvard Collin with his square-cut, regular features? Is he a friend? However could he imagine that he had forgotten him and his family in the fuss over some praise in a provincial paper? He writes to him immediately: 'Your father's generosity and your friendship cannot be forgotten like that. There is no one I am attached to with deeper bonds, and, if you will leave aside circumstances of birth and always be to me what I am for you, then you will find in me the most true and loving friend.' Does Edvard not know that he does not consort with younger people in Copenhagen? That he is the only person to whom he has really felt himself drawn?

Edvard is in the room. Like himself, he is old and stands slightly bent, still with that confident expression, his hands clasped around his stick – and now smiling that cold smile of his. He shivers in the bed. Heart of ice. And then the shadow hanging from the ceiling on its gallows. Shadow dance in light.

Shadow dance in fire.

HE IS IN love. The first time he hears it (others give it a name for him – he scarcely recognizes himself) he passes it off as a joke, but his body burns all over. She has a lovely, saintly face with a touch of childishness, her lively brown eyes seem wise, thoughtful. Her simple grey morning dress matches her face, and her interest in his poems tickles his vanity. He makes himself interesting, and it is as though they have already known each other for an age. Oh, to be fêted by four young girls all at once, giving him bouquets – *she*, plaiting an oak garland for him while he laughs, is amusing, and she smiles back. They are an entire party in nine carriages setting off on an outing, singing and laughing and winding up at a ball at her rich parents, where, he being no dancer, she seats herself beside this wallflower and rejects all offers to dance. Riborg Voigt from Faaborg. But surely she is unhappy and half-promised to the apothecary's son, her neighbour, whom she may not have because – according to her father – he is only after her money. But he cannot help thinking about her, he who until recently made fun of love and infatuation. His moods unbalance him, leave him swinging from one extreme to another, between his passionate feelings for her and his conviction as to the idiocy of his entertaining dreams of a woman of her kind given his wretched origins and his position. Just when he has managed to regain his equilibrium by convincing himself that it will all lead nowhere, he hears that she is coming to Copenhagen to visit her brother and the family there, and once more his feelings are in a whirl. He sends her poems, besieges her brother, and when the visit takes place he reads aloud for her from his new play, *The Raven*. To him it seems that every line in the play is addressed to her, he cannot stop looking at her while he is reading, until their eyes meet and she, blushing, averts her gaze, concentrates on her sewing. When they say goodbye that day, she offers him her hand, thanking him for his reading, and he presses it to his lips as the earth sways under his feet. In that moment he is certain that he loves her and that he has both the courage and the strength to 'do everything to possess her'. But doubts creep in; he cannot sleep that night. The following day he confides in her brother. After a long, heavy silence her brother takes his hand and presses it. 'I had my suspicions,' he says. 'I know that she shows particular interest and kindness towards you.' 'Will you not help me find out for sure?' he says to the brother. 'I must know if she really loves someone else. If she does, then I must overcome my love. Otherwise I shall do everything she and her parents require of me, study for finals at university and be happy just to be given the shadow of a hope.' He is shaking all over, is deeply agitated and flees out on to the street for fear of giving himself away, when a merry group of friends come to visit the brother. The cold air of the street sharpens his anxiety. His whole body is shuddering, and he feels dizzy, clutches a wall, thinks he will faint. On his return to his room he collapses on the bed in a swoon. How long he lies unconscious he does not know. An enormous weariness overcomes him, and it is only later that he writes a letter to Riborg Voigt, in which he is brave and evasive by turns. 'With you I can be anything! You are my only thought, my All, and the heart of a poet beats more deeply than any other . . .! If you truly love another, then forgive me now! Forgive me for daring what would then be presumption. May you both be happy! Oh, forget a creature who can never, ever forget you.' In all his vulnerability he has already adopted the position of the unrequited lover. Riborg Voigt feels the plaintive tone of his letter to be oppressive. 'How can the good Andersen think that I am completely indifferent to him?' she writes in a note to her brother and as a reply to him. She has allowed herself to be carried away by the out of the ordinary, she says, and his singling her out above all others can surely flatter a vain girl. She is concerned for his well-being, hopes for his 'recovery', but her heart she cannot give him, since that already belongs to another who is entirely deserving of it. She is, however, prepared to be his sister, his companion, his friend. And she sends him her best wishes. He sends her a farewell poem:

> Fare well! Fare ever well!
> You I must forsake.
> Oh, that this heart might break!
> Fare well! Fare ever well!

There is a saying – a fairytale
That every oyster pale
Which builds in the salt and watery deep
Shapes its single pearl and then in death must sleep!
Yes, Love, you were a gift to my heart's host,
And yet that pearl my heart's own life will cost.

(. . .)

THEY MEET ONE last time, one evening at the Theatre Royal after the last curtain call. He glimpses her, her father and her sister in the audience and positions himself at the exit to wish them a safe journey. She is the last of them to hold out her hand. He presses it firmly in his and feels as though she returns his pressure. Her eyes are shining, as she whispers 'Farewell for ever.' He rushes out.

He is falling, tumbling, falling . . . Rings the bell, but when the servant comes he can only whisper, and Jens fetches a glass of water. Is that not a pearl in the water?

He visits Odense and Funen, both his sycophantic friends and his alcoholic mother at the hospital, but what a curious creature he is! It is as if he is dead and has now returned to a place where he once grew and gambolled as a child in a completely different life. He is full of unease, longs for Zealand and his friends in Copenhagen, which for him is bathed in a strange, poetic light. When they say in Odense that they are fond of him, is it him or the poet they are fond of? But in Copenhagen he longs for Funen and the people there. The present gives him no enjoyment, for his existence lies in the past and in the future. The moment now exists as a vacuum, a spleen, something dissolved into pain that spurs him to flight, to travel, to write, for it is not enough for a real person, this sense of unreality that torments him and is heightened by loneliness. He collects experiences as a cover for that emptiness, but doesn't he also run from love, even though it is breathing down his neck? That, too, counts as experience for the poet reeling in his fumbling pursuit of talent. And it is then no longer love that rises to meet him, but the gaping hole beneath his feet – despair. It is a short step from emptiness to despair.

To be struck by the ice-sharp claw of reality when (despite yourself and at a distance) you commit yourself to it. It is summertime at Nørager Manor. There are woods with glorious views over Tiisøe Lake – on the lawns the easels are out – and the ladies (Emma, Ida and Mimi) present him with a garland for his poems, as he takes a walk beside the handsome young Ludvig Müller with his vigorous body, his open expression and his quick brain. He attaches himself to him, respects his character and – as he writes to him after Ludvig has left Nørager – loves his face. He takes walks by himself, stands and looks down disconsolately at Ludvig's empty bed, is miserable in his absence. 'Of all those I know it is you I am most fond of, and if you find that peculiar, then remember, as you say yourself, I am an eccentric!' He has a wager with the ladies as to whether Ludvig will respond with similar devotion. The letter arrives, and he is ecstatic, struck right at the core of his heart's thirsting. Ludvig writes that like a child he is looking forward to seeing him again soon in the noisy city, where they will nurture the flower that has sprung up between them in the freedom of divine nature. Otherwise he is well enough, misses only him but will try to overcome the pain, for 'he who cannot dissemble cannot rule'. He, however, finds it hard to dissemble, as he reads the letter aloud to Emma, Ida and Mimi – and weeps for joy. Has anyone ever given his love such a direct response? He hurries to reply. Ludvig's letter enables him on the spot to love the entire world – even his enemies, even the poet Henrik Hertz, who has denounced him publicly and anonymously portrayed him as a drunken, worn-out nag from provincial Slagelse. How can he find words to express how ineffably fond he is of Ludvig? Ludvig is fond of him, and he will always, always be a brother to him in heart and soul. Everything he thinks of, dreams of, he will tell Ludvig, so close, so unspeakably close is he . . . But Ludvig's letter is a fake, a jape thought up by Mimi. Half-child as he is, he is not equipped for such refined emotional games and collapses. Half-child he may be, but he does not relinquish his dream and sends his letter to Ludvig anyway, along with Mimi's letter. Stubborn and blind he adds, 'Would you have written that? Could she not have written it from within your heart?'

EMPTY. EMPTY. WHAT is to become of him? He looks forward to noth-
ing, hopes for nothing, writes nothing. Once he wrote because he was
impelled to, could not let up. But what a beautiful place the world would
be if the heart played a greater role, for everyone. The heart is a leaf with
holes set at angles where eyes once were. A large leaf waving to a little
body's dance.

The line between the sense of emptiness and disappointment and
total poetized love is wafer thin. He swings through the lianas of his
moods. Oh, what is he to do with his 'softness' and the urge he feels
towards another, yes, this wonderful love of the All? Is everything
not poetry for him, the whole prosaic world about him? And is that
not why he is seen as being overwrought? They tell him to moderate himself, but he refuses to make himself as limp and frigid as the
majority. He thinks of Louise Collin, the eighteen-year-old with
her fine skin, her muted elegance, her blue eyes and shining hair
and her warm but reserved interest in him. What he cannot say in
his daily intercourse with her and Edvard and the others, he writes.
'I think about you more than you can know.' He lets her read his
Autobiography, in which he presents his life from its beginnings
until now. An act of trust. Will that not explain him – and his 'over-
wroughtness'? She will see that he is a poet and love him for that.
She will understand him. He awaits her reaction – but the reaction
is silence. She avoids him with the coldness of a Collin. He is a
stranger among strangers. He cannot sleep, is unhappy and – overwrought. He knows it, but he cannot stop. They have let him in but
still keep him at arm's length. 'Is there something in my nature that
makes me so repulsive, so unworthy of your – friendship?' he asks
desperately in a letter to her. Oh, yes. He knows, and he draws his
own conclusions. It is his own feelings that get him into trouble.
He has to be careful, keep his mouth shut. Be limp, be frigid. Take
his own life. The hanged man.

HE HAS TO get out, get away. Even the hanged man has a voice. He writes to Louise and vows to master his weakness. If he went out into the world, does she not think that he will become a decent person? She must promise to look upon him as a brother and renounce her *amour propre*, her coldness towards him, and allow him as a person to be interested in her. Now that she has proved to be indifferent to the poet. For he is a person, too. He stands alone, forsaken by those he clings to. The pain is his – and it is no laughing matter.

To lose oneself in the child. To daydream a way out of pain:

> Little Viggo, will you ride a cockhorse?
> Come climb up on my knee, you lovely lad!
> Near you my heart and head become like yours,
> My child – let's play until it's time for bed.
> (. . .)
> On you no one can scowl, nor black looks send,
> You are a child, untouched by anger's smart,
> The world's wild strife you cannot comprehend,
> The loving heart knows only loving hearts.

ISN'T IT CLEAR and frosty outside? He is flying – no, taking a walk. A strange murmuring passes through the wood. It has grown old, but the streams are young. There is the rustle of leaves falling. And a face before him.

'I have to take your temperature,' says the face.

'Is that Doctor Meyer?'

The face nods and brings the thermometer up before his eyes.

'I do not like having anything put in down there,' he says as the doctor tries to fold back the duvet.

'I have to take your temperature, for your sake,' says Meyer.

'Not for my sake, but for your own. I know I am ill – feverish.'

'But not how ill!'

'It is the German–Danish air. I wish I had died out east.'

'Neither Fru Melchior nor I could do anything for you there.'

'Who can halt the fall of a leaf?'

'No leaves are falling here. It is summer . . .'

'Summer for you, but not for me,' he says.

'For you, too,' says Meyer as he shakes the mercury down in the thermometer and holds it aloft above him, ready.

'I had an idea for a new fairytale. Would you like to hear it?'

'You're not going to escape the thermometer!'

'It is a story about a man who travels abroad to find God but ends up finding him in the Bible.'

'So he goes out into the world in vain,' says Dr Meyer.

'No, he only sees what there is in the book once he has seen the world.'

'And now the thermometer,' says Dr Meyer as he pulls back the duvet and tries to insert it.

But he refuses. Meyer heaves a sigh and leaves, his mission unaccomplished, promises to return tomorrow.

Is there a 'tomorrow'?

PEOPLE ARE SAYING he is already washed up as a writer, they are saying that his works for the Theatre Royal are slapdash, while Molbech at the Theatre speaks of his writing as hackwork, of his verbal sloppiness, his trochees without stresses, of the exceeding vulgarity and lack of musicality in his iambic pentameters, but *The Raven*, which plays on Her Majesty's birthday, is still a success. And now they are rejecting his plays one by one. What is he to make of it? Edvard recommends that he go to Oehlenschläger and request funds to allow him to travel. And he does go to him. There in his drawing-room Oehlenschläger sits and expatiates on his position. 'You have assuredly merits as a poet, but if we look to the future you will nevertheless have to accept that you cannot simply assume that you will be the principal writer of your generation. And in your relations to Jonas Collin, who has by all accounts done so much for you, there you have not done much to express your gratitude to him.' Yes, he is and will remain the underdog – how naïve he has been! How could he ever imagine that he could rise to be the equal of Oehlenschläger – and Edvard? It was childish of him to ask Edvard to be on first-name terms with him, as friends usually are. 'You have meant most to me of all men,' he writes to Edvard. 'You I have regarded as a friend – as a brother. Now the realities of life are insinuating themselves between us. I see my shortcomings, my position, my future and yours, and I can foresee it all. My life as a poet was no more than a shooting star soon to be forgotten!' He has had a miserable night weeping – and wanting to die. He promises not to plague Edvard any more with his sighs and lamentations. What must be in the world must be . . .

HE HAS WRITTEN petitioning the king with the greatest humility to grant him a travel bursary, and now Jonas Collin has told him that he should seek an audience with the king and present him with his latest poems – and at the same time have his request ready to be handed over in person. He is extremely nervous. Is this the done thing? To give something away and in the next breath to request something else in return? But since this is the way, the only way for him, he requests and is granted an audience. So he steps on to the polished floor of the audience chamber with fear in his throat to be confronted by the king walking swiftly up to him, resolute, military and demanding to know what that book is he has with him. 'A cycle of poems,' he replies, and the little grey-haired king gives his head a shake. 'Cycle! Cycle! What do you mean?' For a moment he is struck dumb but manages to hold out the book. 'They are some verses about Denmark!' The king smiles. 'Are they indeed? That could be most agreeable! Thank you kindly.' The king is already giving him a slight bow, preparing to turn away, when he nervously begins to gabble out his life story. 'And that is how I have fought my way through,' he says and pauses, having warmed to his theme. 'Most praiseworthy,' says the king. 'And above all I would humbly request Your Majesty to grant me a travel bursary,' he adds. The king turns his slightly squinting eyes upon him. 'Well, bring me your application then!' 'Yes, Your Majesty, I have it with me. That is what I find so appalling, that I have to bring it along with the book. But that is what they told me that I should do, that was the way to do it. But in my eyes it seems so improper, it goes right against the grain . . .'

Laughter, loud laughter echoing in the half-empty chamber with its elevated ceilings. The king is amused and smiles, nodding kindly as he accepts his application with an open hand. He bows before the king and leaves as fast as he can . . .

HE HAS TO get away – this spring – he can no longer abide being in Copenhagen. What a curious creature he is! His heart is a diary where pages are glued together, but the book is there for all to see. Most of the reasons for his actions are written on the glued pages, but people around him think that the paper is so thin that the writing shows through. So they read him back to front, misread him. They think they know. He is tired of all these people who think they know. He is not the person they are dreaming of. But who then?

Everything that is close to him, he will lose. Even his own hand, fumbling now in the dark along the hard wooden edge of the bed.

Someone has whispered in his ear that that arbiter of taste, Molbech at the Theatre Royal, has drowned his latest submission in an acid bath and described it as plebeian, tasteless, a base production. Yes, it is immature, undeveloped, pitiful – a monstrosity. It has been written by a man who will never come to understand his mother tongue. And the magazine critics land their brickbats on his back, crack their sarcastic quips in his ears. He takes his head in his hands and seeks comfort from Edvard. But Edvard is busy. Edvard, the unremittingly officious public servant who claims to be his friend. Once again he craves attention, and once again his pride gives way to his love for him. Is there not something vile in this craving for sympathy? How can he not despair at Edvard's indifference? Does he not know now that Edvard can never be the friend to him that he would be to Edvard if their positions in life were reversed?

WHO IS IT stirring up the poison around him? Drop by little drop lands on him daily. And daily there are new reasons for his application for the travel bursary not to be granted, and once again he will have to entreat and beg and . . . his entire spiritual existence is at stake.

But he does get away. He is to journey abroad. Isn't it wonderful! Isn't it heavenly! It is spring and next month he will travel via Hamburg and Paderborn to Cologne and from there down the Rhine to Strasbourg and from there to Paris, then on to Switzerland and finally to Genoa. On the way home he will travel through Rome, Florence, Venice, and maybe Vienna, Prague and Munich, too! He sees it all before him. In his head he has made the journey hundreds of times. He rushes round Copenhagen paying calls. Can you see me? The happy man. The chosen one. Mr Ego.

The pines, the cypresses, the golden oranges, they sway in the window of night, the dream, the brief dream . . .

IN A GERMAN landscape. Mountains begin to climb on the horizon. Feeling summer hot on his skin, he is walking with a group of other travellers to see the beautiful view on the road to Eimbeck. He is saturated with thoughts of the goodness of God – he, the poor child from Odense now cavorting with fortune's chosen few who can travel to foreign lands. In Kassel two loaded pistols are handed to them in their chaise – there are disturbances on the route, in the townships students are killing soldiers, they say, and one can never know what they might find themselves in. Travelling to Mainz in scorching heat, they pass statues of saints by the roadside. He takes a room at the Rheinischer Hof Hotel, where the Rhine flows right under his window. Here he eats roast hare and salad and drinks white Bodenheimer and lazily enjoys the perfect summer evening watching the steamship from Strasbourg sail slowly past, full of passengers. The poplars ripple with fresh colour, the full moon throws a column of gold across the surface of the Rhine, people stroll the streets, the frogs croak. But he can give himself neither to rapture nor to dreams. What more does he want? What does he need to be happy? Wishes Edvard were by his side. Didn't he go on board the ship with his arm around Edvard's shoulder when he said his farewells on the quayside at Langelinje in Copenhagen? Edvard comforted him, promising a brotherly reunion, while the whole family stood on the quayside to bid him farewell. Several with tears in their eyes. And after they set sail, the captain handed him a letter from Edvard that was full of affection. After Bingen the mountains start in earnest; from the boat's rail one ruin succeeds another, the slopes on either side rising to no great height but dense with vineyards. In this unusually blue air the towns look dirty and cramped. To sail on the Rhine is to pass through a fairytale. Medieval castles hang like the grapes of memory on the green vine-covered mountains. The Rhine is a melancholy picture of a bygone age – it melts the heart but does not awake the spirit. The Rhine speaks with a forked tongue.

ARRIVAL IN PARIS in a thunderstorm through suburbs where the houses are thrown one on top of the other, covered in dust from his travels, half boiled from the heat, bone-weary, to bed in his hotel room; woken by a most frightful din, the heavens on fire, he leaps up to find crowds streaming out of the theatre, the shouting down in the streets, the rumbling of thunder above and carriages below, and falls back on the bed to a sleep of the dead. Out and away from the hotel into town in the early morning, tramping across the city, passing so many lewd pictures displayed on the streets, and every other minute someone comes and presses a slip of paper into his hand with the address of a doctor who treats social diseases. He discusses politics with the Danes he meets in the city and feels ignorant. They go to the Tivoli Gardens with its red, white and blue lights, its music, a slide and a theatre with dreadful actors who sing out of tune. In the colonnades with their rows of shops the lawyers run to and fro in flying black gowns, while in several courts young lawyers passionately plead their causes. Inside the cathedral of Notre Dame is an ocean of light slanting in through multicoloured windows resembling gigantic kaleidoscopes. Its white interior strikes him. There is no Mass in progress, only a priest dressed in white reading to some poor boys. In the great opera house, L'Académie Royale de Musique, he sees the queen in the royal box and props in *Un Ballo in Maschera* that seem to have been taken from real life – in the opera's great ball scene he counts thirty chandeliers and twenty candelabras. He is at Versailles, in its grandiose gardens with stone terraces, clipped hedges and the fountains in front of the castle. He visits the Trianon and goes into Napoleon's bedchamber with its recently abandoned (for that is how it looks) yellow bedspread and yellow hangings, where he stands in front of the mirror that has so often borne the face of Napoleon and discovers that he looks insignificant. He might have fallen to his knees if he had been alone. Outside the other Trianon he picks a sprig of chamomile as an antidote to all that splendour. He attends the operatic ballet *La Tentation* in Paris, a production that enchants eye and ear alike, a whole world of the imagination in waves of sound, but he is not carried away, for here externals count for everything and the heart is not captivated. He falls sick in his hotel room, sick also for home, for not having received any letters when he himself has written a dozen. Once again he feels himself alone. But at last a large envelope arrives for him. He opens it feverishly, thinking that they must have collected a pile of letters together for him. Only too late does he discover that the sender in Copenhagen is anonymous. The contents is a copy of *Kjøbenhavnerposten*, graced by an anonymous satirical poem directed against him. It is his first greeting from home.

THE WHITE ROSE, the light from the window pouring over his hands, lying there on the white duvet. He must get up, and yet he cannot move.

By chance he bumps into Heine, the dark fellow whom he has decided not to look up in Paris. Doesn't Heine seem friendly enough and talk sensibly about Danish literature and Oehlenschläger? One day he finds his card at the porter's desk, but he wants nothing to do with him. With that ironic smile and those piercing eyes, he is a man to beware of. And then there is Edvard, who has written to him at last. 'You will in my letters search in vain for the language of sentiment (or rather of sentimentality). The way I am in my speech approximates closely to the way I am in my soul, and I know that I am not fond of speaking directly from or of my feelings.' What kind of man is this, who can warn him against putting on one of his well-known expressions of dejection and *ennui* if he doesn't find in his letters what he expects? His sisterly Jette Wulff, the hunchback with the soft, glowing eyes, is the only one who in her letter takes him in her arms. Mr Ego, Mr Composer, let me hear more from you. Soon!

*H*ER *FACE*, *HER laughter he will take with him wherever he goes. The grave? Heaven? In another world they will meet as free and equal spirits. Why did she have to drown?*

Is among the crowds in the seething streets of Paris and on the Place Vendôme in July 1830, when the king on his little white horse lets a blue cloth studded with golden bees fall to reveal the new Napoleon's column, as a deep swelling murmur sweeps across the massed crowds in the square, and hats fill the air to cries of '*Vive la mémoire de Napoléon!*' Napoleon's image stands out at that moment clearly in the undiluted blue of the air. One hundred thousand men in uniform march past the assembled crowds – endlessly. One human life is virtually nothing in such a mass.

In his hotel room works on *Agnete and the Merman*, about Agnete's craving for something other than what she has, a longing for the unknown that drives her out into the waves to the merman. But the fulfilment of her desire makes her deeply unhappy. This dramatic poem will make him famous and stop the mouths of his critics, of those who say he lacks substance and imagination!

He is flying . . .

SWITZERLAND, AND THE mountains seen from afar through the windows of the stagecoach stand out against thin, motionless clouds as though they were painted on to the sky. As they cross the border, it all looks so wretched, scarcely a window in the houses, everything silent, only the cowbells clanking. But abysses reveal themselves – the coach on the rough road constantly touching the edge so that his head swims, the forests below like potato fields, the farmhouses like toys. He feels a strange arousal as he stares down into the depths, hanging by a hair over his grave. And suddenly the perspectives open out on to a play of mist and cloudbanks, floating columns of woolsack. The Alps! It is like flying through the air. You see thick smoke beneath you, but the next moment the smoke is a huge cloud covering the sky above you. By Lake Geneva the mountains possess an inexplicable quality – at their base a sea of fog, over that the sky-high shadowy shapes swim like clouds, and above the glaciers shine. The foreground is dark green, and the entire range of mountains on the horizon is seen through a bluish veil. He lodges in Le Locle, high above the lake at Neuchâteau, is welcomed at a pension as a dear guest. Finished his *Agnete and the Merman* and sends it home with high expectations. Is constantly walking or taking short trips in small, horse-drawn wagons. Will his money last out? He cannot sleep for worrying about money. Dreams that he is arrested at the border and put in a pauper's gaol. Forgets his fear in the revelations that come daily – the Jura Mountains cut like silhouettes against the clear sky, the mirrored stillness of the lake at Neuchâteau ringed by tall silent mountains and the silvery moonlight counterpointed by the throng of children under his window; melons hanging out over the roof of the farmhouses, huge old chestnut trees reflected in the waters of Lake Geneva, the high rocky outcrops around the lake that seem to be painted with mauve and spindrift high in the sky. Like Byron he makes his way to the castle of Chillon with its dungeon, its thick walls, where prisoners were chained to iron rings. In the tower there is a false floor through which prisoners were dispatched to their deaths on the rocks far below. He writes his name on a plank just as Byron scratched his on a pillar seven years before. And is entranced by the wondrous stillness of the vast fir woods. When he gazes towards France through openings in the forest, the sky is grey, the firs almost black and across the entire scene a strain of indigo. By the River Doub the waterfall cascades twenty-eight feet vertically down over a crag, and the water looks like the whitest milk rising from the black depths in arching clouds. A thunderous roar surrounds the waterfall and its plumes of misted water climbing above the treetops. The Alps are an orgy of colour. Their base is sky-blue and their summit snow-white in the sunshine. Around them the deciduous trees are yellow and red among the dark firs. Are the Alps not the folded wings of the earth? What if one day they rose, unfurling those wings with their spangled pictures of black forests, wild cataracts, glaciers, clouds? That could be on Doomsday. Then they will fly towards God and burst like a bubble in the light of His sun.

ITALY. OVER THE Alps, where all is granite, to the border. Like driving along the spine of the earth. Beyond their encounter with the border the landscape softens, the sky recedes, nature becomes more fertile. Chestnuts hang their hands above them as they pass, there are fig trees by the roadside, vines making low bowers, beautiful children minding cattle in mountain valleys, and towards evening the slopes are washed with an indigo blue. Wretched room, wretched tea in Baveno. Approaching Milan, new fertile vistas, women shouting cheerfully after them in their open horse-drawn carriage, a mass of pine, immense cypresses and the Alps now behind them looking like the glass mountains of a fairytale. In Milan he cannot sleep for the impressions that crowd behind his eyelids – the towns they have flown through, a large convent in the moonlight, a girl selling grapes and the fiddlers in a village where two laughing girls were playing with a cat. Milan's streets are narrow, dark and dismal, filled with shadows. The church in the town is impressive, the windows with their coloured glass shed a sombre light in the nave that heightens the mood of solemnity under the great vault, and the figures kneeling before the altar or inclining before the holy statues make him feel like a wild bird among them. On the great stage at La Scala, its boxes with their blue silk curtains ascending in six storeys, the ballerinas look like marionettes with their curiously measured gestures – everything is spotlighted, everything is sumptuous, but it lacks meaning, and he returns through the filthy dark streets to find his bed. Cannot sleep for thinking about what 'true poetry' is. Isn't it divine inspiration? Through cultivation and training it is ennobled and becomes nuggets of gold in the mountain, while in other veins it is tin or baser metals that look like silver and with a sleight of hand can dazzle the masses.

THERE IS A letter from Edvard with criticisms of *Agnete and the Merman*. Oh! He no longer wants to be told what to do and to be treated like a child, for ever compliant! Their characters are quite different. At home his softness, his semi-femininity, were enough to make him adapt to Edvard, but, feeling as he now does, Edvard's manner would have made him run a mile. He will nevertheless always love him as a brother, even though Edvard offends him by claiming that – just like Hemming in *Agnete and the Merman*, who is dying of longing for his Agnete – he is longing for Denmark. Oh no, he is not homesick – feels only pain at the thought of having to go home at some point, home to all those bitter humiliations. He feels himself at home wherever he is, and the world seems to be his home. Denmark is a lovely country but cold, overcast and very parochial even in larger matters. How he would love to stay in southern climes, if only he had Edvard and a couple of others here! There is nothing Nordic in his nature. And oh! The vigour and fresh air he feels sweeping through him here!

Moth wings revolve somewhere in the dark – white wings. Beat up and about, revolve soundlessly again. The black becomes white, the white becomes black. The world is chiaroscuro. Someone or other is breathing. Is his mother standing behind his bed? He rings for Jens, who goes through the rooms.

'I have a strange clarity at the heart of this frailty of mine,' he says to him.

'But your mother isn't here. She died a long time ago.'

'Then I do not understand . . . Perhaps she passed by anyway.'

Jens sighs.

'You must be so tired of me.'

'Not at all, Herr Andersen,' he says and goes. He fumbles for the teaspoon and has enough strength to pour the morphine himself.

FROM MILAN HE travels with Dinesen and Neergaard in a carriage driven by a *vetturino* through Genoa, Lucca, Pisa, Livorno, Florence to Rome. It is arduous, it is beautiful, the sun shines, it is monotonous, it rains. When they reach the river Po, the horses can draw no further. The *vetturino*'s landau is tied by ropes to two oxen, later a team of four is spanned. In the mountains they pass one ruin after the other, can hear waterfalls roaring below them, as the horses plod onwards. In a village in the Apennines in the stench of filth, the streets teem with beggars, most of them with the faces of gypsies, the women almost black, the men in short boots with bare knees, hairy chests and wearing beautiful brightly coloured caps. Outside Genoa the mountains get wilder. They pass through one of the gates to the town, see it spread out in a bow around the bay, the air seems grey, the sea a purplish brown, dead calm, the waves breaking in cobalt blue. In the evening under a sky of midnight blue with fiery clouds, the entire sea is bathed in indigo. From his window he can see the galley slaves working down at the harbour with their red vests and white trousers. They visit the doge's palace that shines on the outside but inside is full of dirt. And the galley slaves' prison, six hundred slaves and among them some of the most frightful faces he has ever seen. In the inner prison there are long planks placed diagonally along the walls as sleeping platforms where the slaves are chained at night in pairs as though they are only one body. In the sickroom three of them lie with jaundiced yellow-green faces and wait for death – one of them, his face almost completely green, he cannot bear to look at for pity, and closes his eyes, and a sick slave, noticing his reaction, rises from his sickbed and bursts into loud laughter, fixing him with demoniacal eyes. In the evening he enters one of the churches in the town and sees here a man kissing the feet of a picture of the Christ; the feet have been almost completely erased by kisses! The landscape plants its kisses on his eyes. too. Genoa nestles beautifully between black olive groves, the waters are clear, several mountains along the way black as pitch. Italy is the land of the imagination. All that the eye could desire is here. Oranges hang golden against the rich green, huge lemons the colour of grass fly to meet them along the way. Everything is painterly, in constant flux. For they even travel through atrocious mountain regions beyond the town of Borghetta, where they meet not rock, not earth but sediment, gravel and shale with stone, where the occasional tree is leafless. And following that, blue mountains, an endless fertile valley, where grapes hang in thick clusters around trees threaded with oranges and olives twining their branches in a wild luxuriance. In Massa they encounter their first avenue of orange trees to the sound of fun and games in the streets, a six-piece orchestra and a crowd of street urchins. The mountains are overgrown with flowering myrtle, the crevices full of a curling mint. In Pisa they inspect the leaning tower, a cylinder encircled by columns which from the top looks like a large deep well – a man from Livorno has recently thrown himself into it and left a deep mark in the stone floor. Livorno is an ugly, tiresome town but framed between the sky, the sea and the wonderful mountains. Which is the loveliest – the clear blue sky, the rich blue sea or the pale blue mountains? It is one colour pronounced in three different ways, love in three languages. On the way to Florence they are besieged by beggars, swarming over the travellers like flies. Through woods of pine and olive and cypress they approach Florence, a dirty little town with an ugly gate and one narrow street. But the gates to paradise are to be found here in the shape of the doors to the church of St Giovanni. Dante's tomb is here, too. In the wealthy Capella dei Principi he is overwhelmed by Michelangelo's *Night and Day* and *Twilight and Dawn*. And by his *Madonna with Child*. And in the same way by his numerous plaster figures in the Accademia delle Belle Arti – Tasso reading for Leonora, Leonardo da Vinci's death. In the art gallery he is saddened by Perugino's Madonna and by his self-portrait in a cardinal's gown with Raphael as an angel. There is the head of a monk by Correggio and Andrea del Sarto's *Life of John the Baptist*. All these works of art, all the great works he sees, teach him that he knows nothing, can do nothing! He wishes he could start all over again as a seventeen-year-old, there is too much to learn, too little time. Against the vastness of the All, we are nothing! The artist's low, dark attic is home to muses and graces, just as Florence is also a cave where beauty and the spirit build their palaces behind spiders' webs and narrow walls. At a distance and from on high Florence takes on a brilliance. The trees are heavy with vines, deserted castles and villas fly past; a little river passes over shallow falls and meanders down the valley. He meets no one on the road. The murderous heat! Spends his nights in inns, filthy holes where the horses are covered in small deaths, crawling with flies that cover him, too. Black pigs, half-naked children pass them, old women spinning, peasant girls, their flannel hats decorated with feathers. By Lake Tracymenes he sees his first laurel tree while they are being examined by papal soldiers. The mountains in the region are mauve, the sun drops down behind an island which turns a dark blue while both air and water flame with gold and strong violet clouds hang in the sky. Far out at sea a fishing boat threads its course.

Rome. Colours of the mountains, crests like long waves, and the dome of St Peter's in the far distance as their carriage crosses the Campagna, and then they are driving wearily through the northern gate into the light and friendly city down an immensely long, dead street. At the post office there are letters to him, mostly from his 'devoted sister', Jette Wulff. He mixes with the Danish circle in the city – Thorvaldsen, the poet Ludvig Bødtcher, the painters Albert Küchler and J.L. Jensen, the priest Zeuthen, the sculptor H.V. Bissen and – after several weeks – the poet Henrik Hertz, his 'adversary'. He is round the city like a shot – witnesses Raphael's second coming at the Pantheon, visits Thorvaldsen in his atelier in the stables of the Palazzo Berberini, is on the Capitol, sees St Peter's, which is not as splendid and colossal as Milan's Duomo, drinks wine and sings German, Swedish and Danish songs with Scandinavian and German artists in Rome's German alehouses. He is in a constant ferment, is inexhaustible. One day finds him in the mountain village of Albano, another in the catacombs with the bones of corpses of hundreds of thousands of martyrs, a third riding on an ass along Lake Albano. Zeuthen and he ride home in the evening across the moonlit Campagna with the distant mountains covered by clouds as though by a sheet of marble, while the ruins are wrapped in a thick bank of fog through which they ride, and it feels as though the elf maiden has wrapped a cloak around him, a clammy winding sheet, and he presses his lips together to avoid her kiss. One sunlit day the Campagna is strangely empty, peopled only by peasant women, who have made a bonfire to keep warm, and peasants wrapped in large sheepskins. In the Tivoli Gardens he enjoys the sight of the ruins of the temple of Vesta and of waterfalls that plunge like clouds down into the abyss. The city's situation is picturesque, set on the rock with water bubbling up around it and encircled by the dark green of olive groves, the near black of cypresses, the reds of the vine leaves, the yellow foliage, the green cactus. Pines and gigantic cypresses alternate in the garden of the Villa d'Este, the deserted villa reveals a whole avenue of fountains – and he is ready to drop from exhaustion in the sun. In Fesch's palace he sees Titian's landscapes with the Holy Family and his Madonna. The Red Sea painted by Raphael when he was fourteen he finds childish, prefers Rubens' Madonna in *The Adoration of the Shepherds*, making judgement on one painting after the other, consuming them with his eyes. In Rome he climbs St Peter's dome, up an internal passageway alongside Hertz, who has kindly come to meet him the day before. From the first gallery the altar below looks insignificant, from the next the figures around it resemble dolls, his head swirls when they reach the highest point and step outside the dome to a magnificent view of Rome, and he forgets his old anger towards Hertz. In the Capuchin church he descends (for the second time) with Hertz down into a passage with six chapels full of skulls, and to the thrill of death. Vertebrae and shoulder bones are stuck in the ceiling like garlands and rosettes. Above them hang candelabras of dead men's bones, and the same gruesome material has been used to construct the altars. In niches complete skeletons sit in monks' habits, and the monks that accompany them are their spitting image. One of them stands with a withered bunch of flowers in his hand, and he imagines that it was the monk himself who planted them while he lived and that a friend visiting him daily stuck them into his hand only to meet the monk's hollow staring eyes. He goes to a ball in princely finery at the Duchess of Torlonia's magnificent villa, where he is announced as 'Monsieur Andersen, *poète danois*'. The arcades and the marble staircases covered with red carpets swarm with servants and the quantity of chandeliers is astronomical; in the Raphael Rooms he carefully registers the entire picture collection; in the Sistine Chapel he lies on his back and marvels at the wonderful prophets and sibyls; in the Borghese gallery he falls for Raphael's *Deposition of Christ*, Correggio's *Danae* and Domenichino's *Diana's Hunt*. He reads his *Agnete and the Merman* aloud several times for the Scandinavian circle, and they listen. His kaleidoscopic experiences, his many rambles between ruins, inhabited palaces, magnificent churches and vineyards stimulate him, the country and its landscape has entered his blood. When he appears in the street below his small apartment across the road from Thorvaldsen's on the Via Sistina, there is something self-consciously contented and dreamy about his face with its little moustache, its spindly sideburns, its sensitive mouth and its fastidiously curled hair.

The evening beautiful, the gilded sky – can't he see it? The domes and the black pines are silhouettes against that clarity. Will it ever be clearer?

COLD IN THE streets, wind, damp. To fall so heavily from such a height. Didn't he write to his mother – a short note between the long letters to others? And now this letter he holds in his hand, from Jonas Collin. She is dead. The colours, the view through the veranda doors of his apartment to pines and yellow buildings leak away. He walks back and forth across the creaking floor with the letter in his hands. Sits. Reads the lines once more. He could not ease her distress, could do almost nothing for her . . . Her crumpled body, grey hair, her rasping voice, the smell of alcohol, her pale, dry skin, her love for him . . . Hasn't he almost forgotten her? How often it has saddened him! He folds his hands and thanks God that now there is an end to her suffering. Now he is alone. Now there is no one obliged to love him. In a whirl of associations he thinks of his father. Dead, he too, and laid to rest in earth. In Collin's letter he reads that his publisher in Copenhagen will not publish his *Agnete and the Merman*. Who is he? What hallucinations have led him to this pass? At such a distance from both of them? He is only an improviser. December is a terrible month. By night he dreams that he is searching in vain for his mother's grave in Odense.

HE RECEIVES A letter from Edvard, his friend and brother, a letter that gives him vampires to fight off by night and ghosts by day. Edvard cuts him down to size. Why all this demented and regrettable productivity? Are you not aware how few friends your muse has? People are saying: 'Oh, has he knocked something else off now' – 'I got sick of him a long time ago' – 'Whatever he writes, it's always the same old hat.' And now you want to write about a journey again! Who do you think is going to buy a book running to several volumes about a journey thousands of people have taken? Two thousand eyes surely cannot have missed so much that you can have something new and interesting to say! It is colossal egotism on your part to impute to people such interest in yourself. The fault must lie with you, for the public – or at least the reviewers – have not given you occasion for it. Oh, I know you. Now you will reply in your self-satisfied way: Yes, but when people have a chance to read my *Agnete*, they will change their minds, they will see how my travels have changed me for the better, have made me more mature, etc. But you are mistaken, you are grievously mistaken. *Agnete* may have its passages of childlike beauty, such as we know from your earlier work, but it also has patches that are desperately deformed – yes, devoid of form. I have been driven to tears at encountering so many of such passages – have, yes, been full of indignation. I have shown your manuscript to a friend, one for whom you have considerable respect, and he said, 'I had wanted to spend this evening with Andersen's *Agnete*, but I cannot abide it!' Your misfortune lies in the fact that Oehlenschläger once sent masterpieces home from Paris; and that is why you have now cobbled this product together.

He can hear Edvard's self-satisfied voice with its edge of irritability and passionate rigour and is on the point of collapse. And now – through Hertz – he hears the voice of Molbech, who slated his *Collected Poems* in Copenhagen. Hertz says that Molbech is simply off his head, a parroter of fashion. 'In your description of nature lies your talent,' Hertz continues, 'but in the domain of romance, there you lose your way.' Everyone wants to teach him. He is in despair.

GRUEL. GRUEL AGAIN. *And after the gruel, which warms him and chases his stomach pains away, Fru Melchior, stepping into his room again with a white rose in her hands to place it in the vase near his bed. Her skin dark with summer, and her black hair standing out against the white walls. Does she exist? He kisses the rose and grasps her hand, kisses that, too, squeezing it in his own several times and looking up at her with a serene smile.*

'Thank you, and God bless you!' he says before closing his eyes and dozing off again.

TOSSES AND TURNS in bed at night, thinking of taking his own life. Prays to God that He will forgive him for these thoughts, forgive those who have put him in such misery. White-faced he makes his way through the thronging streets to Thorvaldsen in his atelier in the stables of the Palazzo Berberini. Thorvaldsen, who is in the throes of modelling a Greek face – a face with blind eyes – and has his hands caked in clay, says (after no more than a rapid glance in his direction), 'Are you ill?' Bathed in the light from the roof-lights he seems dwarfed in this huge space peopled with sculptures, statues, bas-reliefs. He tells him of Molbech's and Edvard's criticisms. 'For God's sake,' says Thorvaldsen, placing a clay-covered hand on his shoulder, 'never let yourself be affected by things like that. The less one knows about art, the more rigid one becomes. That is the beauty of the artist. The deeper he delves into his art, the more he sees its difficulty and the gentler he becomes towards others. Oehlenschläger and Baggesen probably lost many a work of art to their empty squabbling. Feel your own power, don't allow yourself to be led by the opinion of the masses but move quietly onward. I can put myself in your shoes, though – it *is* unfortunate to need a public. Now I have what I need to live off and don't need anyone – that is my good fortune. God only knows what the world would say of me if I did!' Thorvaldsen pulls out a pile of contour sketches and gives them to him, taking his hand in a clayey grip, and the light colours his cheek, his hair streaked with grey, those strong eyes that could have been a boy's. 'Bear the injustice of the world as lightly as you can,' he says as they part.

BUT WHO CAN cure despair in someone who exists so little in the here and now and who swings between heavy despondence and highly charged weightlessness? In someone who searches for his mother's grave in the shadows of the night, in the ragged mists of dreams? In someone who does not know his own face and finds his reflection in the faces of his many passing friends, the many passers-by? In someone who has lent his Self to the Artist and been given loneliness in return? In someone who is forced to play-act because he feels himself unloved? Someone who in his particularly desperate way has so much to give? Someone so lacking a home? So dependent? Thorvaldsen's words, his reassuring touch, percolate into him anyway. They are the gestures of someone who was once – like him – a poor down-and-out, the gestures of the outsider, the outsider who has moved to the centre. To a place in the sun. That is where he, too, wants to be. He must give as good as he gets, meet injustice with defiance and coldness with self-awareness. He grows, becomes several years older in the space of a week. He has to get his knife out in a letter to Edvard, that incomparable egotist who transforms everything into delusion. He will no longer put up with his hectoring; he must soften his tone to match his friend's, otherwise it is finished. A friend who strikes with scorpions is no friend, sooner an enemy than one such. Sooner clarity. But he does not wish to inflict sorrow on the father, Jonas Collin, the man to whom he owes so much, so he encloses the letter to the son, Edvard, in a letter to him. He will have to pass it on to Edvard if he so wishes. Perhaps he will lose them both. Well, then he must lose them. It is up to God. God gives him strength, too, just like the palm trees in Italy, which have to bear a heavy burden – and grow as a result. To arrive at such an insight into himself and the world is bitter medicine. A cure with a splinter of ice.

Something on the wall – sun, fire, shadow? He hears sweet music from the castle square, the sea breaks in the boom of surf on stone, a cloud of smoke pours from the crater of Vesuvius. His heavy hand lies restless on the duvet. Is that not the beating of the world's great pulse he can hear? The sea lifts its mighty wings, coal-black smoke rises into the blue air. Where is he? In the paradise of Naples?

IT IS EVENING. A boy in a white hat pursues him through the narrow streets of Naples with his constant call of 'Donna! Donna!' He slips down a side alley, but the boy runs in front of him and points to a house – it is right there his little *donna* lives. 'Look her, look her. She only thirteen. She new, brand new. You no say no to her?' 'No! No! No!' he cries aghast and hurries into the next street. He is wildly aroused but resists. How can he satisfy his desires on an innocent being?

Wasn't his shadow once so long in Naples that he almost fell over it? Wasn't he in Herculaneum, the underground city?

A labyrinth of dark passageways into the amphitheatre. Holding a candle, he reaches the place where the players once stood, the individual rooms for the various musicians. In the ceiling above him a mask pressed into the lava. He dreams about the mask. It is his own, he cannot pull it off.

What is his face? There in the mirror. His young face, or his old?

IT IS LATE in the evening, and he, Hertz, Zeuthen, a Frenchman and a Norwegian along with their driver are standing before Mount Vesuvius in a biting wind, their faces lit up by the fire from the humped mountain in its covering of ash and blocks of lava. They climb the mountain, sinking up to their knees in ash. Large stones come loose when they step on them and slide away down the mountainside. Hertz comes to a halt in the ash, shouting, terrified, and collapses exhausted. The Norwegian and he take an arm each and raise him up, and he sings to show Hertz how fearless he is. They reach a plateau directly under the crater with the moon right overhead, coal-black smoke billowing up, and a mass of flame shoots upwards, glowing rocks roll down towards them, so that those standing on a slab close to the incandescence look colossal. Night has already fallen; black abysses seem to appear between the fragmented outcrops, and they have to walk across the hardened lava, the heat penetrating them, the lava burning under their feet, knowing that if it gives way they will sink into a sea of fire. Suddenly in a vision – a monstrous river of fire, red and thick as porridge pours slowly down the mountain. The fumes from the sulphur and fire are so overpowering that they have to retreat. Around them a roar of fire erupting from the crater like a flock of birds taking off from a mountain.

'It is the tinder box,' he says.

'What?' Fru Melchior says, wiping his forehead.

'I saw a flame. A soldier went down into the ground and brought the sparks back up with him. Chopped the head off the witch.'

'Oh, you mean your story?'

'I was the soldier. Me, too, the one who burnt to cinders in the flames.'

'Were you ever a soldier?'

'Soldier in the king's student corps. NCO,' he says with a tired smile.

She goes away. She is always going away and is there always. Where is he?

THE CLIFFS ARE covered with red sea apples, and it looks as though the rocks are weeping tears of blood in the surf. They are in their little boat outside the entrance to the grotto. They crouch in the bottom of the boat and glide in, out of the cold wind and in under this warm vault. And what a fairyland it is! The lake is twenty fathoms deep and clear as a mirror. Its entire surface looks like spirit on fire. They strike it, and it is shining silver, the droplets showering up against the light look like crimson rose petals. Everything beams with a heavenly blue – the boat, the oars, the people are all various shades of blue. They sail through ethereal realms . . .

HE IS SAILING. *Here is old man Collin – he, too, dressed in blue standing before the door. With a stick.*

'I have burnt your letter to Edvard,' he says. 'I do not hold a single word of it against you, but I could not be other than fearful that it could have an effect which would have pained me in the extreme – a break between you and him. You do not deserve his correctives; he does not deserve all your anger. At heart he is deeply fond of you and is your warmest protagonist. I do not applaud his lecturing you. But make allowances for him. Everyone has their weakness, you know, and that is just his. We must be patient with each other.'

Everything is blue. Indigo blue.

And Dr Meyer now, too, taking his pulse – or is it Edvard?

'I can under no circumstances be on first-name terms with you,' says Edvard.

'You have to be. You are my shadow,' he says.

'I may be skin and bones, but I am still a man of means and have a gold chain around my neck. In my fine clothes I am taken for a man of substance.'

Edvard jangles his signets in front of Dr Meyer, who turns his back on him.

'That's strange . . .'

'Yes,' says the shadow. 'It's certainly not quite normal. But then you yourself do not belong to normality, and I should know, for I have walked in your footprints ever since I was a child.'

'What is it you want here?'

'I left you in southern climes and longed to see you again before you died.'

'Am I going to die?'

'That you know better than anyone.'

'Your pulse is too high,' says Dr Meyer. 'You will have to have something to calm you. Who are you talking to?'

'There is someone in the room.'

'There is no one here but me,' says Dr Meyer *and pours him some more morphine linctus. He is handed it on a teaspoon but cannot sit up in bed and spills it down his chin, so that Dr Meyer has to feed it to him like a bird.*

Behind him stands Edvard: that shadow clothed in black with lac-
quered shoes and a collapsible hat. He laughs. No, Dr Meyer laughs.

'Don't look so frightened. Just lean back gently.'

He allows himself to fall back on the pillow.

The door closes. It is not Dr Meyer. He shook hands, said goodbye.
Didn't he?

He does not want to be alone with shadow Edvard, Edvard shadow.
He extends his hand towards the bell but is too weak to reach it.

The shadow is on the wall. On the floor. It has its own shadow
under the lamp, a little shadow. He recognizes his own face, the large
nose, the small Chinese eyes. He closes his eyes, not wanting to see any
more. But behind his eyelids it continues, and when he opens them he
is still standing there – stooping, young, thin – before the painting of the
ruins of the Forum Romanum. The white curtain across the doorway
on to the balcony overlooking the coastline sways lightly. He shivers in
the warm summer night.

'What did you see, Edvard, over at the neighbour's that hot summer
evening when you disappeared from me?' he asks.

'It was poetry that lived in that house. I lived there myself for three
weeks, and now I have seen everything, know everything. But you must
not call me by my first name, I will not have it.'

'Then I shall call you Collin. What did you see then, Collin?'

'It was poetry I saw, and I got to know my own nature. In the
antechamber of poetry I came to a realization. That I was indeed some-
one! I was ashamed of my condition, for I needed all that human veneer
that makes up a man – boots, clothes. I hid under the gingerbread
woman's apron, drew myself out into long dark shapes up the wall, ran
up and down, to and fro, looked in through the windows and saw what
no one else sees. When it comes down to it, this is a vile world. I didn't
want to be a man, if being a man couldn't be accepted as being some-
thing! I saw the most unthinkable things in men, in parents, in children.
I saw what no one was allowed to know, but what everyone so much
wants to know – the evil next door. My writing was aimed directly at
people themselves, and they were horrified. They were so afraid of me,
were so fond of me, that they made me professor, presented me with
clothes. I was so beautiful!'

He is talking to himself, with his own face in front of him one
moment and gone the next. He closes his eyes. The shadow conducts him

in its carriage as his lackey to the manor of Sophienholm, to Mrs Bruhn's salon and ballroom, where he knows most of the dancers. Weyse is sitting at the grand piano, while he himself dances with a lovely, dark-eyed woman with a thin band of light across her cheek, while at the same time standing just inside the door, leaning against the wall and waiting for his master's next move.

He can see from the woman's smile, her movements that she is utterly fascinated by the shadow, and they talk and dance far into the night with him leaning against the wall all the time thinking his own thoughts. Now, as it pours itself yet another glass of port and smokes a cigar, the woman comes over to him. The shadow's beardless face looks transparent.

'I asked your master a question. It was much too easy for him to answer, he said, so he referred me to you.'

'Yes?'

'What is the difference between people on the outside and on the inside?' she asks and tilts her head a little to one side.

'Outside they are like the wind,' he says. 'Inside they are either hollow and empty or still, deep water. What shines falls; what is unremarkable grows.'

'That answer I do not like,' says the woman. 'If you are so clever, what does that make your master?'

But who is now the master, and who the shadow? They move into a large white villa that looks like Villa Rolighed. He has his servant's quarters in the cellar and waits on them. He sees his master – made in his own image – leading a jolly life; his master appearing on the stage, drawing an audience even; his master displaying himself in books and fairytales that are on loan from him. One day, as he offers him a glass of wine from the silver salver that he extends with one hand, he reminds him that it is he who is human.

'You are only a pale copy of me,' he says.

The shadow bursts out laughing and waves him away, but a strange darkness floods his face.

He hears him discussing it with the woman.

'He has gone mad, quite off his head. He thinks that it is he who is human here.'

'That's not so good. But he doesn't know anyone here and is tied to this place. He also seems peaceable enough'

'He will never be himself again. He will do someone an injury – either to us or to himself. I am sure of it.'

'Poor shadow, he must be unhappy with the paltry life he leads. I think we should help him out of this world, for his own sake.'

'Yes,' says the shadow, 'but it is a shame for he has served us well.'

'You are a fine human being,' says the woman.

The door of his room opens, and in the square of light from the corridor he sees the head of the shadow but not its face. He is not ready and feels a stab of fear as the creature approaches his bed with a knife pointing at him.

'I don't want to die!' he screams.

Someone lights a candle. Above him Dr Meyer is shaking the thermometer down.

'Take it easy, Andersen,' he says and takes a step backwards. 'Easy now. Gently does it.'

MUNICH IS NIGHTS of toothache and the uninterrupted barking of dogs – even his neighbour sounds like a dog when he growls at them to shut up. The women wear bonnets over their pallid faces, polite harangues stand in queues making it impossible to distinguish an honest word. Military parades in the heat; the streets either squares or highways; and in front of every house – no matter whether it be a small market town or out in the sunlit spaces of the countryside – a garden with flowers and fruit trees. Not in the larger towns. He longs for that paradise on the far side of the mountains – yes, for the mountains themselves. His toothache plays on his nerves. When he is not reading, visiting galleries, churches and the English garden, he paces the floor of his hotel room, brushes and rinses his teeth. Is feverish, flat, unhappy – and cannot sleep. Where are the letters from home?

IN VIENNA HE works on his Italian journey; even when he opens the window of his rented room and looks out at the street, everything is lacklustre in comparison to Italy. What is there here? Windows stand open, scantily clad maidservants sweep the floors, and outside the windows green boxes full of flowers. The butcher sells his meat, the girls offer their flower baskets for sale, people in coats and with potato faces walk past. Only the large wooden saint on the wall of the house is at all exotic. If only he were sitting in a carriage rolling onwards towards something new! He eats cherries on a bridge over the Danube and reconnoitres for mountains in Josephdorf. His encounter with the plays of Schiller at the Burgtheater enlivens him, but otherwise its productions disappoint evening after evening. In St Stephen's Cathedral the churchgoers' response – 'Pray for us' – sounds like a muffled howl from the abyss; a wedding in the synagogue with its rich colours and unaccompanied choir moves him deeply. He looks for Beethoven's grave in the churchyard outside the city and finds only a modest stone with his name. A Dane visiting him is amazed that he doesn't know whether there are any handsome wenches in the neighbourhood. 'You're not enjoying life, you're letting it wither away,' he says to him with a laugh. He is feverish, his hands are shaking. He doesn't think he has long to live. If only he had died in Italy!

IN PRAGUE HIS misery increases. In the sweltering summer's heat his money is running out, headache and toothache worsen, his cheek swells up. He writes to beg for more money from Jonas Collin, and every evening he counts his remaining funds. He is exhausted, sore – and still he wanders the streets of the town from end to end. Restless, homeless. The streets are broad and more like squares. The castle looks pretty much deserted with its scant soldiery, while the church is rich and full of light and resembles a miniature Notre Dame. The view across Prague is beautiful, the Moldau flowing brown, its green islands. But many of the streets are filthy, the coffee-houses few, and the beverages they serve vile. Isn't this a hole he has landed in? Having seen a well-produced *Wallenstein* by Schiller at the city theatre, he takes pity on a girl serving at table in an alehouse. The gentlemen are so offensive and she so sweet-natured! But can he rely on impressions! He doesn't know what he should believe in. Who is he? Where is he going? When he thinks about Denmark he freezes up or feels himself constricted as though he is being strangled. One night he dreams that his throat and mouth are full of hair. What is taking him homeward is not longing – no, God knows! For how will he cope with tramping the cold slush on Østergade once again, tasting the trailing fogs! Last year at the same time he was walking under the laurel trees dressed in summer clothes eating oranges and heavy grapes. Now it is all over . . . Home to the Judas kiss and the cup of pain. But isn't it pure poetry when the poet is a butterfly impaled on a pin, writhing? Isn't that where he is most beautiful?

A BIRD IS *singing, singing outside the window. He tries to get out of bed in the dark but cannot. Perhaps it was no bird but a gentle night breeze? His hands are cold, aching. Is he at Rolighed? Yes, he is in the inner-most, closed-off room which he has always known about but never seen, and something is sitting on his chest, he can hardly breathe, something shadowy, its outline becoming clearer now – a living skeleton wearing his hat and coat. Death. Heads peep out from the darkness behind the skeleton, ugly or grinning heads, mumbling masks.*

'Remember it?' says one.

'Remember it?' says another.

In the silence their laughter rings out.

'Music! Music!' he whispers, wiping the cold sweat from his fore-head. And he has a picture of some mechanical musical contraption that will force the voices to be still.

But they continue, whispering, shouting, their laughter like a knife in his ears. 'Remember it? Remember it?'

But now he hears the bird again, a bird with a beautiful, soothing song that slowly relieves the pain in his ears and hands. Even the skel-eton on his chest succumbs.

'Don't stop, don't stop,' says death.

'Gimme your hat,' says the bird.

And death hands over his hat, and the bird sings. And every time it sings the skeleton gives something away – coat, collar, shirt, pen, trousers, shoes. Ever lighter and more shadowy, it detaches itself from his chest.

And now the bird is singing of flowering elders, scented cypresses, moist grasses, and death rises from his chest altogether like a chill, white mist. And disappears out through the window that is the window out on to Øresund.

His long hand fumbles for his heart. It beats with a peaceful rhythm. The door opens. The skeleton is standing there with an oil lamp in its hand, the light colouring its white cheekbone.

'You rang,' says the servant.

His face is flesh and bone.

'I rang?' he says.

'Yes, you rang. What is the trouble now, Herr Andersen?'

He is the nightingale that soars in the dark.

WRITES AND WRITES in the study of the second-storey apartment in Nyhavn. A fire burns in the cast-iron stove and over the sofa hangs a painting – an angel descending with a pen and a laurel wreath. On the little table his cups, his books and an Italian crucifix, decorated in the Catholic fashion with a silk ribbon. Next to the bookshelf, the window, and through the window a view of three-masters in the canal, boats passing each other. The writing desk is drowning under magazines, manuscripts, prints and books. A glove lies there, too. A loose cuff.

Writes night and day, while the woman below floods the kitchen with water so her children have an indoor ice rink, and the cold rises up to him. The coordinates are north and south, reason and emotion, Rome and Naples. He is the fatherless Roman boy, the penniless Antonio with a talent for improvising songs, spoilt by his mother, sneered at by his uncle, supported by the Borghese family, tyrannized by Habbas Dahdah of the Jesuit school, who as an adult is lonely and suffering, an amphibious being living half in the physical world and half in dreams, a poetic figure, a man unlike others. His innocence is subverted by his vanity. In Naples he regards himself as an artist, surrenders to his passion, finds love. Love, sensuality, the south and artistic success rolled into one – a dream that emerges from his pen in the Copenhagen winter as masts and rigging thicken with ice in Nyhavn Harbour. The whole world of Italy vibrates in the novel, the dream. Every evening out to eat with a different family. Out and home again. No money. Only debt. But the novel must bring money to the writer drunk on his words!

To WRITE THE first of the fairytales in the midst of a cruel winter. To feel a wonderful creative power. To be afraid of not achieving recognition. And to long to be far away. And is once more in the spinning room at the Greyfriars Hospital in Odense, hearing stories from Grandmother and the other old people. Writing about finding the spark in 'The Tinder Box', fooling the high and mighty in 'Little Claus and Big Claus', being labelled as over-sensitive in 'The Princess and the Pea', reconciling himself to death in 'Little Ida's Flowers'. Oh, so many dying around him, friends, acquaintances, so many funerals that cruel winter! Isn't there an odd side to his character? Doesn't he seem somewhat indifferent towards his friends? Cold towards those he is fond of? Isn't he always too busy, always in a hurry? Oh, what it is to be caught in the creative fire! To rise up in it. To forget. When the first fairytales are printed in a little booklet on inferior paper, he sends them to Ingemann as a bagatelle, but by then he has already read them aloud for the naturalist H.C. Ørsted. Ørsted makes a prediction. 'If your novel *The Improviser* makes you famous, the fairy-tales will make you immortal.' 'That I cannot believe,' he replies. 'That isn't something I shall live to see in this world.'

To FIND WARMTH in the fire of recognition, short-lived warmth, ephemeral. Carl Baggers in the *Sunday Magazine*, Ingemann in a letter, Henrik Hertz during a visit – 'Many of those who do not otherwise find you to their liking have surrendered to you here.' To sit on the sofa in checked slippers and dressing-gown with his feet up, a pipe in his mouth and a book in his hand, and to hear the tea-urn sing, to feel at his zenith with constant guests in his house of poetry; and then to feel the gnawing of worms, to rise – from the dead night of exhaustion – with a renewed obsession for his *idée fixe* that criticism has shipwrecked hope for him, to be afraid of being unable to live up to himself, to open the door to the chill wind of humiliation. Can't he remember one of the greatest men in the land saying to him fourteen years ago that he should never forget that he was just a poor child? And didn't Bishop Mynster have him understand twelve years ago that it was an honour for him to be allowed to study?

And his treatment at school – wasn't that cruel and mechanical? Wasn't it a miracle that he didn't go to pieces? Every single step on his path to being a poet in the world is like a street-play, where the hat is sent round to provide for his meagre existence. He has to perform, to bow and scrape and smile, to be grateful and to muzzle his inner thoughts – even for Edvard. To be awkward in his movements, because they often come seconds too late, because they are afterthoughts. At the darkest point is the fear of losing what he already has – and shame at where he has come from. When will his half-sister Karen Marie come knocking at his door? Hasn't he had a recurring nightmare that he meets her, a woman selling her body on the streets of Copenhagen? Prostituted like his aunt, on the street like his mother, poor like her father. He has racked his brains to think what to do with her. Hasn't he already let his mother down when she asked him several times to take her under his roof in Slagelse? All those excuses he found not to see her, and all the excuses he now has to find again. Perhaps she will drag him down with her? Perhaps that is nemesis? He no longer remembers her face, no longer wants to remember it, but it comes back to him anyway in the dreams that take him back to Odense.

You came from nowhere, returned to nowhere, hidden face.

THE QUAGMIRE OF everyday life. His wounds. His sister. He tries to write himself out of it and only entangles himself further and further. In his novel *O.T.*, conceived in an ecstasy of self-pity, he is Otto Tholstrup, the Latin scholar, the academic from central Jutland, light of skin and dark of mind, who has grown up on a farm with his grandfather in Lemvig and is in constant flight from a secret past that is branded on his own shoulder. The brand is *O.T.*, which are not only the initials of his own name but also the first letters of Odense Tower, where his mother was locked up in the penitentiary owing to a confusion of identities. Here he was born – as was a girl, possibly his half-sister, a woman with eyebrows that meet across an ugly face and with a strident, plebeian laugh, a monster, the very image of evil, who persists in thwarting his contented bourgeois existence. She and her father, the scoundrel Heinrich, threaten with their very presence to torpedo his good name and rip his dream of a friendship with the aristocratic Wilhelm to shreds. Under the cloak of his double life and with no faith in his surroundings being able to tolerate the truth of his origins, Otto teeters on the edge of suicide and is only partially saved by his engagement and marriage to Louise. The sense of being a doppelgänger can persist – melodramatic as in the novel, or painful as in his concourse with the Collins of the city. How can people change themselves anyway, how recast their being, when they come from the provinces into the city and have a murky childhood printed in the marrow of their bones, in their very features? To change, it is not enough to change clothes. 'Even in fine clothes you stick out like a sore thumb when you come to the capital from the distant provinces,' says Otto. 'Only there do they get a different cut and let you merge with your surroundings. The same is true in a spiritual sense, but you do not recast your being and your ideas as quickly as the cut of your clothes.' And if and when the recasting is achieved, who and where is he then? Homeless in both places? In the teeming mass of humanity he is alone. In the night he is alone. He is naked, bound to a wild horse chasing through the forest – as in Horace Vernet's painting of Mazeppa.

THE ROOM IS under water – never have the undulating shadows on the walls been so lovely. The water is clear, blue, transparent, and through it he can see the sun now set in purple like a flower of light. He has his boy's voice again and lies with his hands before him on the duvet, humming. In a while he will get up, will put on his clothes and walk down on to the white beach, where the sand is still warm from the sun. In a while he will stand and sing out across Øresund, as he once sang in Odense or in a gully among the Swiss Alps. In a while he will once again be young and a part of the world of men. He will see clearly the green colours in the garden of Rolighed, inhale once again the scent of flowers and escape this intoxicating blue water in which death resides. But who has promised him one more summer's day? And what would he not give for it? His voice? To be a fish in his imagination? Even the pain he will accept, pains in his stomach, pains in his legs. And the disquiet of existing among strangers in the town, of being unable to find rest anywhere, unable to find a woman. He just wants to be able to stand once more on the beach with Edvard, with his hand on his shoulder, and be young again. How many times has he had that very dream! To share everything with Edvard in this world or another. As a fish he leaves the water in his room, leaves the transparent blue behind him and passes down the corridor on the first floor, down the steps of the large, silent house with its gleaming furniture, its vases. With every step a knife runs him through. The darkness of the garden is phosphorescent, and the gentle cool of evening touches his skin, his temples, and carries with it the scents of the garden. With his head swimming slightly, he finds his way down on to the pale beach, to the gentle sound of its rhythmical inhalations swelling and spreading its tongues across the countless pebbles.

The sky is an indigo blue, far out dark formations resemble mountains, but perhaps they are clouds? He stands a while looking out to sea which fuses with the sky at the horizon. He is a pillar of life. Only now does he notice a man further down the beach, a shadowy figure. He moves towards him, and with each movement the knife drives its pain into his legs.

'I have read your fairytales and recognize your voice,' says the shadow, which has Edvard's colourless eyes. 'I find it all ever so interesting.'

He places his hand on the shadow's shoulder and turns his eyes once *again out to sea, but with a sigh of displeasure the shadow steps aside, and his hand slides off to dangle emptily at his side.*

'You have a sickly disposition,' says the shadow, 'aren't really man but half woman. What am I to do with you?'

In that instant he wishes the knife in his legs were a knife he could use against the shadow.

'But affectionate you certainly are. That much I will say of you,' says the shadow, touching its hat and striking away from the beach.

As he stands watching the shadow disappear, there is something – a voice, a sound, perhaps the sound of the sea itself – which calls to him; he starts to wade out into the water, which rises around him, until in the end he stands with water up to his neck and he lets himself fall, fall into the beautiful cool water. The pains cease, and he is no longer in the water and has found his voice again. He is floating on air. Below him lies a man with a waxen face, like a mummy, toothless. A drowned man?

No. He is ringing his bell.

The stillness is broken.

THE NIGHT VIEW from his rooms is frozen solid – deserted ships in Nyhavn Harbour, where rooks overrun the decks.

A new winter, a new frenzy of writing, a new novel in the stocks – *Grey on Grey* or *Only a Fiddler*. He dives down into his 'world of the soul', to the scorn directed against the talented soul (himself as Christian, his middle name), to the cold-shouldering, to the donkeys that always trample the best flowers, to the loneliness in the midst of the crowd. From the lips of the prostitute, Steffen-Karet, the musical talent, Christian, receives the recognition of his genius that others withhold from him. 'Yes, my lovely lad!' she says. 'I don't hold with that Turkish music! Even if you had been a girl!' She draws him to the open bar, gives him punch and sliced apples and then bursts into merry laughter. 'You must be a genius, just like they say!' she said. The other women in the brothel look at him with the same bovine eyes as the boys he has grown up with. He is the peasant boy who looks after the geese, who enjoys sitting alone by the still water of a pond in the shade of hazels and alders letting himself slide away into daydreams. For him the surface of the water mirrors the whole world – birds that fly down deep, trees with their tops pointing down, their roots up, his own upside-down nature. The surface is for him the world's ocean – its water-boatmen, corsairs. The water plants around the pool take on gigantic proportions, become tropical trees, while a frog is a monster such as he has read about in *A Thousand and One Nights*. What he sees in his mind's eye is reality, but the other boys think him mad. They tie him up with willow wands, stick burrs all over him shouting, 'Hurray for crazy Christian!' Madness or genius? Recognized by tittering tarts but not by the gentry. His special qualities are of virtually no use in the coldness that surrounds him, and he shrinks, perishes, even in his desire for the Jewish Naomi, falling from the dizzy heights of his dreams to being the village fiddler, the permanent bachelor, the provincial eccentric. A vision of the shipwreck of talent, a utopia of bitterness. With Christian he plunges deep into his own wounds, his own anxieties. He is himself speaking with his own voice, even if the novel's construction will not quite stand up, since it is condemned to being a tragic trail of tears from first to last. Wasn't that what his poet friend Hauch from Sorø says? 'But you *aren't* Christian!' No, but he feels like Christian, bewildered just as he is, obsessed by the anxiety that he might not be good enough in the final reckoning. Maybe he will be crushed by it? Maybe the culture surrounding him is a snake? Maybe he will be consumed (from within) by his attempt to master it? He is alone in the clock tower. 'Instinctively he felt that if he took just one step forwards, the bell would crush his head. Louder and louder rang the blows on the hollow metal. The quivering air combined with his fear affected him powerfully. Sweat poured from his body. He dared not turn around, his eyes stared fixedly into the hollow bell each time it swung booming towards him. He let out a loud scream for help, but no one could hear him; he felt his scream to be sound-less beside the beat of the bell. Shaken to the core, it seemed to him to be the monstrous maw of a snake.' Fear and trembling in the depths of his soul, in the depths of every soul that lives for its talent.

Edvard is to be married – God bless him, may he be happy and deserve his happiness! To have a faithful, loving wife, to see oneself reborn in one's children, is to have a home. He writes to Edvard. Domestic happiness is something I would right gladly have. Like Moses I stand on the mountaintop and look into the Promised Land into which I myself shall never come. If I stand alone my whole life long, friendship must be everything for me, must fill up every space, which may be why my utterances, why my demands are so great – much too great! But give me as much as you can, you are what I love above all. I have a foreboding about my entire future, with all its longing. That I will be alone and must be so. My under-standing will, I hope, always show this to me as clearly as now.

His feelings are as strong as Edvard's. As he loves his Hen-riette, so is he also loved! Twice he has loved, but each time it was only self-delusion. He will never forget it. It is one of the suffer-ings he cannot even speak about to his dearest friend.

IN THE DARKNESS two women by the head of the bed. Two women with their backs to him, their bare shoulders, their sinuous wrists, the curve of their necks as the light (a moonbeam?) touches the hemispheres of their two faces turning slowly towards each other; their faces, their bodies elide until they smile with one face, sorrowful as a painting by Botticelli. They are there, they aren't there, are there . . .

His spirits rise as he sends off his lament in *Only a Fiddler*. Isn't it a sign of ingratitude not to be content with what the Lord has given him? From now on he will see everything in the brightest light! Hasn't he been translated into German and French? And doesn't the Frenchman Xavier Marmier plan to write a whole article about him in his *Revue de Paris*, on a par with Oehlenschläger and other famous writers in Europe and Russia? But despite all that he is – temporarily – knocked off his perch by the 26-year-old Søren Kierkegaard's judgement on *Only a Fiddler*. Oh yes, he met him downtown, at the Student Association, where the young theologian whispered to him in friendly fashion, 'I shall soon be sending you a critique of your novel, which will do it more justice than other reviews, which give quite the wrong impression of you.' A whole book has come out of it written in convoluted and partially impenetrable language – *From the Papers of One Still Living*. He reads parts of it, puts it down, reads on, wanders to and fro in his small rooms. As if in a stupor. Is hurt, dispirited. The man has been bitter, jealous, has wanted to hurt him. The ending of the novel is wrong, which is to say not good, the author lacks a philosophy of life, as does the main character, Christian, who is a 'blubberer', a vain 'husk', who has to go through so much discomfort and meaninglessness before at last, thank God, meeting his downfall. Christian is presented as a genius, but his only talent is the self-pity he displays as he experiences great trials and sinks under their weight. The hero of the novel just repeats the same joyless fight that his author himself fights in his life – is, indeed, at no distance from the author but is simply an amputation of himself, so that his own 'character is transposed into fiction, in such a way that one is truly tempted at moments to believe that Andersen is a figure who has escaped from a group which some writer has composed but not yet finished'. The author Andersen's hand is shaky, his pen spits out not only blots but slurs, and his so-called genius is a little taper that the wind will puff out instead of a fire that the storm will only cause to rage. Nor is the author Andersen better equipped to drive round in his coach surveying Europe than he is to trace the map of the human heart . . . What is he to think? He looks up Edvard, who lays on his rage a cooling salve. Ingemann tries to calm him – Kierkegaard presumably has kindlier thoughts about it than he voices here. At the close of the book some such curiously restrained amicability is suggested. And, yes, Kierkegaard has divided himself into two here – the critic and the reader – and as a reader he recalls his first impression of the book and is so full of his feelings of gratitude to the writer to whom he owes it all that he will whisper it in his ear at the first opportunity. What is he going to whisper? Why whisper kind words and write down the unkind? And why not be alive through and through instead of being a reader half alive, a critic half dead?

And on it goes, this Copenhagen mudslinging, this pedantic emphasis on the novels' shadowy side. Returning from a liberating trip to Sweden, he reads in the *Maanedsskriftet* yet another article about his lack of understanding, his exaggerated childishness and naïvety, his self-centredness. They don't hold out much hope for him. In the Collin household they think the review well written; the critic has hit the nail right on the head! His heart needs to have a hard skin not to bleed to death. He must get out again, away, abroad – maybe he will die out there?

OH YES, THE cold! To be small, to be kidnapped by a toad and then to live with the butterflies, to be scorned by the maybugs, left alone for winter and half freeze to death. Each snowflake for Thumbelina is like a barrowful for us. To survive, to live with a friendly if instructive field mouse with the prospect of marriage to a mole, a life deep underground. To be saved by a swallow, to flee south. To write his way through and out of the dark, labyrinthine world and into a dream. Thumbelina saves the swallow's life, Johannes rescues the body, the Stranger in 'The Spectre', and is saved himself. A utopia of love? The poet struck by Cupid as in 'The Saucy Boy'. The cold princess transformed into a large coal-black swan with flashing eyes, into a white swan, a human princess. With the swan's down of love. But there is no moral in this, say the critics, no instruction for the young, the language is too everyday. No poetry in this story, none in that . . . For the most part the critics are mute, take no notice. As though the fairytales hadn't happened. But the children and their parents read them. More and more. In Danish, in Swedish, in German and now in Dutch, now . . . To blow life like glass, to breathe on inanimate matter, to waken the dead, changing the mermaid in 'The Little Mermaid' into a human being robbed of her voice and stuck by knives – into a tragic but liberated spirit of the air. To turn the vanity of the world, of the king, into music in 'The Emperor's New Clothes'. To find harmony in the wise child who tears the curtain aside. Hypocrites and snobs you are, the whole lot of you.

HIS MOOD SWINGS like a pendulum, like an empty swing between sun and moon. Sick and full of the fiery 'King of Denmark' cough medicine and of raisins preserved in crystallized sugar and vinegar, he reads 'The Little Mermaid' aloud at the Student Association and is over the moon at being seen and heard. Over the moon one evening, resigned the next. Marmier – charming, fast-talking Marmier with his French accent – has spoken to him about Sophie Ørsted, 'You are in love with her! I know it! Ask for her hand, then!' Now it is already a thing of the past. She is lovely, brilliant, good, adorable, and belongs to one of the foremost intellectual families in Copenhagen, while he is poor, without a fortune – is not even in love – perhaps? Isn't she exactly half his age? And doesn't she treat him like a much older man? Luckily, she has no idea that he has anything more than a good opinion of her. He is discreet, cannot – as Marmier does – immediately encircle his prey. He has dreamt of her, has felt sensual, has . . . This evening wasn't she just adorable, told him she had become engaged, and he took her hand for the first time and, despite the tremor in his hand, wasn't he calm, in the best of spirits? Twice he pressed her hand and felt no pain. But at home, looking out over the view of Nyhavn, he is alone, alone as he will always be. He will die lonely like Christian in his novel. If she hadn't become engaged, if he had proposed to her, it would never have been any good for her! But her skin, the light in her face, her lips, the way she walks, her laughter, her sudden earnestness, that look from her brown eyes that rocks him on his feet like a thunderbolt, the few seconds when everything stands still around them, the lacework edging to her dress that reveals a glimpse of cleavage, of breast . . . He grasps his penis, rubs it up and down, fantasizes. In the darkness of his bed.

SUNLIGHT ON THE *white wall. Dozing at the edge of the world, the shadow of a candlestick turns into a little one-legged soldier with an upturned conical hat and a bayonet fixed to the rifle in his hand. A castle materializes out of the shimmering light, and in front of the castle a ballerina with both arms outstretched and one lifted leg. A spangle flashes on her poised little body. The stillness overwhelming, broken only by the sound of his hand moving across the duvet and his faint breathing. When he closes his eyes and opens them again, the picture is gone, but behind his eyelids – in a dark and teeth-clenching space – the soldier sets sail in a newspaper boat, silent, with rifle gripped tight in his clenched fist. Towards the light. And the fall. His breathing is nervous, rasping, and he dozes off, has a sense of drowning, of being helplessly closed in, and thinks, 'That's it. It's over.' But when he opens his eyes the drawing on the white wall stands out clearer than ever, the soldier staring at the ballerina, the ballerina staring at the soldier . . . Fru Melchior – he notices her only now – opens the door to the balcony, and in the blinding white sheen of the velvety blue sky over Øresund, the soldier and the ballerina are consumed in fire.*

'There is ash on my hands,' he says.

Fru Melchior looks at his long hands. Smiles.

'Then we had better wash them,' she says.

WHAT DOES HE long for? To be honoured? Yes, he lives only for honour – and hasn't he made a name for himself here at home? Even the shadow of a name beyond the borders of Denmark? But here he stands just as poor and helpless as he was when he stepped through the gates of the city at Vesterport with his bundle in his hand – and less happy. The beautiful dreams that filled him then have been replaced by this reality, this acknowledgement of his own shortcomings – and the impossibility of overcoming them. If he can only bring his spiritual treasure to the surface, the ferment he can feel . . .

'Cultivate the lark of hope,' Ingemann writes to him from Sorø But how? Without money. How long does the hat have to go round? It is a misfortune to be a poet in a small country. He has to have a fixed poet's annuity otherwise he will be ruined. He writes a begging letter to the king, to Chamberlain Rantzau-Breitenburg, his admirer, whose invitation to tea he has just refused, preferring to spend that evening cultivating his female correspondents, Henriette Hanck and Jette Wulff. And now his entire happiness depends on him. Rantzau-Breitenberg will have to support his case to the king. 'I shall be ruined if something is not done for me. Five hundred *dalers* a year until I reach a path of some kind, and I am saved. I am convinced that the king would give them to me in that he has known me, has a fair picture of me, as you have. My friends have said to me that I must grasp this moment; my need is so great! My entire life's happiness, all my future undertakings, I lay in your hands. Say only to the king what I know you have so kindly said to others about me! Do not turn down this plea of mine . . .'

HEADMASTER MEISLING ON Østergade in front the welter of shops, Meisling across the road, directly facing him, looking worn out, the skin round his eyes like elephant hide. 'I have to say this to you,' says Meisling barring his way. 'I was not kind to you at school, I was wrong about you, and it pains me. You are head and shoulders above me.' He gives this uneasy and corpulent man a friendly smile and is touched. 'Forget my harshness,' says Meisling. 'I have already forgotten it,' he says. 'To you the honour, to me the shame,' says Meisling and bows his head to avoid his gaze. And now Meisling stands slightly dishevelled in his crumpled coat, touches his hat brim, turns about and continues along the street limping slightly, directionless. Disappears into the milling crowds.

HE DREAMS THAT *he is once more in his customary seat in the pit at the Theatre Royal and is a little thought that moves through the hearts of the front row of spectators. The first heart he visits is a woman's, and in it lie plaster casts of all her friends as though at an orthopaedic institute, revealing all their physical and spiritual faults; in the next female heart a white dove flutters above the high altar; in the next he can see a poor attic with a sick woman and through the window lovely roses in a box on the roof – and the sun-drenched sky; now he crawls on hands and knees through a heaving butcher's stall, meat slabbed on meat, the heart of a rich and respectable gentleman; his wife's heart is an old, dilapidated dovecote on which the man's portrait is used as a weathervane; after that he enters a hall of mirrors that magnify to huge proportions; this person's insignificant ego sits on the floor, impressed at the sight of its own great size; next he seems to be in the heart of an old spinster, a tight needle case full of sharp needles, but the heart belongs to a young military man with several medals, a man solid to the core, as they say. Bewildered, he emerges from the last heart, his own – a white room full of shadows with windows standing open to the winds that come wafting in from all corners of the earth, where a long-legged, stooping man raises his eyes from the white paper to gaze out towards the blue mountains. Behind him is a boy, singing, reaching his arms out towards his back. And further away still a boy with an axe hacking at the frozen lake.*

There is someone lying and singing – an old man. Is it him?

'That's a lovely song you're singing,' *the servant says close to his ear. He recognizes his voice.*

'Am I awake?' *he says and opens his eyes.*

WORKS ON HIS autobiography *The Life of My Youth* for Germany. Here he is the precocious shoemaker's son who wants to become a poet and does so. He is the misunderstood genius, the butt of laughter and irony, who battles against all odds like the hero of a fairytale and succeeds through the grace of God and with the help of some few discriminating men. One of them was the poet Baggesen, who regarded him as 'the little adventurer . . .' The old woman at the hospital who foresaw that his hometown of Odense would one day be lit up in his honour is the proof that the forces of destiny are working in his favour and that from the lowest of the low he has been born to greatness. He is high on the fairytale plot of his destiny. Doesn't it look as though the adventure of his own life will arouse just as much interest in him as his writings? He jokes in a letter to 'My Sister' in Odense, Henriette Hanck: 'So, soon you will be ashamed to do less than place a candle in the window for me, the day I enter town . . .' But he nevertheless complains a moment later of an indisposition and of his closest friends, who dismiss it as imagination. Henriette comforts him (as so often before). His indisposition is not imagination, his nerves just aren't very strong, and those with weak nerves so often feel afflicted in the extreme without really knowing why. That she knows from her own experience. But this little woman of his own age – whose first novel (published anonymously) dealt with a woman who squanders the love of her youth, and who already sees a modest future for herself as a spinster in Eilschow's apartments for professionals of single status in Odense – holds a picture up for him, a picture of what ambition does to a person. The picture is of an unhappy, lonely individual, filled solely by ambition – in other words, self-love. The object of his love is not someone whose happiness he wants to promote but someone who can flatter his self-love when he shows the world how much she dotes on him. If he caresses a child it is not because he has feelings for it but because he wants to win over its parents, who might be useful to him. His pride, which at the start accompanied his ambition, leaves him the moment he can climb a few rungs by using base flattery or sycophancy. Half of his fellow men envy him, the other half look down on him. No one is fond of him, and his friends leave him one by one. At the hour of his death he has not a single faithful heart against which to rest his head and only a hired hand to close his sightless eyes . . . He reads this parable and it strikes home – in part. Is this jealousy speaking? Even through her mouth? He dismisses it.

WAKES SUDDENLY, SURROUNDED by stillness, the dark, hears sounds outside as though burglars are breaking into the house. He rings the bell – how soon will the servant come? Rings again. Again. And now has no more strength.

Sunshine is his life. Thank God, he has been granted by royal decree a fixed annuity of four hundred *rigsdalers*. He can afford to be ill, to travel, no longer has to beg for crumbs at everyone's door . . . two thousand *rigsdalers* would have met his needs, but four hundred is a small crumb-tree in the garden! He moves into a set of rooms at the Hotel du Nord, the cheapest, up under the eaves, but with a view of Kongens Nytorv and the Theatre Royal across the square. And hasn't he already become a first-class dandy, a prince of fashion! Wears a jacket lined with velvet costing sixty *rigsdalers*, a hat, an umbrella . . . gets handsomer by the day! That's what his most foppish friends say. Jette Wulff says, 'But you were so original before.' Mrs Colbjørnsen: 'You dress well, are of fine character, are written about in the papers, even in France! Perhaps you will be invited to court one day.' Ørsted: 'Now you can't complain. You're recognized by everyone and have an established name.' This is the life! In Germany his name seems just as well known as at home.

CLENCHES HIS HAND, *smiling softly. Remembers Thorvaldsen's face when he sailed out in the boat, one of the first to welcome him, in the harbour, to Rheden, after his twenty years abroad. It wasn't Heiberg, Grundtvig, Oehlenschläger, Hertz or the others in the boat whom Thorvaldsen embraced with his smile, but him. On the torch-lit procession in his honour through the Botanical Gardens, didn't Thorvaldsen, the star of the day, link arms with him before disappearing into the jubilant crowds? And the day after took him in his arms, kissed him twice? Spiritual brothers, the young and the old. Wasn't he happy in that moment? Thorvaldsen's broad, aging face under its wild grey mane lit up by the sun, his thin lips, his sharp, worn voice and those magical hands that could charm such music out of clay. Hadn't he, too, with his long scissors, his long fingers – with that unconscious dance of hand with hand – created little carriages out of paper? Where are they? In which corner of which room do they stand now? Do they exist? Everything is falling apart – is that why he can't remember his own face? His father's face keeps getting in the way.*

BY NIGHT HE devours books on Africa and America, feels at home among the blacks with ostrich and lion, dreams of slimy snakes in the wet grass, gazes at stars dragging their tails across the transparent air. Wakes to days at his writing desk at the Hotel du Nord and the play *The Mulatto* about a black slave from Mauritius, who is taken in by a rich French family, educated in France and who, on his return to his slave colony, witnesses racism, assaults on the slaves. Polishes his verse line by line, for the play must be tight, musical, must be exotic, a blend of Victor Hugo, whom he met in Paris, and Casemir Delavign. Must be new, with not a trace of the old 'Andersen' left. The hero, the mulatto, has to be warm-blooded, full of life and vigour – all the things that the fiddler and the improviser were not. The mulatto is in love with a white countess, Cecilie, and she returns his love and competes for him against the demonic Eleonora at a slave market in Martinique. Surrounded by the bleached drabness of his hotel room, he writes the vibrant colours of the south into his play, blue, violet, green, yellow, red. Gets up from his chair, his head in a daze, and paces the room, passing the bureau with Thorvaldsen's bust, the paintings on the walls, the bookcase with his own bust (along with a crucifix and various curiosities), the wood-stove, over the green carpet and past the sofa with its table and, above, the oval mirror. When he has guests, he sits like a long-limbed baboon draped across a chair talking, gesticulating with his arms, rising from time to time to cast a glance at himself in the mirror. He knows. It is his vanity. Alone with *The Mulatto* late in the evening, his imagination heats up, he becomes 'dreadfully passionate' and has to go outside to cool his 'hot blood' Here he can be found drifting around the narrow streets of the harbour in Nyhavn with the hollow sounds of the basement drinking dens in his ears, or aimlessly walking the paths of the gardens of Kongens Have or across the broad, empty cobbles of Kongens Nytorv with the shadowy statue of the mounted king in the middle of the square. By day he attempts to combat his sexual irritability by taking warm baths. He gives way too easily to the call of his organ, its urgings . . . He must stop it. Maybe there is something wrong with his penis? It is so sore, always.

A LETTER FROM Henriette, who sees herself as the woman he celebrates in his poem 'The Month of October' and is offended by his rumoured engagement. What offends her, though? He will not become engaged. *The Mulatto* is finished, but he has lost his most prominent tooth. He will have to have a false tooth – oh yes, to swan around, decked in the plumes of youth without a single tooth in his mouth! Who wants a toothless organ grinder? A fake? An eyesore?

FEVER. THE ROOM sails before the eastern wind so icy cold that he crawls into a hollow – a hollow one moment so narrow, huge blocks of rock suspended over him, and the next high as the open air, with sepulchres spiring above him with muted organ pipes, petrified pennants. A blue light spreads across him, and he hears the sound of singing. Plants that resemble animals unfold before him. He is in a castle where the walls are full of colour, and the ceiling is a flower. In the windows time has burnt its moments into pictures, living pictures. He recognizes his mother and father on the outskirts of a wood, his mother wearing a calico dress, his father gathering mushrooms from the forest floor. And there are biblical pictures from the schoolroom in Odense, only now in motion – Adam and Eve in front of the tree in Eden, Jacob on his ladder climbing to heaven, floating angels. In the mirrored images of the windows people he has met come and go in an endless procession – the mad woman at the Greyfriars Hospital, Grandfather with flowers in his hair, Grandmother with her stick, pale-faced Edvard, hunchbacked Jette, dark-skinned Rachel, Jenny of the lovely voice, even the black waiters at the Hotel du Nord . . . In a sunlit hall the walls are transparent pictures peopled by millions of happy faces, many of them as small as the dot of a rosebud painted on paper. In the centre of the hall, the tree of paradise with shining apples that look like oranges. It grows dark. A woman with light touching one coloured cheek, black hair and languid movements, lies down to sleep in front of the tree, her skin, her breasts gleaming, making him hot and nervous. He closes his eyes, hears her calling to him without moving her lips – there is a song in her voice, and he walks towards her, leans over her, and she smiles in her dream. Her lips are dark, her mouth half open. He feels the desire, the sensuality in the tips of his fingers, the weight of his body. One more moment like this to balance against eternal darkness, he thinks. And kisses her eyelids, her lips. Everything dissolves around him, a cold rain falls on his skin, an icy chill cleaves his body. A man looking like Dr Meyer is standing a few paces away.

'I will come one day when you least expect it,' he says.

He closes his eyes, opens them again. No one is there.

No one. The maid's laughter rises from the floor below.

He feels relief. A moment later, fear.

FURIOUS, STORMING AT Molbech the theatre censor's critique of *The Mulatto.* Molbech with his greasy hair, his evasive eyes, his envy. Molbech, who writes: 'Herr Andersen's characters are warped creatures dissolving out of definition, who are at the same time narrative figures who can only be regarded as affected, who would only ever permit representation on the stage with the aid of unnatural pretentiousness and bombast . . . Of Herr Andersen's play it must also be said that two ladies of rank falling in love with such a mulatto turns into a situation which is not only indecent and indelicate in the extreme but also deeply embarrassing and wanting in piquancy.' This is now the third time that this toad has tried to bar his entry to the Theatre Royal. His play must be performed otherwise it is curtains for him! He neither can nor will suffer this injustice. His friends will have to look after him or give up on him! Hasn't Oehlenschläger told him that they can't not perform the play? Hasn't Ørsted heard the play three times and declared that there can be no conceivable grounds for not performing it? Heiberg is the only one to make excuses for Molbech, but he is after all a friend of Molbech's. Molbech wants to grind him into the dust, but his name will still be alive when Molbech's is a dead word in an old folio. Fire and poison are running in his veins. Molbech and Heiberg and their mob are parrots echoing each other's verdicts on him. He knows the verdicts by heart, collecting them irritably into one stinking bouquet: 'H.C. Andersen has a poetic nature, which shows us how different it is to possess invention and to be blessed with a richness of imagination; this last no one can deny him. He knows how to decorate and arrange thoughts and feelings, but he lacks creativity . . . His three novels are a kind of arabesque, an overcrowded and inartistic tracery, in which instinct has led him to produce beautiful passages that indicate poetic power, but a serene prospect of the whole guided by the understanding shows, as we have already noted, that he cannot create, but only decorate and arrange; this is not invention, but imagination, surely; what he lacks is reasoning . . . The dramatic pieces we will not discuss, being only a dismembering of the poetic works of others . . . In the children's fairytales, which could probably be termed the most poetic works of this author, we see a greater degree of unity, but there is nevertheless in the narrative mode itself, which is here the prime feature, something of the arabesque – qualities of satire, of naïvety, of the baroque and of conviviality lie side by side with too great confusion and there is no moral – we, at least, could not find one with the best will in the world, for he speaks to adults one moment and to children the next . . . We would wish for this poet – for that name we truly believe we can give him – that he saw himself and the world about him with greater clarity . . .'

He shows it to his friends, but only Ørsted sees the funny side.

He is alone among strangers and has difficulties in returning their well-intentioned greetings. Oh yes. The Collins count upon his good nature, but they pay homage to their domestic gods, Oehlenschläger and Heiberg. But he no longer wants to be a tame household pet and to feel despondent in their company every other day . . . He must get out, out, away!

In Sweden at Thorup Manor he half falls in love with the eldest of the daughters of the house, Matilda Bark, a young woman of the world who speaks of Paris, music and poetry. He reads his stories, they praise his books, remind him of his many readers in Germany; and he becomes mellow, high-spirited. It is summer, he turns as brown as a Bedouin, he is a child of the sun and, when he travels, returns to his natural colour with the first ray of sunshine. Didn't his hair turn black on his journey to Italy? If he had enough money he is sure he would fall wholly in love . . .

WORKS ON A new play, *The Moorish Girl* at Nysø Manor, argues daily
with Baroness Stampe, who has repeatedly asked him not to travel
abroad but to come and stay – that domineering woman who insists
on presiding over Thorvaldsen's correspondence. Thorvaldsen – a
man whose company he relishes – has bid him welcome at the lunch
table. His friend works unobtrusively on his drawings and sculptures
in his thatched, stone-built atelier – 'The Sibyl's Studio' – created
specially for him, while he sits before his view of park and woodland,
writing. In the evenings he reads aloud. Amusing to watch the way
the baroness and her sister follow Thorvaldsen's least movement; at
table he sits between the pair of them. One evening, as they are all
sitting around the table – even Thorvaldsen – the baroness says, 'Ah,
yes, Christine. You always did have to have a doll to play with. Last
year it was that one, this year it's this one – and now it's Thorvaldsen.
Whether it be large or small, it is still only a doll to you!' He, too, is
a doll. He wanders alone through the woods by the lake, thinking
about Ahasverus, the cobbler of Jerusalem. How much their characters resemble each other! He will write a tragic epic about him, about
his niece Ada and Judas Iscariot.

For five weeks – twenty times in all – Henriette has looked for a letter from him, but in vain. Why does he not write? Why this silence?
And now, at last, a letter from him, in which he says he wants to
travel, that the negative criticism of his fairytales gets him down,
that his appearance is unsightly . . . He must believe her when she
tells him, as a non-flattering sister, that he has an interesting and
soulful face. And doesn't that mean more than being beautiful,
especially for a man? In *her eyes* he is beautiful and she looks with
partiality upon those features that are so dear to her. And why does
he now want to cast himself out into the transient friendships of a
journey and increase the distance from those he leaves behind at
home? She cannot think of his journey without misgivings and
pain, but that must not, of course, be a consideration . . .

HIS GREY 'SISTER' in Odense with her brushed-back hair – she loved him . . . His unhearing heart . . . Didn't he once say to her that her hair looked awful? Just as in Joseph's dream the sun and moon should bow down before him . . . Didn't he win half a city and lose his . . .? The window rattles. The wind comes from nowhere, is inside himself. A creature born of the wind. Borne by the wind, but where? And whither was she borne? In the city of the dead, windows are hearts that rattle.

Denmark. Sorø. A bottle with the gatehouse as the mouth of the bottleneck – through it you enter confinement and drear. The lake, sluggish, sleepy, seems to yawn in boredom. By the foul-smelling swamp, in an area newly landscaped on a quagmire, the trees seem to be rotting. Heigh-ho. Hope: amiable people.

Fêted in Lund by Swedish students with torch-lit processions, speeches. From his hotel room he is on the look-out for the suppressed smile at the corners of a mouth, but there are only well-disposed faces. When they seek him out in the foyer of the hotel, he thanks them profoundly and afterwards weeps in the solitude of his room with agitation, his feelings overwhelmed. Cannot sleep that night for the pain in his head, in his organ. He reads in a Swedish newspaper: 'Andersen belongs not only to Denmark but to the whole of Europe, and the homage paid to him by the youth of Sweden at Sweden's southernmost university ought, we hope, to draw the stings of pettiness and envy in his own homeland that are attempting to turn his laurel wreath into a crown of thorns . . .'

To BOW TO the star of the stage, Mrs Heiberg, send her his latest fairytale with a dedication, as her devoted servant, to watch her bring *The Mulatto* to triumph at the Theatre Royal – acknowledging her personal beauty, her spirituality, her sensibility, her plasticity. To receive wild applause in the theatre, to be praised in *Kjøbenhavns Morgenblad* for a 'genuine work of genius'. And to weep some days later when the newspaper *Fæderlandet* accuses him of stealing the whole idea of *The Mulatto* from the short story by the Frenchman H. Arnaud. So much nonsense and envy. To be unable to get away owing to a shortage of money – despite such success in Sweden – to stake everything on Mrs Heiberg in *The Moorish Girl*, to be sick with a concealed passion, masturbating till it hurts, to wander restlessly round town, to attend an audience with King Christian VIII, who acknowledged him several times with a greeting from the royal box during a command performance of *The Mulatto*, to be given a brooch with nineteen small diamonds, to float on air for just one night.

To be standing one day in front of the Heibergs' house on Christianshavn, to read aloud from *The Moorish Girl* to Mrs Heiberg – lovely, a little pale, with shining dark hair, sitting there in her white silk dress, its flounced collar highlighting the heart-shaped opening of her corsage. Large brown eyes, she has, long eyelashes, strong eyebrows. Dispassionate and absentminded in equal measure she listens (she has just returned from taking the waters with her husband as a cure for her exhausted stage voice). As he reads for her he slides forward until he is sitting on the edge of his chair. When he shuts the manuscript after the final sentence his gaze moves nervously from the paper to her face.

'It is a big role for you . . .' he says.

Silence. Her lips remain motionless.

'It is a challenging part, you will play both a man and a woman . . .'

She clears her throat. Leans slightly towards him.

'I shall say it point-blank. Your play does not appeal to me. It will not be effective on stage. The subject is confusing and lacks interest. And as for me – well, you know how many roles I have played. I am myself in poor health, and this part will take all my remaining strength. I do not wish to. I cannot.'

'You cannot mean that,' he says. 'That is unfair of you.'

'But you know I am unwell, and the likelihood is that your play will not be performed before the warmer months. My throat problem, you understand. It is really no good.'

'But the play will fail without you!'

'I am obliged to turn you down,' she says, fatigued, letting her hand pass across her forehead.

'I beg you,' he says.

'I am sorry.'

His breath comes quickly.

'You are a great actress. The one everyone wants to see. How low do I have to sink? I can feel how you humiliate me. Tell me, how low do I have to sink before you will listen to me?'

'You need not sink low because you ask *me*,' she says.

'Don't you understand that it's life or death?' he says. 'I am prostrating myself before you, begging you from the depths of my heart. Take this part!'

'No,' she says. 'And I am not alone in my judgement.'

She stiffens in her chair.

'It's Heiberg, the director of the whole thing – it's his jealousy,' he says. 'He can't stand me, and he's talked you round.'

She smiles coldly.

'What makes you think that? Where did you get that from?'

'I know his opposition to the play.'

'Can you really not understand that both the nature of this role and my state of health make it impossible for me to help you? Are you asking me to squander my resources on such a hopeless undertaking?'

'It's so unfair of you! Take on this role!'

'I shall act no boy's parts,' she says.

Furious, he gets up. His hat falls out of his hands, he bends down to pick it up.

'You are heartless,' he says. 'You are not a good person. But one thing I will say to you. You stand now at the height of the wheel of fortune. Beware. You may one day find yourself at its low point, and *I* may reach the heights. Then I shall crush you!'

She, too, gets up.

'Leave me, you crazy man! You are wicked, evil!' she says.

'Yes, that is what I am,' he says, 'and it is you and your kind that have made me so. It is not in my nature.'

She laughs dismissively and shows him the door. She laughs – yet her first breath was drawn in the same poverty as his. Match-sticks going up in flames.

IN EXTREME DESPAIR, haunted by desire, sick, he drifts around the city. Has no friends. Drinks wine into oblivion, staggers into bed in his hotel room. And the next day does have friends after all. Thorvaldsen comforts him; he reads *The Moorish Girl* aloud for Jette Wulff, and she says: 'Don't you worry about "*die berühmte Frau*". Your play will bring pleasure without her, and then the glory is yours alone!' But he doesn't believe her. 'It is curious, this mistrust you have of yourself,' she says. 'For God's sake, don't let the world see it. Stand on your own two feet. They are big enough! Cheer up now.' But he doesn't cheer up. Heiberg is putting spokes in the wheel, finding all kinds of excuses for delaying the rehearsals for his play. Mrs Heiberg informs him through her husband that with the greatest respect she will not take a more minor part in the play either. They are shutting the door on him, as though he weren't even worthy to fasten their shoes! Heiberg is entertained at the Collins. Even they. He is alone. He must get away, away from the clammy cold of Copenhagen. To Italy. He will not be the half-baked poet whom they all make fun of. Let them do as they wish with his play; all that's left is for the public to hiss it off the stage. In Italy he will be able to breathe . . . He writes his letters of farewell – to Ingemann, Jette, Henriette, the Swedish countess Matilda – full of drama, his posture churlish, a chill at his fingertips. His dearest wish is to die abroad, never to return home. God must give him the strength to create a new, honest work. Even Mrs Heiberg gets a last letter. She has caused him deep sorrow, but he reaches out his hand nevertheless. Farewell!

IT'S DUST GETTING in his eyes, and something is blowing down his neck. Who is holding an umbrella over him? The servant? Fru Melchior?

'I'll only come to you once,' says the servant.

'With a horse?'

'Yes. A horse and two stories. One of them nasty, the other lovely. Beyond description.'

'You aren't the servant . . .'

'I am the other servant and I resemble the first.'

He stands before him in uniform but bathed in a light that passes through his flesh, exposing all his bones. The same broad, ruddy face he knows. And now he is rummaging for something at the foot of the bed; he wants to stop him but does not have the strength.

He is fiddling with his feet, flinging him up on to the horse.

'Shall I cut your toenails?' he says.

But now he is seated on the other servant's horse. Giddy up! Up and away, through the walls, down to the beach and the glinting moon.

'What am I doing on the back of this horse?' he asks.

'You have been wicked, and you're getting the nasty story,' says the servant.

They ride on; the servant tells the story, his voice sharp as a knife, and every word cuts him to the quick. He tries to jump off but has become part of the horse.

'Who's that sitting up at the front of the horse?' he shouts.

'That is also you.'

'Give me the lovely story,' he says, feeling the breath on his neck now.

The servant looks at him, shows him his scissors.

The other servant whispers the lovely story in his ear. It is music. Wind.

'I am not afraid of the other servant,' he says.

'There is only me,' says the servant, who begins to cut his nails.

'I am not afraid of death. Death is the loveliest of servants.'

'Lie still now . . . Herr Andersen.'

'I am on horseback. I can't.'

The servant holds his restless legs in a tight grip. He is glued to the horse, whether he sits at the front or the back. Why can't the servant see *that? He rides and rides and does not turn back. The sea is still, the moonlight trembling on its surface, in his ears a rushing, the air cling-ing like skin to his body. Hasn't he always dreamt of being two?*

What is the servant doing with those scissors? Can't he leave his feet alone?

He draws up his feet. That makes it easier to ride and fly away.

The servant says something he cannot hear.

He has dust in his eyes.

Would sleep now, if he could.

To sleep. And not to dream.

Heavy farewells in a strong wind one November evening. The Collins accompany him out to the ship in Copenhagen, Edvard remaining behind until last, and they stand at the railing for a moment, fumbling, uncertain what to do with their hands. How many unspoken moments lie between them? But the unexpected happens. Edvard with his pale face, his winter cloak around his shoulders takes a step forward, embraces him, kisses him on the mouth. Moved, he says a farewell, his heart ready to burst. Edvard leaves the ship by the gangway like a shadow. His eyes follow him all the way. Will they see each other again? That night – seasick, the seas crashing against the sides of the ship. Where is he going? He has still not wiped the kiss from his lips. Longs already for home.

HASN'T HE BEEN the guest of the Count Rantzau-Breitenburg at Breitenburg Castle, stayed in a magnificent room with a bedroom adjoining? The count, his benefactor, received him like an old acquaintance, the servants serving him oysters and champagne, of which he ate an abundance, and he read from his fairytales and was spoken of in that elevated company as Denmark's great poet. They pampered him, but still this worry about money, his sore penis, an inexplicable anxiety that comes and goes. The first evening he placed his note, 'I am only apparently dead', on the bedside table and could smile at his own fearfulness the following morning, until he heard the count's retarded brother knocking on a door close to his and continue knocking – like a ghost – and he thought: Better to be really dead than living in dementia. Wasn't he sick at heart when he left Copenhagen? Some days later he flew, accompanied by servants, in the count's four-in-hand to Itzeho, and now he is sitting in the great hall of the music society in Hamburg alongside diplomats, tradesmen and music-lovers listening to Liszt – in the front row, face to face. Great men resemble mountains – they look their best at a distance. Seated at the grand piano, Liszt looks as though he has been a patient at an orthopaedic institute and has been straightened out. There is something spidery about him, something demonic – his pallid face, the passions showing through the surface, make him look like a devil who has to release his soul through music! The notes stream from his blood as from a torture victim, his face becoming more and more alive, more plastic, as though a divine soul were rising from the demon spirit. The notes sound like ringing drops of water. Is he himself not equally obsessed and condemned to writing himself to freedom – while smiles play around the trades-men's lips at the thought of the fairytales and the chink of gold in their depths?

To HAVE RAILWAY fever and to place oneself at the mercy of God, travelling for the first time with the steam engine on the stretch between Wolfenbüttel and Braunschweig. From a distance it looks like a rocket shooting across the fields in a straight line. Now he knows how it feels when the globe turns; close to, grass and field are like a whizzing spinning wheel, while objects in the distance remain at rest. There is something magical about the movement that reminds him of the flight of birds; a dragon is hitched to his carriage, while mortals outside move like snails. The sound when the steam is released – like a demon, groaning. The signal whistle – like a stuck pig with a knife in its heart. He is alone with a man in an eight-seat compartment and the steam engine flying on the tracks. The thought strikes him – what if the man is mad, and the fit comes over him right at that moment? His whole body burns. It is railway fever . . .

Himmer, the bookseller in Augsburg, shows him some daguerreotypes of portraits by the painter Isenring, pictures created in ten minutes with all the expressive clarity in their eyes, the detailed patterns of the silken fabrics. They are lit up as though by a powerful fire. The daguerreotype and the railway – the magic of a new age.

Munich, the Athens of Germany. He has seen a whole new city grow up like a border of roses, which continues to shoot new branches, set new buds. The old part of the town is the rose border, and every branch is a street resplendent with churches and monuments, every leaf a palace with walls adorned with pictures, seeds from the fruit of Pompeii – and he himself bursts into blossom with the city. In the Odeon arcade the pianist Thalberg plays with great skill and calm, not transported, not as original as Liszt; Thalberg speaks to the understanding, Liszt to the imagination – what is missing is feeling.

THERE IS THE drone of a bee – a white bee, isn't it? – in the room. The windows, which shone before and mirrored the summer nights, are now frozen over with white flowers, the walls are drifts of snow, the door made of wind; empty is the distance before him, empty for miles – gleaming, shivering halls in the strong perspectives of an auroral light. He is a boy again sitting there on a floor as smooth as glass, blue with cold, assembling sharp segments of ice. It is Chinese Mah Jong. He carries slabs of ice backwards and forwards, constantly positioning new forms – triangles, squares, circles, rhomboids. His eyes shine like chips of ice, obsessed, his hands are almost black with cold, but he keeps on and on, the shapes constantly creating new words but not the word he is longing for. The word is eternity. If he finds that, he will be released from cold, from winter, will hold the whole world in the palm of his hand. The restlessness of the boy's icy sensibility runs over him, lying there in the bed, and he feels a sharp pain in his heart, fumbles at his chest with that long-fingered hand. In Fru Melchior, who enters the room at that moment, he sees in a flash of insight a dark figure who can only amplify his pain; he is helpless, caught, but she lays her hand on his. For some moments he is carried quite away, is still a boy walking around in the darkness with his flat slabs of ice, but the emptiness seeps away, his hand moves, the boy before him takes on colour, the segments of ice begin to dance and – as though they were tired – lay themselves down in a certain word. Is he the only one to see it? He raises his hand and points into the room with the windows and their mirrors of summer nights.

'You are far away,' says Fru Melchior.

'Eternity . . .'

'Eternity?'

'The ice maiden wants to take me; she knocked on the pane, sent her bees on ahead. She didn't get me. You came at the last moment.'

'Was it I who saved you?' says Fru Melchior with a chuckle, sitting on the chair beside his bed.

'Your hand . . .'

'I just placed it on yours.'

'Mine was frozen solid, like something left behind on a frozen lake.'

'And then you had a glimpse of eternity?'

'There are both brown and white bees there,' he says and smiles faintly. 'I prefer the brown ones.'

'Can we choose ourselves?'

'No, we have to take it as it comes. What we must have is what we don't need.'

Snow-capped mountains near Innsbruck like gleaming clouds of silver, as the carriage carries him close up against the abyss, deepened by the moonlight. Now and then a star over a mountain peak resembling a lighted beacon. The primeval slopes are crumbling, shattered, look as though they are covered with runes and hieroglyphs, but aren't they rather great walls with sepulchres, the sepulchres of extinct races inscribed by rain and storm and half obliterated by time? The river sings its lament to the passing of all earthly things.

Verona with its sumptuous churches, ceiling paintings, Virgil's square with its new theatre. He drifts about during the feast of the Holy Conception, people stream out of church, a group gathers around a Punch and Judy show. He walks through the arcades, feeling like a foreigner. People don't know him, don't like him perhaps? Poets of Rome and Greece have walked here, thinking about their works. Among the swarm of humanity. As for him, he thinks about Ahasverus. Wishes never again to see Denmark, where he was more unhappy than happy. In his hotel room he opens a window with large iron bars outside looking out over a deep, dark valley. Somewhere out in the darkness a river rushes; above him the heavens are bright with stars. He leans his forehead against the bars and feels himself no more alone than in a Danish drawing-room. He who has a home at home can feel homesick, but he who has none feels equally at home no matter where. Within minutes his hotel room has become a home for him.

ON THE ROAD to Florence he walks behind the carriage through the mountains for a large part of the way. The blue of the air strikes home in him, seems to come from the mountains themselves. The blue has a scent, his eyes swim and at the same time see clearly; the stillness of the heights is overwhelming, brings on a melancholy, not a northern darkness but one that slumbers in the midst of brightness. All that penetrates is the sound of a stream humming far below. Here he walks at one with the world. On his descent from the mountain tops, shepherds hooting into conches, a cart full of robbers and a robbers' girl accompanied by soldiers, frequent beggars, monks and black pigs, filthy lodgings . . . After Florence and a few days with a one-horsed *vetturino* he is in Rome. It is like a dream, being there again. He feels at home. Around St Peter's the air is so blue that a rainbow hangs over the fountains. He wanders round to the Capitol, the Vatican, the Forum Romanum, the Colosseum, the Rotunda, the Spanish Steps, Café Greco, the Lateran Church, the galleries, day after day, with or without a companion from the Danish colony. But nothing is the same. The artists live more isolated than before. At the end of these many wanderings awaits the apartment at Signora Magaritha's on the Via Purificatione. And the lack of letters, the loneliness that it brings. To travel so far to encounter that. Every night since his cold hotel room in Florence a dream has hurried post-haste ahead of him – on the street in Rome he will meet Jonas Collin, who tells him that *The Moorish Girl* has been booed off the stage on its opening night at the Theatre Royal. It has only had one performance. The booing was followed by applause so loud that a diplomat said that if you could draw a line under it, the line would extend far out across the square in front of the theatre. To escape the boos of Copenhagen, only to hear them in Rome. To escape into the blue. In the green December gardens of the French Academy he comes to a halt before the view. An uneven green field stretching towards the pine woods of the Villa Borghese and on to the blue snow-covered mountains. Out there is where he lives.

NEW YEAR'S DAY 1841. Time has stopped at the stroke of midnight on his watch, and he gets it ticking again with the knuckle of his index finger. In the Sistine Chapel the castratos sing, the Pope reads from the gospels, Queen Maria of Spain surveys the broad array of humanity from her elevated chair. Under the dome of St Peter's he kneels and prays to God: 'Give me everlasting poetic renown, give me health, and give me your peace.' Takes a walk by the Tiber in thin sunlight. Back in the loneliness of his room he thinks of his wish to die abroad. And has to be out again, to be in motion, wanders about and is washed up in the Via Ripetta, where a dilapidated *palazzo* with a tall arcade and artificially carved marble pillars surrounds a little square courtyard. Over mutilated marble sculptures and bas-reliefs tower the colossal heads of Roman emperors festooned with creepers, grass. Filth and dusty cobwebs everywhere, cabbage stems, lemon peel, straw baskets from wine bottles are strewn across the courtyard between the marble sarcophagi. On a wide, dirty marble stairway leading up to the *palazzo*, bare-legged, shivering beggar boys are playing cards with ragged blankets around their shoulders and clay pipes in their mouths. Reclining. Two peasants with long staves chase a flock of turkeys across the yard, while from a window above a wrinkled woman shakes out her sheets on to the boys. He continues his search in the labyrinth of streets, recognizing himself in the shop windows, his gaze frozen fast at times to his own reflection, which he finds displeasing, finds constant fault, unconsciously, with his hair or his face in these blurred images; he measures himself at random against beautiful boys in the street – as he did in Florence, where an attractive boy decked out in white stockings, pale-blue velvet knickerbockers, checked scarf and a red woollen beret with a black border reminded him of all the things he has failed to be and have. He ends his evening in the darkness of a marionette theatre. In its dancing white figures he sees all too clearly the strings of dependency on recognition and money at home, which make him kick against the pricks, make him unable to prevent his mask from cracking; that night is a night of pain with toothache that drives him out of bed and to the brink of madness; he burns and twists with fever, wraps his head in the sheet to avoid the cold air in the room. And the following day, when he checks the post office and finds a letter from Jonas Collin, his fears are confirmed: *The Moorish Girl* was not a success, was performed only twice. He shuts himself away, speaks with no one, gives up his trip to Greece and Constantinople. Who is he, if he doesn't succeed? That night he does not sleep. Towards morning he dozes and dreams that his head is a stone and that someone is hitting it with an axe without it breaking. Protected by sleep, the stone head does not crack. Only when he wakes does he feel the pain from the blows.

WALKS THE STREETS again, aimless and dizzy, visits galleries, talks with his fellow Danes – Küchler, Rothe, Constantin Hansen, Carstenschiold – who support him, although he doesn't hear them – their voices sound like a whisper. Makes his way back to his rooms, every evening from half past five reads, eyeing the clock every other minute. Isn't it nine o'clock yet? Then he can go to bed and sleep until the new day. Loneliness bigger than a mountain. Has ceased to worry about being attacked when he walks the streets. Wouldn't it be best if he were killed? His art is no longer clear to him, so what is there to live for? If he died, he would be talked about – seen. Here is his weakness, and he knows it – this immense craving to be spoken about. A narcotic. And what does his sorrow consist of? He is like the mosquito he saw struggling in a spider's web in the Colosseum the other day; he struggles in the same way to escape the memories that his life's destiny has spun around him. But aren't his weaknesses, his faults, his mistakes borne along by his stubborn will to create? Isn't his flight itself a means to get himself worked up to a new work, a work that – each time he runs away – is to outdo all his others? Is his flight not the gateway to discovery just as much as the starry sky above the Colosseum? That sky has appeared just as powerful to his eyes in Scandinavia, but here it seems more elevated and the more he looks at it the more it fills with stars – fills to infinity.

HE HAS HIT rock bottom, but Ahasverus – still an image of restlessness, homelessness – will raise him up again. Each day has its own unease, its own five or six fruitless excursions from his apartment to the post office for a letter from Edvard. And when at last it comes, it comes across as icy cold in its record of his fiasco in Copenhagen and of the success of Heiberg's new poems, which – so say letters from female friends in Copenhagen – paint hell as a place where the condemned are forced to watch his two plays *The Mulatto* and *The Moorish Girl* on the same evening. He is beside himself, his headache and fever lay him low once more; his Ahasverus grinds to a halt. One day he rushes into the poet H.P. Holst, who he has agreed can lodge with him in his apartment in the Via Purificatione. H.P. Holst – Copenhagen's new literary darling – answers him back.

'Before leaving Copenhagen I heard these poems by Heiberg, *A Soul after Death.* They are lovely . . .'

'How can you say they are lovely when they attack me!'

Holst smiles faintly and spreads out his hands to conciliate him.

'I assure you that there is only one point – and there in passing – where there are a couple of swipes at you.'

'But why the swipes? What sick mind needs to bring others down with such swipes?'

'But they are bagatelles, not worth speaking of.'

'And which you have quite unreasonably kept hidden from me . . .'

'I was aware of your sensitivity, as is your friend Edvard, too, by the by.'

'I do not believe in your tact. Heiberg has the jealousy of an artist – I am too big for him, and he puts down poison, and wants nothing better than to see me removed from the earth . . .'

Holst laughs.

'How childish you are . . .'

'If I am childish, then you are insensitive – just like so many others in the prison of Copenhagen.'

'No, now you must calm yourself . . . You do not know what

you are saying,' says Holst and stands up before him. But he is a head shorter.

'My words stick much more firmly in the brain than yours, coming as they do from an original place!'

'Original place? In my eyes that seems more like a whinger's corner. And I, who thought you so amiable,' says Holst.

'And so I am – as long as I am not spat upon.'

'No one is "spitting" on you.'

'Spit is the absence of love. And absent it is in that prison,' he says and goes to his room.

THE CARNIVAL SPREADS – in the theatre the audience is already
dotted with people dressed for the carnival, in the streets shepherds send bunches of flowers flying up to women sitting at their
windows, pierrots chained to chimney-sweeps can be seen here
and there on the squares. A man has been killed outside the
Palazzo Rospigliosi by the galloping semi-wild horses that fly
through the streets. People greet each other graciously, while a
procession of donkeys with pierrots take their places before the
Spanish Steps amid catcalls and whistles. His sadness peels away
like a mask, and behind the mask is gaiety, the urge to drown in
the crowd, the urge to recast himself. He wanders around in the
heat of the sun in cloth boots, white trousers and a dress with the
whiff of caprice about him – a steamship rolls down the street; a
man with a basket full of living cats; bears standing tall on two
legs; a minstrel sitting playing a harp; and flags that turn in the
wind as on a wheel of fortune. A *donna* tears his buttonhole of
blue violets from him, and he throws confetti at her, his eyes
consuming her. The confetti rains down from windows and balconies on to the heaving streets, he among them dressed in a hired
Polichinello costume with a white tricorn hat, yellow and black
feathers and a red mask, mixing with the Danes and the exuber-
ant Romans; costumed ladies with hand-held masks present him
with bouquets; a pretty lady made up as a French courtesan asks
whether he is English, Spanish or French, and when he, light-
headed with surrender, says yes to it all, she laughs, crowns his
head with a pretzel and vanishes into the crowd with him following until suddenly she is gone. Irresolute, he stands in the twilight
under an archway with his red mask, scouring the crowds for her.

On Capri and later in Naples, where his feverish condition wors-
ens, he quarrels with Holst again, inflamed one moment, concili-
atory the next; he hesitates between travelling to Sicily or Greece,
plagued by his sickly indecision; funds for his onward journey have
come unexpectedly from King Christian VIII. He will travel to
Athens and Constantinople. Is God not – once again – on his side?

HIS PHLEGMY COUGH gone, has been given Seltzer water and has stubbornly racked his brains for several hours for a word he cannot find; it
is morning, sunlight filling his rooms – he felt like some poor madman
but did at last find the word and fell asleep. The swelling in his leg has
gone down, says Dr Meyer. Just a little temperature. He has had guests.
Young Jonas Collin has been – how he reminds him of Edvard, his concern just as dry, his sensitivity just as efficiently salted away. And the
master of the house, Moritz Melchior, looked in, his clothes immaculate
as ever, sat modestly in a chair by his bedside, saying little but with a
touching attentiveness in his brown eyes and a boyish smile; and now he
can hear one of Copenhagen's richest and most enterprising business
barons play with his grandchildren in the drawing-rooms below.
When did he ever send him away him empty-handed? He is content, is
immeasurably happy in his earthly paradise, wants not to read the
newspaper they have brought him but to narrate. He rings for Fru
Melchior and immediately asks her to write down something for his
biography. She is wearing a light summer dress, gets out pen and paper
and sits on the chair by his bed. Her soft black hair is set up and shines
in the rays of the sun.

'Can I start?' he asks impatiently.

She nods. He clears his throat, coughs weakly, finds his voice.

'One day in my apartment at Mrs Anholt's I get a letter signed
"Adelgrunde". "I love you as a poet and as a man," it says. "Have
never seen you and leave the city today." And then, "I have to see
you and press your hand." She determines a time, approximately
between twelve and one that day, when I am to meet her walking from
Gothersgade along the ramparts at Nørrevold. There I will meet a
young lady in a silk dress with a folding parasol. I recounted this
straight away at lunch at Councillor Collin's. Admiral Sommer, who
was present and heard that I did not intend to meet her, said, "Then
death and damnation I will!" My feeling was that the young students
living near the ramparts would see me come running along, and soon I
would be told that there had been no trace of such a lady. I went out,
returned. Mrs Anholt received me with a message from Adelgrunde
complaining that I hadn't met her at the given time and place.
"What did she look like?" I asked. "Charming, black silk and a fold-

ing parasol." "Wasn't she unhinged?" I asked. "She must surely have looked in some way improper?" "Not a bit!" said Mrs Anholt.'

'Was that it?' asks Fru Melchior and writes down the last part.

He sees that she is smiling. A dizziness slowly surfaces. Isn't she sitting a long way away from him? He lets himself sink back on the pillows.

'What am I to make of all these stories?' he says, speaking to her, to the window, the room at large, the feathery clouds pencilled outside like calligraphic symbols.

'It is your way of breathing.'

'Perhaps there really is a place in another world where many more breathe as I do. Do you think so?'

'If there is no such place, then you will certainly be the man to invent it!'

His large toothless face smiles faintly.

'Tomorrow I want to sit on the balcony for a few hours.'

'Yes, tomorrow,' she says. 'You are too tired now, I'm sure.'

He nods. He imagines that he nods and that the day has flown by, and that they are sitting on the deck of a ferry on the Strait of Bosporus under a sky the colour of mother-of-pearl – passengers dressed in white with suntanned skin on their way across the river Styx. The ferryman is like a shadow on the bridge. A peaceful passage towards the silhouetted domes, the song of cicadas.

So far away, so near.

CONSTANTINOPLE UNDER AN overcast sky, but vast, fantastic – a Paris composed of Venice and the imagination. Tall, dark cypresses, one magnificent mosque after the other, their minarets aspiring skywards, the pale, floating seraglio, the prison where the condemned are executed. The colour of Constantinople is chestnut; against the dark cypresses the white churches shine. He arrives from the hotel in Galatia in a flimsy gondola accompanied by a hired servant. It is like visiting a beehive where each bee is an Egyptian, an Armenian, a Turk, a Jew. The streets are narrow, with danger in every step; the house-fronts cut-away as on an architect's drawing, their interiors exposed. Shops *en masse* and everywhere. Passing through the Egyptian bazaar and its brisk trade in colours, he arrives at the Grand Bazaar, an entire town under cover of a myriad roofs with districts for cobblers, jewellers, butchers, outfitters, book-dealers, money-lenders, where the jostling throng pressing in on him propels him down closed lanes and alleyways, even through the shops themselves where people sit in threes and fours on wooden crates, smoking or working. The streets crisscross each other or run in parallel at times as in a labyrinth. The air is full of the whinny of horses, the shrill whistles of beggar boys, the barking of yellow-eyed dogs, the beating of drums, and then like a sound from afar comes the sudden braying call of the muezzin high in the minaret of a nearby mosque. Some way from the bazaar, encircled by shops, is the large, white body of Sultan Ahmet's mosque with shoes and boots ranged in the shadows of arches and doorways outside. Finding himself in a crush where a street linking two mosques erupts into a terrifying maelstrom of life, nerves get the better of him as he feels people slipping between each other like eels struggling in a knot. He passes the church of St Sofia, a huge and antique aqueduct, wide grassy squares, and he visits a café where the hookahs bubble. But not until he is once again out on the water with his hired servant can he breathe freely again.

WHEN THEY DANCE, the dervishes have tall white hats on, some of them looking like a mixture of Mamelukes and gypsies. In the streets of Paras he sees them side by side with Armenian priests with the long black crape trailing from their hats. Every street comes across as a hall for masquerade; what was only tinsel in towns in Europe is the real thing here, right to the marrow. Accompanied by his hired servant, he visits the dervish monastery at Scutari; their feet clad in slippers, they and the other visitors are let into a square hall with galleries, where the women sit separate from the men shut behind special grills. On the walls Turkish inscriptions, tambourines, cymbals. On white and blue carpets a large group of dervishes are lying in all manner of clothing, some in military uniform, all with turbans on their heads. An extraordinary chant, started by a few but then joined by them all, rises to the ceiling, reminding him of a running scale and a variety of imitations of melodies spun by trained voices. The dervishes kneel and bow their heads to the ground as though worshipping an idol. A priest steps forward, the incense from a vessel curls up around his face, most of the dervishes kiss his hand, but two of them remain seated on the floor singing with a hollow sound that resembles snoring or a death rattle. They all take off their turbans and put on white felt skullcaps. And now a man appears with upper lip cut away and long black hair bound up; his gown is white with figures of horses and knights sewn on it in red. He lays his gown to one side and stands there in his red tunic, swaying backwards and forwards in time to the hollow sound and baring his arms to his shoulders; his one hand is withered, his body moves from side to side in increasingly passionate positions. And now the bodies and limbs of the others are also moving, as though driven by a machine; the dervishes groan, inhaling deeply, the sweat pours down over their pale faces. Finally they collapse exhausted and lie on the floor. Extinguished. He is both attracted and repelled . . .

The following day he is at the dervish monastery in Pera, which comes across as more elegant. The dervishes make a brief prayer accompanied by quiet, repetitive music – a drum sounding monotonously, two notes on a flute reminiscent of the splashing of a fountain – the hall airy. The dervishes cast off their tunics and stand in the centre of the floor in open green shirts, wearing tall white hats that hide no shadows and around them a long green skirt, extending outwards and creating a funnel. With arms extended and half raised, they turn on the spot, slowly at first but then with increasing speed. They spin in a circle with two in the centre; the circle moves as they move around themselves to the chanting and music. Their faces are completely white. Suddenly they stand stock still – and the next moment begin to turn again. They are like lifeless dolls representing the movement of the planets.

THE MASQUERADE IN the streets arouses his sensuality, a blissful ferment running through his nerves; smoking Armenians, Greeks, Turks fill the barbershops, the cafés, the lanes. A Bulgarian peasant dances at a street corner, while another plays the bagpipes. Behind Constantinople snow glints on the slopes of the mountains in the clear sunlight. In the white mosques along the quayside thousands of worshippers bow rhythmically in motley rows; a nightingale warbles its trills, turtledoves coo in the tall darkness of cypresses, the air across the Asian mountains touches him like a scent of colour; six men with skin burnished to bronze manhandle a slab of marble hanging from three poles up the steep streets. The churchyards are extensive; there are green turbans on the graves of dervishes, and on the tombstones there are one or two hollows for water, where the dogs can quench their thirst to bring salvation to the dead. An array of ships with their sails set are mirrored like swans in the water over on the Scutari side, while the small boats glide across the surface like black snakes. Every evening he writes and masturbates, while by day he reads from his fairytale collection in French or German at the Austrian, Greek or Russian minister's. He receives a ministerial visit – hasn't he (far from Denmark) made some kind of name for himself?

The evening before the prophet's birthday. All the minarets are lit up, a red glow on the western sky, twinkling stars in a southern air, the moon clear, shining, necklaces of lamps around the smaller minarets, the warships with lights in every canon mouth. The minarets of St Sophia like colossal blooms of fire on stalks, while in the moonlight their white shafts shine against the transparent air. Lovely views across the churchyard with its coal-black cypresses and scattered lights in houses; and over the tops of the cypresses, the sparkling water around the illuminated warships. It is an entire city of minarets garlanded and glowing with light standing out against the horizon. And now all has gone soft and quiet, scarcely anyone about. The whole city a fairytale.

THE MOON, ITS beams gazing in at him, turning all the objects in the room into silhouettes. Sitting there in the bed, his hands are phosphorescent. The moon, that told him about the ruins of Pompeii, where carts once rolled on the streets paved with slabs of lava; where water fountained from courtyard basins decorated with mussels and conch shells, where the names on the doors and hanging signs were freshly painted, where songs reverberated in colourful chambers guarded by dogs made of metal. Now German soldiers in the pay of Neapolitans play cards and dice in the city of the dead, as a party seeks to pass them in the moonlight on their way to the stone stairway of the amphitheatre, where a soprano steps on to a stage that – with its walled wings, its two arches in the background – has not changed for thousands of years. In a sleight of mind, she steps forward and starts to sing, her song has the lightness, the sureness of a flying Arab stallion and the pain of the mother beneath the cross. Everyone is clapping and shouting around her. And three minutes later the stage is bare. All have gone, not a note can be heard. The ruins are still standing, as they will stand for centuries. The applause of the moment, the song of the singer, her smile, will be forgotten. A vanished memory.

He takes a sumptuous illustrated volume from the bedside table, the French translation of his fairytales that they brought him the previous day but that he was too tired to read. Now he leafs through it. All the memories preserved in it, all the moments and rooms and journeys that rise up from the pages, the words. His life and thoughts compressed, held in the moment, passed on – like a bee in the universe. Against the vastness of the All, we are nothing.

BY SHIP THROUGH the Bosporus Strait across the Black Sea to Kustendje, overland by horse-drawn cart to Czerna-Woda, where he embarks on the steamship *Argo* and sails down the Danube through the evergreen Bulgarian and Rumanian landscape; rumours speak of violent uprisings in the Balkans, thousands of Christians are said to have been massacred, but the joy of discovery is stronger for him than his fear. In large wicker carts drawn by white oxen they travel on their way, at times crossing a desert, war-torn landscape where wild dogs roam. Only the overturned grave-stones witness to the existence of towns. The heat along the journey threatens to drive him mad. They re-embark on a sailing boat, travel under virtually no wind with a sail that the captain calls '*una phantasia*'. The islands of the Danube with their wild horses alternate with garrison towns dotted with minarets and green wooden areas with wine gardens. In Orsova on the other side of the Hungarian border he is placed in ten days' quarantine along with the other passengers for fear of the plague. Laughing, they make their way with a guard following their baggage, drawn by bullocks, towards the quarantine station, a large yellow building hidden behind white walls. The porter locks them in behind the walls with his large bunch of keys, and he is to share with an Englishman, the explorer William Ainsworth, in room No. 2. A hundred times a day he walks with him back and forth around the little garden and the gravel courtyard, when he isn't sitting inside writing his travelogue or sticking flowers in his album. Friendly and cheerful are their conversations during the first days – in the evenings to the sound of some Bulgarian's monotonous, never-ending flute playing and with the view of a forested mountain outside the high walls.

'This blueness in the air is extraordinary,' he says to Ainsworth. 'This is what makes me travel.'

'If the colour of the air is your driving force,' replies Ainsworth, 'then travel to the Ganges. There the sky has the most unique blue-green colour.'

But as the days pass, heat and imprisonment in the little yard bring him almost to boiling point. In the middle of the day he dreams that he is in the 'lead prison' in Venice and at night that he is alive and kicking in hell. He feels his blood infected with the heat, and he torments himself with imagined mistakes in letters he has written. In a dark hour in room No. 2 he fantasizes about the devil having proposed that in this hell they should perform the ending of Heiberg's *Fata Morgana*, but the damned protest that even in hell it can become too hot! Instead the devil suggests that Heiberg's newest and most infernal comedy be played with accompanying prologue, written by a friend of the Heibergs', so that all and sundry can know why and how Heiberg's comedy is to be admired.

He falls sick with stomach pains, and his greatest fear is that the quarantine will be extended, but he is released into Orsova's beautiful countryside. A large acacia tree laden with white flowers stands at the end of his new lodgings at the Hotel Kaiser of Austria. For the first few days he feels sluggish, feels like the man condemned to execution who is suddenly pardoned on the block and who cannot immediately sense his freedom. As the days pass, the beauty of his surroundings steals into him – the flowering elders and acacias, the ubiquity of green, the clear Danube in which everything is reflected, even the green mountains of Serbia.

As to sensuality, his blood is oriental! Traipses round Budapest, in the Matthias Church, where he hears beautiful women's voices, to the theatre where he sits alone in the pit watching Raupach's *The King's Daughter, a Beggar-Woman*, listening to this appalling trash being applauded for no reason. Walks across the floating bridge in crushing heat to Offen; soldiers swim in the river – some returning to the jetty in shirts, others in swimming suits – and wave their tricolour ensign and their caps; music plays, and women gather on the jetty to watch. He studies their shapes, their movements from a distance, their laughter entering his body; he would give anything to be the object of their glances. Back at the hotel he drowns his senses in burgundy. Wakes in the night in confusion to the scent of the new eau de Cologne that he bought on his first day in town, wanting to be freshly shaved and groomed to see Mendelssohn Bartholdy's *Paulus* at the Hungarian Theatre. His old eau de Cologne, along with the pomade in his trunk, evaporated into thin air in the sweltering heat of the steamship.

Perhaps he, too, will evaporate into thin air?

ON HIS WAY down the Danube towards Vienna on board the little overcrowded steamer *Maria Anna* he drinks punch and tries to sleep. Is afraid that the door to his cabin will suddenly burst open, has barricaded it with a chair. For among the many guests in the saloon he has seen his doppelgänger – a man who looks like his caricature, a loose bas-relief. The guests in the saloon have enjoyed their laugh at the poor man's expense, sketched him. He is missing all his teeth in his lower jaw, looks exactly like a shadow . . .

Is someone in the passage . . . Edvard?

Fire in the distance, thick smoke, ominous black clouds billowing towards the red sunset. In the border town of Tében on the Danube over two hundred houses have burnt down; between the scorched trees the chimneys resemble columns of a temple, and he thinks of Thebes in Greece. Smoke unfurls black flags across the town, charred horses are dragged away, men and women search for their children, the church burnt out.

The following day, thinly scattered forests, German air, unremitting heat. Their landing in Vienna is near the Prater, and they drive in their carriage through the amusement park, through Leopoldstadt to the Jewish Market, ending up at the Hungary Hotel on Stephansplatz. Letters from Jette and Henriette but none from Collin. He is deeply distressed. All the old miseries of Copenhagen return to him. Feels the German–Danish air. He wishes he had died in the east.

HENRIETTE WRITES ABOUT his letters, about how full they are of interesting things because he hears and sees so much of interest now, while hers bear the mark of her monotonous surroundings and seek refuge in the thoughts and feelings that crowd in on her as she writes. He must, therefore, know her much better than she knows him; it often causes her to feel bashful that she does not have a completely clear picture of him, but she is not able to say precisely why that should be so. But why does she write to him so often, when she does not believe in the principle that she should answer every one of his letters? She writes to him right now in order to find peace of mind; she cannot bear his anger that she – in order to support him on the home front – has allowed an Odense newspaper to publish a couple of his travel letters, which have since become objects of amusement in Copenhagen. She is miserable both because of her own indiscretion and because of his anger. There is, however, another reason for writing that she cannot name.

He lays the letter to one side and does not concern himself with what lies behind what cannot be said, what never is said in so many words by his closest female friend, his female tin soldier. He plunges into Vienna, goes to the Burgtheater, leaves again after the second act. It is evening, the air raw and cold, as he reaches the square at Stephansplatz. The cathedral looms before him out of the darkness, its tower like a spider's web, its massive gateway carrying the stone figures of Christ, angels, devils; the windswept square in front of the cathedral is empty save for a pair of pedestrians and a fiacre slowly approaching one of the side streets, the hard clatter of the horses' hooves on the cobbles sending a faint echo far up in the funnel of the towering walls. With a bottle of wine in his hand he comes to a halt, observing a poor young girl kneeling before the holy statues facing the square; he is moved by the lovely figure she makes, remains standing for a while before tearing himself away and turning back to the hotel with the thought that she is only lying there to display herself and catch a man. Alone in his hotel room he is angry with himself for his thoughts about the woman. Writes in his travelogue, which is to be called *My Evenings in the Orient*. Drowns his desire in the Tokay wine.

A VISIT TO Grillparzer, the writer, where he discusses his bitterness towards Heiberg and the Copenhagen milieu and his unwillingness to return home. Grillparzer says, 'You are the only natural poet at the moment. Your fairytales are the flowering of Europe's new literature, and they sell like hot cakes in Vienna and other major cities.'

In Dresden, two heartfelt letters from the Collins that fill him with bliss. He reads them through six times, kisses the paper they are written on, is in Seventh Heaven. Is this not the happiest evening of the entire journey for him, the solitary? Isn't it this he has fled from in order to find, like a thirsty wanderer crossing the desert for water? Several weeks later – after his steam crossing to Aaresund – Henriette meets him in Odense. They shake hands. He avoids her company and hurries onwards. Onwards.

He wrote off her friendship in his reminiscences by saying 'awkward friendships cause only harm'. How cold could he be? A remarkable coldness. Where does it come from? His hand is freezing. Tucks it under the duvet. Won't think about that. Thinks about it.

HOME TO TEPID receptions, flaccid handshakes, the dinner round, at Oehlenschläger's a reading of Heiberg's satirical poem about his play, a caricature of him as traveller to the Orient in Goldschmidt's satirical magazine *Corsaren* – 'Poor Andersen, who has suffered such great hardships in Greece and Turkey' – and a scathing article on *The Moorish Girl* in the *Tidsskrift for Litteratur og Kritik*. What he would give to be Liszt, who has money, respect and admiration and who can travel from place to place leaving every pettiness behind! September 1841 in Copenhagen was the month of irritability and foul humour. Isn't he half deranged, impossible to his closest friends? To endure life in this ice-cold country, in sad, mean-spirited Copenhagen, requires an extraordinary inner fire. If his self-awareness had been greater, he would not have been knocked off balance by all the poisonous drops that had fallen on him over the years . . . Henriette consoles him, writing about the criticism, 'It is dreadful spiritual arrogance to wish to upend another human being as completely as that.' She would prefer not to say any more about the criticism but would rather talk about his facial expressions, his eyes, his way of being when she feels most for him. He himself does not know what he is like at such moments: not a Copenhagen type, not distinguished, not too refined, not wooden, not dandified, but brotherly, serious, affectionate . . .

A rose in her letter, a rose elf, listening and gossiping to the bees. Who is to be killed?

FOUR FAIRYTALES TO write and finish off at the last minute, under contract, and finds himself falling into despondence because of them, becoming flat, exhausted by their creation, even though they spring from the paper like dried flowers that acquire depth and colour and in the end wings to fly out behind November panes as cold as night, out into the starry sky above Kongens Nytorv; to masturbate, to fall asleep wearing his silk dressing-gown (a gift!) and, waking in the middle of the night, to sit himself down at a page three-quarters covered with corrections, erasures, that closes in mid-sentence; to dip his pen in ink-blood and write on across an ocean without a shore, in a circle without circumference, to reach out and bring home something between his fingers that feels like the beat and rhythm of the heart. There is Wee Willie Winkie with his two umbrellas – the one with the pictures and the one without – he throws his fine eye-dust and tells the boy Hjalmar dreams of mouse weddings, of hens and storks and finally the loveliest one about death. There is the Rose Elf in the house of flower petals, who witnesses a jealous murder among men and calls down justice on the murderer. There is the conceited Buckwheat strutting where oats and wheat bow to the wind, breaking at last in two. There is the Swineherd, the prince in disguise, who swaps genuine presents like a nightingale and a rose for a musical box to expose a la-di-da princess. The worst that can happen is the empty umbrella. Nights without dreams, days without stories – the imagination dead . . . not to exist.

NOTHING COMES OF nothing – a letter from his half-sister Karen Marie, the sender's address given as Borgergade 30, Copenhagen's slum district five hundred yards from his hotel. So close as to be unreal. He could meet her on the street, has perhaps already met her on his daily walk round the harbour area, to Nyhavn or Havnegade, where the screeching fishwives congregate. His hand is shaking, as he reads it through several times with all its spelling mistakes, its clumsy description of her plight, its appeal for money. Will she blackmail him? He has to give up writing for the whole of that evening and night, paces uneasily up and down the floor of his hotel room with the letter in his hand, not knowing what he should do with it, finally places it in a drawer but continues to open the drawer at regular intervals to reread it. He is overcome by self-reproach for these years of ignoring her alternating with feelings of bitterness, incomprehensible to himself, at the very fact of her existence. Hasn't he made himself believe that he has no more family of flesh and blood – not even Edvard knows of Karen Marie's existence – and yet it is the same as in his novel *O.T.* He cannot run away from his 'dark past'. It clings to him, can undermine him, make him look ridiculous, drag him into the dust . . . or is that something he is making up? Everyone knows about his origins, the son of a shoemaker . . . But why not about her? What does he have to be ashamed of? She wants a little money, he can give her some and then she will disappear. That'll be that . . . But won't she come back? Won't she keep on beating a pathway to his door and then – if he doesn't give in to her begging – start throwing muck, about the dealings of his aunt, streetwalker and brothel madam? His enemies, even his friends, will love the chance to stir up the muck, for there is no mercy in Copenhagen! They'll say, there you have him, that Andersen with his family of beggar women, washer-women, tarts – what does he want with us? He thought he could keep all that under wraps, but with the help of this closet sister it has been brought to light! What a farce that he should be the poet consorting with the best families in Copenhagen, the royal family even! A swindler, a cheat! Born in the gutter! He is in despair and furious at the same time, goes to bed, to masturbate, to fall fleetingly to rest only to wake again, sweating, agonizing over the misfortune that hovers over him and grows beyond all proportion in the darkness. He hears one laughing voice saying, 'What a past master you are at tormenting yourself.' Another says, 'You aren't making this up.' Exhausted, he falls asleep at last, only to wake with a start early the next morning, to hurry into his clothes and down into Kongens Nytorv, the deserted square in front of the Hotel du Nord. He rushes to Edvard's house, wakes his servants, steps nervous and pale into his drawing-room and, when he appears in his dressing-gown still heavy with sleep, confides everything to him.

'Are you sure? Is she really your half-sister?' says Edvard. 'And the letter, is that genuine?'

'I don't know what's genuine or fake,' he says, 'but it's true that my mother's daughter was called Karen Marie.'

'In that case, I will have my brother-in-law, Adolph Drewsen, take a closer look at the matter . . .'

'Drewsen?'

'As a magistrate with the Copenhagen police he is best placed to shed light on all this. We must find out who her husband is, if she *is* married, as the letter says. And we must find out about their address.'

'Yes, if you think that is the way to do it . . .' he says. 'But Drewsen will have to keep my name out of it!'

'Naturally. Adolph is conscientious and discreet.'

He leaves Edvard and seeks company at the Ørsteds, the Wulffs, to whom he says nothing, not even to Jette. She notices his mood – he looks melancholy, almost in anguish – and attempts to cheer him up, but without success. At dinner at the Collins' house on Bredgade he is taciturn and withdrawn, and he hurries out across the frozen cobbles, over Kongens Nytorv, crossing the square to the Hotel du Nord and his rooms. As he empties a bottle of wine, everything that has lain hidden inside him for so many years rises to the surface – indistinct images of his older sister running errands for their mother in her clogs; his mother shouting at her, complaining about her father, Rosenvinge, the womanizer who has no money to give her for his daughter, so they have that extra mouth to feed; his big sister laughing when he plays at being a French soldier, or suddenly bursting into tears when she has to sleep on the floor, while he has the wall bench; his big sister, who has to go down to the washing stone by the river with his mother and learn to become 'a little washerwoman'; her hand already rough when he reaches up to hold it; that long interval when he doesn't see her but hears that she is in service at a gentlewoman's house in Svendborg, where she has to learn to work in the kitchen and can't go to school much; and when he does finally see her again, she is like a stranger to him – he can't talk to her about his books, and she thinks his dolls and his theatre daft, a waste of time, thinks he is spoilt by their mother, when he, too, ought by now to be in service. But the light in her face he cannot forget, he has forgotten, does not want to forget . . . No, he doesn't know what he wants. Obliterates himself in wine.

And the following day Edvard is at the hotel, bearing certain knowledge that she is to be found at the address she has given, is a washerwoman and forty-one years old, that a husband also exists, although there are no documents to that effect, a workman, Peder Kaufmann, thirty-nine years old. Edvard thinks he should write a letter to her, but what should he write when what he most wants is to be free of the whole thing? The next day he does dispatch a letter to her at the address in Borgergade with the first foot post, saying that her husband can come, can come that same day to him at the hotel and get some money. And then that must be it – he is still feverish and will not be plagued by ghosts. Oh, but isn't he spineless? Can't he even bear the thought of seeing her?

He waits all day at the hotel, but Kaufmann does not turn up. Are they making a fool of him? Is the whole thing just a bad joke? Has his agony of waiting been in vain?

The next day Kaufmann comes into the room like a morning caller, wearing a threadbare, newly washed coat and newly washed working trousers and with his cap in his hand, and takes his place modestly on the chair indicated. Kaufmann has an honest face and explains their plight in gentle tones and without pressing his case. Immediately he feels calmer and gives him a book and four *rigsdalers*. Kaufmann's face lights up. He gets up and is clearly delighted as he shakes his hand in parting – and he, too, is delighted, relieved when Kaufmann is out of the door.

An hour later and he has come to a halt with the draft of the travel book on his writing desk. If only they don't return and beg money from him again.

AFTER TWO YEARS' work he has completed his travel book of the Orient, *A Poet's Bazaar*, 409 pages in all. Such are his exhaustion and his anxiety about its reception that he takes Dutch courage, drinks himself to a bad stomach, so that when he is invited first to luncheon with the prime minister and later the same day has to do a reading from the book at Amalienborg for King Christian VIII and the queen he is struck by a fearful bout of diarrhoea which reduces him to panic. In the midst of which it occurs to him – as he shuttles between his rooms and the toilet – that he could send his excuses, but the very thought of failing to comply with an invitation from the king aggravates his nervousness and his stomach pains, leaves him exhausted, hanging on a thread, full of self-reproach, until his stomach is finally empty and at the last moment he can decide to bear the agony. He has himself transported to the castle, where, pale but composed, he reads long sections of the book aloud and entertains the royal couple with conversation about his experiences. As always King Christian VIII is inquisitive about his personal life and with that intimate manner of his gives him the chance to spread his wings and forget his anxieties. It is late before the king lets him go, and he arrives back drunk at his hotel around midnight and during the days that follow floats through readings for the Oehlenschlägers and the Bournonvilles, only to be brought up short by the first of several public slatings of the book in *Corsaren*: the reader, it says, warms to his flowery poetic descriptions for the initial dozen pages or so, but after that it becomes tiresome, his vanity gets in the way, and he does not do ordinary people justice in his portrayal of them. Set beside the intense admiration of Heiberg in Denmark, the extensive admiration of him in Germany is of little worth, for that he has acquired by dint of peddling his wares in the mistaken impression that by winning German admiration he can procure the same for himself in Denmark.

This attack on his alleged vanity is only the opening thrust. The review in *Dagen* lashes out with scorpions' tails: 'Andersen is a child, devoid of consciousness, devoid of self-criticism. In that stage he has remained or, rather, has regressed. He remains a child as before, but now an old child, and that is repulsive. Accordingly, this great travel book is nothing more than an aggregate of childish vanity and vague pictures and idiotic exclamation marks. The title in itself reveals clearly enough the author's viewpoint: *A Poet's Bazaar* – what affectation! What a thorough sham! . . .'

Once again he wanders the streets of Copenhagen, incensed, tired of life. From the palace he hears that the king is reading *The Bazaar* aloud and has reached the Orient.

OFF AND AWAY to the Manors of Gisselfeld and Bregentved, to light and comfortable rooms looking out over woods, lakes, avenues, parks; away to a cosseting fit for kings, to servants saying 'a most humble good night', to champagne, sumptuous dining-tables, floral arrangements; to solitary wanderings under oaks so still he can hear the children's play in nearby houses, to imagin-ation that lies twined in the trees' inclining limbs; to hobnobbing with nobility – the duke or the count and his wife – to fresh invit-ations, to a letter from the king with a gold diamond ring, to rooms with tooled and gilded leather and silks with bronzed birds, and to the semi-darkness of long passageways hung with princes and princesses, still flattered in their frames, still young and long dead – an older resident was, perhaps, in love with one of these evergreen youths and passes him daily – and away to erotic rapture, to adulation at his reading, to the flirtatious eyes of young aristocratic ladies in the ballroom; away to long drives in an ele-gant carriage and four through the softly rolling landscape of Zealand, between ripening cornfields or on woodland rides by the seashore with golden sunsets across the water and dark trees against the glowing light of the forest; away to the unearthly twilight moon in hushed, unpopulated landscapes and to solitary nights with that wild, almost animal urge to kiss a woman that he had in the south.

He is in a fairy grotto with no money of his own, lives like a count – and the magazines' critique is only so much hot air; on a walk through the woods at Gisselfeld with their swan-enchanted lake the idea for a new story comes to him, one where ugliness trans-forms itself into beauty and derision exposes itself. Yet another mirror and a reflection. A pipedream. During the course of a year it is transformed: 'The Story of a Duck', 'The Cygnet', 'The Ugly Duckling'.

HE IS DREAMING. *Evening, a long crooked street in Naples, hot. He is there as a boy in a white shirt. A shadow in a doorway.*

'You are too tall and weird,' it says and is gone.

He walks on, tensing his body. A window in the boarded-up houses opens. A man shouts down at him, his face contorted.

'You are repulsive inside!'

He hurries on, but the street changes; a biting cold creeps up through his legs – it is frost. He knocks on a door and unexpectedly it opens. There is nobody behind the door, just a dark room and a stairway; he takes a few steps up the stairs, but the cold paralyses him, and he collapses on the third step, sleeps, thinks he is dead when a man with a rough face wakes him.

'You've gone the wrong way,' he says scornfully. 'The musicians are in the square.'

It is warm again; sweating, he pulls himself upright and walks on down the lane; the airy sound of music hangs about him like the colour blue. He is no longer a boy but a man and, to his own amazement, is singing along to the music that is still only audible in the distance. When will he reach it? Who is that, barring his way in the dark? Has he no strength?

A heavy woman with a hanging-wattle throat like a turkey shoves up against him in a corridor. He is so surprised that he doesn't manage to resist.

'What am I to do here?' he asks.

'You live here!'

'Never seen the place,' he says.

She leads him out to the kitchen and opens the door to a room the size of a pantry, where a boy's white shirt is slung across something that looks like a bed but could just as easily be a cupboard. Spiders' webs are draped in every corner; a rag doll dressed as a princess sits on the only chair in the room.

'This is where you live – people like you can't expect better. This is where you have lived all your childhood, and you still owe me money.'

He fumbles in his pockets for change but finds only two coins, which he immediately gives her.

'They are not valid,' she says throwing them on the floor. 'They are

fake, just like everything else that comes out of you. Crooked and cracked – even the tune you are standing there humming sounds cracked.'

'That's all I've got. Can't I owe you?'

'You owe me already for half a life!'

'Then you can have the other half as security,' he says.

'I don't want to be owed nor to have your miserable life,' she says, her wattles jiggling under her as she pushes him into the pantry and locks the door after him. In desperation at being locked in, he hammers on the door until his knuckles bleed. In the dark he doesn't know whether it is night or day and falls asleep exhausted.

When he wakes and takes hold of the door, it opens with ease but in the place of the kitchen he is now on a patio where organ grinders are winding up their instruments to the hilarity of the local beggar boys. He puts his hands over his ears and tries to slip out through a gateway, but a dark man with a parrot nose grabs him by the arms and chains him to a spare organ.

'Play!' he says. 'Let's see what you can do!'

When he turns the handle, a scratching noise sounds from the box.

'Keep turning!' says the parrot-man, exposing his false teeth. He seems to have met this man somewhere before, in another life. As a trainer at a circus, as theatre director, as visitor to a spa. The man has a wealth of faces; it pains him that he cannot see his true face, but perhaps the true one is false.

And he turns faster and strikes up a tune that transplants itself to the others' and sings along on theirs.

The beggar boys shout and clap their hands.

'Now that don't sound quite right,' says the parrot-man, scratching the back of his neck. 'Exactly what's wrong with it, I cannot quite say.'

'I'm no good at the organ,' he says.

'Organs is all there is. They've been refined over hundreds of years,' says the parrot-man. 'If you're no good at them, you're no good at nothing.'

'There is a blue tune . . .'

'Rubbish! Tunes can't have colours!'

'I can hear a blue tune!'

'You are just so ugly! And there's no such things as blue tunes!'

'If you let me free of this box, I'll sing it for you.'

'Oh, all right then,' says the parrot-man and sets him free.

Now he closes his eyes and listens. Faintly he can hear the tune out-side the town and begins to sing, but his nervous voice cracks in two, they all laugh at him, the parrot-man sets the beggar boys on to him.

There is a wind blowing through him. It feels as though the world no longer exists; buffeted he walks round the patio. The boys, the parrot-man, the tuneless music are gone, and he feels as though he has been in the hall of mirrors at the Louvre, in the catacombs of Rome, in the arcades of Copenhagen – wherever humanity has been, leaving its traces behind – but this is a dead world, and he is alive; like a sleepwalker he reaches out his hand, and another hand grasps his, leads him to a little room with a bed. A young woman with gleaming skin removes her shift and stands naked before him. The colours of the threadbare carpets are yellow ochres, a water jug with chipped enamel in one corner looks like an amphora. An oil lamp burns, casting wavering shadows where the walls meet.

'Won't you lie with me?' she asks with a little smile.

But he cannot.

'I just want to look at you,' he says.

'Don't you make love?'

'I love your beauty.'

'I am not very pretty.'

'To me you are beautiful.'

She pulls on her shift and walks sadly away.

When he finds the way out again, there is an explosion of laughter as though from an audience in the theatre; his mother's face, his father's face are visible at a window, and he waves to them without them notic-ing him. There is a whole world behind the windows that had been shut-tered before – never has he been so close to, so far from that world of scents, trees, fruits, sculptures, shorelines, mountains – and half-naked women offering themselves. But it all exists only behind the windows, exists perhaps nowhere at all. He reaches out his hand to them and feels only a warmth in the air and hurries on. A boisterous crowd in carni-val clothes fills the alley. One man in a black mask and harlequin out-fit presses him up against the wall laughing, holding a knife to his face, while behind the mask a pair of menacing cold eyes glitter with intent, and he sees himself sliced to ribbons.

'You are so ugly, nothing will help. Put a mask on,' says the harlequin, *releasing him again He gets up in a daze, his white clothes now grimed, and continues through ever-increasing exhaustion towards the monotonous, drawn-out music that becomes constantly clearer and feels like part of himself. A square under a huge plane tree opens before him, with lights around the square and dervishes dancing in rows, their arms waving gracefully above their heads with wilder and wilder movements. The green and blue colours on their tent-like kirtles attract him. Isn't it as though they dissolve into the colours of the sky, the air? Soon he, the stranger, has become part of the group of dervishes, dancing like them, spinning like them to his inner music.*

And he tosses and turns in the bed, feverish, sweating.

He is flying.

A swan.

THE DIAMOND RING given to him by King Christian VIII is in pawn, his money-box cleaned out to pay for his passage by ship, coach, railway, and now he is sitting full of awe on the fire-dragon's back, holding on, saying the Lord's Prayer six times, as he flies through the black night of the tunnel; flying onwards across thin ramparts of earth that turn into deep chasms of dusky evening, past factories where fires glow and shine in the snow; hovering in his imagination, on the nib of his pen, in hotel rooms along the way, being with Ahasverus in Canossa in the time of King Henry IV, the time of the crusades, of medieval courtly life, of Columbus, the Thirty Years War, the time of King Ludvig XIV and XV; to wander with Ahasverus through America's primeval forests or through the time of the French Revolution, of the German Brotherhoods, of Napoleon, the Greek Revolution, the beginnings of modern times – a long story in which Ahasverus and Columbus talk of the New World, and Ahasverus's thoughts reflect the distant future; to dream of putting all this on the stage, of winning over the European stage with Ahasverus, the peregrine spirit, homeless and eternally present; to arrive at St Denis and the warmth of spring, entering the city's fortifications, and to be installed in the city itself at the Hotel Valois on rue Richelieu, walking about with Danish acquaintances in the Palais Royal, feeling himself to be free. To travel, to live, to be at least two – the man of the night, alone in his hotel room with cakes, cognac, absinthe, red wine, with his pen and penis, sensual excitation and the prick of Onan; and the man of the daylight, moving from face to face, museum to museum, theatre to theatre until his feet cry out.

Euphoric with travel he visits Theodor Collin in his apartment overlooking Notre Dame, and together they share their sorrow over big brother Edvard's loss of his daughter, little Wulle; he talks with Orla Lehmann about the Danes' struggle to retain Schleswig, dines with Marmier, who has made him famous in Paris, is given letters of introduction to Victor Hugo, Lamartine, Dumas; lunches with Hugo, who appears in a dressing-gown, in rooms hung with erotic rococo wallpaper; catches the jovial Dumas on his bed long past midday, writing his latest play with paper, pen and ink on the quilt – 'I live as a single *garçon* through and through,' says Dumas, 'so you must take me as you find me!' Dumas offers to take him to the Théâtre Francais and introduce him to the celebrated actress, Elisabeth Felix Rachel.

Dressed to the nines and with his hair groomed, he walks behind Dumas up the steps to Rachel's little room behind the scenes during the interval in a production of *Phèdre* As she receives them, holding out her hand to them in turn, he is instantly captivated by her distinctive dark face, her deep, sensual voice, her unforced movements. Isn't she some kind of dream-like *déjà-vu* image of the Jewish girl, Naomi, who featured in his *Only a Fiddler*, only here more alive, accessible, smiling with an air of hidden pain? They sit on three stools behind the screen that marks her territory, and in his fumbling French he compliments her on the love and respect she commands in Denmark, on the many portraits of her hanging in Copenhagen.

'That I cannot believe,' she says, 'but when I come to Copenhagen I will think of you as someone I know.'

'If you come to Copenhagen one day, you will find so many friends that I will only be in the way!'

'No, why?' she says, laying her hand briefly on his.

'Monsieur Andersen is a shrinking violet,' says Dumas and laughs. 'On the way up to you he confided in me that the thought of coming to talk to you made his heart hammer as though he were a little boy!'

'Artists understand one another,' she says, smiling earnestly and laying her hand once again on his.

From one moment to the next she can change from supple gravity to laughing directness but devoid of a woman's usual sugary sweetness. He sees her on stage both as Phèdre and as Maria Stuart, finds her unpredictable right down to her choice of costume, appearing as Phèdre one evening dressed in white, the next in sky-blue with a red cloak. When she begins to speak her lines, it is as though she were humming a tune; her face is a multitude of faces, altering constantly in the present moment and forging associations to widely different people. On stage Rachel possesses an aura of the vanished; in her person Greek figures, who otherwise seem dead, live and breathe. With her passion she sculpts living statues out of the marble slabs of Racine and Corneille; she is flesh of our flesh, a life, a soul, and he feels a tingling in his spine when, like a sleepwalker, she expresses our deepest hidden feelings. When she appears as Maria Stuart, he is struck by her natural calm, her harrowing performance, her beauty on stage, and when along with other writers – Scribe, Gautier – he is invited back to her rooms with their plum-coloured walls and carpets, their expensive curtains, their tasteful furniture and bookcases full of works by Shakespeare, Goethe and Schiller, he is possessed by the circle of intimacy and private understanding that she casts around him. Gracious in her black dress, she bids him sit beside her on the sofa by the fireplace, and as one gentleman after the other joins and leaves the company of the soirée, the two of them lose themselves ever more deeply in talk of the different ways of acting on the European stage, of poetry, fairytale and of their particular but similarly extraordinary rise from poverty – he the son of a cobbler, she the daughter of a Jewish gypsy. Now they are at one and the same time celebrities and strangers in a world that was not originally theirs. Across the ruins of his fumbling French but supported by the lively gestures of his hands and face and by the range of intonation in his voice, the two of them find each other, two grown-up children who suddenly meet each other in the same fire, singed and clutching their extraordinary talents in a world of formalities and conventions. Intoxicated, he sneaks away from the company around midnight and fails to find sleep as the hours echo their sensuality in the deadness of his hotel room. What is he to do with all that fire in his blood?

The following day she returns his album with an aphorism inscribed: '*L'art c'est le vrai*'. She hopes that such an aphorism will not seem paradoxical for a writer as distinguished as Monsieur Andersen.

At la Comtesse de Bocarmé's salon he meets Balzac, a little cannonball with square shoulders. Countess Pffaffin, dressed in black and radiant with beauty, draws him down on to a velvet sofa, reaches a hand out to Balzac and pulls him down on the other side of her.

'I feel so small between two giants of our time,' she exclaims loudly. He turns his head and behind her back encounters Balzac's laughing face parodying the countess with his miming mouth. When they escape from her, Balzac gives him a series of compliments.

The painter David spontaneously sees a poet in him, Gautier, Alfred de Vigny likewise, while Lamartine writes a poem for him. Heinrich Heine places a poem about his painful foreignness in Paris in his album, a poem recording how happily his visitor and his wife played with their children, and despite sensing reservation in his eyes – isn't he too much a panderer to princes? – he nevertheless appreciates Heine, underlining his skills as a storyteller at his own expense. He floats like a bee in the heat of summer, until one evening in the Théâtre Palais royal confirmation arrives of his own fearful premonitions in reports of the booing his play received at the Theatre Royal in Copenhagen and (a little later) in the cold legal language used by Edvard to report the dramatic fiasco of *Agnete and the Merman* and of the uninspired performance of Mrs Heiberg, regarded by him as one of Europe's leading stage artists. He is convinced that she has done what she can to bring down his play and is caught once again in the web of hatred for Copenhagen. In a letter penned in fury to Jette Wulff he pours out his gall – May I never again see that home that only has eyes for my faults but no heart for the greatness God has given me. I hate that which hates me, curse that which curses me! It is from Denmark that all the cold blasts come that turn me to stone! They spit on me, trample me in the dust! I am still a poet by nature, and God has not given them many such! With my dying breath I shall pray Him never so to honour such a people again! Oh, what poison runs in my blood right now! When I was young, I could weep, but that I can no more! I can only be proud, hate, abominate! Give my soul to the powers of evil to find a moment's ease! Here in this great city the most famous, most noble spirits of Europe encircle me with their warmth, encounter me as one of their own, and in my own homeland boys sit and spit at the finest creation of my heart!

Nevertheless he comforts Jette Wulff: his letter must not make her disconsolate, for by the time she reads it eight days will have passed; his is an elastic disposition, by then his mind will be calmer, his hatred will have abated to a quiet breeze, his fever be gone.

TWO DAYS AFTER the letter his rage has dissolved. He roams the streets of Paris, ends up on the Champs-Elysées, which have been transformed for the occasion of the king's birthday into a gigantic marketplace with the clamour of stalls, shops, swings, theatre and human freak shows. Misshapen women and children in bleached clothes are put on parade. He is overcome with sorrow, stops in front of a fat, deformed three-year-old sitting on display in the sun dressed in red corduroy. As though it were a circus act, a woman suddenly strips the clothes off the child, exposing a body on which pouches of fat hang in such obese clusters that he can scarcely recognize this as a child. In desperation at the brutality of this exhibition he turns away and asks a random spectator, 'Is it a boy or a girl?' '*Un garçon, monsieur*,' says the man and looks at him in amazement.

Eternal life there must be. It waits for all, even for the freak, who is like the faulty painting that the master tears to pieces himself. You gather together the pieces and preserve them. The freak cannot be rubbed out like a miscalculation – there must be an eternity, if there is an eternal, loving God . . . Pains in his stomach . . . His hand reaches out for nothing.

On his journey home from Paris, a funeral at Gisselfeld – Countess Danneskjold is laid to rest, the rain falling in heavy drops on the white coffin; he feels it in the pit of his stomach, is nauseous. And filled with *joie de vivre*. The horrifying thought haunts him – to lie in a wet grave, heavy earth on the coffin. He loves life! Life is letting oneself go, flying away on wings of the railway, circling the earth. Flying.

JENNY LIND. ONLY twenty-two she is, when he meets her in Copenhagen at a party one evening at Bournonville's, the ballet master – is not at first sight pretty, an ordinary face with broad cheekbones, pale complexion, deep-set grey eyes and flaxen hair hanging in curls. Her expression – when he observes her on her own – is heavy, as though she is carrying something heavy inside, but when she speaks her unusual personality comes to light, her eyes shine, and there is something magnetic and quite spontaneous about both her voice and her movements, light, quick, as full of signs as a dancer's. She gives him her hand affectionately when Bournonville introduces him to her, talks immediately about his writing and – a little later – about her fear of performing and singing in Copenhagen, where she is only visiting. From the first he is attracted to her, by her admiration for him and by the part he can now play. For hasn't Bournonville asked him to persuade her to give some guest performances at the theatre and promised that he will be delighted with her?

'I have never performed outside Sweden!' she says. 'At home everyone is so gentle and kind to me. But just think, what if I am hissed off the stage when I appear in Copenhagen!'

'That won't happen,' he says.

'Oh, yes! I don't know your theatre and your audiences, and I have seen Johanne Louise Heiberg – I cannot measure up to her. My gifts and my looks are insignificant beside hers. I have neither her beauty nor her genius. I do not dare.'

'I cannot make a judgement as to your singing,' he says, 'for I have never heard it. Nor do I know how you act . . .'

'There you are!' she says.

He spreads his hands in entreaty and continues, softening his voice.

'But, such is the mood in Copenhagen at the moment, I am convinced that even with an average voice and a modest performance you will give pleasure!'

'Do you really think so?' she says and holds her breath.

'Bournonville has told me of the effect your singing has had on everyone in Stockholm. I think you should risk it.'

She seats herself at the piano and sings for the modest gathering that evening, but he feels that she is singing for him – a Swedish folk-song carried on the sweetness of her soprano, the mellowness of the sounds, the shadings and the elegiac cadences fill the drawing-room with a plastic world of emotions and forms that seem ethereal. After a week of struggling with her own nervousness and uncertainty, during which she can suddenly burst into temperamental tears and beg Bournonville to abandon the idea of her performing, she stands one evening on the stage of the Theatre Royal as Alice in Meyerbeer's *Robert*, lost in the character's spiritual world and – with no conscious thought of her effect on the packed and silent auditorium – fills that space with the melodic purity of her voice. As she holds her breath so does the audience in the song's beautiful, muted conclusion, which with its crystal pianissimo thrills the ears even of those sitting furthest from the stage. Her magical singing is quite effortless – her breathing cannot even be heard – and appears to come from a force of nature capable of raising the dead just like Orpheus's song. He sees her immediately in the image of the nightingale – truth and nature united – and, with the rest of the euphoric audience, does not want to let her go. His health and hers are drunk that same evening at Bournonville's; he is in love, kisses her hand at every opportunity, becomes her confidant, gives her bouquets of flowers, sends her poems, goes to exhibitions, takes an omnibus with her and asks Bournonville's children daily what her feelings for him are – 'Has she never said, "I am fond of him"?' And they tease him, saying 'Nah!', have grave difficulties seeing him as a *primo amoroso* with his awkward gestures and those foppish clothes hanging off his tall, bony frame with its large feet and hands – and he feels it but is dragged helplessly along and considers proposing to her. After more performances and concerts Copenhagen is ecstatic; the king presents Jenny with a diamond bracelet, three hundred students pay homage to her in torch-lit processions and serenades – rumour has it that she has divine powers, and the city is in a fever. Overwhelmed, Jenny weeps tears of joy in a dark corner and promises, 'I will work, I will do my utmost . . .' And when early one September morning she leaves Copenhagen by ship for Toldboden, he stands on the jetty, waving goodbye just moments after pressing discreetly into her hands a letter containing a declaration of his love.

BEING IN LOVE. And longing. Being in a vacuum with only his organ left to grind, fighting the urge with cold baths. His letter to Jenny unanswered. And in the expanding vacuum, he lets his pen dance (doesn't it dance on its own?), finishes 'The Ugly Duckling' – ugliness growing into beauty – and recalls one youthful love saying nay in favour of another, like an old ball that has lain too long, gone soggy in the gutter, and himself as the gilded top saved by chance from the compost heap – in 'The Top and the Ball'. Creates a night and a transport of joy, when a large and withered field flower ascends to heaven with an angel, there to be given a kiss and a voice by God, so that it can join in the chorus of heavenly bliss – in 'The Angel'. Resurrects Jenny as an insignificant nightingale to exorcize the sick emperor, and death – in 'The Nightingale'. Reaching out for metamorphosis, catching it on the wing, on paper, as a counterbalance to the echoing emptiness of the universe, a confirmation of the divine love interwoven in all things. A vision for the lonely scribbling 38-year-old man in his rooms at the Hotel du Nord.

Karen Marie has made an appearance at the hall porter's desk at the hotel. He doesn't see her, only hears about it the following day. The last time she sought him out she looked young and well dressed, told him about her dreadful life as a washerwoman, and he gave her four *rigsdalers*. She thanked him like a stranger and disappeared.

WHY DID SHE never come again? Was he so cold? Is she dead? He can't stop tormenting himself with the thought. He slides into a morphine sleep, and when he wakes she is standing in the deepest shadows of the room – he recognizes her white headscarf.

'You didn't want to see me,' she says.

'I did see you.'

'Once.'

He pushes himself up on to his elbows in the bed.

'Do you exist?'

'I do, and I don't.'

'Are you dead?'

'Not entirely.'

'Have you come to fetch me?'

'It won't be me as . . .'

'Will we meet in another world?'

'There is none – we won't meet no more.'

'I know there is . . .'

She laughs, her laughter filling the whole room, so that he has to hold his hands to his ears.

The door opens – the maid.

'You called?'

He takes his hands away, looks long and hard into the shadows, but there is nothing but darkness and the faint light from a lantern out on the balcony outside the window.

'I didn't call,' he says.

'Jens says you laughed and shouted!'

'It wasn't me, it was . . .'

'Who, Herr Andersen?'

'My sister,' he whispers and allows himself to be straightened out in the bed. The maid's hands are warm, strong. The other day he heard her in the passageway with the servant.

'He talks to himself, wild talk, most at night,' she said. 'But he don't know it.'

'You might do that, too, when you get to die. There ain't nothing funny about that.'

But he is to go to Bregentved, or is it Gisselfeld? He will answer the *invitation in the morning.*

    He can come a few weeks late. As he has every summer for thirty years. No one can stop him doing that. Summer is not over.

    Such flies in his head.

THE FAIRYTALES HAVE been published, and all the magazines are in favour, praise them for their lyricism, gravity, humour, depth – universal applause, requests to write more! And they are read and purchased, not just borrowed from neighbours but sold out, reprinted. Has he now learnt the trick of composing fairytales? He thinks so. The first ones were revampings of stories he had heard as a child, but what people applaud in the fairytales is what he himself has created. He has found his method – to get hold of an idea for an adult and narrate it for the young without forgetting that it must contain food for thought. Subjects for fairytales seem to be inexhaustible – it is as though every tree, every fence or flower is speaking to him, saying, 'Just look at me a little while, and my story will appear in you!' His friend, the poet Hauch in Sorø is already calling 'The Ugly Duckling' a classic, maintaining that there is a deep symbolic truth in the progress of the cygnet through derision and pain to victory and that the words of the ending – 'It doesn't matter if you're born in the duck pen as long as you've hatched from a swan's egg' – immediately possess a proverbial quality. From Germany he receives a handsome review of *A Poet's Bazaar*.

He is relieved, floats from one dinner engagement to the next, enjoying the homage, lazes about, drifts around Copenhagen and lands at Nysø Manor after a night with the handsome young law student Baron Henrik Stampe in his brougham – how good can it get? – unmelancholy loneliness some few hundred yards from the woods with an autumn storm surging and tearing the treetops. Isn't this loneliness preferable – free of *ennui* and touched by forest and the sea, his familiars – to estrangement and abandonment in his hotel rooms in Copenhagen?

He has air under his wings, is riding a wave in the midst of the November cold, naked trees in a windblown landscape. A new play, the fairytale 'Elder-Tree Mother', the sketch for a winter tale about an enchanted mirror ('The Snow Queen'), the fourth act of *Ahasverus* – even a jolly ditty for Thorvaldsen's birthday – flow from his pen. Together with their hosts, the servants and Henrik Stampe, he surprises the old man in the morning by singing songs outside his door to the accompaniment of chattering fire-tongs, a dinner gong and bottles rubbed with cork. Thorvaldsen opens his door in his dressing-gown, slippers and underwear and immediately proceeds to sing along with the chorus as he twirls his grubby nightcap.

To BEG FOR money, for friendship . . . He gets nothing from the foreign editions, and asks the director of the Royal for better payment for his play *A Comedy in the Open Air*, only to discover that it has never – as was promised – been performed. He flies into a rage, writes to Edvard Collin from Nysø. A third party has insinuated himself between him and the play, and it must be Heiberg – as usual. It may look as though he has money and is living well, but no one could imagine just *how* frugally he has to live. However, completely bereft of money, he cannot manage. And bereft of a friend such as Edvard. How often he has to come crawling on his knees for his friendship!

Are you listening, Edvard?

To WALK THE corridors of the country house alone, to sit in the conservatory beside young Henrik, lying in the lamplight weak and pale and beautiful in the wake of his fever, to sense his open mind and his trust in him, to be moved that someone has held out a hand to him, to admire his courage on the lake, even his little compositions when he sits at the piano and plays for him; to be stunned by Henrik's ever more passionate declarations to him, when they are once again back in Copenhagen, the touch of his friendship, his 'a penny for your thoughts', and his desire to excite him, embrace him; he misses him more and more when he doesn't come to call, feels Henrik's jealousy when Henrik has been to see him and he hasn't been at home, feels his own jealousy, when Henrik speaks of Jonna Drewsen with increasing frequency and expects them to write letters to her, enclosing Henrik's own notes; to be in awe at the strength of his feelings for a friend, in despair at the loneliness of his absence and to confide more freely in him in letters than sitting face to face in his rooms, when there are a thousand small things – even towards him – that have to be taken into consideration. If he cannot always be agreeable towards him, it is because he cannot bear the waiting, the sitting and waiting in vain for him to turn up, when he could accomplish so much for his friend – a friend for whom at certain moments he is ready to lay down his life. Loneliness, the waiting fills him with what the English call 'spleen', a feeling of being out of sorts, a diffuse sorrow, which can lead to the wish to take his own life. He suffers from this spleen, but when he can lay bare his thoughts to Henrik it is gone.

He introduces Henrik into the Collin circle, where only the chosen have entry and where he can encounter Jonna without difficulty and without their erstwhile secrecy. Aren't they a strange threesome? Doesn't Mrs Collin believe in all seriousness that he is in love with Jonna, scolding him for making far too much of her – yes, for spoiling her solely because she praises his poetry and goes round calling him a poet? But it is Henrik who is in love with Jonna, and he who loves Henrik – and Henrik who speaks of the great love he has for him. Henrik can provoke in him arousal and irritability at the same time. They are out on the icebound Øresund together, to dinner at the Stampes, and Henrik indulges him, is agreeable towards him – and the next moment abandons him to be with Jonna. He becomes violent towards him, morbid, irritable, thinks he is going mad and will be abandoned to his *ennui*. Henrik has put a distance between them, is friendly but aloof, distracted, stops coming so often, is busy elsewhere.

But he has known the rush in his blood.

Desire courses wildly through his body – alone, unbridled, like a zombie he wanders the streets, releasing himself from its hold in the clutch of his hand in the darkness of his hotel room.

And Jenny is just a dream at the end of the rainbow! How he leaps for joy when at last a letter from her comes full of heartfelt expressions of sisterly friendship! Isn't she actually proud of being able to express her friendship for him through her songs, to be able to give him even such a paltry sign of her admiration for the divine beauty of his stories? And how deep his confusion, his disappointment when once the joy over her reply has abated he feels once again the mounting of his desire for her?

WHEN HE COMES down to the foyer the next morning the waiter at the Hotel du Nord says: 'It was a funny thing about Thorvaldsen dying like that yesterday!'

'Thorvaldsen!' he exclaims in amazement. 'He isn't dead – I dined with him yesterday!'

'They say he died yesterday over at the theatre.'

'He must be ill!' he says, dismissing it, only to feel a strange anxiety run through him moments later. He grabs his hat and rushes out of the hotel and over Kongens Nytorv to Thorvaldsen's house. His body lies on the bed, already yellowing; strangers have forced their way in, almost filling the whole room, he has to push his way through, the floor awash with melted snow from their boots, the air nauseous. Henrik's mother, Baroness Stampe, sits at the bedside weeping. He stares at the body, shaken, moved.

The day before he had dinner with him at Baroness Stampe's with Henrik, Oehlenschläger and the painter Constantin Hansen – who is to deliver paintings to the museums for Thorvaldsen – all present. Thorvaldsen, who was not usually garrulous, told stories and was full of life – he would never have dreamt that an hour later Thorvaldesen would be numbered among the dead. Thorvaldsen wanted to go to the theatre, but neither he nor Oehlenschläger cared to go with him. So Thorvaldsen went on his own to the première of *Griseldis*, entering the theatre in the middle of the overture, was in high spirits, shook hands with the one theatre director, old man Collin, rose to let the second director squeeze past him, and as he sat down again, slumped forward in his seat. There he died as the music reached its crescendo.

He returns to the hotel from Thorvaldsen's house and later the same day writes a poem for his funeral. The following day Thorvaldsen's body lies in an open coffin in the academy's great hall with a fresh laurel wreath around his forehead and surrounded by flaming candelabras. He cannot bear the sight and hurries away. In the street outside he suddenly stops, feeling faint. He has lost a friend. Such is the unpredictability of death.

When is it his turn?

PROFESSOR HEIBERG HAS once again rejected one of his plays, and he writes to him, suggesting that they meet, perhaps they can make a start at a rapprochement – yes, even begin to establish friendly relations? Early one morning in May he visits Heiberg at his house in Christianshavn; after some introductory words of politeness they sit opposite each other in silence; he has placed his hat on the table beside a wineglass full to overflowing, but he has no desire to drink, allowing his eyes to wander from a shadowy painting of Mrs Heiberg at the far end of the drawing-room to Heiberg's delicate head with its thinning hair, its sharp nose that almost seems, yes, to curve slightly to one side. Heiberg's one hand is resting on the foot of his wineglass; he isn't drinking either. A sardonic smile clings almost invisibly to his lips as he talks, presenting his reasons for rejecting the play.

'I do not go back on my decision,' says Heiberg. 'I believe that your *Flowers of Joy* is nothing more that a pale imitation of an original work, one which in all humility I wrote myself, and it is marked by – you must forgive me – a confused muddle of thought, imagination and taste, despite the fact that you are, of course, an experienced writer.'

'Your judgement is too harsh. I have not imitated your work but simply drawn inspiration from it,' he says. '*The Flowers of Joy* has a clear central theme and does not bulge out in all directions. Nor is it the "nonsense" you describe it as in the theatre selector's report. There is a coherent poetic idea to it!'

'But as drama it is muddled!' says Heiberg without looking at him.

'There is something individual in the play that you just aren't seeing!'

'I regard it as impossible – yes, dishonest even . . .'

He leans across the edge of the table.

'It may be that you just feel it to be ridiculous egotism on my part to defend my work, but you seem to have harboured an antipathy towards me for a number of years that makes you emphasize nothing but my shortcomings.'

Heiberg sighs and withdraws his hand from the table. His nostrils are trembling slightly.

'In no way do I harbour antipathy towards you – I entirely appreciate your talent!'

'Why attack me then, as you have done in *Intelligentsia*? There you denied me any form of invention but apparently felt that it was to be found in my novels. But you have not even read them! You told me so yourself.'

Heiberg smiles, waves his hands as though to wipe away his embarrassment.

'I have not yet read them, but I will now read them!'

'And later,' he persists, 'in your writings you poured scorn on my *Bazaar* and spoke of my infatuation for the lovely Dardanelles, whereas in my book the Dardanelles are actually described as not being lovely at all. It is the Bosphorus that I found delightful. Perhaps you haven't yet read my *Bazaar* either?'

Heiberg straightens himself in his chair.

'All right, so it was the Bosphorus, I don't remember, and other people don't remember either, you know. For me what mattered was to give you a poke.'

There is something seductively honest about Heiberg's admission, and he smiles, struck by a sudden sympathy for him, looks into his intelligent eyes and thinks of the many beautiful things he has written.

Their talk continues, becomes livelier, Heiberg praises his fairytales, asks him to visit more often, leads him upstairs to his observatory, his telescope, through which he enjoys the 'riddles of the universe'.

They part company – aware of their differences – but never become friends. And no matter how hard he tries to work on the theatre's two directors, the play is and remains rejected.

He gets nowhere by using politeness, resistance, warmth, persistence. Once again he is alone and humiliated. One evening after a couple of glasses of punch in his hotel room, it occurs to him to seek the company of Thorvaldsen. He gets up, takes his hat and a light frockcoat and gets as far as the corridor outside his room before it dawns on him that Thorvaldsen no longer exists. The dimly lit corridor closes around him. A scream is trapped in his throat. After several glasses of punch that fuel his sensual arousal, he fantasizes about his German friends. Didn't Clara Schumann invite him to Leipzig?

He must get out, away – again.

Away, away. A younger man accompanies him to the harbour, remaining until he boards the steamship *Christian VII* at Reden, stands there all alone and small on the quayside waving goodbye. The darkness steals around his body, and his summer jacket is a white square getting smaller and smaller. It was Henrik. Henrik – after all.

NIGHT. IS HE asleep? He can smell the elder trees in Rolighed's garden – or has the teapot on the bedside table cast aside its lid and set its elder-flowers free? They are even growing out of its spout and soon turn into a tree spreading into his bed and drawing the curtains to one side. A girl climbs down the tree, takes him by the hand and leads him downstairs; with a mysterious stillness they float along dark passages and empty rooms full of shadows. A row of windows stands open, their long white curtains swaying as a raw wind flows in from the garden. In the middle of the floor stands an open coffin with the body of a woman. Around the coffin, husband and children, silent, sorrowing. The man kisses the woman's faded hand. They leave without a sound. Strangers fill the room, place the lid over the dead woman, nail the coffin down, the blows of the hammer exploding with sharp insistence in the empty rooms of the house.

'Where are we going?' he asks the girl.

She points to a chair in a recess in the room, where a woman is sitting in long black robes. She is crying – someone is crying – is it himself? He has not cried since he was a boy. A tear lands in her lap, becomes a pearl, translucent. In the girl's hand it has seven colours – like the rainbow.

In the pearl of sorrow there are wings that will carry me away from here, he thinks.

But how far away will he go?

There is a tugging at his hand.

AT THE BRITISH Hotel in Hannover early in the morning – with the cabby asleep on his box outside the window – he dreams that he sees a man plunge to the ground from the top of the Round Tower in Copenhagen. From high above he tries to catch a glimpse of the man crushed on the street, but is interrupted by someone pricking him on the shoulder. He turns and finds himself standing in that dimly lit space before Thorvaldsen. Behind him he catches sight of his father and mother. Everyone, even his grandmother, Weyse and Kamma Rahbek, who now arrive all speaking at the same time, so that he grasps only fragments: 'Don't think about me,' says Thorvaldsen. 'Think about me,' says his mother. 'Don't distract him,' says his father.

'I have to go to Weimar,' he says. 'We shall have to talk somewhere else.'

'Always so busy,' says his young mother and approaches him. She is wearing her rust-coloured calico dress, the one she always wore for their annual summer outing, even though it is cold and damp in the stone tower. Nevertheless none of them is shivering, only him, and he can't understand how they can be so alive when they are dead.

'Can't you see that he hasn't got time?' says his father, restraining her.

'He comes over to us often enough,' says Thorvaldsen and laughs.

But it is a sad laughter. He doesn't recognize him and – when he suddenly wakes – has the impression that it was he himself who accidentally fell from the Round Tower and thinks immediately of the imminent railway journey from Hannover station. If he is to be crushed on this journey, then so be it; he could be crushed if he remains in Hannover, too. He wants to leave. His beloved Henrik's Jonna will inherit all he has. Farewell, Edvard. Farewell, Ingeborg, Louise, old man Collin, everyone. Oh Lord, Thy will be done.

WEIMAR, A SMALL town in the Thüringen mountains, 'the German Athens', home to Goethe, Schiller, Heine, a town with a promenade of linden trees, a wealth of low, flat-roofed houses, an imposing theatre and a library built like a castle with views across broad meadows and down to the river Ilm. At the edge of town stands Goethe's summer residence, now empty, beside the river in the park that he designed himself with its many picturesque vantage points for walkers to enjoy the view. Belvedere, the summer residence of the duke and duchess and their court, lies just outside the town, the hunting seat of Ettersburg towers some miles away high in the mountains up against a dark forest.

He arrives in the town in a stagecoach and installs himself early in the morning at one of the town's two hotels, the Erbprinz. After five hours' sleep he is off on his rounds, looking up Weimar's Chancellor Müller, who offers to introduce him to the duke and the most important personages of the town. He meets – by chance on the street – Baron Marconnay, the duke's Lord Chamberlain, whom he already knows from Copenhagen, and Marconnay immediately invites him to stay at his own elegant apartments. Later in the day in oppressive heat he walks with Goethe's biographer and companion, Eckermann, in the castle gardens and discusses Goethe with him on the garden's wide arching bridge. Eckermann wonders what the philosopher Schlegel meant when he spoke of Goethe's 'silent laughter'. 'Perhaps it is the same as the Greeks said of the Sphinx,' he tells him, and Eckermann nods quietly as he considers the idea. Around them the apple trees already have clusters of small fruit, and he suddenly remembers a stanza of Goethe's and says it aloud to himself, as he stares across the beautiful gardens with a sense of light-headed joy:

> I step up to the tree
> And say, 'Sevilles! Sevilles!
> You ready ripe Sevilles!
> Sweet oranges of Seville!
> I shake you, feel my shaking –
> Oh, fall into my lap!'

'Goethe wrote that remembering Italy,' says Eckermann.

'I know,' he says. 'And there he and I have something in common. Where are longing and life energy closer than in the word "Italy"?'

'Many people here have read your *Improviser* and your *Bazaar*, where you bring Italy, the Danube and Constantinople to life in colourful portraits and pictures – both the life of the people and their art. We even get an impression of madmen and their wretched conditions,' says Eckermann, wiping the sweat from his cheek with a white handkerchief. 'I am sure that Goethe would have appreciated your books.'

'Frau Goethe made me the same assurance the last time I met her, in Leipzig,' he says, 'and I was deeply moved.'

They move in under the shade of the trees.

'I often spoke with Goethe about the relation between invention and truth – yes, you are perhaps acquainted with my book?' says Eckermann, as they stand looking towards the bright walls of the rococo castle standing in glaring sunlight like a mirage on the far side of the bridge.

He nods.

'Many people think that truth can be torn away from the human sphere and is to be found divorced from it in an aesthetic dimension. What is your view on that?'

'In art I see God and a world reflected in all their miraculous wonder, but man is himself such a miracle, and without that miracle art is dead. Without the imagination and feeling nursed by that miracle, art is as superficial and dry as Horace's poems.'

'Horace's poems?'

'They consist of learning and formulae – I thought that even when I read them as a twenty-year-old. Dryness and decoration and distance from the world are dangers for art.'

'But on the other hand, are you not afraid of sentimentality?'

'My critics in Denmark are familiar with the term, but I know only the feeling behind it. I have to be as I am; they have to be as they are. Perhaps theirs is a fearful life of the mind . . .'

That same evening he is at the theatre, where an opera is performed in honour of the young duke's birthday. The duke is received with a standing ovation when he enters the theatre, but

229

from where he is sitting he cannot see his face or his build.

The day after Marconnay takes him through the same sunlit garden into the castle itself, where he first takes tea with the grand duke and duchess and afterwards sits as guest of honour at the royal table. In the high-ceilinged dining-hall among the rows of gilded mirrors that enlarge the room, most of the men – and servants, too – are, like the grand duke himself, in uniform, the women in gauzy evening dresses adorned with flowers and with their hair set up in coils. As the duchess yet again engages him in conversation, and he relates his impressions of Copenhagen, of the Manor of Bregentved and his railway journey through Germany, he has the feeling of being part of a dream that fulfils his mother's fantastic desire to see him climb in society and reflects her simple peasant admiration for all things aristocratic and royal. That world had always been at an insuperable distance from her life, while for his it had become a wild fantasy that he has pursued passionately, anxiously and at times with disregard for all else. Now he is perched at its height, has his moment of happiness among those singled out by God – and, in the mirrors of these faces, in their enthusiasm, the admiration of the ladies of the court, even he can feel himself to be singled out by God as a poet, can rise above the misery of life in Copenhagen. Like a drunken man he can immerse himself in these drops of sympathy, whether it be the duchess's thanks for his reading from his novel *Only a Fiddler*, her gratitude at having made his acquaintance at all, or Chancellor Müller's reference to Oehlenschläger's vanity, when on his German trip he had circumvented Weimar because in his opinion Goethe did not pay him sufficient attention.

As for himself, he receives all their attention. The day after the royal dinner he is driven in the duke's carriage with Chancellor Müller to the hunting seat of Ettersburg, is escorted into a hallway hung with antlered trophies, where a 28-year-old man with a fine figure, dark hair, piercing brown eyes and curling moustache addresses some friendly words to him in a straightforward manner. 'I am pleased to meet you.' He does not know who it is but guesses it is the duke, Carl Alexander. The handsome man disappears, only to reappear shortly afterwards and introduce him to his wife, a daughter of the deceased king of Holland, who also says some kind words, and he is led to the royal table, where he provides entertainment for the company. The surroundings are magical – rococo furniture, crystal chandeliers, servants in silk livery, flower arrangements, a sweeping view from the park of the Harz Mountains. Outside the young people of the village have gathered at the castle to celebrate the young duke's birthday, *mâts de cocagne* erected in the park, their poles decorated with scarves and waving ribbons, violins playing, dancers swinging in pairs under the flowering lindens – and over everything, it seems to him, a Sunday radiance.

The young duke breaks off his dance to lead him outside, accompanied by Eckermann, to a place in the garden where Goethe played his music – on one side of the tree he, Schiller, Herder and others have written their names, the other side has been struck by lightning. They stroll through the park in the cool of the evening deep in conversation. The duke knows the majority of his works and reads aloud from his song cycle 'This is what the Zombie did'. The duke's conversational manner is confidential, friendly, stimulating, and even there in the growing twilight he thinks how he might have him as a friend, if he had not been a duke. At the castle he reads aloud from his fairytales and is admired. When he is driven back later that evening in a closed carriage with four horses, he thinks again, intoxicated, overwhelmed by it all, of a friendship with the duke, of all they could share – prince or no prince!

As he flies from one engagement to the next, from castle to castle, his exhaustion mounts; one day at Ettersburg Carl Alexander and others are reading from their own stories, while he listens, feeling sick and nauseous, on the point of throwing up – it feels as though it will never end – but when his turn comes, he manages to read from 'The Ugly Duckling', 'The Princess and the Pea' and 'Little Ida's Flower' before fatigue overcomes him. Carl Alexander presses his hand.

'I am your friend, if you so wish . . .'

His face swims away as he struggles against sleep.

'I hope to be able to give you a sign of my friendship in the future,' continues the duke, still holding him by the hand.

'Thank you,' he manages to say.

'My idea is to have great artists living here, just like my grand-father. Then it was Goethe and Schiller. Now it will be Liszt and Andersen.'

'Do you really mean that?'

'Yes, of course. You must come to Weimar again, and do not forget us!'

He smiles. Touched. A softening in his heart.

'I shall never forget Your Highness,' he says and remembers then that he has *Only a Fiddler* with him, bound in morocco, which he gives to the grand duchess. She hands him in return a branch from one of the linden trees in the castle gardens.

On the ride back to the town in the cool darkness of the carriage, the branch falls out of his hand. They have difficulty waking him, and the cabby helps him to bed at Marconnay's. He dreams that he returns to the gardens in the windswept night to fix the branch back on to the tree, and suddenly doesn't know where he is. Carl Alexander appears unexpectedly between the trees – he doesn't recognize him at first, but his calm returns when the duke takes him in his arms and whispers in his ear.

'I love you.'

ON HIS FINAL day in Weimar he visits the ducal crypt, the chapel where the coffins of Goethe, Schiller and the grand duke and duchess lie side by side. He is alone in the shadowy room, wants to go over to Goethe's coffin but leans instead over Schiller's, stands there between the two of them mumbling the Lord's Prayer, praying God that he may be worthy of them as a poet, God's will be done for better or for worse. He takes a leaf from the laurel wreaths on the coffins of the poets, looks at the other coffins, leans against Goethe's and Schiller's . . .

IS THERE REST ANYWHERE?

IN DRESDEN AMONG his many calls he meets Counsellor Drewsen on the street in morning coat with a cane and his wife by his side, visits them in their apartment opposite the Hotel de Pologne, where *en passant* she gives him the news that Henrik and Jonna are now engaged.

It can't be true, he thinks at once and is struck dumb.

'The engagement was announced the week before last,' she declares with a smile. 'Didn't you know?'

In confusion he leaves her and walks around the town aimlessly. He eats ice-cream, goes to a playhouse, but while he is reading aloud from one of his fairytales for a critic the following day, there is a creaking inside his head, and he is afraid he is going mad. He rinses away the strange agitation in his head with glasses of stout, falls asleep for half an hour only to wake to vomiting and diarrhoea. He lies there sick on the sofa all morning and in the afternoon takes short walks around the hotel. Henrik has totally betrayed him – doesn't he love him any more? Not one word has he heard from him, not one drop of love! Why so naïve? Couldn't he see where it was going? But how could he know that Henrik only wanted to use him as a stepping-stone to get to Jonna . . .? Isn't that what he has done? That self-assured aristocrat with his smooth skin, his broad brow, his curly hair – Sir Baron, whom Thorvaldsen used as a model for his favourite Greek-looking statues.

No, he will not be bitter . . .

ONE MORNING IN Leipzig he visits the composer Robert Schumann and Clara Schumann and their children at their home. The same evening he takes a walk around the town with Robert Schumann, which concludes again at home with Clara Schumann. This evening the singer Livia Frege, who has sung for him at Mendelssohn's, sings Schumann's setting of his poems 'March Violets', 'The Soldier' and 'The Fiddler'. Clara Schumann sits by the piano. The evening is warm; the windows in the drawing-room are open; far off he can hear voices, the rumbling of a horse-drawn cart on cobbles, the song of the blackbird, an almost imperceptible cacophony that only heightens the gaiety, the elegy of the music and makes him feel as though he has slipped his moorings and is floating on an island paradise. Listening to the singing and feeling the warmth shown by Robert and Clara Schumann melts his defences, and he is ready to share his world with them. When they say their farewells, he cannot quite comprehend that it is over, and like a sleepwalker he cannot let go of Robert Schumann's hand.

'Thank you,' he says.

Schumann laughs.

'You have already said so many times. It is we who say thanks to you.'

'No, it is I,' he says and then seems to wake, echoes Schumann's laugh.

'I will never forget this evening,' says Schumann.

He lets go of Schumann's hand, turns his back to him and walks away into the night, into the deserted street.

'Come again soon!' a voice calls behind his back.

WHO IS THAT shouting? Where are these voices, these sounds coming from? His head groans. The door opens, and the maid pirouettes into his room, round and round, looks at him in bewilderment, dances on out into the hall and down the stairs, through the drawing-room and out into the dark garden. If he could get up he would see her spin a blood-torn path through the thorns and bushes and disappear down on to the beach and on down the beach in her shining red shoes. She dances in the churchyard where not even the dead are dancing – they have better things to do – and her shoes are grafted on to her feet, forcing her to dance over meadow and field, skipping down the empty roads. Her shoes have taken over from her legs, and even when she could take them off, she had to shuffle a step or two, couldn't leave them – they meant more than anything, more than the old woman who has looked after her, more than her lover, more than all she believes in. In the end she wishes that her feet would leave her so that she could be rid of her red shoes – that an executioner would slice off her feet and carve her a pair of wooden legs and crutches, that the shoes would dance away with their feet and disappear into the woods, that she could regret the shoes being all she ever lived for.

The door opens – now it really opens. It is Karen Marie asking him where her shoes are.

No, it is the maid.

'Jens told me to say that you only need ring once. We'll hear you all right!'

'Did I ring?' he says.

'Lots of times, Herr Andersen.'

He stares at his right hand clenched round the bell. And lets go.

FOLLOWING ON THE heels of the happy days in Germany, an invitation from the Danish Queen Caroline Amalie to be the guest of the royal couple on the island of Föhr in Schleswig, and he is flattered and downhearted at the same time, because he has to count every *rigsdaler* and can scarcely afford to travel – again. But how can he say no to Danish royalty, and to Christian VIII, one of his most devoted readers and benefactors?

Up in the middle of the night to take the stagecoach to Korsør, onwards by ship and coach to Odense and Flensborg, and from Flensborg in the cool of the moonlit night along deserted roads in an open carriage – to be a centre of stillness under dark clouds chasing across the sky and, as they travel over dreadful roads towards the dawn, to hear a single bird singing unseen among carpets of flowering heather; and on through Fresian villages where not a soul raises a hat or greets them, on towards the marshlands by the coast with their loose soil and reedy embankments, where the horses sink helplessly into the mud and he has to climb up on the embankments, fearing to fall as he looks down at the houses sheltering in the lea below. Driving on through an almost Finnish landscape with flooded meadows looking like lakes, even the cornfields under water after the heavy rain, with houses of burnt clay covered in moss, the colours of it all an orgy of browns, greens, mauves crowned by an overarching sky and the lisping sound of the waves on the reed-covered shore. The end, the beginning of the world.

Waiting, dressed in his travelling clothes, beside his large trunk in some filthy little hamlet, by ship to the spa at Wyck with its slanting roofs, its gables facing the street, its salon and a promenade for the royal family and their guests; no sooner has he arrived exhausted in his rooms than he is summoned to dine with the king and queen, to hear the cellist Christian Kellermann play for the company, to read aloud from 'The Top and the Ball' and 'The Ugly Duckling'. The king laughs, is in high spirits and thanks him for his fairytales.

In bright summer weather there are walks on the promenade every day with the Duchess of Augustenborg and the Princesses of Schleswig-Holstein, lunch in the salon, boat trips with the queen, fairytale readings for the high-spirited royals, bathing from small bathing huts drawn out into the water by horses, looking back at the coastline with its weathered green whale tusks like large gateposts. At evening the sun-drenched spa is wrapped in a red mist of moonlight, the waves break on the shore, the water spurting like champagne; by day he goes sailing round the islands with the royals in a steamboat, disembarking where rotten coffins and human bones have washed up on the tide, drinking sheep's milk and wandering where red and green cottages lean, clinging to each other for support to create dark and narrow streets. On the island's outermost sandbank, where the waves race in, a tower-like wooden structure has been built containing baskets of bread and brandy for those stranded by the tide. On the royal boat in the evening there is a banquet and dancing around the ship's funnel, while between the dancers the servants bustle to and fro with plates, sailors carry table leaves, and on the wheel casings other sailors sing out the fathoms. Someone asks him to write an impromptu poem for the royal couple:

> Homeward from the sea a pearl we bring,
> A pearl to treasure, rich with poetry.
> Deeply moved by it, our hearts will sing
> Seeing painted there the face of royalty.

Life for these weeks is a fairytale of the sea, dreamt up in an open boat on the waves of the North Sea. On 5 September they celebrate the twenty-fifth anniversary of his arrival in Copenhagen with a little bundle, a penniless boy in a foreign land. The same evening the king turns to him.

'I can only say to you how welcome it is to me to hear of your recognition, even in Germany. I must congratulate you.'

He bows his head slightly, smiling in his own melancholy way.

'What was your first performance in Copenhagen?' says the king, reluctant to let him go.

'Ah, well, I had a mixed reception from the singing master Siboni for my voice, which was clear and sweet then,' he says. 'Later I tried the ballet, but I wasn't cut out for that – I looked pretty comical, I am sure.'

The king smiles.

'But it was Kamma Rahbek at Hill House who first pronounced me a poet because of some lines I had written. For that I am grateful to her. I wanted to write great works for the theatre and did write some, but had it not been for the intuition of the critic Knud Lyhne Rahbek and Councillor Collin I would never have received help in improving my abilities. I was a strangely overgrown and dreamy child – I often sat alone during that time in my room, which was not larger than a pantry, putting on plays in my puppet theatre.'

'What plays were they?'

'Oh, Shakespeare and Schiller and many more,' he says. 'I had already read them in Odense – now I extracted from them what I could understand. The action was more dramatic than at the proper full-scale theatre!'

The king nods, seems to have had an afterthought – his well-groomed grey beard, his blue eyes, the lines on his forehead, his cheeks blotchy from the red wine and the heat are suddenly very close, his voice intimate and concerned.

'How much do you have to live on a year?' he asks.

'Four hundred *rigsdalers*,' he says, sensing which way the wind is blowing.

'That isn't much.'

'But I do not need more! And anyway my writing also brings something in.'

'About how much?'

'Twelve *rigsdalers* per sheet!'

'That is not much either,' says the king, shaking his head gently and looking at him, but he for his part falls silent and just smiles, considers asking for more for a moment but refrains. As an invited guest he does not want to impose himself. To stand there yet again with his hat in his hand and rip the hour of joy to shreds.

Some days later a grand rabbit hunt has been arranged on the island of Sylt, in which the Prince of Nør, the governor of Schleswig-Holstein, takes part, and he walks along among the reddish green willows of that sand-duned landscape to the sound of exploding shots and sits and waits in the cold air, looking out over the mournful landscape reminiscent of Greenland with its

black-green grass and dark houses. Cattle graze in a dark valley –
as though on a descent into Vesuvius's ashes – and gulls cry like
children.

As they sail from the island, the dunes of Sylt lie glinting in the
sunlight like glaciers. On board the boat the king comes up to him
again as they approach the island of Føhr in the setting sun.

'Ah, yes,' says the king. 'These glorious days will sadly soon be
over!'

'My sentiments entirely, Your Majesty,' he says. 'It says in the
Bible that once we have tasted the bread of heaven earthly bread
will never taste the same!'

HE DRIFTS FROM one court to the next, catches himself out – on a stretch of heath on the way to Augustenborg Castle on Als – thinking like a courtier. How many courts, both great and small, there are on the earth! How many mansions . . .! If you look up at the countless stars above and think that they, too, have their courts and add it all together, then there is an infinite number of courts – yes, and your head swims at the almighty power of God!

At Augustenborg Castle he sits next to the governor, the Prince of Nør, at a dinner hosted by the Duke of Augustenborg for a mixed company from Germany, Denmark, Schleswig and Holstein.

'Do you really dare sit next to someone whom the Danes have hissed off the political stage?' the prince asks him, smiling.

'Ah, yes, but that was just the common people. I felt uncomfortable when I heard about their hissing,' he says.

'But you are as Danish as anyone,' says the prince.

'Even Danes can take a broader view,' he says. 'We live in a time of affiliations – in Denmark we look towards Scandinavia, so who can wonder that in Schleswig-Holstein there is a tendency to attach oneself to Germany? Everyone has to go his own way.'

Nevertheless he does feel bad when the Duke of Augustenborg talks politics at the table and speaks of his preference for the songs of Schleswig-Holstein. Isn't there a certain condescension audible in his voice towards all things Danish? He writes a poem over dinner about his own ambivalence:

> Each colour speaks to a place and a time
> They are all, in my eyes, all right.
> But at my parents' knee I learnt in my time
> To love most the red and the white!

A momentary anxiety in him unfolds as a headache as he walks the tightrope of compromise and has to propose a toast at the table for the Princesses of Schleswig-Holstein. And when the duke rises and proposes a toast for the Danes currently under his roof and especially for the one who has honoured the Danish language through his writings and the house with his presence, he is moved to tears and breathes a sigh of relief.

Hasn't he always shied from disputes between nations? In Copenhagen people who haven't a clue about what life is like in Schleswig-Holstein are getting all worked up and adding fuel to the fire. On the island of Als, a garden of fruitfulness where the castle stands surrounded by woods, where the sea sends a watery tentacle curling deep into the forest and where gardens and cornfields surrounded by hazel hedges abound, his sense of disunity and underlying unrest seems out of place and fills him with foreboding.

IN THE MIDDLE of the night, a dream. A fir tree is growing in the garden of Villa Rolighed. At first he can see only the tip of it from his window, but it quickly grows taller, thinking only of growing and growing, of getting bigger and older. He goes down to it and says to it, 'Enjoy the sunshine and fresh air, for Heaven's sake', but it doesn't hear him and stubbornly carries on growing, cursing when in the glittering depths of winter snow a hare just hops over it. It grows into the largest and finest of the firs in the garden, and one winter evening a servant cuts it down and carries it into the drawing-room, where the children and Fru Melchior decorate it. It stands in a covered bucket full of sand among Chinese vases, rocking-chairs, silk sofas, large tables strewn with picture books – and it trembles. On its branches hang small string bags with sugar crystals, decorations made of coloured paper and gilded apples and walnuts, while attached to its branches are a hundred tiny candles in red and blue and white looking like miniature people. At the very top they have set a large star of golden tinsel. It is fabulous, unbelievable.

'Tonight,' they all say, 'tonight it is going to shine.'

The tree's only wish is that night had already come, that the candles were already lit. Won't it strike roots then and stand there in all its glory winter and summer long? And won't the other trees from the garden come and look at it? And the sparrows? Perhaps they'll come flying right up to the windowpanes just to see its magnificence? Its bark aches with longing.

And evening falls in the curtained drawing-room; the lights are lit on the tree. What splendour, what joy! A couple of the green branches catch fire from one of the candles; the fire is quickly put out, but now the tree doesn't even dare to tremble. What if it loses its finery? The folding doors fly open, the children rush in followed by the grown-ups. For a moment they all stand in silence and marvel at the tree, but it lasts only a moment; then they dance around the tree, the candles burn down – and the children pluck the tree. No one looks at it any more, the children are busy with their toys, Uncle Melchior is telling stories – about Humpty Dumpty who falls down the stairs but gets his princess anyway.

Is that the world as it is? If the tree falls down the stairs, then surely it will get a princess, too? And tomorrow it will be dressed up again, decorated with candles and gold and fruits, and then it will hear stories again and not tremble.

All night long it stands there, full of expectation, thinking its own thoughts. Surrounded by the chilly silence of the room.

When morning comes, the servant fetches it and takes it up to the attic, where he places it in a dark corner. What is it doing here? It is completely empty, emptier and colder than in the drawing-room at night, and the tree has only its own thoughts for company.

Oh, it is because it is so cold out there, the earth so hard, that the good people are waiting until spring to plant it. Yes, people are good and thoughtful, and there is a purpose in all their actions.

And it can allow itself to be admired by the mice, who peek out of their hidey-holes, wanting to know everything. It has to tell them about Humpty Dumpty, and it has to tell them about him again and again, for more and more mice – rats, too – want to hear the story. But they don't like it.

'Have you only got that one lousy story?' they say in chorus. 'There's no fat in it, not even tallow. Can't you tell us a larder story?'

'No,' says the tree.

So they disappear – the mice, the cold, all disappear where they came from. The sun shines in at the attic window, and the tree can warm itself in its rays – and it isn't old, is in its prime, just stunted, just waiting to be planted out in the spring sunshine.

The servant comes and carries it out to the courtyard, to the sun, to the fresh roses, the flowering limes, the swallows – and now it must remember to enjoy every minute, now it must live.

But it lies in the undergrowth tangled in nettles and weeds and sees its own branches withered and yellowing. It thinks of the hare that hopped over it, of the snow, of the piercing blue of the sky. And one of the children tears the gold paper star off 'that rotten old Christmas tree'.

The servant comes carrying an axe, on his way to cut the tree into small pieces, and the children gather round, laughing.

The door opens. The servant stands there with his axe. White in the face.

He starts up, shouting.

'It's Jens, your servant,' says the voice over by the door.

'Go away!' he says. 'Away!'

'I have got your shoes. You wanted to go down to the garden.'

'It isn't morning yet.'
'It's already late morning, Herr Andersen. The night is long gone.'
'Gone.'
'Yes, gone.'
'I am burning,' he says and looks astonished at the servant.
'No one is burning here.'
'Yes, the tree is burning. You just can't feel it.'

DRIFTS ABOUT IN the October cold of Copenhagen, his senses pulsing, consoling himself with cakes from Apitz and Lardelli, the confectioners in the middle of town. His play *The Flowers of Joy* has been accepted at the Theatre Royal, but no one wants to act in it, least of all Mrs Heiberg. Falls into a mood of dejection bordering on tears at the unfriendliness of the theatre and again has to drown his sorrows in porter ale in his rooms at the Hotel du Nord. Only when the dandified critic P.L. Møller, handsome and nine years his junior, calls on him at the hotel several days in a row late at night and rouses him to life again with his quick, sharp tongue, his sensuality and his enthusiasm for his work does he find calm again. Møller wants to write his biography and show how, with his rich and prolific imagination and the exceptional recognition he enjoys abroad he towers above his Danish contemporaries.

'I must thank you for your kindness,' he says to Møller as they sit drinking wine at his table one evening. 'I recognized the refinement of your mind from the first moment you appeared in Copenhagen.'

'And you are among the few who approached me from the very beginning. With friendship and kindliness. People say that I am malicious – and it's true that I'm not the sort to rub people up the right way – that kind of rubbing we can leave to the bootblacks. I don't attach my affections to anyone very quickly – but when it does happen then I know that I can be relied upon more than so many others.'

'I am glad to be able to rely on you – in Copenhagen there aren't many people who can be relied on.'

'The Heiberg clique have given you the runaround long enough. Now it's time for me to show that "family" of backscratchers that you are not a wit inferior to Heine, Musset, Pushkin, Byron. If you will allow me?'

'That's up to you. It is you who wield the pen. I only hope for a little more sunshine in your own life.'

'Am I so unhappy, then? Is that how I come across to you?' says Møller with a nervous smile. His eyes are vulnerable and have that glow which can suddenly turn to ashes and reveal their bitterness.

'Ah no, maybe not. Far be it from me to judge. At times you seem as restless as I am myself. The "family" have not treated you kindly either.'

'No, there is too much "family" and too little feeling and imagination,' says Møller, getting up lithely and stepping to the window to look out over the deserted cobbles of Kongens Nytorv. With his back still turned he empties his glass. Møller's slim, well-proportioned body and the soft, dark hair at the nape of his neck in the shadowy light make him think for a moment about the rumours in circulation about the man's many female conquests.

'Imagine,' says Møller, still with his back to him, 'that we could live free, without ties, without fear. Wouldn't we be happier?'

'Fear comes from inside us – it never lets go of us entirely,' he says. 'God has the means to banish it, but we don't know when and never quite how. We have to trust in God.'

'Does that makes us happier?' asks Møller, turning towards him.

'We are but hieroglyphs in a grand design, and God is love.'

'Then we are not free?'

'We are as free as those wild horses on the deserted islands of the Danube estuary – bounded by the earth we walk upon. If I had been endowed with divine powers, I could never even with the most benevolent of intentions have led myself to my goal more surely than God has led me. Think of the surroundings and the conditions in which I was born.'

'I envy you your trust in destiny, but I cannot share it. Do you never have doubts?'

'Oh yes. Alone with my own self I can despair, feel the absence of God. The darkness is in all of us – people can do the craziest things out of despair. That is what Goethe has taught us. But light comes from God.'

They continue for hours, talking and talking, and when Møller leaves the second night the moods and words of their conversations hang in the orange light of the room like the echo of a music already distant, something that has been there and will not come again if he does not hold on to it. He begins to write.

His pen chases across the paper. In a rush of inspiration he writes – in 'The Fir Tree' – about the tree that loses everything because it fails to live in the moment and – in 'The Snow Queen' – about Kaj with the splinter of ice in his eye and his heart, who in the cold blue northern light of the Snow Queen's kingdom is redeemed by Gerda, the wise child, and wins back the world and a sleigh and his own self.

The stories are published within a month. Reviews are scant and grudging. The city is cold.

Summer, freezing, his back is freezing, sweat on his forehead.

WHO JUMPS HIGHEST – the grasshopper heavy in his green uniform, the flea with tidy manners or the silent skipjack made from a genteel wishbone? It's the skipjack, and he jumps up to the princess – and he needs to have brains for that, needs to have his head screwed on – and that's why he gets the king's daughter, while the flea will have to join the army and the grasshopper sit on the verge and ponder the ways of the world.

He writes 'The Jumper', 'Elf Hill', 'The Red Shoes' and 'The Shepherdess and the Chimney Sweep' for simultaneous publication in Danish and German. A German edition of his complete works is in the offing, in London he is hailed as one of the most important of the romantic poets for his novels *The Improviser* and *Only a Fiddler*, Russian and American editions appear, while in Copenhagen he achieves (secret and anonymous) success with his comedy *The New Lying-In Room*, but the new fairytales are neglected, banished to a few lines in minor reviews, and Heiberg describes with relish his latest opera libretto *The Water Elf* as an abortion, as trivial as life itself. Plagued by headaches, he wants to get away again.

The eruption of words and manuscripts has exhausted him. Day after day he drifts about in the spring sunshine with lust and longing raging like a fever in his blood, is bored, masturbates – 'You need a body,' as the grasshopper says – writes letters to Jenny Lind which remain unanswered, his mood swinging, suddenly on top of the world when Henrik Stampe presents himself in his rooms or when anyone approaches him affectionately. The thought of recognition abroad – though isn't it more than he deserves? – can sometimes permit a lightening of his spirits, some sense of resolution, of a grasp of the world as it is. Even death in the form of old Henriette Collin's departure has something painless about it, something gentle, like a sleeping child. 'Oh Death, you are a Glory not a Shade,' he writes in a poem in her memory. To be called in – like a son of the house – to her deathbed one Sunday night and to witness her final hours among the distraught Collin family provides him with a sense of belonging to the world. Are God and eternity not a presence by the deathbed, between children and grandchildren – a sacred moment? And doesn't he love 'Father' Jonas Collin? How is he to survive his despair if the old man were to die before him?

He dreams of being free of pain, but its shadow journeys with him on the back of the stagecoach as he leaves Copenhagen for Skanderborg and later for the Manors of Glorup and Bregentved, and it hurries ahead to wait for his return in Copenhagen, to wait for him to open his friend Carsten Hauch's new novel *Castles on the Rhine*. It is in all the papers, and people around him have already been asking him what he has done to Hauch to be portrayed so shamelessly as a mad poet. He gets angry because he considers Hauch too big-hearted to borrow his features to present the character of a self-obsessed poet dying in the madhouse of out-and-out vanity – until he reads the book.

There is no mistaking it, the poet Eginhard has his outer features – the prominent nose, the slightly stooping gait, the close-set eyes, the large hands and feet, the long-limbed body – but here presented as a satanic caricature by a writer who, owing to a leg amputation as a young man, tried to take his own life with two shots of a pistol, both of which missed their mark. A number of aspects of his personality as well as the knowledge about prophecies when he was a child that his home town of Odense should one day be illuminated in his honour are in the most grotesque fashion transferred to Eginhard, who is prepared to turn his back on an angel's garlands of paradise in favour of the bitter gifts his muse holds out to him. Eginhard's immense and intolerable poetic narcissism finds expression in a manic consumption of any form of experience, using anyone around him for his own purposes, spying on friends and relations, publishing their private thoughts and unscrupulously plagiarizing any word and image and publishing it as his own. An abrupt fall awaits Eginhard's morbid vanity; his world gives him his just deserts when it fails to present him with the two German knighthoods he had been counting on – and he ends in madness.

The prophecy of his homecoming to his home town in triumph is reworked into a literal nightmare. Sitting in an open carriage on his way to the madhouse crowned with a laurel wreath, which in his madness he has placed on his head himself, he is surrounded by a large mob, laughing and shouting at his misfortune. The noisy crowd frightens the horses, which have to be unhitched, and the mob takes their place. Shrieking and laughing, they pull the carriage to the madhouse, while Eginhard sits there, confused but glowing with pleasure, waving to left and right.

This was to have marked Eginhard's exit from the story – and a premonition (not devoid of *schadenfreude*) of his own disappearance in the mists of oblivion. What fuels the contempt that creates such a picture if not a repressed envy that has gone amok and reflects not only Hauch's relationship to him but also that of Heiberg, Hertz, Holst – of the whole 'family', in fact?

Although he feels it, he chooses to ignore Ingemann's remark that the portrait of Eginhard has made an inexplicable but painful impression both on him and his wife Lucie. Their feeling is, though, that it will damage not him but the novelist who has exploited his friend's discarded rags. He feels neither bitter nor angry at Hauch, is even prepared to go along with his lame excuses. For isn't it him? Isn't it Andersen? Aren't all his weakness assembled there in Eginhard? Eginhard – Mr Ego, his closest friends call him in jest – what is the difference?

Reading the book has left him at fever pitch. He is pilloried all over Copenhagen. The portrait touches deep chords in his fear of madness. Wasn't his grandfather mad? Didn't his father go mad shortly before his death?

There is no one he can talk to about that particular fear. Not any more. There is nothing for it, no words for it – he has to shut himself off. It is a flood he has to allow to pass over his head. Intimacy is locked away; friends can be counted on one hand – even Jette Wulff has been silent for a year and now sends him a letter scarcely concealing her anger that in his letter to her he had been rather too pleased with his own reception in Weimar. Too pleased with himself? Too self-obsessed?

It is cold at the top of the mountain. Even joy has the contours of ice.

Who understands him?

HIS MOTHER IS with him, her back half turned towards him, grey, aged, a wild look in her eyes like the time when he saw her in her bed at the Greyfriars Hospital. And then she is silent suddenly, once again the dark-haired, sunburnt woman with wounded Spanish eyes.

'Do you remember?' she says.

And he does remember. Remembers her stories, which have become his.

A cold street one New Year's Eve. A poor girl walks without a hat and barefoot through the dark. She has lost one of the oversized slippers she had on, a boy has run off with the other.

She is carrying a bundle of matches in her apron, while another is clutched in her frozen hand. The snow is settling in her hair; there is light in the windows of the houses, and the smells of roast goose inside hangs in her nostrils.

She sits, huddled in a ball in the angle between two houses, and draws her legs up under her. She is freezing. Not one match has she sold, not earned one penny, and if she goes home empty-handed her father will beat her.

Her hands are almost numb with the cold. One match would do her good – if only she dared!

She strikes one against the wall – it flares up and burns, and she warms her fingers. There is a strange light in the flame. She is sitting – isn't she? – in front of a big cast-iron stove with shiny brass knobs. Oh, the heat! Even now she is stretching out her feet to warm them – but the flames die, the stove vanishes, and she is left with a burnt-out match in her hand.

Quickly she strikes another. The wall in the gleam of the flame becomes transparent. A table is laid in the dining-room with a white tablecloth, fine porcelain, and steam rises from a roast goose filled with prunes and apples. The goose hops off the dish and is waddling across the floor towards her with knife and fork sticking out of its back, when the match goes out and there is just the cold wall.

In the light of the fresh match that her feverish fingers have lit she is sitting under a Christmas tree with thousands of candles among the green branches. When the match goes out, the candles climb up and up, turn into stars in a far-off sky – and one of them falls, leaving behind *it a long trail of fire.*

'Someone's dying,' says the girl, echoing her grandmother's words. When a star falls, a soul flies up to God.

She strikes yet another match against the wall, and in the glow of the flame sees her old grandmother standing there, luminous and gentle.

'Grandma!' she cries. 'Take me with you. I know you'll be gone when the match goes out!'

And quickly she strikes all the matches she has left so that she can hold on to her grandmother, until there is a bonfire lighting up the wall and everything around her, as though it were broad daylight. Grandma has never looked so lovely, as she lifts her up and together they fly up and up – and there is no fear, no hunger, no cold. They are with God.

Before him stands his grandmother with the girl in her arms. She has frozen to death.

The girl has his mother's face.

'Take me with you,' he whispers.

TAKE ME WITH you to see Jenny Lind. Take me with you to that evening in Copenhagen, when people camped in front of the theatre to get tickets for her *Norma*, the rich honesty of her performance in presenting a woman not raging but deeply hurt, who in her immediate impulse to kill allows herself to be disarmed by the sight of her faithless lover's children. Her movements on the stage follow the moment's impulse, while her singing is as unforced as the wind, casting spells in those long held notes that climb imperceptibly to a crescendo or sink to a soft pianissimo that sculpts the stillness. There is no mirror here, and the word 'play' is a contradiction in terms, for it is nature itself singing. Witnessing her, he understands what art is, for she teaches him to lose himself in something greater. Didn't she tell him that singing teachers are useless, because God has inscribed in her so clearly what she should study that she cannot sing according to any method – only imitate the birds as best she can?

His passion runs wild, in her he hopes – and is disappointed. During a party at the Collins' with a host of invited guests she scarcely even looks his way, and even before dinner is served he returns to his hotel room on the verge of tears. Worshipped in the eyes of the whole city, she is his reflection. His condition veers from ecstatic hope to misery to agonizing dependence on her attention. At her farewell party at the Hotel Royal, when the ballet master Bournonville makes a speech in her honour, she makes him happy – and sad at the same time.

'I will choose one among you all as a brother. Will you, Andersen, be my brother?' she says, approaching him with a champagne glass in her hand. They drink to him – he is quivering before her, a daft smile on his face, and when no one is watching slips her champagne glass into his pocket.

Some months later he has given in and is once again riding the stream, travelling again, and is installed at the Hotel Britisch in Berlin. Berlin, where she is, too. And he sends a hired servant over to her to get a ticket for her performance at the opera. She replies that if tickets are to be had, he will get one – but no ticket comes. He waits and waits, becomes angry and is suddenly overwhelmed by loneliness at the *table d'hôte* and goes up to his room to look out over the crowds milling in the rain on Unter den Linden.

Dressed up with tiepin, cloak and top hat he mixes with fashionable high society promenading on the broad avenue in the December rain or makes his way to the opera house and, standing in the pit by the door, rubbing shoulders with bawdy soldiers, fishwives and a drunken Frenchman, hears Jenny sing in German an aria from *La Sonnambula*. Beneath all the rococo magnificence of the theatre, the audience holds its breath, and he sees only her, hears only her as though in a dream. Unreal she is, her voice so close to him and yet infinitely distant. Back in his sumptuous hotel room with its carpets and silk furnishings he feels his desire for her will tear him apart and again feels himself alone.

His love for her resists expression in a way that continues to surprise him and does not conform to his daytime notion of how he should behave to her and what she means to him. At the same time he struggles with the fear that a door will open, letting in the star's professional coldness, which he has long been aware of – but ignored. Isn't that something that has slowly crept in like a shadow and become part of him, too? Over the next two days his thoughts are diffuse, his desire for her and his fear of rejection driving him to her apartment in an uninteresting part of town, despite himself. The first day his visit is in vain – she is at rehearsal. The following day he is at first turned away by the concierge, who guards her peace against the thousands of admirers who will do anything to get close to her.

'She is receiving no one!'

'Yes – me she will!'

'I have no idea who you are, Herr . . .'

'Andersen! Hans Christian Andersen! Give her my card!'

He rummages for his card in his pocket but cannot find it.

'Give her my name!' he says desperately. 'She will not refuse to see me.'

The concierge disappears. Soon after Jenny herself appears, generous, blooming. He kisses her hand, and she takes him in to the sofa, where they talk. She is full of her performance, her Berlin acquaintances – she has made so many friends already! She is thinking of settling in the city, for this is where her musical home is, not Stockholm.

Seven years at home, and not a soul knew her – pure pettiness, all of it – while seven months away, and she is offered all the most prestigious engagements. She is having fun in Berlin, feels wonderfully well, her voice has doubled in strength, her acting has changed completely, has more life, more passion. Last year her success was considerable, this year it is overwhelming. And does he know that she makes music every day with Mendelssohn, who has such high regard for him? Every day she goes to Hasenheger Strasse, to Professor Wichmann and Anna, his wife, who are her new family. There she has felt for the first time the blessing of home; Mendelssohn comes, and they talk, she sings while he plays – yes, improvises even on the piano; those hours are among the happiest of her life – oh, Mendelssohn is simply spellbinding! When she closes her eyes and thinks of his dark eyes, his handsome face so full of life, then . . .

She looks at him, smiles, a rapt expression on her face, and then taps his hand, praises his latest fairytale, wants to know his plans but takes advantage of a pause in the flow of his sentences to wonder aloud where she will spend Christmas Eve.

'Won't you spend it with me?' he says tentatively. 'That was what I had been counting on.'

'We shall see, we shall see,' she says lightly and gets up absent-mindedly to ask her companion Louise to look at her diary of engagements.

'One day around Christmas I expect there will be,' she says when she returns and is suddenly fatigued, has half an eye on the clock, lets him know that his visit is over. He gets up, kisses her hand again; she smiles at him again, lost in thought, and he doesn't know what is in her mind. Out in the street he begins to walk but stops abruptly, turning to contemplate the house, the windows of the third floor mirroring the sky. In love with Mendelssohn? He cannot believe it. What does Mendelssohn, a father of four, have that he doesn't? He intuits it and feels sweat prickling his skin even in this winter cold.

He has many visitors at the hotel, among them Alexander von Humboldt, who he thinks is going to arrange an audience with the King of Prussia – but no ticket from Jenny, not a word. Once again he has to go to the opera to see her one evening, and his disappointment and anger dissolve before the beauty of her singing, only to return the next day – Christmas Eve – when he calls at her apartment to find her not at home, the place deserted.

On Christmas Eve he eats alone in the hotel restaurant, waiting to hear from her at any moment, but in vain. At about eight he goes to one of the many parties to which he was invited on his arrival in the city, a party with artists from Berlin and aristocrats from the Prussian court, reads one of his stories, receives gifts and wallows in an adulation which both overwhelms and surprises him, partly because it seems so at odds with the atmosphere in Copenhagen and partly because Jonas Collin has pronounced it to be hollow. Restless, he leaves the party to call on Jakob Grimm, who didn't know who he was when he was last in Berlin but who now with his learned, gentle and rather shy manner talks to him about the fairytale as to an equal. When he returns to his empty hotel room at about eleven the transition is too great. It is a return to all that his shadow has been fleeing from – a room without Jenny, without love. Yes, a room abandoned even by the dream of her. A room for loneliness.

How many times can he bear being frozen out? He is worth nothing to her even as a brother artist, and he no longer feels anger but hurt and sorrow. He has been full of her, has lived for her in Copenhagen, surrendered himself, recommended her to Meyerbeer and his German friends before they even knew her, was there in Berlin for her sake. He no longer loves her. She has cut out the sick flesh with a cold knife. There are no friends or children around him. He is the stranger, whose Christmas tree is the starry sky seen from a hotel room and who – flying in fantasy and in reality – surrounds himself with new towns, new faces. Oh, so many faces whose smiles he desires, like so many glow-worms in the tapestry of darkness.

'I do not hate you, for I have never loved you,' Jenny once said to him when he complained about her lack of attention. He didn't understand that then, but now he knows what she meant.

Nevertheless on Boxing Day she invites him to share her Christmas tree on the third floor, gives him presents – soap shaped like a cheese, eau de Cologne. And admiration. 'You are a good person.' A pat on his shoulder, his cheek.

'You are such a child,' she says to him with a smile.

CHILD? HE REMEMBERS *one day some months ago, lying weak in his bed in the apartment in Nyhavn, being visited by the young painter Carl Bloch, who talks to him about the sketch drawn by the sculptor Saarby for a statue of him for the occasion of his seventieth birthday. But he cannot abide it; he said so, only not to Saarby.*

'What have you said?' asks Bloch.

'I have told members of the award committee that it reminds me too much of Socrates and the young Alcibiades.'

'Is that so terrible?' asks Bloch from the chair by his bedside, stroking his smooth, dark beard with one hand.

'There's a boy crawling right up my crotch as I'm reading!'

'I think it gives a nice sense of your relationship to children and young people.'

'No, no, I cannot stand it,' he says angrily again and again, throwing himself about in the bed.

'What have I said?' asks Bloch, getting up from the chair.

'Everything around me is lies,' he says. 'There is no one I can trust. You only want to hurt me, all of you!'

'No one wants to hurts you.'

'Yes, you do!'

'Shall I go now? Would you prefer me to go?' asks Bloch, already putting on his cloak.

'Yes, I beg you, please. I am most distressed. I beg you to leave me alone,' he says with tears in his eyes.

Bloch stands for a moment in confusion, looking down at him, and then decides to leave. He continues to cry, doesn't know what has come over him, cannot calm down. Suddenly Bloch returns.

'I was going to leave,' says Bloch, 'but stayed in the anteroom since you continued to be distressed. Is there anything I can do for you?'

'No,' he says. 'I have to be alone.'

Bloch bids him a sad farewell. Now he regrets his behaviour, regrets that he didn't, as he intended, write a letter to him apologizing. He thinks highly of his pictures. How many people has he driven away with his strange moodiness?

The following day Iwén the sculptor comes and wants him to pose for a statue, but he is too tired, and it doesn't go well. Later Saarby visits him and shows him his drawing again, but not much has changed in it, so he is forced to say it.

'Neither you nor the other sculptors know me!'

'But I have read most of your fairytales,' says Saaby.

'You haven't seen me read them aloud.'

'No, that I cannot claim.'

'If you had, you would know that I cannot stand anyone behind me and would never have children on my back or up my crotch. You would also know that my tales are as much for adults as for children. Children simply understand the externals – it is only grown-ups who perceive and understand the whole picture. Simplicity is only a part of my stories – they are spiced with humour.'

He can see that this is new to Saaby – that he is no writer of children's books.

But he has offended Bloch, who wanted to help him. The thought torments him, will not leave him.

This self-torment.

These faces.

The clouds in the sky are like the icebergs in Greenland.

Soon Fru Melchior will come with Chinese tea – as long as his hands don't shake too much to hold the cup . . .

As long as he doesn't wet himself and give her trouble . . .

DOESN'T IT SAY in *Preussiske Tidende* that he is more at home in Germany than in Denmark? Hasn't he received his first order, Knight of the Red Eagle, from King Friedrich Wilhelm IV of Prussia? At Potsdam castle he and Humboldt sit drinking tea with the king and queen at one table – two ladies-in-waiting and three escorts at another – conversing about Denmark and its landscape, and he reads aloud for them – 'The Fir Tree', 'The Ugly Duckling', 'The Top and the Ball' and 'The Swineherd'. Humboldt is especially enthusiastic. Coming on top of the hundreds of embraces, kisses, honours and praises from artists and aristocrats in Berlin over the past month, this is the culmination of his stay. The following day he is to leave for Weimar, but that night he cannot sleep, there is a rushing in his blood, and he is worn out. As he falls into a doze, all those faces tower before him in an impenetrable wall, which he tries to break down. Behind the wall he can hear Jenny's vibrato singing, quivering in *La Sonnambula* – calling, perhaps, for him? The massive wall is too much for his strength, her singing changes into the sound of a bell, an alarm, and he wakes in a muck sweat, lurches out of bed and across to the window overlooking the dark, sleeping street, where the sound of a mechanical chime on one of the towers reaches him faintly.

With a sore penis and a pain in one testicle he travels by train from Berlin via Köthen to Halle and on by stagecoach to Weimar. Tired out, he arrives at the post office, where Chancellor Beaulieu's servants meet him and drive him to Beaulieu's residence, where he is embraced by the master of the house and has scarcely had his large travelling trunk brought to his room before Beaulieu asks him to accompany him to a ball at General Beulewitz's. Here – to the sound of chamber music and of the court dancing in their evening finery – Duke Carl Alexander rushes to greet him.

'I cannot receive you here as I would at home,' he says, pressing both his hands. 'Oh, my friend, I have missed you so much!'

When he is summoned to the grand duchess's table in the ballroom, his legs are so weary, and he feels so dizzy that he is on the point of collapse.

'What is wrong?' she asks.

'Ah, it is my chest,' he says, unable to force himself to say that it is his boots that are killing him and that he is exhausted by the long journey and lack of sleep. She calls Beaulieu and asks him to fetch a doctor, but using signs and whispers he makes his problem clear to Beaulieu.

'We had better fetch a cobbler,' he says.

Beaulieu smiles and promises to order a cobbler to stretch his boots – and the introductions continue.

The next day, his head thick with a heavy cold, he walks from the Erbprinz Hotel to Belvedere Castle and is there received by Carl Alexander in his magnificent chambers. The grand duke embraces him warmly, kisses him a number of times and thanks him for his affection. Arm in arm, they stroll to Alexander's room and discuss the writing of fairytales, Goethe, and Alexander's plans for Weimar. Alexander has to attend the council of state and accompanies him to the door, leaving him to walk back to the hotel, tired but happy. The embraces, intimacy, confidences continue. He meets Alexander in the castle's little hothouse, takes walks with Alexander and Beaulieu in turn through the castle gardens and parks, expanses of snow under flocks of crows, reads his stories for them or for the court. Carl Alexander grasps his hand enthusiastically from time to time or presses his cheek against his.

'You must come and stay with me for ever here in Weimar,' the duke says one day, when they are alone in his room, sitting side by side on the sofa.

'I cannot leave my homeland,' he says.

'But we Germans are fonder of you than your Danes, you know that!' says Carl Alexander with an intense look in his dark eyes. He has removed his jacket and is wearing only a shining white shirt.

'I am still a Dane,' he says softly.

'Well, then you can alternate between being here and being there. Give me your hand!'

Alexander takes his hand and holds it tight.

'I love you!' says Alexander – and swims before his eyes.

But on certain evenings when he is outside the range of the court circle, his exhaustion wakes in him a despair, an anxiety that constricts him, and in the midst of his euphoria he feels a stranger to himself, feels the emptiness of it all. Where does it come from? He thinks about Jenny, prefers not to think of her – soon she will be coming to Weimar, and what is he to expect? Isn't it he and not she who is the sleepwalker? So much is showering down on him, and yet this melancholic loneliness of the hotel room. Who is he? Will he never be entirely happy? Is there no woman who can love him?

Euphoria and oblivion return the day after Jenny's arrival, as she makes him the gift of her portrait and joins him in riding the waves of courtly high life. They attend a concert, he with rapier and tricorn, she in a simple embroidered dress with a rose in her bodice. She sits alone by the window with her hands in her lap, her eyes downcast, as a soprano performs Mendelssohn songs to a piano accompaniment in the great hall filled with princes, dukes, courtiers. He stands in the front row with the grand duke by his side, sensing Jenny's eyes on him – isn't she always looking in his direction? After the concert he is introduced to one after the other – the Duke of Gotha, Prince Albert of England – but has eyes only for her and is always asking Carl Alexander or the duchess what they have said to her about him.

'I have spoken to her about your character,' says Carl Alexander smiling with delight. 'Oh, I am so glad she is here! I wouldn't mind taking her for a twosome!'

The night following the concert he lies in a sweat unable to sleep. In the morning he visits Jenny with Beaulieu, but she has a headache, and he takes his leave of her in a foul mood. Later he walks in the park with her, and she speaks enthusiastically about Mendelssohn again. In the evening he sits, crushed, in a corner of the theatre while on the stage she sings *Norma* to thunderous applause. What is he to do with himself?

Some days later at a modest gathering at Countess Redern's Jenny sings songs and a hymn that captivate everyone.

'She leaves me speechless,' says the young duchess. She embraces Jenny, kisses her, Jenny weeps. That same evening she gives an incomparable performance of *La Sonnambula* at the theatre, Beaulieu is beside himself, everyone ecstatic, but his truculence grows when it is his turn to read 'The Little Mermaid'. Why is she not paying him more attention?

The following evening, as he reads for a large company assembled at Chamberlain Plötz, his images bring tears to Jenny's eyes; he listens to her sing, loses her – why is the distance between them so great? And why does she have to occupy his thoughts like this? He drives home with Beaulieu, feeling ill.

'I do believe you are falling in love with her,' Beaulieu says to him when they are seated in his chambers.

'No, that won't happen,' he says.

'You are fighting it, but it shows,' says Beaulieu.

'Yes, you may have observed it, but I have no wish to love her.'

'I, too, loved a woman whom I could not attain,' says Beaulieu, turning pale. 'She gave me promises of a kind, but they were my own imaginings. My thoughts followed her blindly in spite of myself and brought me to the point of madness. In the end I was a ghost and was frightened of my own reflection in the mirror. Love can have the teeth of a vampire. Oh, I was so miserable – it was like a disease.'

He looks at Beaulieu leaning forwards watching the flames in the fireplace, colour flooding his dark face, and he finds himself weeping inside both for Beaulieu and himself.

Once again he cannot sleep. He stares out of his window at the snow falling silently in the darkness and thinks of leaving Weimar and travelling onwards to Italy, even though Carl Alexander has requested with such insistence that he stay.

The following day he calls upon Countess Redern at her own request, only to hear from the lackey that she is not at home. Instead he is received by Carl Alexander and his wife, who have hidden themselves away with Jenny at the countess's and who receive him and drink several glasses of wine with him. Carl Alexander puts his arm around his waist, his wife kisses Jenny, but he is somewhere else, cannot enjoy himself, feels dizzy.

That evening – the same evening she is due to leave – he and Beaulieu are at Jenny's. The vestibule of her house is full of people, outside a large crowd has gathered to sing her a serenade, and she opens the window on to the cold air to express her heartfelt thanks to everyone in Weimar. He paces restlessly about behind her, wanting to be alone with her but knowing it is impossible. As they part, she reaches out her hand, and he strains to catch the tone of her voice, to find the warmth of her eyes.

'God knows when we shall see each other again,' she says. 'But what is between us will, I hope, last a lifetime.'

He cannot swallow for the lump in his throat. Beaulieu kisses him, and she sees it.

'Thank you for being so good to Andersen,' she says to him.

Back in Beaulieu's rooms they talk of her; he is unable to hold himself back, does not believe that he can survive his feelings for her.

'Weep your fill!' says Beaulieu.

And he weeps, Beaulieu embraces him, kisses him affectionately.

And the day after Carl Alexander can speak of nothing but Jenny, the brightness of her face when she sings or speaks, her divine singing, her warmth, her naturalness. Pressing his hands, he talks of his plans of getting Jenny to live at Weimar, as his wife's guest.

'You must always write to me about her,' Alexander says. 'Do not mention her name, just "our lady friend"!'

Some days later when they come to bid their farewells to each other, he calls early in the morning on Carl Alexander in his bedroom at Belvedere to find him in his nightshirt and nightcap. They kiss and Carl Alexander holds him tight, reminding him that on that very spot Wieland met Napoleon, his grandfather talked to the youthful Goethe – and now they are friends for life. They both weep.

He bids farewell to Beaulieu, too, the same day, and Beaulieu asks him to be his friend always and kisses him warmly.

Aboard the stagecoach on the way across that rain-swept, windblown landscape the horses' hooves seem to hammer against his temples. Alexander and Beaulieu are already somewhere else, and he feels his loneliness. Alone in the world.

In longing we feel the strength of love.

In Leipzig four publishers are competing to publish his complete works, and Mendelssohn is enchanted with his fairytales and with the way he reads them. In the Gewandhaus he applauds the overture to *Tannhäuser*, even though the audience boo and whistle. It conjures an entire painting. To a deathly hush in the hall Mendelssohn demonstrates his genius, his playing of Beethoven out of this world. You could hear a pin drop, a door to heaven open.

In Dresden he receives a letter from Jonas Collin who cannot comprehend how he can bear this empty journeying, this life waited on by princes. Suddenly downhearted, he writes a long, complaining letter to Edvard. Is vanity his weakness? Is it just leading him into emptiness? When will his friends in Copenhagen understand that praise gets him on his mettle, makes him give of his best? Is that weakness? No, but it is seen as such. Weaknesses that we do not have are like the dry wall we strike our matches on. The wall does not go up in flames, but when we touch it afterwards we feel a residue of sulphur left behind. Bitterness can arise between friends, spreading across the spoken, the written word. A singed mark that stains the lining of the soul.

He has money worries. Can he continue his journey? Reads Hauch's portrait of him as a writer in German, finds it one-sided, giving the same impression of him they have in Copenhagen. He has twisted and turned his subject so that it fits Eginhard in his novel – and yet it does not resemble him.

He cools his tumescent sensuality by wandering the town. Begins his autobiography *The True Story of My Life* in his hotel room. Here he will be seen as a whole person. How many grounds he has for rejoicing! Isn't his life like a beautiful fairytale, rich and happy? Could his destiny have been managed more happily, more wisely, better than it is? Isn't it – as he has said to the critic P.L. Møller – an affirmation that there is a loving God, who guides us all to our best end?

He writes far into the night by the light of two oil lamps, one either side of the paper, his hand and his pen casting double shadows across the gleaming white surface of the paper.

TRIESTE, TRIESTE – HERE comes the warm sunshine, the sea, the Istmen, the small waves quiet along the shoreline, the entire promenade full of strollers, the almond trees in full blossom. Along the streets with their villas, shops and coffee-houses there is a teeming blend of Albanians, Dalmatian peasants, Turks and Greeks with fez or turban. Sunset makes the houses on the mountainside look as though they were illuminated, the narrow sea turns purple, then shines like burnished gold. He looks out on the scene from his room as he writes.

Through the mountains on the way from Monza to Rome the heat of the sun increases, and it seems as though spring has kissed all the fruit trees to flower. The cornfields look like velvet, each stem full of sunshine.

As he travels by mail coach across the Campagna outside Rome, the mountains look as though they are painted on air, and he is ecstatic.

He rushes around the city, revisiting St Peter's, the Pantheon, the Colosseum, the Forum Romanum, but there is nothing to take his breath away any more. It is as if everything has been modernized, grass and bushes have been weeded away, the sound of tambourines is absent from the streets, no young girls dance the *saltarello*, and even the Campagna has been rationalized by invisible railway tracks. He is overwhelmed by the heat of the city, nervous in the massed crowds of the Easter celebrations. Among the Danes in the city he feels a strange emptiness that is intensified when he enters a church to cool off in the shade and finds himself before a memorial stone. On the sepulchre beneath the figure of a beautiful woman sculpted in marble stands the word '*Umbra*', while above is the impressive bust of a man with the inscription '*Nihil*'. Who were these two? A shadow and a nothing.

He reads 'The Snow Queen' for Frau Goethe, who lives in the city with her son and torments himself the same day with premonitions of death and with his old thoughts of dying in Rome. But no. Surely there are still many roses waiting to bloom for him? Isn't there still the freshness of life in his thinking? He wants neither to end as the bust that the sculptor Kolberg made of him – heavy, material and already half dead – nor get stuck in Oehlenschläger's unbearable narcissism. Didn't Kästner – the Hannoverian minister and son of Werther's Lotte – tell the story about him having exasperated Thorvaldsen so much that Thorvaldsen had drawn a knife on him? 'You can cut any figure you like,' Oehlenschläger had said, 'but I can talk about it – and when I talk, you will be silent!'

It's no good him being in Rome. He must fly again.

Naples in the heat. Naples in the evening in his room. Sitting there now with glasses of pastis and wine. He has walked round the town, nervous, slightly dizzy, strengthened by several cups of coffee in a café on the main street. From here the evening panorama – Vesuvius with its column of smoke, the shining blue water gilded by the moon, eleven fishing lights, their reflections like obelisks in the water, the lighthouse revolving, blinding in the dark, thousands of lights in the streets where the fish and orange vendors sit, a line of children in a candle-lit procession, shouting and tumbling as though at a party and setting everyone in motion; black shadows over the water and under the shadows boats with sails set.

It is as though the sky is lifted on high and the water transparent down to the seabed with its fish and plants. Scarcely a star can be seen. Instead the lights of carriages passing each other in the dark streets, their lamps looking like rolling balls of fire.

By day the heat takes possession of him. As he moves around the town sweat pours down his face, and on his second day in town, standing in the large castle square, he is already on the point of collapse, goes through a crisis when the square expands in front of him, seems never-ending, he counts each step, stops, wipes away the sweat and eventually manages to reach the shade on the other side, where his exhaustion recedes. But when he starts up the stairway to his room on the fifth floor and leaps up the first flight, he loses all his energy, and his head spins as he stares down the stairwell. He works at his autobiography and burns internally like Vesuvius in the evenings, when coolness and the dark take over the town. By day he seeks the shadows of narrow side streets, but is still taken aback by the sun gutting the life out of him.

He moves to a new room. From here he walks out to get oranges, malmseys, parmesan, bread, salami, olives and wine from Capri, getting lost sometimes – like the guests who come to see him – in the labyrinthine lanes of the neighbourhood, where you need stilts to see where you are.

In the cool of the evening the view is intoxicating. The sea sweeps up to the house. To the left a mountain rises verdant with bushes and trees, to the right Vesuvius, smoke rising like a fir tree, while ahead in the distance Camoldi, Cap Mysene, Prosida and Ischia swim in pinks and reds. The air is ethereal, the clouds dissolve into distances, ships stand silhouetted against the golden light.

To save money he moves to yet another room, this time in a long alley with balconies, where only two lights shine in the pitch-black evenings and which is so narrow that he cannot make out a complete constellation. Every day the barber, his hands stinking of onions, comes to lather him and scrape off his stubble. The smell of onion clings to his nostrils at night and only disappears when he goes to swim in the sea. The sun is pitiless, the water salty, but he returns strengthened to his room. He reads for his Danish and German acquaintances, finds it strange that several of them live off other people – one of them by making air balloons and drawing. But what does he do himself?

He thinks about Tasso, of the short distance between Tasso's birthplace and his grave, the salt sea rolling between them like the salty tears he wept while he lived.

He has to go to Amalfi one more time, to the view of the Sirens, the rocky islands and the mainland coastline stretching into the distance. He crawls along the edge of a precipice, looking down at the dizzy, toothed cliffs, the deep blue water, the sea birds gliding beneath him. He stands upright and loses his balance, throws himself face down, feeling the earth moving under him, crawls onwards. Soon he is back again in his room in the long alley, back to his autobiography in the dry scirocco and the hot blood that will never leave him in peace; back to his painful stomach, to his nerves and the heat that beats down, making him afraid to go out. He limits himself to short walks, so that he can quickly make it back to his room. But nevertheless one day he does take a longer walk through the alleyways, the heat shooting out of his pores, and his anxiety makes him want to throw himself down in the street, makes him send for a carriage, but when it arrives he is only three hundred yards from his door. He offers the cabby a peapod, but it is not enough and in his fury he refuses to pay more, walks on but gets no further than a doorway near his house, where he has to go in to the concierge and rest. It is dark in here – the harsh light of the street in front of him – the concierge a shadow, a shadow himself.

He works on the autobiography, visits no one, cannot pull himself together to pay calls and turns down invitations from the Prussian and Swedish embassies. As each day proceeds, he has to lay the book aside and take to the sofa or his bed, where he lies covered only by a sheet. By day he tries to read if he is not resting, but there is an awful din in the streets and lanes around him – cows with bells, goats with their smaller bells, carts rolling, boys shouting, people on their balconies talking about domestic matters, seeming to quarrel, and across the way, through an open balcony door, the sound of endlessly repeated scales on a piano which someone seems to be tuning for the benefit of the entire town. When finally a whole tune is played it is always the same one and keeps going round and round in his head.

Lying half awake at night by the open door to the balcony, it is as if light were streaming from the balcony across the alley and as if sweet soft music were coming from deep inside the apartment and lulling him to sleep.

In his dream he is sitting on his balcony with a light behind him. His shadow is the only living thing on the balcony across the way, and as a joke he asks it to go in through the door, which is ajar. The shadow disappears, and he sees it again only a couple of years later, long after he has returned home, a cadaverous figure in lacquered boots, with diamond rings on its fingers and in a black frockcoat that is too big for it. The shadow forces its way in to him, bearing its hard-won knowledge from the rooms it has visited, which turn out to have been a seat of poetry. The success of the shadow outdoes his own. He himself is in despair at the general lack of interest in his books dealing with goodness, beauty and truth. The shadow persuades him to go with it to a spa, but on the condition that the shadow is the master and he the shadow. At the spa the shadow, in the form of a fine gentleman, meets a princess and seduces her with the knowledge and human insight that he – the shadow's shadow – possesses. The princess decides to marry the shadow. The day the shadow and the princess celebrate their wedding, his life meets its end in the castle prison. However, by that time it has already ebbed half away and been drained to a shadow. Hardly anyone notices that his soul has gone.

He wakes bathed in sweat.

But he has already the previous day – on a sudden impulse – started on his fairytale 'The Shadow'.

HERE AGAIN THAT dark, almost transparent gentleman wearing a hat and that devilish smile that manages to be at the same time friendly and seductive, standing before his bed, his face resembling now Edvard's, now his own – he cannot quite decide which, before the figure disappears like a vision that has never existed leaving him chilled to the marrow. Has he come to fetch him? Or has he already taken him? He mumbles a prayer.

HOLLAND. VIA OLDENZAAL, Goor to Deventer with its large market, the town a fortress, magnificent houses, waffle shops. Takes the stagecoach to Utrecht, passing through flat, green meadows, beech woods, heath-land, the highway paved, the houses clean.

In Amsterdam shady trees overhang the canals, a wealth of ships, parks. He drives through the Jewish Quarter, the rich Jews live alongside the canals, those less wealthy in handsome, airy buildings on the other streets.

Holland is Europe's idyll! In The Hague there is a large party in his honour at the Hotel d'Europe, the speeches emphasize his fairytales, the painterly quality of his language, the freedom of his form, his imagination. In the town of Schewningen his eyes are struck by the grey-green colour of the sea. In Rotterdam everything seems to be trade; he stays at the Hotel Pays Bas near the river Maas, opposite fields and avenues and with a view of a forest of ships.

'Is there a theatre in town?' he asks his hired servant.

'Oh, here in town there's nothing for foreigners,' says the servant, 'only watching girls dance.'

'What girls are you talking about?'

'Public ones,' he says.

'Oh, I see.'

'I know one who is kept by a young gentleman, one of the top class ones – the gentleman is away at the moment, and if you want you can spend the evening with her for ten *guilders*. It's a chance in a million.'

'Yes, well, I am not disposed for that sort of thing,' he says. 'I am in weak health, you see.'

'But it'll build you up!' he says.

He sends the servant away in order not to be tempted further.

LONDON, THE THAMES – England, ruler of the waves, sending her ships to all corners of the world! He can see that from the deck of the steamship as he sails into the city. Every minute a ship arrives, flying its high flag of smoke – like a flower in its cap – and trailing its long white wake, or ships with all sails set, puffing out their chests like proud swans, or the thousands of fishing boats, like a market, like chickens, like so many torn pieces of paper. Steamship after steamship, like rockets at a huge firework display. It looks like a heath fire, but it is smoke from the steamships! A thunderstorm in the midst of all that, lightning striking several times, while a train races along one shore, billowing blue smoke into the black clouds; along the other shore monumental, smoke-blackened buildings.

He drives to the Sablonière Hotel on Leicester Square and lodges himself in rooms overlooking the courtyard – the windows so covered with soot that his sleeves turn black – and the sun shines in on his bed as proof that there is a sun here.

The following day the ambassador, Count Reventlow, gives him a long explanation of England and the English.

'One doesn't make compliments,' he says. 'One speaks honestly, but everything is governed by etiquette, and kings and artists do not consort here as they do in Germany.'

Carl Alexander is also in town, and he takes an omnibus to visit him in his royal suite at Marlborough House, where they exchange many embraces and kisses. He says the same.

'People are dying of etiquette here – even the queen is bound by it.'

'But she is the queen!' he says in astonishment.

'Yes, I said as much to her – you must be able to see whoever you want to! But no, she said. It won't do. All England would speak of it, if I broke the rules of etiquette.'

'What are we supposed to make of that?' he asks.

'It is the price of freedom, and the land of freedom is where you die of etiquette,' says Carl Alexander, extending his arms with a smile. 'I consider myself lucky to have my little Ettersburg.'

Jenny is also in London, attracting considerable attention and giving many performances at astronomical ticket prices at the Italian Opera. He sees her again in rural surroundings in Haymore Lane and finds his portrait and hers in shop windows all over the area around Leicester Square. He is in high spirits, amazed. He really is famous in a way that neither he nor Danes as a whole can understand! But isn't this good fortune a worrying form of advance payment?

London gets under his skin. He is in Trafalgar Square in the sunshine with Nelson's column and two fountains; on the streets there is music, a little girl dances, a Punch and Judy show attracts a crowd. There is the life of Naples without Naples' turmoil; it resembles Paris but with more power. In the evenings he is driven once again out on to the streets, their gaslights countless as the stars in the sky. Over the city hangs a transparent pall of blue smoke. Omnibuses, horse-drawn cabs, coaches follow each other in endless movement, as though there were an important event at one side of town and everyone had to be there! Musicians, even entire choirs, take their place on the pavements and perform their tunes, their songs. Beside Rome, London is the city of cities; London is the busy day, Rome the vast and silent night.

At his hotel many letters are already waiting for him from enthusiastic readers, translators look him up and compete to get commissions for his newest works, critics – with some exceptions where he is mocked for being excessively full of himself in his recently published autobiography – speak of his warm and artless nature, of the rare and surprising art of his novels and fairytales, of a magic and wealth of observation reminiscent of Dickens. Count Reventlow prepares him carefully for his introduction to London's aristocratic circles and talks to him about the power of the aristocracy.

'None save those who have a precise purpose there dares drive in their sequestered street,' says Reventlow. 'There are barriers at each end.'

On the afternoon when Reventlow and his daughter drive him in a small carriage to a soirée at Lord Palmerston's, his nerves are jittery, he has had a poor night, but he glides effortlessly through the sumptuous rooms and introductions to one lady after the next, and between the families of Lord Palmerston and the Earl of

Suffolk he is also met by Carl Alexander's affectionate greeting. Everyone is familiar with his writings, English ladies of title dressed in the richest and finest taste, with glinting diamonds and sumptuous bouquets, encircle him, almost trampling his feet in their urge to tell him of their enthusiasm for 'The Ugly Duckling', 'The Top and the Ball' or *The Improviser*. He wilts in the heat, can scarcely stand on his own feet in the thrill of this excited attention, but in the weeks that follow he flies on from one party to the next, the young ladies clutching him, pestering him, so that sometimes he feels that he is regarded as some strange animal but still cannot free himself of his fascination with the royal wealth of his surroundings – Anthony Rothschild's house with its marble stairs, fountains in the bedrooms, magnificent fireplaces, floral arrangements, carved panelling on the walls, rococo silverware. He sends Edvard a newspaper cutting with a picture describing him as 'one of the most remarkable and interesting men of the day' and catches himself being vexed – *o vanitas!* – that the Danish papers are not covering his visit but Oehlenschläger's trip to Sweden.

In Lady Blessington's salon his joy reaches its climax when an elegantly dressed man with dark hair and beard and lively, searching eyes makes his entry and salutes the assembled company. Seated at a desk, signing a book at that very moment, he recognizes Charles Dickens and leaps up, hurries over to him and takes both his hands. They look into each other's eyes and laugh.

'I had too many engagements already, but I said to myself that I must see Andersen. You have no idea how I am taken with your stories!'

Together they move out on to a veranda covered with climbing vines and roses and with a view of the garden and green fields, and there they stand for a long time talking, he in his broken English, Dickens with the aid of smiles and hand gestures. He is in seventh heaven.

Some days later after a visit to town he finds a parcel at his hotel containing Dickens's complete works inscribed 'to H.C.A. from his friend and admirer C.D.' and enclosed with it a letter from Dickens. He is ecstatic. He knows of no one he would rather have as an admirer and friend, no one with whose works he can identify himself more closely and whose eye for the transience, the living detail and the searing tragedy of the human condition he can more readily identify himself with.

His meeting with Dickens cleanses him, brings him closer to himself, to the sources of his own vision, so different from the image of pure innocence and artlessness which these English aristocrats read into him and which he has adopted; it brings him down to earth, too – and closer to exhaustion from the previous week's frenzied celebration. He walks around a churchyard near Clapton, observing the sunflowers planted there, turning their heads towards the sun. They are flowers rising from the dust and ashes of the dead pointing towards light and life, towards their nobler and departed elements. Wandering alone in the area around Leicester Square, his eyes are opened to the extraordinary stares of the poor. They dare not beg, but hunger is written on their faces; they position themselves outside a confectioner's and stare with a look – a look into the unknown. Often there is a message pinned to their chest: 'Have not eaten for two days.' That poor man could be him – the stranger is him. In his area only few are to be seen, but in the rich quarter there are none. There they do not exist.

London represents the torpid and relentless logic of the mass, of existence itself. This stream will pass endlessly through the streets, even after his death. There will always be these waves of omnibuses, cabs, men with billboards, placards on posts, boxes wheeled along with posters for air balloons that go up by day, by night, bushmen dancing in a park, Vauxhalls, waxworks, beggars with petitions starting 'Ladies and Gentlemen . . .'

For the next fortnight he travels by train, omnibus and steamship from London via York to Edinburgh, from Edinburgh via Stirling to Dumbarton, from there via Glasgow back to Edinburgh, thence to return to London. He realizes with delight in Edinburgh that even in the country of Walter Scott he is known as 'the Danish Walter Scott' and that his books are to be found in most local bookstores – yes, he is even recognized on the journey by adults and children at hospitals, at small stations and on steamships. From Edinburgh with its old town riddled with narrow, black and filthy lanes and the new town's beautiful streets he walks in the glens of Kirkcaldy on the lookout for Scott's glorious landscapes and finds ruins with crumbling dungeons on overhanging cliff-tops and ivy-covered houses looking like baronial castles. He stands in Mary Stuart's bedroom at Holyroodhouse, and the impressions of the dramatic productions of his youth with his puppet theatre in Ulkegade return as he imagines her lover's murderers crowding in through the low-lintelled door. In the neighbouring room there are still bloodstains on the floor where Riccio was dragged in and murdered. The rock formations, the mists, the huge valleys, stone-built houses, the small lakes, the mountains greenish-brown, the expanses of heath, the houses that creak at night like old cupboards, the streets of Dumbarton deserted on Sunday, the curtains drawn, making him think that the inhabitants are either reading their Bibles or getting drunk – all these images fall into place and provide an overall picture of a country that is harsher, wilder and more romantic than the one he has just left. A province of dreams *à la* Walter Scott.

Exhausted and replete with sense impressions he embarks at Ramsgate in beautiful weather – after a visit to Dickens and his family at Broadstairs. Dickens walks from Broadstairs in his green Scots kilt and checked shirt to shake his hand in parting on the quayside. As the ship glides out of the harbour and into open water, he sees Dickens standing on the furthest point waving his hat and finally raising one hand up towards the sky. Is it a sign? Is it only there that they will see each other again?

After a reunion with Carl Alexander in Weimar he is some four weeks later back among the familiar houses, people, streets and routines of Copenhagen. But his head and his memory are full to overflowing. He cannot find peace of mind and feels like a tired but happy dancer after a great ball, the echo of the music ringing in his ears, his thoughts breaking over him like waves – even when he sleeps.

IS HE ASLEEP? Is he dreaming? Isn't he walking round the room, round the garden looking for a tin soldier? No, other things are at stake here. The house has altered, is no longer Villa Rolighed, but old, so old it has a date, has tulips and twining hops carved on its beams, has a grimacing wooden face and a leaden gargoyle in the shape of a dragon's head, is dilapidated compared to the other houses in the street with their smooth walls and large windows. The new houses want nothing to do with the old one. It's a monstrosity, its stairway is far too broad, its iron balustrade makes it look like the gateway to a funeral.

He is sitting in his chair at the dormer window letting his thoughts drift where they please, when suddenly he has a visitor. It is the boy from across the road, who has a parcel for him. He tears the paper off and inside finds a tin soldier.

'I had two tin soldiers,' says the boy. 'This is one of them, and you are to have it because you are alone so much.'

'Oh, it's not so bad,' he says, patting the boy's head. 'I'm fine really.'

And now they are walking round the house, trying to find a place for the tin soldier. The carved trumpeters in the doorways have fatter cheeks than before, as they blow: tan-tan-te-raa, the lit-tle boy is coming, tan-tan-te-raa! The door opens to show the passage hung with old portraits of knights in armour and ladies in silk dresses, and the armour and the silk dresses rustle. Down a stairway they come to a terrace overgrown with greenery as though it were a garden and from the terrace on to a room lined with pigskin printed with golden flowers.

'The gilt decays, but the pigskin stays,' say the walls.

'Sit down! Sit down!' says the high-backed armchair. 'Ah, how our bones creak! We'll be getting arthritic next like the old wardrobe. Oh!'

'Creak! Crack!' says the furniture. There is so much of it that chairs and tables are almost falling over each other's legs to see the boy.

In the middle of the wall hangs the picture of a lovely young lady dressed as in the olden days in a crinoline dress and with powder in her hair.

'Where did you find her?' asks the boy.

'Over at the junk shop,' he says. 'There are lots of pictures like that over there. No one knows about them or can be bothered with them, for the subjects are all long dead and buried. But I knew her long ago – she died fifty years ago.'

Under the painting a bouquet of withered flowers hangs behind glass and looks as though it was about the same age. The pendulum of the large clock swings to and fro, the hands move round and everything in the room seems to turn with them, becoming ever older, but they don't feel it.

He has found a place for the tin soldier at last and stands it on a chest of drawers.

'Thank you for the tin soldier,' he says to the boy. 'And thank you for coming across to see me.'

'Yes. My parents say that you are so alone.'

'Oh well, old thoughts come visiting,' he says, 'and now you come as well!'

He gives the boy jam, apples and nuts, and once he has gone and night has fallen he hears the tin soldier complaining.

'Oh, I can't stand this – it's so lonely and miserable in here – when you have been in a family, you can't get used to this. The day seems endless and the evenings even longer. Goodness me, that old man isn't half lonely! Nothing comes his way, neither a kiss nor a Christmas tree. Only a funeral . . . Oh, I can't stand this . . .'

He gets up and places the tin soldier in the window so that it can get light during the day and hear the birds singing.

The boy comes again, and he plays for him on the piano with a landscape painted on the inside of the lid. He hums a folksong to the rusty piano and is happy, looking up at the portrait of the woman.

'Yes, she could sing that one,' he says to the boy, who looks as though he understands.

'Your eyes are so clear,' the boy says.

'I can't stand it! I want to go to war. I want to go to war!' shouts the tin soldier with his tinny voice and throws himself off the windowsill on to the floor. Both he and the boy look for him, but in vain.

'I'm sure I'll find him,' he says to the boy when he goes home again.

And the boy doesn't come any more. The windows in the house freeze up, the rooms grow cold, for the heating has gone out, too, and he no longer has the strength to fetch firewood. He curls himself into a ball in the bed with two blankets and a duvet over him. How long does he have to lie here? He senses quite clearly that the boy is watching the house through a spy-hole in the window of the house opposite and that the snow has drifted into all the curlicues and inscriptions, yes, even the

*eye sockets of the dragon lying across the stairs, and he thinks that no
one is at home there any more.*

'I can't stand it!' he whispers.

'What can't you stand?' he hears a voice ask near by.

'The tin soldier is lying under the ground . . .'

'Yes, but you are lying here in bed.'

'No one knows him. They have forgotten him.'

'But you remember him . . .'

'Do I?'

'Yes.'

'Right now I can remember nothing. Where am I?'

*'Here,' says Fru Melchior, who is sitting by his bedside holding his
hand. Around her it is dark. But her white dress shines, and the warmth
of her hand spreads all the way up to his temples.*

FIVE FAIRYTALES WRITTEN in the damp November greyness of Copenhagen. After drifting about such a long time, bad-tempered and full of toothache, doing nothing, and then to finish them off in a frenzy and as a thank-you to his English publisher Bentley and to London – as *A Christmas Greeting*. And to feel them between his fingers – later – a snail sick with ambition, a pair of boasting shirt-collars and a drop of water mirroring the jungle of the city swimming up from the pages of the slim volume. To submerge himself in a physical tide of transience, of loss and of confrontation with the icy chill of death in 'The Old House' and 'Story of a Mother' and – like a wave – to remain there.

King Christian VIII is dead – he weeps in his room – and there is war between Denmark and the dukedoms of Schleswig-Holstein supported by Prussia. His German sympathies have lost their home. He follows developments from the Manor of Glorup on the island of Funen. Those shot in the chest lie on the earth as though they are asleep; those hit in the stomach are almost unrecognizable so distorted are their faces; some of the dead lie on the ground and have literally 'bitten the dust', while their hands clutch the grass. The field hospitals stink of the wounds of the sufferers, excrement flows from the sides of those shot in the belly. His friend the young painter Lundby, who inspired him to write 'The Little Match-Seller', is standing one day in the camp outside the town of Schleswig, leaning on his rifle, when some peasants walking past stumble by accident into some rifles stacked in front of him. One of them goes off, Lundby collapses – the ball has taken him from below, travelling up through his jaw, split his mouth open, shooting away a lump of flesh and beard; he lets out a few faint sighs and dies.

Danish troops exercise daily across most of Funen and around Glorup. He is gripped by the turmoil around him and in his initial patriotic enthusiasm writes songs that accord with the mood of a small country defending itself against a larger foe – 'In Denmark Was I Born' – and feels himself to be freed from the oppressive mood of Copenhagen. But it pains him to make his picture of a cultured court at Weimar match the devastation caused by the German General Wrangels in Jutland. How can he relate culture and the war machine? To find Prussians plundering and torching towns in Jutland is beyond his idea of civilization – as though he were dreaming an evil dream.

In his letters to Carl Alexander he bemoans the fact that so many people whom he loves – Germans and Danes alike – now face each other as strangers, when mutual understanding would make everything blossom in love. Carl Alexander asks him to promise that the mood of the moment will never exert an influence on their friendship. And when Carl Alexander places himself at the head of a volunteer contingent from Weimar against the Danes in Schleswig-Holstein in the second year of the war and makes him consider breaking off their relations, even then he defends his right to have such relations against fanatic nationalists in his circle. But by that time his own initial patriotic tendencies have faded, too, to be replaced by a mood of depression that permeates his newly rented apartment in Nyhavn. He suffers spiritually and physically from the quantities of blood being spilled, the numbers of men being mutilated and of towns being razed to the ground. His days are full of an inner tension that makes it impossible for him to wrench his thoughts away from the war. He can write nothing.

In the May heat he dreams one night of the theatre of war and of speaking with the Tsar of Russia about coming to the aid of the Danes – just like the Swedes did. At a party arranged for him when the Swedish author Frederika Bremer visits Copenhagen, all the panegyrics make him sick. How little he has to give the wounded and mutilated being freighted by ship to Copenhagen! What has he left to give anyway? Hasn't his creative wellspring run dry? How little it all matters in this sick world!

And yet it returns anyway, when he escapes to Sweden and travels by ship down the Göta canal past Trollhättan, across Lakes Vänern and Vättern, passing the skerries to Stockholm. Here he loses himself in the lovely blue smoke, in the mist that lies like a veil across the houses scattered through the woods, in a white horse that suddenly appears near Trollhättan, standing there like an enchanted king looking down from a grey crag surround by firs. He is carried away, absorbed in the light trunks of the beech woods, in the water's reflections of moon, birds and the hulls of ships. In the middle of the night nothing disturbs the water's peace here on Lake Vättern and in the depths of his own self. In the light of day he is out on the open sea off the coast with its string of small islands, crumbling grey crags of primeval cliffs topped with pine woods and small clusters of rock relieved by great forests of fir. The sea is like a mirror and his head once more a broad highway for thoughts peopled with weird caravans taken from his own works, from memories, from momentary flashes of fresh insight. In his head pious processions of children with waving banners are replaced by dancing Bacchantes singing wild songs that he is frightened of putting on paper. But he writes the whole journey down and takes it home with him.

FREDERICIA CHURCHYARD, WHICH he visits on his way to Glorup Manor. Here lies the long row of officers fallen in the war, grave by grave, stone by stone, their mangled and bullet-holed bodies already stiffened in the earth; they are, like Shakespeare's spirits, melted into air, into thin air. He makes a note of the names, one by one – he has known a number of them, picks grass from one of the graves and seems to hear the dead man's voice in the air. He returns to the churchyard several times. A long rectangular grave holds the bodies of the common soldiers in four or six layers one on top of the other separated by lime, without coffins. Even after death distinctions are made – but are we not all of one flesh, made of the same earth? Isn't that what he wrote in his novel *The Two Baronesses*, while he sat at Glorup, and the troops exercised in the park and the fields near by?

What gravity lies between the graves . . .?

It follows him into a dream. He falls asleep in a room at an inn by the harbour with a view of the army's batteries on the Funen side and of a fir tree decapitated by a shell. In the dream he is attacked from behind by a soldier with an invisible face. He wakes with a start and leaps up in the deathly silence of the half-light to discover that he is alone in one wing of the house. He looks out of the window, down towards the beach, where he sees two objects – people or trees, he cannot quite decide. They move towards the house and are suddenly gone. Soon afterwards one of them reappears and goes round the other side of the house and stands there looking for something in his room – if it *is* a person, that is.

He takes the mail coach to Odense, where he thanks God that he has been spared being a poor artisan mocked by his fellows. He discusses poetry with Aarestrup the poet and uses the large pair of scissors that always accompanies him to cut out paper dolls for the youngest of his twelve children. From Glorup, where he works on his Swedish travel book, he goes to Nyborg where the hollowness of the world of gentility gets on his nerves.

'You are not writing to the Duke of Weimar, surely?' asks the Countess Sophie Scheel.

'Naturally,' he replies. 'He is my friend.'

'As long as you are a true Dane . . .'

'I am as Danish as anyone,' he says.

'You did say, though, that you didn't have the courage to fight in the war but that you would likely go along as a troubadour!'

'I never said any such thing,' he says. 'That is simply tittle-tattle!'

The contrast between the stagnant life of the goldfish bowl and the war close at hand is too great. In Nyborg he hears of the Battle of Isted and of the thousands slain, among them the acquaintance of his younger days Frederik Læssøe. They fought for thirty-six hours before the Danes could capture Schleswig. He becomes tetchy, gets upset for no reason, weeps alone in his room, writes a consolatory letter to Læssøe's family but cannot sleep for his fantasies about disasters of war.

Some days later he becomes aware of the circumstances surrounding Læssøe's death, and in his frenzy he wants to journey from Svendborg to Schleswig to be with the troops. Couldn't it have been him? Læssøe died when he and his scouting party pushed forward into a village that had all the appearances of being friendly and had been given milk and water to drink by the inhabitants; but suddenly all the doors and gates of the town are thrown open, and the soldiers of Schleswig-Holstein supported by the inhabitants throw themselves upon them, men and women, young and old shooting and mowing them down without discrimination. Many die, blood flows in the streets, and in the end the Danes raze the village.

All around Schleswig cannonballs have ploughed up the fields, the horses have devoured the oat harvest, hedges have been cut down, woodlands and houses burnt to ash. Outside the town the Danes have forced their way three times through a peat bog towards the enemy's well-chosen position dug deep in the bog, and three times their lines of advance have been cut down by enemy fire, the men falling like flies.

When will there be peace?

Will there be peace?

NIGHT. A BONY man with a horse blanket over one shoulder enters through the closed door, carrying something, but he cannot see what it is.

'What are you carrying?' he asks.

'You,' says the bony man and walks on through the wall.

For a long time he lies staring into the air, thinks he has fallen asleep but is floating in a morphine trance.

'Where is my child?' asks a woman. She is some yards from his bed and looks like Edvard's wife, Henriette, but has Fru Melchior's long black hair – or is it his mother's?

He knows the answer but cannot lift his arm right now to point to the door. The woman disappears – was she there at all? He closes his eyes and sees it all before him. She walks down the passageway, down the stairs and across the rooms below, empty and silent with the night, and then out into the garden. Here she calls for her child. It is thick with snow out there, winter – in the snow sits an old woman wrapped in black.

'Death has been to your house and taken your child,' she says. 'He hurried away and will not return.'

The woman wants to know which way Death went, but first she has to sing all the songs she has ever sung for her child; the old woman, who is the night, sits listening silently and gathers up the mother's tears.

'Go to your right,' she says, 'into the dark spruce wood below.'

And the mother walks along the beach and deep into the spruce wood, and where the forest paths meet, she loses her way. Right there at the crossroads stands a hawthorn bush encased in ice, and she asks it the way.

'I saw Death with your child,' says the thorn bush, 'but first you must warm me by your heart or else I'll turn to ice.'

And the mother presses the thorn bush to her breast so that the thorns pierce her skin and her blood flows in little droplets, and the thorn bush shoots fresh leaves in the winter night and tells her which way to go.

The woman comes to a great frozen lake, but the ice is too thin to bear her, so she lies down at its edge to drink it dry, but she cannot, even though she believes in a miracle.

'It's no good,' says the lake. 'You'd better give me your eyes; they are the clearest I have ever seen. If you weep them out for me, I will carry you over to the hothouse of Death.'

The woman weeps, and her eyes sink down to lie on the floor of the lake, already turned into pearls, and the lake lifts her like a swing and lays her on the other shore. A curious house stands there – but the woman cannot see it.

'Where can I find Death who has taken my child?' she says feeling someone close at hand. It is the old grave-woman who looks after Death's enormous hothouse.

The grave-woman knows nothing of the child, but she knows that Death will soon return to replant many of the trees that have wilted during the night.

'Everyone has their life tree or their flower in the hothouse, and their heartbeat – follow the sound . . . But what will you give me for telling you what else you must do?'

'I have nothing to give you,' says the grieving mother, 'but I will go to the ends of the earth for you.'

'Give me your long black hair,' says the grave-woman, 'and take my white hair instead.'

And in her joy that the grave-woman does not ask for more, she gives the old woman her beautiful black hair and takes her snow-white hair instead.

Now they enter Death's great hothouse, where magnificent hyacinths grow beside strong peonies, sickly water plants, gorgeous palm trees, oaks, planes, parsley and flowering thyme. The woman leans over the very smallest plants, and among all the millions growing there she recognizes the beating of one heart, her own child, in a little blue crocus drooping to one side. She stretches out her hand over it.

'Do not touch it,' says the grave-woman. 'Wait until Death comes and threaten to pull other flowers up if he touches yours – then he will be afraid. He has to account to God for each and every one and must have God's permission before he pulls one up.'

When Death comes with its long and icy hand, looking like a poor man with a horse blanket over his shoulders, she does as the old woman told her, threatening in her despair to tear up all the flowers.

'Do not touch one of them,' says Death. 'You are full of sorrow – would you give that sorrow to another mother?'

'Another mother?' says the woman, releasing the two flowers she had grasped.

Death gives her back her eyes. He has fished them up off the floor of the lake because they shone so brightly.

'Look down into the well,' he says, 'and I will give you the names of the two flowers you were going to pull up. You can see their future, their whole life in front of you, see what you will interrupt, destroy.'

And she looks down into the well and sees one happy life beside another unhappy one.

'Both are the will of God,' says Death.

'Which of them is the flower of unhappiness and which the flower of the blessed?' she asks.

'That I cannot say – but you must know that it was your own child's future that you saw.'

'Which of them was my child?' she cries.

But Death remains silent, however much she forces herself upon him.

'Then free my child from misery! Bear him away instead, bear him to the kingdom of God. Forget my tears, forget everything I have said.'

'I do not understand you,' says Death.

'No. Nor can you.'

'Will you take your child? Or shall I take it with me into the unknown?'

The mother wrings her hands and prays to God.

'Do not hear me, Oh Lord, when my prayers go against your will. Do not hear me.'

She bows her head, wanting to see nothing. Death takes her child into the unknown country.

And he sees that light is streaming from the greenhouse in Rolighed's garden, that that is where the woman went. And that the darkness around the greenhouse and himself is all that unknown country. And that his mother with her black hair and he himself will disappear into it as into a great sleep. What has their life been, then, if not a short dream?

How can he sleep now?

He rings the bell feverishly.

THE WAR IS over. In his story 'In a Thousand Years' he imagines the future – airships crowded with young Americans land in England; travelling by air and via a tunnel built between England and France, they tour Europe's memorials, its sinking cities, in the space of eight days; meanwhile a gigantic telegraph pipe reminiscent of a sea snake links Europe and America. In spite of everything he longs to see Carl Alexander and Weimar again as they were before the war and writes to Beaulieu, whom he remembers for his many embraces and confidences, and receives an arrogant, antagonistic reply.

Anxious, he travels to Germany anyway, passing through Flensborg, which resembles a garden of death with all its graves and burnt-out buildings, and Rendsburg, which feels like a snake-pit of anti-Danish sentiments.

The journey is not a happy one, and he turns back, only to set off again and again return. But finally he is in Weimar, standing opposite a disagreeable Beaulieu, who has received a head wound during the war and complains of recurring pains. He feels himself imprisoned in the room he occupies on the stairway up to Beaulieu's. One day, with Beaulieu once more lying on his bed complaining, he has a vision of Beaulieu in a fit of madness trying to open his door in the middle of the night to murder him.

Carl Alexander, now the grand duke, receives him beside the glow of the fire in his room in quite a different and affectionate manner. They embrace and kiss each other, but he feels nervous when they speak of the war and doesn't feel quite as at home as before.

Franz Liszt and his lover, Carolyne Sayn-Wittgenstein, on the other hand, are two meteors that flare up under him at the Altenburg house up on the mountain overlooking the town. In that large house with its many salons, its countless bedrooms, its collection of instruments (some of them previously belonging to Beethoven or Mozart), with music-making and nightly parties where radical ideas fly to and fro, they are in the vanguard of the musical life of Europe. They ask him to consider their house as his own, and he reads for a gathering of young musicians his story of 'The Nightingale'. He cannot, however, be really close to Liszt, or the heat of his presence will turn into a branding iron. How can he follow that man's savagery, his unreflective tone poetry or the much-admired music of Wagner, so clever, so racked by thought, so lacking in melody? He cannot entirely share the audience's ecstatic reception, their wild accolades, and he disagrees with Liszt that Mozart is 'passé', has been overtaken by Wagner and other composers of effects.

In the hunting castle of Starnberg in the company of the young Bavarian King Max, he feels free to air his views. Everything he says King Max finds interesting, especially his fairytales 'The Little Mermaid' and 'The Garden of Paradise'. When they pass a small flowering islet on a sailing trip across a mountain lake, the king picks lilac for him and tells him of his plans for a fairytale castle at Hohenschwangau.

'This will be placed in my album, Your Majesty,' he says, taking the bunch of lilac, 'next to a sprig of linden flowers that was given to me years ago on my first visit to Ettersburg.'

Oh yes, and he feels the words strike home when Jette Wulff, his 'sister', writes to him after his visit to King Max that he is betraying himself completely, betraying his very nature and the spiritual gifts that God has given him, if he can feel pleased and honoured to sit at the same table as German kings and nobles or to accept an order that is worn only by the greatest scoundrels and by a bunch of insignificant individuals. Do titles, money, high society, fortune bear some kind of external relation for him to genius, spirit, the gifts of the soul?

He has to concede that he is certainly not sufficiently thankful to God and that he has allowed himself to be affected too profoundly by the trivia, the trifles, the trappings of show, but is that perhaps due to the wretched conditions in which he was brought up? And isn't it true that in all the glitter of court, he thinks first and foremost of the person in the glittering frame and can easily distinguish between these people and see a Humboldt, a Schumann, a Liszt, a Dickens?

NINE YEARS AFTER his visit to London he receives an invitation from Dickens to come to England and stay with him and his family; Dickens will do his best – his whole family will – to make him happy and assures him that his love and esteem for his friend are so great that even if the road from London to Copenhagen were paved with paper it would not suffice to express it. He is moved and, fired with enthusiasm, devotes all his energies to completing his novel *To Be or Not to Be*, which he has been working on for years and which is to be published simultaneously in England, Germany and Denmark with a dedication to Dickens.

Surely in the novel's Niels Bryde he has managed to create a character capable of convincing the reader that there is eternal life? And that that insight can only come through the experience of loss, hardship, sickness, war even – in the remorseless school of life? Brought up as a Christian, Niels Bryde is first an atheist, later a pantheist susceptible to a belief in progress and scientific thinking in the form of the insensate machine, before recovering his childhood faith when, like a latter-day Aladdin, he finds 'the lamp of life' in a belief in God and eternal life. Neuredin's shrewdness and Aladdin's faith are mutually inspiring; for, as his friend Ørsted says, are the laws of nature not the thoughts of God? In the all-embracing power of God's love and in the perception of a life after death lies the answer to Hamlet's question – in the simple fact of being. In his novel the gypsy woman rediscovers her image of God and sees it as a sign of her deformed child's life after death, and so life itself continues, into eternity, on the far side of death. Is that not exactly what he believes – that suffering on Earth receives compensation through eternal life? And hasn't he defended that thought against Oehlenschläger, who believes that it is vanity to want to lay down conditions like that to God? 'It is a demand that is nothing other than justified' was what he said to the astonished Oehlenschläger.

Summer 1857, and the novel has just appeared in England and Denmark, as he travels by ship to London and on by train to Higham station, which is nothing but a couple of houses, to continue in the bitter cold – accompanied by the guard, who shows him the way and carries his suitcase and, slung round his shoulders, his night-bag and hatbox – and to travel the last miles on foot to Dickens's country retreat at Gadshill.

The house with its bay windows, its entrance supported by columns and its wide dormer window above is surrounded by a thick hedge, behind which two huge cedars of Lebanon can be seen. Dickens greets him warmly in the hall, and in that instant the nine years that separate them only serve to increase their veneration for each other. There is an *élan*, a humour in Dickens's approach that he immediately finds infectious. It wraps itself around him for the entire month of his visit and at first makes him think that his stumbling English is not a handicap for him. But on the morning after his arrival, when he attempts to signal with clumsy gestures to Dickens's wife and children that he would, as is his wont, like to be shaved and appoints Dickens's eldest son to be his barber, the temperature has already started to fall.

In Dickens's absence during the day he gathers the children around him at first and communicates with them by means of his skill with scissors and paper. Princesses, hangmen, double dancing pierrots, ballerinas, skull-faces, Wee Willie Winkie, cartwheel men with double hearts, unhappy mask-faces, swans, griffins, silhouette arms with pointy fingers – they all grow from the paper between the movements of the scissors like a tapestry of miniature dream pictures. He makes bouquets of brown field flowers and willow wands for the family, and picks other unusual posies in the extensive gardens or in the woods near by for Dickens's wife, Catherine Dickens, who invites him to the Crystal Palace and to the theatre in London. And he leads his hosts up to the top of a hill near the house – a place that Dickens immediately christens 'the Hans Christian Andersen Monument'. Here they lie on many an evening with bread and wine beside them watching the sun going down and with a view of the Thames and the far-off sea. In the sun's golden rays the ships are like silhouettes on the spreading limbs of the Thames and the smoke from the chimneys of the scattered cottages a blue, dream-like haze.

He kisses Dickens on the forehead when Dickens invites him after his first week to stay and attend his play *The Frozen Deep* at a special performance in London, in which he will himself play one of the leading parts. And, as the close of his stay approaches, he weeps like a child to see Dickens getting inside his role in the play's death scene. But his eyes and ears miss nothing, and when his poor English makes the children and Dickens's sister lose patience with him he can sense them parodying his well-meant deaf-mute gaucheries behind his back. He has the feeling that fine cracks are beginning to appear even in Dickens's obliging manner but at the same time cannot give up his company. At odd moments he escapes to the country house belonging to his publisher's family, the Bentleys, on the way to London and to their rather different unconditional cordiality or to London, where he gets tangled in a confusion of cabs and feels overwhelmed by anxiety. On one occasion he arrives at Dickens's house on Tavistock Square in London apparently with a corn on his foot. In reality he has hidden in his boots his pocket watch, a timetable, a wallet, his scissors, a penknife, a couple of books and some letters of introduction in the certain conviction that the cabby had been going to relieve him of them.

On a daytrip to London he chances to see a review of *To Be or Not to Be*, which describes his main character as a fiasco and the work as revolutionary and a danger to the reader. The following night he sleeps uneasily in his bed at Dickens's country house with the review hanging over him like a vampire. In the morning he wakes to yet another negative review in *The Examiner* and to a letter from Copenhagen enclosing a copy of *Fædrelandet* and a review calling *To Be or Not to Be* confused, a patchwork of spiritual bits and pieces, and the main character (echoing Kierkegaard's characterization of the main character in *Only a Fiddler*) a 'worm'. He feels himself to be completely misunderstood. It is he who is being attacked, he who is the fiasco, the worm. It isn't just that he feels yet again the Danes' wet blanket gagging him, but he is also in Dickens's house with no Dickens and no one to talk to, and his thoughts are condemned to circle around the perpetual darkness throbbing at their centre – he is a stranger among strangers. He is being tried by God and must curb his bitterness, must be full of love, but he cannot and stumbles out on to the lawn in front of the house, where he collapses on the grass between the bushes and weeps. This is where Catherine Dickens finds him. After he has tried to explain using mime and broken sentences, she takes him into the house and reads the English reviews.

'Stupid, stupid,' she says, smiling and shaking her head. 'My husband never reads the papers.'

That same evening Dickens returns from London with someone from *Punch* magazine who has written an article about him. The reviews in *The Athenaeum* and *The Examiner* come up in the conversation over dinner. Dickens wipes the corner of his mouth with a napkin.

'Apart from what you write yourself,' he says, 'you should never read the magazines. In twenty-four years I have not once read a review of anything I have written.'

The man from *Punch* thinks he is exaggerating, but Dickens insists.

After dinner Dickens takes him in his arms.

'Never allow yourself to be influenced by the magazines – they'll be forgotten in a week, while your book will remain and live on. God has given you such infinite abundance – follow what is within you, give what you have within you. Go the way you must go – you are above such trivialities.'

They take a walk up to the hill in the twilight, and Dickens makes a mark with his foot in the sand, then rubs it out.

'That is criticism,' he says and laughs. 'A work that is good will live by itself.'

They drink wine on the hilltop and compare Danish and English words. He fumbles to tell Dickens about Danish folk legends, until their silence merges with the stillness of the evening spread across the landscape – on his part with mixed feelings of frustration at not being able to express himself and the peace of being close to a friend. The setting sun sends orange glints from the roofs of Rochester; a mist rises from the Thames and the sea far out.

As dark grey clouds gather in the sky, they return to the house. Dickens reassures himself one last time that all is forgotten and that he will sleep well.

Doesn't his stay in the house seem long for Dickens but short for him?

A fortnight later Dickens drives him to the station through the picturesque landscape around Maidstone – it is as though they were looking down over the woods from a balloon – and he is silent, moved, the lump in his throat allows few words of farewell.

He writes to Dickens several times, receives one reply. The rest is silence between them.

HE IS AN oak tree, he is flying upwards with the scent of honeysuckle, woodruff and violets beneath him, an entire forest singing below him – at that moment a sudden chill passes through him.

He is a mayfly – drunk on the scents of meadows full of clover and wild rose-banks, he sinks earthwards, sunlight gleaming on the tired wings that can no longer bear him, and glides down on to a soft blade of grass that sways him into sleep.

'Doctor Meyer says that there is nothing the matter with your back and that you have improved a little.'

He opens his eyes. Edvard is there in front of him, come to visit. In a smart, light summer jacket, his brow furrowed – isn't he old like him?

'I am tired of barbers, tailors, hairdressers.'

'Have they all been here, the same morning?'

He nods. Edvard smiles faintly, hands him a piece of stiff paper, like parchment.

'Your will.'

He skims through it. There are minor sums to be distributed immediately, and then the larger amounts to Edvard, his wife, their children, and to the Melchiors.

He hands it back. Is satisfied.

'There is also my wish to lie in a grave beside you and your wife,' he says, beginning to cough.

Edvard frowns. He cannot tell what he is thinking.

'I shall see to it,' says Edvard, his voice seems mournful, his hand clutches the will, which he now places in his briefcase.

Edvard gets up, goes towards the door with the briefcase and papers. At the door he turns.

'I hope that you feel no pain – we are all thinking of you,' he says. And is gone.

Gone, gone. Will he see him again?

He must write a letter and – why not? – get out and sit on the balcony. Just for half an hour.

Doesn't Dr Meyer say that his progress is satisfactory?

GERMANY AGAIN. AND again. But he has seen Carl Alexander for the last time, and he is on his way home from Maxen, when Jette Wulff asks him, in a letter from Eisennach, where she is waiting for the ship to America, to come to her, to come and say goodbye, to take his leave of her. Doesn't it only take two hours from Maxen to Eisennach? And didn't she ask him to go with her to Rome, too? But he does neither. And she understands him, that weak, hunchbacked woman – she understands him. He is famous, he is busy – and she forgets that when she looks into her own heart and contemplates the feelings for him that have always been there. His heart, she knows – knows it to be a sure anchor that will not let her go, even if from time to time the surface makes it seem otherwise.

And he sits in his rooms in Nyhavn and reads how the steamship *Austria* caught on fire in the Atlantic – her ship. She is on board. Only 90 of the 560 passengers survive – and she is not among them. She chokes to death in her cabin. His imagination is overlaid with images of horror – he sees her alive, feverish, desperate in her struggle against the fire, sees her image before him as he walks in the street. Generous she was with her great wealth of feeling; she overestimated him. He tortures himself. Why couldn't he have made a detour in Germany and met her one more time before she left Europe? What is wrong with him? What a man of straw . . .!

To escape from Copenhagen to the Manor of Basnæs in the time of cholera – the certainty hanging over him for several days that his time has come; to fly on his writing, rising into the air with the old oak tree and crashing down with his crown filling the sky – in the fairytale 'The Old Oak Tree's Final Dream'. To be back in Viking times, gliding like a swan in the form of an Egyptian princess on a quest for a magic flower to heal a dying father, to be taken like her by the Marsh King, and to be her daughter, Helga – violent by day, soft and reptilian by night; then to be rescued and carried to Egypt by the chattering storks, and to save the dying man with the magic flower – in 'The Marsh King's Daughter'. Love is the seed of life – the wind touches in passing. To be the wind, to be howling summer and winter long with the wind – in 'The Story of the Wind' – and to be half-crazy and alchemical and obsessed by gold along with Valdemar Daae, to blow through his dream, through pantry, cellar, attic and castle gate until cracks and chinks appear, to sing at the grave of the Lord Daae and his youngest daughter – although where their graves are, no one knows. To have black ravens, black crosses dance in old Anne Lisbeth's nightmare – in the story 'Anne Lisbeth' – because she disowns her ugly son, and he calls to her, an angel in heaven; every night she has to be visited by his apparition until she wins back her soul in the churchyard.

To tell fairytales, stories, until they are over – for all stories are over some time – and begin again (if his fingers are not glued together with ink) when the mist maiden opens her locker of poetry.

THE NORTH SEA. Jutland. In a fierce storm the sea rolls in on foaming breakers, the whole coastline seems made of white foam, a vision of great white castles rising against a deep blue ground. He walks down the main street in Løkken, his feet sinking deep into soft drifts of windblown sand; the sun reflects off the sand, burning the air and making him feel he is in the deserts of Africa. Aren't the dunes on fire? Smoke pours off them, the fine sand whirling around them. The sea is a gigantic waterfall crashing against the coast. Far out the waves rise into the sky like towering buildings. The wind cries, the sea roars, and he stands in coat and hat on the wide-open beach, drinking it in. Or out on the point facing the sea's swelling abyss, its dizzying surfaces. Is there firm earth beneath his feet, land behind him? Isn't he just a worm in the eyes of the gulls crying and wheeling in the wind?

Skagen. The sand-dunes looking like snowdrifts in winter against the sunlit blue of the sea, a golden land of deserts with a hidden treasure of poetry – quite unlike the light beech woods of the east coast. Arriving from a distance across brown swathes of heather, past marsh and meadow, Skagen is just a pale clearing on the horizon. The town itself goes on and on, a main street deep in sand and side streets constantly changing and marked by ropes strung from post to post as the shifting sand dictates.

Behind dog-toothed lines of dunes looking like distant Alpine ranges the white church tower rises out of the sand above the sand-blown church and its covering of sea hawthorn and wild rose. He imagines a night centuries ago, the wind howling across the town, a man seeking refuge in the church. Exhausted, the man lets himself slide into a pew. The heavy stone that fills his head cracks open. The lights are lit. Aldermen and mayors step out of the sculpted epitaphs and take their place in the choir; the doors and gates of the church fly open, and the dead all enter in their party clothes. A woman, the object of his unhappy love, sits beside him in the pew, the priest lays their hands together, gives them his blessing. The organ roars like the storm outside. The ship hanging in the nave floats down before the man and the woman. The newly wedded pair climb aboard, all the congregation follow, and the ship rises up, sails through the air and out to sea. At that moment the man draws his last breath in the darkened church. The following morning the priest and the congregation find the church buried in sand.

No one disturbs the dead man's peace in the country's largest sarcophagus. No one knows he is there. Only he and the storm that has sung for him between the dunes.

SPAIN, AND EVERYTHING green and flowering. The immense panorama across the sea to the coast of Africa, the sweet taste of prickly pear in the carriage on the mountain road to Málaga, tropical gardens – pepper trees with their small pea-shaped fruit, the thick stems of the palms, thickets full of passion flowers, lily-like flowers growing up the trees, fine grasses in the watered earth, big shadows of banana and rubber trees and the powerful scents of oranges, geraniums, lemon trees.

He sleeps uneasily these hot nights, goes to the bullfight with Jonas, Edvard's son, in the middle of the day, where in a small arena only half full the bulls rip open the horses' chests and bellies; four lie dead in the arena already, their guts hanging out, the blood streaming from their chests. The bulls bellow with pain, one of the bull's innards are caught around its horns, a picador falls with his horse and has to be helped from under the fallen animal; one bull is run through by a sword so that the blood flows from its mouth, and it roars. The spectators yell and clap, the matador cuts off the ear of the fallen bull and throws it out to the crowd, who throw their hats, their fans, their cigar cases down into the arena to him.

Spain is passion fruit and rawhide, and the Alhambra near Granada floats on pillars with its red courtyard, its windows open to the air, its portals and walls with their Arabic inscriptions. The Alhambra is a revelation. The tiled walls look as though cleverly woven lacework has been thrown across a foundation of red and green and gold and been petrified in the instant. In the Hall of the Two Sisters the ceiling rises, unfolding like the cup of a colossal flower; in the Hall of the Abencerrages stands the large marble basin, whose reddish-brown colour derives, according to legend, from the blood of the Abencerrages murdered by Baobdil; light streams in a downy blue haze through the star-shaped openings in the cupola of the largest bath chamber and through the Moorish windows; water trickles through the gardens and the pipes which for centuries have brought hot and cold water to the many basins can still be seen. He can hear the voices of the Moorish women in the empty rooms.

During the day, as he walks around Granada in the baking sun in his respectable dark travelling jacket, boys and women cannot conceal their amusement at the sight of this tall, cadaverous figure; a family points at him from a balcony, and he seeks refuge in churches, in the wild green abundance of the area with its Moorish arches, in the teeming crowds that assemble for Isabella II's visit to the town, or in his hotel. But Jonas, the insect-collector, makes poor company, and there are scenes between them over the dinner table.

'It is egotism on your part,' says Jonas one day, 'to be so concerned with what some chance letter-writing student chooses to write to you.'

'Why do you say that?'

'You walk around brooding on it and get anxious, and you aren't aware that your anxiety makes life uncomfortable for others.'

'We are all different,' he says, hurt. 'But I never thought that by being the person I am I could make life uncomfortable for my travelling companion. Didn't I pay for your trip – and don't I make allowances all the time?'

'That is nothing to boast about. My grandfather did you lots of favours, and now you are bitter because he has been hard on you recently.'

'That is nonsense. I am not in the least bitter . . .'

'Yes, you are, but you will never be honest about it like I am.'

'Are you now to be a soothsayer for me?'

'I constantly strive for truth.'

'The truth is that you are too dry and undemonstrative for me and that you have not the least appreciation for the allowances I make for you.'

'What are these allowances?' asks Jonas, his jaw clenched under that pale young face with its stiff upright hair.

'We don't need to go into that now,' he says, getting up and hurrying out on to the street in front of the hotel.

In low spirits and alone, he wanders through the crowded streets of Granada until his legs hurt and he no longer knows where he is.

After many hours he returns to the hotel to find that Jonas has forgotten the whole thing and wants to go out with him. He doesn't feel up to it, instead makes his way into the dark part of the Almeida, where multicoloured lights hang under the trees like shining joker's caps.

But surely he has that boy in his heart, he is surely . . . that boy at heart. Heart.

Dreams that a wet child is sitting on his shoulder, but when he lifts it down it is only a dry leaf – no, a rag.

MOROCCO. GREEN MOUNTAINS, strong surf, Tangiers with its low, flat-roofed houses, the desert with its shining sands running up to the town. They are carried to shore from the boat, the coastline teeming with figures in Arab costume, some of them coal-black; outside the gates of the town six men sit in long kaftans with heavy turbans on their heads and check incomers. Not far away at the caravanserai hundreds of Arabs dressed in white are encamped in Bedouin tents with their herds of camels; they are being joined by Arab traders arriving from Tetuan swaying on their over-laden camels. In Tangiers men and women in oriental dress fill every corner of the narrow alleys and tiny shops; outside the town in dry hollows there are butchers' stalls with bloody meat and a Jewish cemetery with horizontal stones bearing Hebraic inscriptions. Barbaric-looking men on horseback or on mules pass them, carrying long rifles. From the towers of the mosques the prayers ring out night and day, drums beat, hyenas howl in the darkness. He dreams he is a Moor in the sunset looking towards the coast of Europe – milky-green clouds hang in the red evening air.

SEVILLE. SUMMER HEAT in the gardens around El Alcazar, the oranges hanging deep among the dark leaves, the roses in full bloom. A marble channel where the Moorish women used to bathe is as long as a ballroom and leads to the new Moorish baths and fountains. On terraces covered now by gardens there were fountains in Moorish times, and water pressure could – like a conjuring trick – send the jets shooting out in the shape of a net; in hollows and cliffs the water was made to play with itself in any number of ingenious patterns. Inside the buildings the colours are as fresh as though the Moors abandoned them only yesterday. The Alhambra is a dream vision of the Moorish age in moonlight; El Alcazar, with its overwhelming wealth of colours, is the Moorish reality in the light of day. He stands open-mouthed before the strange lacework ornamentations on the walls, the doorways' motley mosaics, sees a fantasy building borne on columns light as air, where kaleidoscope pictures and patterns like Bruges lace are printed on gilded walls. The observer is confronted by a chaos of arabesques, apparently identical and yet so different that the eye slips into a trance-like confusion while at the same time resting with delight on these labyrinthine traceries. El Alcazar belongs in *A Thousand and One Nights*, in the constantly re-embroidered story of the astonishing resurrection of beauty.

From the Plaza Nueva, where he is staying with Jonas, he can look up and see rows of orange trees and lose himself in the cloudless blue sky above.

Peace.

Dreams that he is following Edvard, it is Edvard's back, his walk, in the narrow alleys of Tangiers. Every time he gets close to him and is about to reach out and touch his shoulder, he disappears down another alley between low houses, white and windowless, that didn't seem to be there a moment before. He thinks : Surely he must know me, so why is he running away from me? At last Edvard disappears from sight behind a white door. Now Headmaster Meisling appears in the schoolroom in Helsingør. He says to Meisling, 'I don't want to go to school with you any more.' Meisling laughs. Doesn't take him seriously. 'You are my student for ever,' he says.

THE BLOODBATH OF war – again. Prussia and Austria against Denmark, a kingdom and an empire against a little country – and all because of Schleswig and Holstein. The first days of January 1864, minus ten degrees and he in the lap of luxury, thinking of the soldiers in their freezing barracks. Every day squads of soldiers file through the snow past the windows of the great house on their way to the front – singing on their way as though they were going to a jolly party. His travelling companion, Viggo Drewsen, is among the long, dark ranks. He can do nothing, write nothing, imagines the battlefield, returns to Copenhagen.

Telegrams saying that the Dannevirke fortifications have been abandoned by General Meza without a shot being fired follow reports that the Germans have crossed the Eider. How can he understand this other than as an evil dream? His dark and heavy mood is deepened by the fanaticism of those around him, crowds fill the streets, smashing windows and gaslights, singing, shouting abuse at the king and the government, spitting into the carriage carrying the little princesses. Gade the composer describes Meza as a madman, out of his head; Edvard is dry, detached, has no comment. He wanders restlessly around the city from one acquaintance to another, trying to share his depression with his few close friends, thinks of visiting the crown prince but refrains, unable to see how best he can talk to him. Perhaps he wouldn't even care for a visit from him?

The theatre is almost empty, voices echo in the great auditorium, and he finds dramatic dialogue intolerable at this moment; it is music he must have. At home – behind windowpanes flowering with frost – he sits with the pain of his gnawed gums and the sores from his new dentures and feels alone and sad. Wouldn't it be better to die now rather than wait for his body to fall to pieces bit by bit? Even though he is still sixteen at heart – despite not daring to act that way. Wouldn't he write a comedy, if he could have his way, if times were different?

Isn't he pathetic? Why not simply join the ranks of old men and forget these youthful feelings, which make him so totally ridiculous? Oh, how he can rub salt in his own wounds, going round like this with his false teeth – can't even manage an egg with them – shunting his African cactus back and forth from the cold window, hoping for red blossoms, which in all likelihood will never appear. Oh, how he can torment himself with his *idées fixes,* his half-baked notions, seeing himself consigned to the bottom of a ship, thrown into a dark dungeon, tortured and abused – all because he has signed a petition to the people of Switzerland asking them to drum up sympathy in Europe for the people of Denmark and now believes the Germans will come and arrest him. What Germans? Where are they supposed to come from, when they aren't even in Copenhagen?

But won't they soon reach Copenhagen? Won't they totally destroy Denmark? Will there be a Denmark in fifty, a hundred years? The army has been routed in the trenches of Dybbøl, thousands killed, wounded, taken prisoner, Viggo surely among them; restless, he goes down to the harbour, where a steamship hauling two barges arrives at the quayside with five hundred wounded from the Battle of Dybbøl. The most seriously wounded are carried slowly along the quay – one of them completely covered and so heavy that he must be dead – and are freighted away in cabs, omnibuses. He searches for Viggo but doesn't find him among the pale, frozen figures, and his own legs can scarcely carry him as he continues on into the city, on to the Garrison Church to see the bodies of the officers who have fallen, and makes his way finally to Edvard in his house in Bredgade.

'What I have seen has made such a deep impression on me,' he says to Edvard in his gloomy study.

'Yes, yes indeed. We are all living with the war,' says Edvard.

'Not Viggo, though. I worry about him constantly – but what I saw down at the harbour and in the Garrison Church . . '

'What was that then?'

'You know Lasson – he is lying there now, shot dead, an officer in burial sheets lying among the others, surrounded by flowers. The others lie in coffins in the gear they were found in, one with his finger chopped off. The gravedigger told me that the Germans had stolen his ring, and that was why. They looked as though they were asleep, tanned by the wind, with a blush in their cheeks.'

Edvard sighs, purses his lips, looks across his desk and picks up a sheet of paper.

'The dead are dead – that's how it always is,' he says off-hand.

He hesitates a moment, wondering whether it serves any purpose going on.

'Mrs Schmidt, an acquaintance of mine from the Casino Theatre, her son is a cadet . . .' he says and comes to a halt before Edvard's evident lack of interest.

'Well, what about him?' asks Edvard.

'He was attacked by five Prussians – two of them each shot a bullet through his left arm, the third hit his chest, but his mother's watch, which he always carried on him, deflected the shot, and it merely grazed him. The soldiers were drunk – one of them picked up a stone and was going to smash his head in, but the stone slipped when it hit him – a fifth came with his bayonet fixed shouting "*Verfluchte Däne! Ich soll dich kitzlen!*" . . .'

'Yes, and . . .'

'Just as the soldier was going to ram the bayonet into his stomach, a Prussian officer shoved him aside, and the blade of the bayonet only gave him a flesh wound. He is still alive!'

'Lucky for him.'

They observe each other for a moment, these two men who have walked side by side so long. He picks up his hat from Edvard's desk and leaves his study – Edvard's detachment makes him feel he is making a nuisance of himself. But isn't it Edvard, after all, who is best at shooting down his obsessions when they become intolerable? Edvard with his narrow-minded prejudices, the bureaucrat from Frederik VI's day who cannot stand all his despondency – how fortunate for him that Edvard has Henriette by his side, in whom he can confide without a qualm and who – in her affectionate and teasing way – can call him 'crazy' when he goes overboard with his imaginings but can also comfort him when he has imbibed too much misery and fear from the newspaper reports from the front. She understands him when he has to break with his German friends and tear them from his heart, when he abandons his God and cannot pray, when Satan rules in his heart; she listens to him when springtime makes him angry because it can blossom regardless of the blood flowing, and when he feels that he is empty, dull and alone, when he thinks nobody cares for him, nobody wants to speak to him and when he wants to speak to no one. Then she asks him to devote his thoughts to his work. Then she reminds him of what he has to contribute – she who has herself lost several of her children.

How many coffin lids has the gravedigger now raised so that he can look down at a dead officer lying there in the gentle peace of the sleeping? He shares each family's bereavement, they thank him, and he weeps; he reads for a gathering of wounded soldiers, students and workers in aid of war widows, and he is applauded and swamped with flowers – but his depression will not leave him, is waiting for him like a ghost when he returns to his rooms in Nyhavn.

'You are not *so* affected by the events of the war,' says a Mrs Hammerich, his neighbour at the dinner table at Mrs Neergaard's one evening. 'Won't we have some new work from you soon?'

'Are you trying to insult me?' he says, rising in his anger from the table and storming out. He goes to the Collins' and later walks the streets, while on other evenings he sees his own plays – *He Is Not Born* and *Wee Willie Winkie* – at the Theatre Royal and the Casino Theatre, if only to feel the flatness of the atmosphere spread by the war over the entire city – even the actors are heavy and lifeless. Mrs Heiberg herself does not contradict his expressions of bitterness and abandonment when he visits her in his restlessness one evening at Søkvæst House in Christianshavn, where it is so strange to find Heiberg's telescope standing on the first floor with its covers on while the sky is shining full of stars outside.

'The house is not the same since his death,' she says. 'I feel this loneliness.'

A lackey comes to take him to Amalienborg, to the queen, and as they sit talking about his book *In Spain* and about the war a platoon of soldiers crosses the Palace Square, and they stand up to watch them.

'There go our wonderful soldiers,' she says, and he nods and doesn't mention how worn their clothes are, how exhausted they look. When he takes his leave, he kisses the queen's hand with his chapped lips and is afraid he might have punctured her delicate skin.

Constantly dispirited, feeling bitter towards men, towards God – either he will abandon himself to his dark thoughts or else there is a new, more powerful life ahead! Isn't it springtime? The apple trees festooned with red and white flowers? Clusters of primrose in the grassy banks? He enjoys the walks in the warm sunshine, greeting the flowers, the green profusion – just like in the old days before misery struck. He starts writing a hymn about Saul, visits Basnæs and then is back in Copenhagen to receive one dreadful telegram after the other: the island of Als attacked, no help from France and England, major defeat, strong resistance. The enemy on their way across Funen – when will Denmark be overrun by Germany? He wanders in the windswept streets, returns to his rooms and waits for the death sentence to be passed on him and his country. To live, to enjoy, the passing moment – gone – gone. Three thousand killed.

To live, to enjoy, the passing moment. One day overflows into the next, but there are a million scents in his head, a million thoughts. And then the beat of the waves through his window, the sound of the world in the shell at his ear. The light drawing quivering shadows on the white wall. The light.

ARMISTICE, AND NIGHTMARE upon nightmare – the Danish government has resigned, and a new one is formed. Dreams he is in a Russian prison in Copenhagen – a prison scene reminiscent of *Fidelio* – and of rivers of blood flowing into the bathing machine he uses when he bathes in Øresund – the blood comes from war-wounded soldiers bivouacked close to the shore. Edvard says, 'Life's brevity is as it is, forget all your weighty concerns.' Edvard is his friend! He leaves for Helsingør, where the sea has a blue transparency, and the shoals of mackerel swim for the shore – the entire Swedish coastline clear in the sunlight, Kullen like a mountain of light.

The armistice conditions, as bad as they can be. Holstein and Schleswig are lost. In oppressive heat at the Marienlyst Hotel he dreams he is a boy again watching over his shattered father. His father gets up in bed and shouts orders at Napoleon's troops. He wakes and finds himself standing up on the bed. With flailing arms and bathed in sweat. Oh, this whole year. A night of heavy horror from start to finish. 1864.

PARIS, 1867. PARIS is the modern fairytale, the fairytale of the times. Paris illuminated like a shining mist, with locomotives flying to all the ends of the earth. A mass of teeming humanity rampaging on the boulevards by day and in cafés and dance halls in the moonlit nights; Paris is a Universal Exhibition with the colossal edifice of Aladdin's Palace erected on the Champs de Mars' sandy expanse, gardens with canals, grottos, waterfalls driven by machines and subterranean aquaria. Paris is liberation and corruption, the infernal smell of food from under the pavements, the dying trees flowering a second time, women with their hair piled up in rolls, gaslight, lamplight, falseness, freshness, temptresses to whom he gives a wide berth but nevertheless seeks out with his new young friend, the handsome, curly-headed Robert Watt, who has aroused his sympathies because he, too – for all his female conquests and his affectionate and cheerful nature – is, like himself, scarred by dark experiences in his youth.

In Paris he finally has the sense that he is no longer a young man, but in Watt's energy and wild nightlife he finds an extension of himself, a mirror for himself in stories of the younger man's debauches. But do women really throw themselves at his feet, as he claims, when his greatest asset is his youthful *élan*, when he is so short on elegance? With him the doors open on to the red light, white slave market, to its women and to the rapture spiked with fear that comes of being close enough to touch. At Mabille with its babble of running water, its lamps winking among the leaves and dancing couples, its willow weeping over the pool, there are tarts for the taking, and girls dance the cancan to Offenbach's music just like on the big stage; but in the fleshpots which he – each time to his own amazement – finds himself visiting, he is confronted by women powdered or plain, fine *madames* or poor young girls – and can choose for himself; in one place he picks out a lady, two other places it is young girls of eighteen, and each time he goes into a room with them, watches them strip for him and then talks to them, feels sorry for them. One of them says, 'You certainly are innocent, for a gentleman!' and tries to draw him down on to the bed, but he resists, gives her money and leaves as fast as he can, relieved to have sinned only in thought.

He is with Watt at a fourth brothel after drinking wine and champagne, and while Watt is having fun with a woman he is in a room talking to a pretty little Turkish girl about Constantinople; she presses herself upon him, caressing his neck with one hand, wanting to '*faire l'amour*'. The feel of her skin, her scent, her naked breasts close to his face, her flashing hair and that lissom young brown body makes his head spin for a moment.

'I only came to talk to you,' he says, closing his eyes, 'nothing else.'

'*Dommage*,' she says with a tired little smile.

He gives her extra money when he gets up to go and can find neither his hat nor the door.

'Come again soon,' she says and hands him his hat, 'but not tomorrow – that's my day off.'

The girl's wondering eyes remain in his memory for a long time.

Back home he has to write about the Universal Exhibition, about Paris and these women's sensuality, their transient pleasures. And he does so in the fairytale 'The Dryad'.

HE IS THE dryad come alive for half a day, for half of a mayfly's life, steps out of a chestnut tree in the centre of Paris and floats above the omnibuses, the joyrides, the riders on horseback, all the bustle of the gas-lit boulevards of Paris. In her he flies to the sound of back-alley guitars and organ grinders and sees houses, horses, people dancing before him; she looks like the goddess of springtime with her green dress and a half-opened chestnut blossom tucked in her nut-brown hair; now she is human, leaping and dancing through the streets, unable to stay still, is like the flash of a mirror – now here, now there, past shops, cafés, trees, flower displays, statues, now bathed in yellow gaslight, now in the city's blues; she dances to the organ grinders, to the cancan music, her colours shifting like a hummingbird's, catching the lights from the windows' reflections; every time she halts she takes on a new shape, so none can follow, none recognize her – and no one does she recognize in the city's wild intoxication; in the Madeleine Church with its scent of incense and its women clad in black, kneeling before the altar, she becomes fright-ened of the silence and longs to be away, longs to be where? So off she must go, like the mayfly that cannot rest. And she is under the ground, in the depths below the city, in vaulted armouries with their flickering lamps, their chambers and criss-cross passageways, a mirror of the city, where she drives in open carriages along the Boulevard Sébastopol; she is at the Mabille among the swarms of dancers who seem addicted to the tarantella, and she is carried along on the flood, dancing in magic circles with her shoulders bared to the man swinging with her, her desire like an opium euphoria, her lips moving, telling, and her partner whis-pers in her ear words that sway to the beat of the music, stretches out his arms for her but embraces nothing but empty air; she is borne towards Aladdin's Palace on the Champs de Mars and the red lighthouse of the Universal Exhibition, is in the halls of human knowledge, in subter-ranean tunnels with aquaria and fish that cannot grasp her looks, her frippery; workmen sing in the night, unaware that she has come to the exhibition to disappear; in the tropical gardens they have made, she has to lay her weary body down with all her experiences ringing in her ears like echoes of a night at the ball; she is rootless, frightened, but abandons herself to what she has been and seen, to the scents of her half-day's life, and of her memories of the tree she once stood inside, the chestnut that, *as the first rays of the dawn touch her, dies with her death. Her body shines with the lustre of a soap bubble, and she turns to drops, to tears. Disappears.*

As he will disappear.

But he will get out on the balcony. Tomorrow.

ODENSE TOWN HALL. Evening. The torches in the square outside make a sea of light, a sea of people, a city lit up for him, the keys of the city ringing, all those voices singing for him, honorary citizen of Odense. The window stands open to the air, and he feels himself overwhelmed, happy, on edge. Streams of icy air brush against his teeth setting his toothache on fire. The pain is unbearable. Down in the square the workmen are shouting 'Long live Hans Christian Andersen!' over and over, as he steps to the window, screwing up his eyes with the pain so that the lights start to dart and dance out there like a hallucination; through it all he hears his own voice thanking them for the honour.

'This is a day I shall treasure as my fondest memory!' he says.

The torches are thrown on the bonfire. The flames of the torches die slowly.

'I AM A lucky Larry,' he says, sitting in the sunshine on the balcony watching the white sails fly like swans on the blue horizon of Øresund. And he says it again when Fru Melchior helps him to bed. His eyes catch a face in the looking glass. Whose is that mummified face?

He hears Fru Melchior whisper 'Poor Andersen', but he cannot tell to whom – maybe the servant . . .

'Thank you. God bless you,' he says when once again she comes in, carrying a white rose, and it is morning. Or is it evening, perhaps? He grasps her hand and kisses it; his smile is serene as he repeats his 'Thank you. God bless you.'

Day after day he drinks quantities of oatmeal gruel.

'Do not ask me how I am,' he says. 'I don't understand a thing any more. It is all beyond me.'

He takes hold of her hand again.

'You must be so tired of me!'

His voice is faint, and she assures him to the contrary.

'I am glad that I can take care of you, so that you aren't among strangers.'

After a long night's sleep his mind is suddenly clear. Isn't the force present in the tiniest nerve so slight when you die that it is on the edge of disappearance? It leads to clarity, and that, too, brings light.

'Oh, how blessed! How lovely! Good morning to you all,' he says in the moment of waking, reaching out his hand both to Fru Melchior and the servant.

Shortly after he falls into a doze only to wake again without being able to assemble anything in his head. Friends and acquaintances call to pay their respects, coming up from the drawing-room to his bedroom, but he doesn't know whether he recognizes them, shadows as they are in the clear sunlight.

'Will I ever get up again?' he asks one day.

'I hope so,' says Fru Melchior without averting her eyes.

'You must promise me that you will have my arteries cut open if I die.'

She nods.

'If it were a journey I was going on, I could write it down,' he says.

She smiles.

'You could leave a little note on the table saying "I am only apparently dead", just as you used to,' she says.

He smiles faintly. There is a roaring in his ears as voices, faces, sounds blend in one great echo chamber; faces are speaking but as though from another world and not to him.

'Can I be alone?' he says.

And they leave him; he is alone.

'I understand nothing,' he whispers. Over and over.

He cannot sleep. All night he cannot sleep for the veil across his eyes and the veil across the world. That night he rings incessantly for the servant, and time and again the servant enters to stand exhausted by his bedside, powerless to do more than observe that fevered, mute and cavernous face.

He senses that Dr Meyer comes several times a day and is uneasy.

'The doctor is coming again this evening,' he says to Fru Melchior. 'That is not a good sign.'

'Over the past fortnight he has visited you twice a day,' she says, and he feels calm again.

'Would you leave me alone?' he asks again.

She gets up from the bed and leaves the room.

Far away in the quiet of the evening a window slams, a child cries, a blackbird sings. It is their summer Sunday, and his mother has put on her party clothes, her brown calico dress. They are in the woods, his father, his mother and himself, for this one day a year when she puts on her calico dress and comes with them, for their annual outing; he is running around picking wild strawberries, stringing them on a straw and tying garlands in a clearing between the trees. His father says little, just sits on a tree stump lost in thought. Nothing happens. There is just the sun, a few butterflies, the scent of green leaves. What thoughts are passing through his mind? Does he have any thoughts at all? They have no thoughts. This is paradise.

The blackbird again.

A tremor in his hand.

He dies.

AFTERWORD

Journey in Blue represents my vision of Hans Christian Andersen and his works. It has been said of him that his personality was banal but that his writings possessed genius. This is not an opinion I share. For me his poetic genius corresponds to a complex, rich and enthralling personality, which – while it may have been oppressed by his impoverished childhood and by the senseless opposition to which his writings, particularly in Denmark, were subjected for many years – managed with its nervous vibrato and its nomadic, almost modern lifestyle to overcome both inner and outer demons. His religiosity did not provide an escape for him but developed from childhood and was an integral part of his positive way of experiencing the world. Just like another great writer, Isaac Bashevis Singer, he couldn't hurt a fly and had an eye for all the small things that in the end make up the large.

In my journey with him I have from time to time made use of his own words because they provide the most precise and complete description of his experiences or states of mind. Elsewhere I have taken the liberty of paraphrasing or rewriting some of his stories, something I feel to be entirely in the spirit of a writer such as him, who never stood still and who was always open to new forms of expression. I have attempted to place myself at his point of view – which for some may be heresy but which for me was the only way in which I could write the present book. The reader must judge if it has succeeded.

Stig Dalager